THE
E. L. KONIGSBURG
COLLECTION

Also by E. L. Konigsburg

Jennifer, Hecate, Macbeth, William McKinley, and Me, Elizabeth
From the Mixed-up Files of Mrs. Basil E. Frankweiler
Altogether, One at a Time
A Proud Taste for Scarlet and Miniver
The Dragon in the Ghetto Caper
The Second Mrs. Gioconda
My Father's Daughter
About the B'nai Bagels
(George)
Throwing Shadows
Journey to an 800 Number
Up From Jericho Tel
Samuel Todd's Book of Great Colors
Samuel Todd's Book of Great Inventions
Amy Elizabeth Explores Bloomingdale's
T-Backs, T-Shirts, COAT, and Suit
TalkTalk: A Children's Book Author Speaks to Grown-ups
The View from Saturday
Silent to the Bone
The Outcasts of 19 Schuyler Place
The Mysterious Edge of the Heroic World

THE E. L. KONIGSBURG COLLECTION

From the Mixed-up Files of Mrs. Basil E. Frankweiler
Jennifer, Hecate, Macbeth, William McKinley, and Me, Elizabeth
The View from Saturday

e. l. konigsburg

Atheneum Books for Young Readers
New York London Toronto Sydney

Atheneum Books for Young Readers
An imprint of Simon & Schuster Children's Publishing Division
1230 Avenue of the Americas, New York, New York 10020

Manufactured in the United States of America
First Edition
2 4 6 8 10 9 7 5 3 1
Library of Congress Control Numbers:
From the Mixed-up Files of Mrs. Basil E. Frankweiler 67-18988
Jennifer, Hecate, Macbeth, William McKinley, and Me, Elizabeth 67-10458
The View from Saturday 95-52624
ISBN: 978-1-4169-9385-8

From the
Mixed-up Files of
Mrs. Basil E. Frankweiler

To David, with love and pluses

From the Mixed-up Files of Mrs. Basil E. Frankweiler

To my lawyer, Saxonberg:

I can't say that I enjoyed your last visit. It was obvious that you had too much on your mind to pay any attention to what I was trying to say. Perhaps, if you had some interest in this world besides law, taxes, and your grandchildren, you could almost be a fascinating person. Almost. That last visit was the worst bore. I won't risk another dull visit for a while, so I'm having Sheldon, my chauffeur, deliver this account to your home. I've written it to explain certain changes I want made in my last will and testament. You'll understand those changes (and a lot of other things) much better after reading it. I'm sending you a carbon copy; I'll keep the original in my files. I don't come in until much later, but never mind. You'll find enough to interest you until I do.

You never knew that I could write this well, did you? Of course, you don't actually know yet, but you soon will. I've spent a lot of time on this file. I listened. I investigated, and I fitted all the pieces together like a jigsaw puzzle. It leaves no doubts. Well, Saxonberg, read and discover.

Mrs. Basil E. Frankweiler

1

Claudia knew that she could never pull off the old-fashioned kind of running away. That is, running away in the heat of anger with a knapsack on her back. She didn't like discomfort; even picnics were untidy and inconvenient: all those insects and the sun melting the icing on the cupcakes. Therefore, she decided that her leaving home would not be just running from somewhere but would be running to somewhere. To a large place, a comfortable place, an indoor place, and preferably a beautiful place. And that's why she decided upon the Metropolitan Museum of Art in New York City.

She planned very carefully; she saved her allowance and she chose her companion. She chose Jamie, the second youngest of her three younger brothers. He could be counted on to be quiet, and now and then he was good for a laugh. Besides, he was rich; unlike most boys his age, he had never even begun collecting baseball cards. He saved almost every penny he got.

But Claudia waited to tell Jamie that she had decided upon him. She couldn't count on him to be *that* quiet for *that* long. And she calculated needing *that* long to save her weekly allowances. It seemed senseless to run away without money. Living in the suburbs had taught her that everything costs.

She had to save enough for train fare and a few expenses before she could tell Jamie or make final plans. In the meantime she almost forgot why she was running away. But not entirely. Claudia knew that it had to do with injustice. She was the oldest child and the only girl and was subject to a lot of injustice. Perhaps it was because she had to both empty the dishwasher and set the table on the same night while her brothers got out of everything. And, perhaps, there was another reason more clear to me than to Claudia. A reason that had to do with the sameness of each and every week. She was bored with simply being straight-A's Claudia Kincaid. She was tired of arguing about whose turn it was to choose the Sunday night seven-thirty television show, of injustice, and of the monotony of everything.

The fact that her allowance was so small that it took her more than three weeks of skipping hot fudge sundaes to save enough for train fare was another example of injustice. (Since you always drive to the city, Saxonberg, you probably don't know the cost of train fare. I'll tell you. Full fare one way costs one dollar and sixty cents. Claudia and Jamie could each travel for half of that since she was one month under twelve, and Jamie was well under twelve—being only nine.) Since she intended to return home after everyone had learned a lesson in Claudia appreciation, she had to save money for her return trip, too, which was like full fare one way. Claudia knew that hundreds of people who lived in her town worked in offices in New York City and could afford to pay full fare both ways every day. Like her father. After all, Greenwich was considered an actual suburb of New York, a commuting suburb.

Even though Claudia knew that New York City was not far away, certainly not far enough to go considering the size and number of the injustices done to her, she knew that it was a good place to get lost. Her mother's Mah-Jong club ladies called it *the city*. Most of them never ventured there; it was exhausting, and it made them nervous. When she was in the fourth grade, her class had gone on a trip to visit historical places in Manhattan. Johnathan Richter's mother hadn't let him go for fear he'd get separated from the group in all the jostling that goes on in New York. Mrs. Richter, who was something of a character, had said that she was certain that he would "come home lost." And she considered the air very bad for him to breathe.

Claudia loved the city because it was elegant; it was important and busy. The best place in the world to hide. She studied maps and the tour guide book of the American Automobile Association and reviewed every field trip her class had ever taken. She made a specialized geography course for herself. There were even some pamphlets about the museum around the house, which she quietly researched.

Claudia also decided that she must get accustomed to giving up things. Learning to do without hot fudge sundaes was good practice for her. She made do with the Good Humor bars her mother always kept in their freezer. Normally, Claudia's hot fudge expenses were forty cents per week. Before her decision to run away, deciding what to do with the ten cents left over from her allowance had been the biggest adventure she had had each week. Sometimes she didn't even have ten cents, for she lost a nickel every time she broke one of the household rules like forgetting to make her bed in the morning. She was certain that her allowance was the smallest in her class. And most of the other sixth graders never lost part of their pay since they had full-time maids to do the chores instead of a cleaning lady only twice a week. Once after she had started saving, the drug store had a special. HOT FUDGE, 27¢, the sign in the window said. She bought one. It would postpone her running away only twenty-seven cents worth. Besides, once she made up her mind to go, she enjoyed the planning almost as much as she enjoyed spending money. Planning long and well was one of her special talents.

Jamie, the chosen brother, didn't even care for hot fudge sundaes although he could have bought one at least every other week. A year and a half before, Jamie had made a big purchase; he had spent his birthday money and part of his Christmas money on a transistor radio, made in Japan, purchased from Woolworth's. Occasionally, he bought a battery for it. They would probably need the radio; that made another good reason for choosing Jamie.

On Saturdays Claudia emptied the wastebaskets, a task she despised. There were so many of them. Everyone in her family had his own bedroom and wastebasket except her mother and father who shared both—with each other. Almost every Saturday Steve emptied his pencil sharpener into his. She knew he made his basket messy on purpose.

One Saturday as she was carrying the basket from her parents' room, she jiggled it a little so that the contents would sift down and not spill out as she walked. Their basket was always so full since there were two of them using it. She managed to shift a shallow layer of Kleenex, which her mother had used for blotting lipstick, and thus exposed the corner of a red ticket. Using the tips of her forefinger and thumb like a pair of forceps, she pulled at it and discovered a ten-ride pass for the New York, New Haven, and

Hartford Railroad. Used train passes normally do not appear in suburban wastebaskets; they appear in the pockets of train conductors. Nine rides on a pass are marked off in little squares along the bottom edge, and they are punched one at a time as they are used; for the tenth ride the conductor collects the pass. Their cleaning lady who had come on Friday must have thought that the pass was all used up since rides one through nine were already punched. The cleaning lady never went to New York, and Claudia's dad never kept close track of his pocket change or his train passes.

Both she and Jamie could travel on the leftover pass since two half fares equal one whole. Now they could board the train without having to purchase tickets. They would avoid the station master and any stupid questions he might ask. What a find! From a litter of lipstick kisses, Claudia had plucked a free ride. She regarded it as an invitation. They would leave on Wednesday.

On Monday afternoon Claudia told Jamie at the school bus stop that she wanted him to sit with her because she had something important to tell him. Usually, the four Kincaid children neither waited for each other nor walked together, except for Kevin, who was somebody's charge each week. School had begun on the Wednesday after Labor Day. Therefore, their "fiscal week" as Claudia chose to call it began always on Wednesday. Kevin was only six and in the first grade, and everyone made a big fuss over him, especially Mrs. Kincaid, Claudia thought. Claudia also thought he was terribly babied and impossibly spoiled. You would think her parents would know something about raising children by the time Kevin, their fourth, came along. But her parents hadn't learned. She couldn't remember being anyone's charge when she was in the first grade. Her mother had simply met her at the bus stop every day.

Jamie wanted to sit with his buddy, Bruce. They played cards on the bus; each day meant a continuation of the day before. (The game was nothing very complicated, Saxonberg. Nothing terribly refined. They played *war*, that simple game where each player puts down a card, and the higher card takes both. If the cards are the same, there is a war which involves putting down more cards; winner then takes all the war cards.) Every night when Bruce got off at his stop, he'd take his stack of cards home with him. Jamie would do the same. They always took a vow not to shuffle. At the stop before Bruce's house, they would stop playing, wrap a rubber band around each pile, hold the stack under each other's chin and spit on each other's deck saying, "Thou shalt not shuffle." Then each tapped his deck and put it in his pocket.

Claudia found the whole procedure disgusting, so she suffered no feelings of guilt when she pulled Jamie away from his precious game. Jamie was mad, though. He was in no mood to listen to Claudia. He sat

slumped in his seat with his lips pooched out and his eyebrows pulled down on top of his eyes. He looked like a miniature, clean-shaven Neanderthal man. Claudia didn't say anything. She waited for him to cool off.

Jamie spoke first, "Gosh, Claude, why don't you pick on Steve?"

Claudia answered, "I thought, Jamie, that you'd see that it's obvious I don't want Steve."

"Well," Jamie pleaded, "want him! Want him!"

Claudia had planned her speech. "I want you, Jamie, for the greatest adventure in our lives."

Jamie muttered, "Well, I wouldn't mind if you'd pick on someone else."

Claudia looked out the window and didn't answer. Jamie said, "As long as you've got me here, tell me."

Claudia still said nothing and still looked out the window. Jamie became impatient. "I said that as long as you've got me here, you may as well tell me."

Claudia remained silent. Jamie erupted, "What's the matter with you, Claude? First you bust up my card game, then you don't tell me. It's undecent."

"Break up, not bust up. Indecent, not undecent," Claudia corrected.

"Oh, boloney! You know what I mean. Now tell me," he demanded.

"I've picked you to accompany me on the greatest adventure of our mutual lives," Claudia repeated.

"You said that." He clenched his teeth. "Now tell me."

"I've decided to run away from home, and I've chosen you to accompany me."

"Why pick on me? Why not pick on Steve?" he asked.

Claudia sighed, "I don't want Steve. Steve is one of the things in my life that I'm running away from. I want you."

Despite himself, Jamie felt flattered. (Flattery is as important a machine as the lever, isn't it, Saxonberg? Give it a proper place to rest, and it can move the world.) It moved Jamie. He stopped thinking, "Why pick on me?" and started thinking, "I am chosen." He sat up in his seat, unzipped his jacket, put one foot up on the seat, placed his hands over his bent knee and said out of the corner of his mouth, "O.K., Claude, when do we bust out of here? And how?"

Claudia stifled the urge to correct his grammar again. "On Wednesday. Here's the plan. Listen carefully."

Jamie squinted his eyes and said, "Make it complicated, Claude. I like complications."

Claudia laughed. "It's got to be simple to work. We'll go on Wednesday because Wednesday is music lesson day. I'm taking my violin out of its case and am packing it full of clothes. You do the same with your trumpet case. Take as much clean underwear as possible and socks and at least one other shirt with you."

"All in a trumpet case? I should have taken up the bass fiddle."

"You can use some of the room in my case. Also use your book bag. Take your transistor radio."

"Can I wear sneakers?" Jamie asked.

Claudia answered, "Of course. Wearing shoes all the time is one of the tyrannies you'll escape by coming with me."

Jamie smiled, and Claudia knew that now was the correct time to ask. She almost managed to sound casual. "And bring all your money." She cleared her throat. "By the way, how much money do you have?"

Jamie put his foot back down on the floor, looked out the window and said, "Why do you want to know?"

"For goodness' sake, Jamie, if we're in this together, then we're together. I've got to know. How much do you have?"

"Can I trust you not to talk?" he asked.

Claudia was getting mad. "Did *I* ask *you* if I could trust you not to talk?" She clamped her mouth shut and let out twin whiffs of air through her nostrils; had she done it any harder or any louder, it would have been called a snort.

"Well, you see, Claude," Jamie whispered, "I have quite a lot of money."

Claudia thought that old Jamie would end up

being a business tycoon someday. Or at least a tax attorney like their grandfather. She said nothing to Jamie.

Jamie continued, "Claude, don't tell Mom or Dad, but I gamble. I play those card games with Bruce for money. Every Friday we count our cards, and he pays me. Two cents for every card I have more than he has and five cents for every ace. And I always have more cards than he has and at least one more ace."

Claudia lost all patience. "Tell me how much you have! Four dollars? Five? How much?"

Jamie nuzzled himself further into the corner of the bus seat and sang, "Twenty-four dollars and forty-three cents." Claudia gasped, and Jamie, enjoying her reaction, added, "Hang around until Friday and I'll make it twenty-five even."

"How can you do that? Your allowance is only twenty-five cents. Twenty-four forty-three plus twenty-five cents makes only twenty-four dollars and sixty-eight cents." Details never escaped Claudia.

"I'll win the rest from Bruce."

"C'mon now, James, how can you know on Monday that you'll win on Friday?"

"I just know that I will," he answered.

"How do you know?"

"I'll never tell." He looked straight at Claudia to see her reaction. She looked puzzled. He smiled, and so did she, for she then felt more certain than ever that she had chosen the correct brother for a partner in escape. They complemented each other perfectly. She was cautious (about everything but money) and poor; he was adventurous (about everything but money) and rich. More than twenty-four dollars. That would be quite a nice boodle to put in their knapsacks if they were using knapsacks instead of instrument cases. She already had four dollars and eighteen cents. They would escape in comfort.

Jamie waited while she thought. "Well? What do you say? Want to wait until Friday?"

Claudia hesitated only a minute more before deciding. "No, we have to go on Wednesday. I'll write you full details of my plan. You must show the plan to no one. Memorize all the details; then destroy my note."

"Do I have to eat it?" Jamie asked.

"Tearing it up and putting it in the trash would be much simpler. No one in our family but me ever goes through the trash. And I only do if it is not sloppy and not full of pencil sharpener shavings. Or ashes."

"I'll eat it. I like complications," Jamie said.

"You must also like wood pulp," Claudia said. "That's what paper is made of, you know."

"I know. I know," Jamie answered. They spoke no more until they got off the bus at their stop. Steve got off the bus after Jamie and Claudia.

Steve yelled, "Claude! Claude! It's your turn to take Kevin. I'll tell Mom if you forget."

Claudia, who had been walking up ahead with Jamie, stopped short, ran back, grabbed Kevin's hand and started retracing her steps, pulling him along to the side and slightly behind.

"I wanna walk with Stevie," Kevin cried.

"That would be just fine with me, Kevin Brat," Claudia answered. "But today you happen to be my responsibility."

"Whose 'sponsibility am I next?" he asked.

"Wednesday starts Steve's turn," Claudia answered.

"I wish it could be Steve's turn every week," Kevin whined.

"You just may get your wish."

Kevin never realized then or ever that he had been given a clue, and he pouted all the way home.

2

On Tuesday night Jamie found his list of instructions under his pillow pinned to his pajamas. His first instruction was to forget his homework; get ready for the trip instead. I wholeheartedly admire Claudia's thoroughness. Her concern for delicate details is as well developed as mine. Her note to Jamie even included a suggestion for hiding his trumpet when he took it out of its case. He was to roll it up in his extra blanket, which was always placed at the foot of his bed.

After he had followed all the instructions on the list, Jamie took a big glass of water from the bathroom and sat cross-legged on the bed. He bit off a large corner of the list. The paper tasted like the bubble gum he had once saved and chewed for five days; it was just as tasteless and only slightly harder. Since the ink was not waterproof, it turned his teeth blue. He tried only one more bite before he tore up the note, crumpled the pieces, and threw them into the trash. Then he brushed his teeth.

The next morning Claudia and Jamie boarded the school bus as usual, according to plan. They sat together in the back and continued sitting there when they arrived at school and everyone got out of the bus. No one was supposed to notice this, and no one did. There was so much jostling and searching for homework papers and mittens that no one paid any attention to anything except personal possessions until they were well up the walk to school. Claudia had instructed Jamie to pull his feet up and crouch his head down so that Herbert, the driver, couldn't see him. He did, and she did the same. If they were spotted, the plan was to go to school and fake out their schedules as best they could, having neither books in their bags nor musical instruments in their cases.

They lay over their book bags and over the trumpet and violin cases. Each held his breath for a long time, and each resisted at least four temptations to peek up and see what was going on. Claudia pretended that she was blind and had to depend upon her senses of hearing, touch, and smell. When they heard the last of the feet going down the steps and the motor start again, they lifted their chins slightly and smiled—at each other.

Herbert would now take the bus to the lot on the Boston Post Road where the school buses parked. Then he would get out of the bus and get into his car and go wherever else he always went. James and Claudia practiced silence all during the ragged ride to the parking lot. The bus bounced along like an empty cracker box on wheels—almost empty. Fortunately, the bumps made it noisy. Otherwise, Claudia would have worried for fear the driver could hear her heart, for it sounded to her like their electric percolator brewing the morning's coffee. She didn't like keeping her head down so long. Perspiration was causing her cheek to stick to the plastic seat; she was convinced that she would develop a medium-serious skin disease within five minutes after she got off the bus.

The bus came to a stop. They heard the door open. Just a few backward steps by Herbert, and they would be discovered. They held their breath until they heard him walk down the steps and out of the bus. Then they heard the door close. After he got out, Herbert reached in from the small side window to operate the lever that closed the door.

Claudia slowly pulled her arm in front of her and glanced at her watch. She would give Herbert seven minutes before she would lift her head. When the time was up, both of them knew that they could get up, but both wanted to see if they could hold out a little bit longer, and they did. They stayed crouched down for about forty-five more seconds, but being cramped and uncomfortable, it seemed like forty-five more minutes.

When they got up, both were grinning. They peeked out of the window of the bus, and saw that the coast was clear. There was no need to hurry so they slowly made their way up to the front, Claudia leading. The door lever was left of the driver's seat, and as she walked toward it, she heard an awful racket behind her.

"Jamie," she whispered, "what's all that racket?"

Jamie stopped, and so did the noise. "What racket?" he demanded.

"You," she said. "You are the racket. What in the world are you wearing? Chain mail?"

"I'm just wearing my usual. Starting from the bottom, I have B.V.D. briefs, size ten, one tee shirt . . ."

"Oh, for goodness' sake, I know all that. What are you wearing that makes so much noise?"

"Twenty-four dollars and forty-three cents."

Claudia saw then that his pockets were so heavy they were pulling his pants down. There was a gap of an inch and a half between the bottom hem of his shirt and the top of his pants. A line of winter white skin was punctuated by his navel.

"How come all your money is in change? It rattles."

"Bruce pays off in pennies and nickels. What did you expect him to pay me in? Traveler's checks?"

"O.K. O.K.," Claudia said. "What's that hanging from your belt?"

"My compass. Got it for my birthday last year."

"Why did you bother bringing that? You're carrying enough weight around already."

"You need a compass to find your way in the woods. Out of the woods, too. Everyone uses a compass for that."

"What woods?" Claudia asked.

"The woods we'll be hiding out in," Jamie answered.

"Hiding *out in*? What kind of language is that?"

"English language. That's what kind."

"Who ever told you that we were going to hide out in the woods?" Claudia demanded.

"There! You said it. You said it!" Jamie shrieked.

"Said what? I never said we're going to hide out in the woods." Now Claudia was yelling, too.

"No! you said '*hide out in.*' "

"I did not!"

Jamie exploded. "You did, too. You said, 'Who ever told you that we're going to *hide out in* the woods?' You said that."

"O.K. O.K.," Claudia replied. She was trying hard to remain calm, for she knew that a group leader must never lose control of herself, even if the group she leads consists of only herself and one brother brat.

"O.K.," she repeated. "I *may* have said hide *out in*, but I didn't say *the woods.*"

"Yes, sir. You said, 'Who ever told you that . . .' "

Claudia didn't give him a chance to finish. "I know. I know. Now, let's begin by my saying that we are going to hide out in the Metropolitan Museum of Art in New York City."

Jamie said, "See! See! You said it again."

"I did not! I said, 'The Metropolitan Museum of Art.' "

"You said *hide out in* again."

"All right. Let's forget the English language lessons. We are going to the Metropolitan Museum of Art in Manhattan."

For the first time, the meaning instead of the grammar of what Claudia had said penetrated.

"The Metropolitan Museum of Art! Boloney!" he exclaimed. "What kind of crazy idea is that?"

Claudia now felt that she had control of herself and Jamie and the situation. For the past few minutes they had forgotten that they were stowaways on the school bus and had behaved as they always did at home. She said, "Let's get off this bus and on the train, and I'll tell you about it."

Once again James Kincaid felt cheated. "The train! Can't we even hitchhike to New York?"

"Hitchhike? And take a chance of getting kidnapped or robbed? Or we could even get mugged," Claudia replied.

U.S.
MAIL

"Robbed? Why are you worried about that? It's mostly my money," Jamie told her.

"We're in this together. Its mostly your money we're using, but it's all my idea we're using. We'll take the train."

"Of all the sissy ways to run away and of all the sissy places to run away to. . . ." Jamie mumbled.

He didn't mumble quite softly enough. Claudia turned on him, "Run *away to*? How can you run *away* and *to*? What kind of language is that?" Claudia asked.

"The American language," Jamie answered. "American James Kincaidian language." And they both left the bus forgetting caution and remembering only their quarrel.

They were not discovered.

On the way to the train station Claudia mailed two letters.

"What were those?" Jamie asked.

"One was a note to Mom and Dad to tell them that we are leaving home and not to call the FBI. They'll get it tomorrow or the day after."

"And the other?"

"The other was two box tops from corn flakes. They send you twenty-five cents if you mail them two box tops with stars on the tops. For milk money, it said."

"You should have sent that in before. We could use twenty-five cents more."

"We just finished eating the second box of corn flakes this morning," Claudia informed him.

They arrived at the Greenwich station in time to catch the 10:42 local. The train was not filled with either commuters or lady shoppers, so Claudia walked up the aisles of one car and then another until she found a pair of chairs that dissatisfied her the least with regard to the amount of dust and lint on the blue velvet mohair covers. Jamie spent seven of the twenty-eight-and-a-half railroad miles trying to convince his sister that they should try hiding in Central Park. Claudia appointed him treasurer; he would not only hold all the money, he would also keep track of it and pass judgment on all expenditures. Then Jamie began to feel that the Metropolitan offered several advantages and would provide adventure enough.

And in the course of those miles Claudia stopped regretting bringing Jamie along. In fact when they emerged from the train at Grand Central into the underworld of cement and steel that leads to the terminal, Claudia felt that having Jamie there was important. (Ah, how well I know those feelings of hot and hollow that come from that dimly lit concrete ramp.) And his money and radio were not the only reasons. Manhattan called for the courage of at least two Kincaids.

3

As soon as they reached the sidewalk, Jamie made his first decision as treasurer. "We'll walk from here to the museum."

"Walk?" Claudia asked. "Do you realize that it is over forty blocks from here?"

"Well, how much does the bus cost?"

"The bus!" Claudia exclaimed. "Who said anything about taking a bus? I want to take a taxi."

"Claudia," Jamie said, "you are quietly out of your mind. How can you even think of a taxi? We have no more allowance. No more income. You can't be extravagant any longer. It's not my money we're spending. It's *our* money. We're in this together, remember?"

"You're right," Claudia answered. "A taxi is expensive. The bus is cheaper. It's only twenty cents each. We'll take the bus."

"*Only* twenty cents each. That's forty cents total. No bus. We'll walk."

"We'll wear out forty cents worth of shoe leather," Claudia mumbled. "You're sure we have to walk?"

"Positive," Jamie answered. "Which way do we go?"

"Sure you won't change your mind?" The look on Jamie's face gave her the answer. She sighed. No wonder Jamie had more than twenty-four dollars; he was a gambler and a cheapskate. If that's the way he wants to be, she thought, I'll never again ask him for bus fare; I'll suffer and never, never let him know about it. But he'll regret it when I simply collapse from exhaustion. I'll collapse quietly.

"We'd better walk up Madison Avenue," she told her brother. "I'll see too many ways to spend *our* precious money if we walk on Fifth Avenue. All those gorgeous stores."

She and Jamie did not walk exactly side by side. Her violin case kept bumping him, and he began to walk a few steps ahead of her. As Claudia's pace slowed down from what she was sure was an accumulation of carbon dioxide in her system (she had not yet learned about muscle fatigue in science class even though she was in the sixth grade honors class), Jamie's pace quickened. Soon he was walking a block and a half ahead of her. They would meet when a red light held him up. At one of these mutual stops Claudia instructed Jamie to wait for her on the corner of Madison Avenue and 80th Street, for there they would turn left to Fifth Avenue.

She found Jamie standing on that corner, probably one of the most civilized street corners in the whole world, consulting a compass and announcing that when they turned left, they would be heading "due northwest." Claudia was tired and cold at the tips; her fingers, her toes, her nose were all cold while the rest of her was perspiring under the weight of her winter clothes. She never liked feeling either very hot or very cold, and she hated feeling both at the same time. "Head due northwest. Head due northwest," she mimicked. "Can't you simply say turn right or turn left as everyone else does? Who do you think you are? Daniel Boone? I'll bet no one's used a compass in Manhattan since Henry Hudson."

Jamie didn't answer. He briskly rounded the corner of 80th Street and made his hand into a sun visor as he peered down the street. Claudia needed an argument. Her internal heat, the heat of anger, was cooking that accumulated carbon dioxide. It would soon explode out of her if she didn't give it some vent. "Don't you realize that we must try to be inconspicuous?" she demanded of her brother.

"What's inconspicuous?"

"Un-noticeable."

Jamie looked all around. "I think you're brilliant, Claude. New York is a great place to hide out. No one notices no one."

"Anyone," Claudia corrected. She looked at Jamie and found him smiling. She softened. She had to agree with her brother. She was brilliant. New York was a great place, and being called brilliant had cooled her down. The bubbles dissolved. By the time they reached the museum, she no longer needed an argument.

As they entered the main door on Fifth Avenue, the guard clicked off two numbers on his people counter. Guards always count the people going into the museum, but they don't count them going out. (My chauffeur, Sheldon, has a friend named Morris who is a guard at the Metropolitan. I've kept Sheldon busy getting information from Morris. It's not hard to do since Morris loves to talk about his work. He'll tell about anything except security. Ask him a question he won't or can't answer, and he says, "I'm not at liberty to tell. Security.")

By the time Claudia and Jamie reached their destination, it was one o'clock, and the museum was busy. On any ordinary Wednesday over 26,000 people come. They spread out over the twenty acres of floor space; they roam from room to room to room to room to room. On Wednesday come the gentle old ladies who are using the time before the Broadway matinee begins. They walk around in pairs. You can tell they are a set because they wear matching pairs of orthopedic shoes, the kind that lace on the side. Tourists visit the museum on Wednesdays. You can tell them because the men carry cameras, and the women look as if their feet hurt; they wear high heeled shoes. (I always say that those who wear 'em deserve 'em.) And there are art students. Any day of the week. They also walk around in pairs. You can tell that they are a set because they carry matching black sketchbooks.

(You've missed all this, Saxonberg. Shame on you! You've never set your well-polished shoe inside that museum. More than a quarter of a million people come to that museum every week. They come from Mankato, Kansas where they have no museums and from Paris, France, where they have lots. And they all enter free of charge because that's what the museum is: great and large and wonderful and free to all. And complicated. Complicated enough even for Jamie Kincaid.)

No one thought it strange that a boy and a girl, each carrying a book bag and an instrument case and who would normally be in school, were visiting a museum. After all, about a thousand school children visit the museum every day. The guard at the entrance merely stopped them and told them to check their cases and book bags. A museum rule: no bags, food, or umbrellas. None that the guards can see. Rule or no rule, Claudia decided it was a good idea. A big sign in the checking room said NO TIPPING, so she knew that Jamie couldn't object. Jamie did object, however; he pulled his sister aside and asked her how she expected him to change into his pajamas. His pajamas, he explained, were rolled into a tiny ball in his trumpet case.

Claudia told him that she fully expected to check out at 4:30. They would then leave the museum by the front door and within five minutes would re-enter from the back, through the door that leads from the parking lot to the Children's Museum. After all, didn't that solve all their problems? (1) They would be seen leaving the museum. (2) They would be free of their baggage while they scouted around for a place to spend the night. And (3) it was free.

Claudia checked her coat as well as her packages. Jamie was condemned to walking around in his ski jacket. When the jacket was on and zippered, it covered up that exposed strip of skin. Besides, the orlon plush lining did a great deal to muffle his twenty-four-dollar rattle. Claudia would never have permitted herself to become so overheated, but Jamie liked perspiration, a little bit of dirt, and complications.

Right now, however, he wanted lunch. Claudia wished to eat in the restaurant on the main floor, but Jamie wished to eat in the snack bar downstairs; he thought it would be less glamorous, but cheaper, and as chancellor of the exchequer, as holder of the veto power, and as tightwad of the year, he got his wish. Claudia didn't really mind too much when she saw the snack bar. It was plain but clean.

James was dismayed at the prices. They had $28.61 when they went into the cafeteria, and only $27.11 when they came out still feeling hungry. "Claudia," he demanded, "did you know food would cost so much? Now, aren't you glad that we didn't take a bus?"

Claudia was no such thing. She was not glad that they hadn't taken a bus. She was merely furious that her parents, and Jamie's too, had been so stingy that she had been away from home for less than one whole day and was already worried about survival money. She chose not to answer Jamie. Jamie didn't notice; he was completely wrapped up in problems of finance.

"Do you think I could get one of the guards to play me a game of war?" he asked.

"That's ridiculous," Claudia said.

"Why? I brought my cards along. A whole deck."

Claudia said, "*Inconspicuous* is exactly the opposite of that. Even a guard at the Metropolitan who sees thousands of people every day would remember a boy who played him a game of cards."

Jamie's pride was involved. "I cheated Bruce through all second grade and through all third grade so far, and he still isn't wise."

"Jamie! Is that how you knew you'd win?"

Jamie bowed his head and answered, "Well, yeah.

Besides, Brucie has trouble keeping straight the jacks, queens, and kings. He gets mixed up."

"Why do you cheat your best friend?"

"I sure don't know. I guess I like complications."

"Well, quit worrying about money now. Worry about where we're going to hide while they're locking up this place."

They took a map from the information stand, for free. Claudia selected where they would hide during that dangerous time immediately after the museum was closed to the public and before all the guards and helpers left. She decided that she would go to the ladies' room, and Jamie would go to the men's room just before the museum closed. "Go to the one near the restaurant on the main floor," she told Jamie.

"I'm not spending a night in a men's room. All that tile. It's cold. And, besides, men's rooms make noises sound louder. And I rattle enough now."

Claudia explained to Jamie that he was to enter a booth in the men's room. "And then stand on it," she continued.

"Stand on it? Stand on what?" Jamie demanded.

"You know," Claudia insisted. "Stand on it!"

"You mean stand on the toilet?" Jamie needed everything spelled out.

"Well, what else would I mean? What else is there in a booth in the men's room? And keep your head down. And keep the door to the booth very slightly open," Claudia finished.

"Feet up. Head down. Door open. Why?"

"Because I'm certain that when they check the ladies' room and the men's room, they peek under the door and check only to see if there are feet. We must stay there until we're sure all the people and guards have gone home."

"How about the night watchman?" Jamie asked.

Claudia displayed a lot more confidence than she really felt. "Oh! there'll be a night watchman, I'm sure. But he mostly walks around the roof trying to keep people from breaking in. We'll already be in. They call what he walks, a cat walk. We'll learn his habits soon enough. They must mostly use burglar alarms in the inside. We'll just never touch a window, a door, or a valuable painting. Now, let's find a place to spend the night."

They wandered back to the rooms of fine French and English furniture. It was here Claudia knew for sure that she had chosen the most elegant place in the world to hide. She wanted to sit on the lounge chair that had been made for Marie Antoinette or at least sit at her writing table. But signs everywhere said not to step on the platform. And some of the chairs had silken ropes strung across the arms to keep you from even trying to sit down. She would have to wait until after lights out to be Marie Antoinette.

At last she found a bed that she considered perfectly wonderful, and she told Jamie that they would spend the night there. The bed had a tall canopy,

supported by an ornately carved headboard at one end and by two gigantic posts at the other. (I'm familiar with that bed, Saxonberg. It is as enormous and fussy as mine. And it dates from the sixteenth century like mine. I once considered donating my bed to the museum, but Mr. Untermyer gave them this one first. I was somewhat relieved when he did. Now I can enjoy my bed without feeling guilty because the museum doesn't have one. Besides, I'm not that fond of donating things.)

Claudia had always known that she was meant for such fine things. Jamie, on the other hand, thought that running away from home to sleep in just another bed was really no challenge at all. He, James, would rather sleep on the bathroom floor, after all. Claudia then pulled him around to the foot of the bed and told him to read what the card said.

Jamie read, "Please do not step on the platform."

Claudia knew that he was being difficult on purpose; therefore, she read for him, "State bed–scene of the alleged murder of Amy Robsart, first wife of Lord Robert Dudley, later Earl of . . ."

Jamie couldn't control his smile. He said, "You know, Claude, for a sister and a fussbudget, you're not too bad."

Claudia replied, "You know, Jamie, for a brother and a cheapskate, you're not too bad."

Something happened at precisely that moment.

Both Claudia and Jamie tried to explain to me about it, but they couldn't quite. I know what happened, though I never told them. Having words and explanations for everything is too modern. I especially wouldn't tell Claudia. She has too many explanations already.

What happened was that they became a team, a family of two. There had been times before they ran away when they had acted like a team, but those were very different from *feeling* like a team. Becoming a team didn't mean the end of their arguments. But it did mean that the arguments became a part of the adventure, became discussions not threats. To an outsider the arguments would appear to be the same because feeling like part of a team is something that happens invisibly. You might call it *caring*. You could even call it *love*. And it is very rarely, indeed, that it happens to two people at the same time—especially a brother and a sister who had always spent more time with activities than they had with each other.

They followed their plan: checked out of the museum and re-entered through a back door. When the guard at that entrance told them to check their instrument cases, Claudia told them that they were just passing through on their way to meet their mother. The guard let them go, knowing that if they went very far, some other guard would stop them again. However, they managed to avoid other guards for the remaining minutes until the bell rang. The bell meant that the museum was closing in five minutes. They then entered the booths of the rest rooms.

They waited in the booths until five-thirty, when they felt certain that everyone had gone. Then they came out and met. Five-thirty in winter is dark, but nowhere seems as dark as the Metropolitan Museum of Art. The ceilings are so high that they fill up with a lot of darkness. It seemed to Jamie and Claudia that they walked through miles of corridors. Fortunately, the corridors were wide, and they were spared bumping into things.

At last they came to the hall of the English Renaissance. Jamie quickly threw himself upon the bed forgetting that it was only about six o'clock and thinking that he would be so exhausted that he would immediately fall asleep. He didn't. He was hungry. That was one reason he didn't fall asleep immediately. He was uncomfortable, too. So he got up from bed, changed into his pajamas and got back into bed. He felt a little better. Claudia had already changed into her pajamas. She, too, was hungry, and she, too, was uncomfortable. How could so elegant and romantic a bed smell so musty? She would have liked to wash everything in a good, strong, sweet-smelling detergent.

As Jamie got into bed, he still felt uneasy, and it wasn't because he was worried about being caught. Claudia had planned everything so well that he didn't concern himself about that. The strange way he felt had little to do with the strange place in which they were sleeping. Claudia felt it, too. Jamie lay there thinking. Finally, realization came.

"You know, Claude," he whispered, "I didn't brush my teeth."

Claudia answered, "Well, Jamie, you can't always brush after every meal." They both laughed very quietly. "Tomorrow," Claudia reassured him, "we'll be even better organized."

It was much earlier than her bedtime at home, but still Claudia felt tired. She thought she might have an iron deficiency anemia: tired blood. Perhaps, the pressures of everyday stress and strain had gotten her down. Maybe she was light-headed from hunger; her brain cells were being robbed of vitally needed oxygen for good growth and, and . . . yawn.

She shouldn't have worried. It had been an unusually busy day. A busy and unusual day. So she lay there in the great quiet of the museum next to the warm quiet of her brother and allowed the soft stillness to settle around them: a comforter of quiet. The silence seeped from their heads to their soles and into their souls. They stretched out and relaxed. Instead of oxygen and stress, Claudia thought now of hushed and quiet words: glide, fur, banana, peace. Even the footsteps of the night watchman added only an accented quarter-note to the silence that had become a hum, a lullaby.

They lay perfectly still even long after he passed.

Then they whispered good night to each other and fell asleep. They were quiet sleepers and hidden by the heaviness of the dark, they were easily not discovered.

(Of course, Saxonberg, the draperies of that bed helped, too.)

4

Claudia and Jamie awoke very early the next morning. It was still dark. Their stomachs felt like tubes of toothpaste that had been all squeezed out. Giant economy-sized tubes. They had to be out of bed and out of sight before the museum staff came on duty. Neither was accustomed to getting up so early, to feeling so unwashed, or feeling so hungry.

They dressed in silence. Each felt that peculiar chill that comes from getting up in the early morning. The chill that must come from one's own bloodstream, for it comes in summer as well as winter, from some inside part of you that knows it is early morning. Claudia always dreaded that brief moment when her pajamas were shed and her underwear was not yet on.

Even before she began undressing, she always had her underwear laid out on the bed in the right direction, right for getting into as quickly as possible. She did this now, too. But she hurried less pulling her petticoat down over her head. She took good long whiffs of the wonderful essence of detergent and clean dacron-cotton which floated down with the petticoat. Next to any kind of elegance, Claudia loved good clean smells.

After they were dressed, Claudia whispered to Jamie, "Let's stash our book bags and instrument cases before we man our stations."

They agreed to scatter their belongings. Thus, if the museum officials found one thing, they wouldn't necessarily find all. While still at home they had removed all identification on their cases as well as their clothing. Any child who has watched only one month's worth of television knows to do that much.

Claudia hid her violin case in a sarcophagus that had no lid. It was well above eye level, and Jamie helped hoist her up so that she could reach it. It was a beautifully carved Roman marble sarcophagus. She hid her book bag behind a tapestry screen in the rooms of French furniture. Jamie wanted to hide his things in a mummy case, but Claudia said that that would be unnecessarily complicated. The Egyptian wing of the Metropolitan was too far away from their bedroom; for the number of risks involved, it might as well be in Egypt. So the trumpet case was hidden inside a huge urn and Jamie's book bag was neatly tucked behind a drape that was behind a statue from the Middle Ages. Unfortunately, the museum people had fastened all the drawers of their furniture so that they couldn't be opened. They had never given a thought to the convenience of Jamie Kincaid.

"Manning their stations" meant climbing back into the booths and waiting during the perilous time when the museum was open to the staff but not to visitors. They washed up, combed their hair, and even brushed their teeth. Then began those long moments. That first morning they weren't quite sure when the staff would arrive, so they hid good and early. While Claudia stood crouched down waiting, the emptiness and the hollowness of all the museum corridors filled her stomach. She was starved. She spent her time trying not to remember delicious things to eat.

Jamie made one slight error that morning. It was almost enough to be caught. When he heard the sound of running water, he assumed that some male visitor was using the men's room to wash up. He checked his watch and saw that it was five past ten; he knew that the museum officially opened at ten o'clock, so he stepped down to walk out of his booth. It was not, however, a museum visitor who had turned on the water tap. It was a janitor filling his bucket. He was leaning down in the act of wringing out his mop when he saw Jamie's legs appear from nowhere and then saw Jamie emerge.

"Where did you come from?" he asked.

Jamie smiled and nodded. "Mother always says that I came from Heaven." He bowed politely and walked out, delighted with his brush with danger. He could hardly wait to tell Claudia. Claudia chose not to be amused on so empty a stomach.

The museum restaurant wouldn't open until eleven thirty and the snack bar wouldn't open until after that, so they left the museum to get breakfast. They went to the automat and used up a dollar's worth of Bruce's nickels. Jamie allotted ten nickels to Claudia and kept ten for himself. Jamie bought a cheese sandwich and coffee. After eating these he still felt hungry and told Claudia she could have twenty-five cents more for pie if she wished. Claudia, who had eaten cereal and drunk pineapple juice, scolded him about the need to eat properly. Breakfast food for breakfast, and lunch food for lunch. Jamie countered with complaints about Claudia's narrow-mindedness.

They were better organized that second day. Knowing that they could not afford more than two meals a day, they stopped at a grocery and bought small packages of peanut butter crackers for the night; they hid them in various pockets in their clothing. They decided to join a school group for lunch at the snack bar. There were certainly enough to choose from. That way their faces would always be just part of the crowd.

Upon their return to the museum, Claudia informed Jamie that they should take advantage of the wonderful opportunity they had to learn and to study. No other children in all the world since the world began had had such an opportunity. So she set forth for herself and for her brother the task of learning everything about the museum. One thing at a time. (Claudia probably didn't realize that the museum has over 365,000 works of art. Even if she had, she could not have been convinced that learning everything about everything was not possible; her ambitions were as enormous and as multi-directional as the museum itself.) Every day they would pick a different gallery about which they would learn everything. He could pick first. She would pick second; he, third; and so on. Just like the television schedule at home. Jamie considered learning something every day outrageous. It was not only outrageous; it was unnecessary. Claudia simply did not know how to escape. He thought he would put a quick end to this part of their runaway career. He chose the galleries of the Italian Renaissance. He didn't even know what the Renaissance was except that it sounded important and there seemed to be an awful lot of it. He figured that Claudia would soon give up in despair.

When she gave Jamie first pick, Claudia had been certain that he would choose Arms and Armor. She herself found these interesting. There was probably two days' worth of learning there. Perhaps, she might even choose the same on the second day.

MAIN FLOOR

E—Elevators
T—Toilets

INFORMATION DESK
879-5500 ext. 457

RESTAURANT HOURS:
Mondays-Saturdays, 11:30 A.M.-2:30 P.M.
Sundays, 12 P.M. -3 P.M.
COFFEE HOUR: Saturdays, 3-4:30 P.M.
Sundays, 3:30-4:30 P.M.

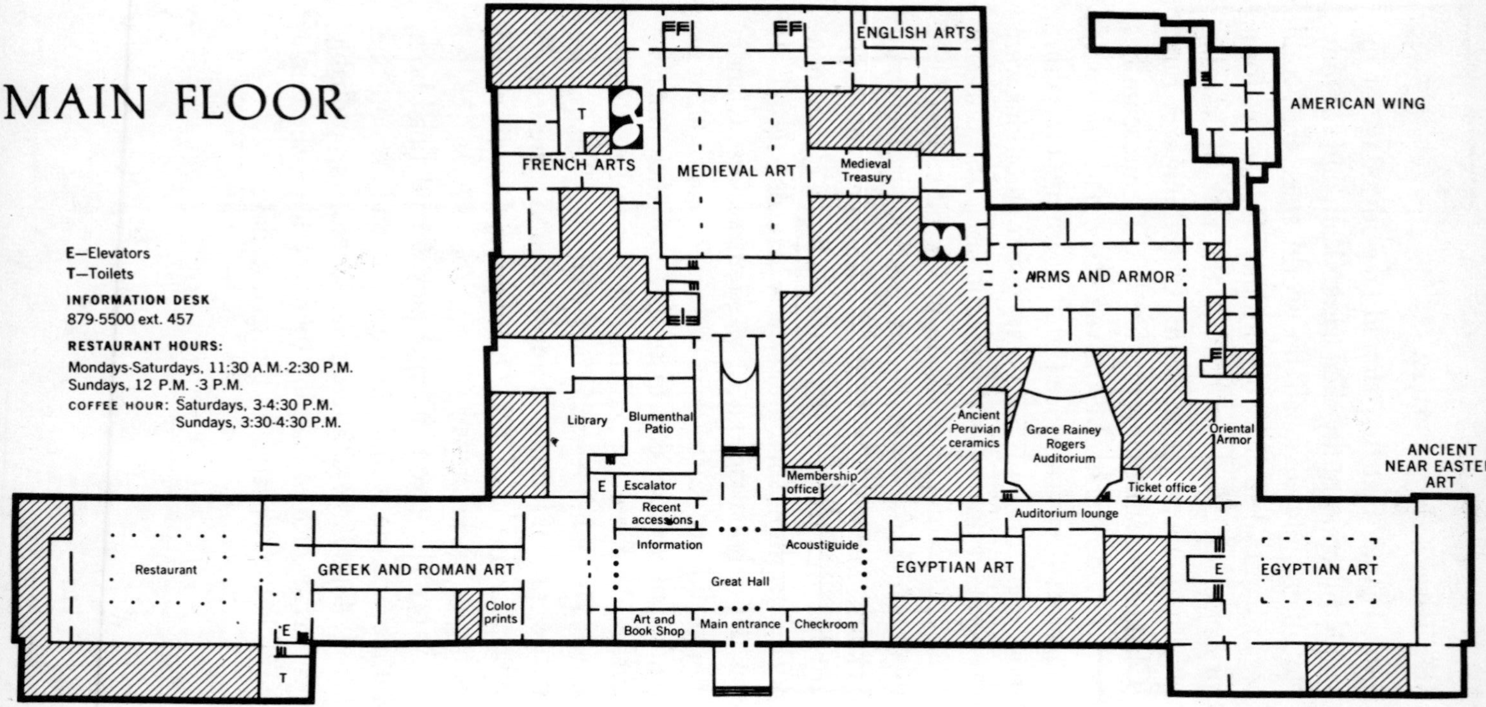

SECOND FLOOR

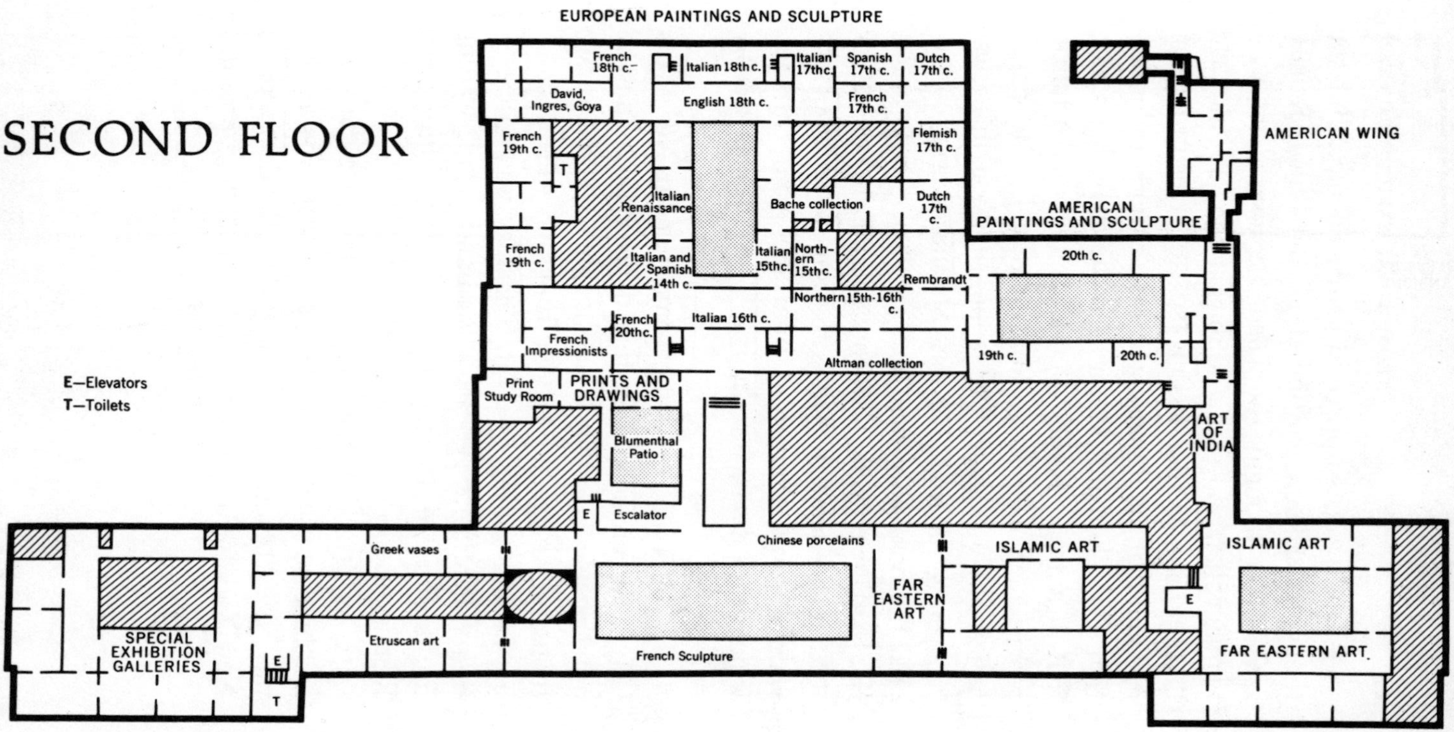

E—Elevators

T—Toilets

Claudia was surprised at Jamie's choice. But she thought she knew why he chose the Italian Renaissance. She thought she knew because along with tennis, ballet, and diving lessons at the "Y", she had taken art appreciation lessons last year. Her art teacher had said that the Renaissance was a period of glorification of the human form; as best she could figure out, that meant bare bodies. Many painters of the Italian Renaissance had painted huge billowy, bosomy naked ladies. She was amazed at Jamie; she thought he was too young for that. He was. She never even considered the possibility that he wanted her to be bored. She had given him first choice, and she was stuck with it. So she marched with him toward the long wide stairway straight in from the main entrance, which leads directly to the Hall of the Italian Renaissance.

If you think of doing something in New York City, you can be certain that at least two thousand other people have that same thought. And of the two thousand who do, about one thousand will be standing in line waiting to do it. That day was no exception. There were at least a thousand people waiting in line to see things in the Hall of the Italian Renaissance.

Claudia and Jamie did not think that there was anything unusual about the size of the crowd. This was New York. *Crowded* was part of the definition of New York. (To many art experts, Saxonberg, *crowded* is part of the definition of the Italian Renaissance, too. It was a time much like this: artistic activity was everywhere. Keeping track of the artists of the fifteenth and sixteenth centuries in Italy is as difficult as keeping track of the tax laws in the nineteen fifties and sixties in the United States. And almost as complicated.)

As they reached the top of the stairs, a guard said, "Line forms to the right. Single file, please." They did as they were told, partly because they didn't want to offend any guard or even attract his attention and partly because the crowd made them. Ladies' arms draped with pocketbooks and men's arms draped with coats formed a barrier as difficult to get through as barbed wire. Claudia and Jamie stood in the manner of all children who are standing in line. They stood leaning back with their necks stretched and their heads tilted away, way back, making a vain effort to see over the shoulders of the tall adult who always appears in front of them. Jamie could see nothing but the coat of the man in front of him. Claudia could see nothing but a piece of Jamie's head plus the coat of the man in front of Jamie.

They realized that they were approaching something out of the ordinary when they saw a newspaper cameraman walking along the edge of the crowd. The newsman carried a large, black, flash camera which had *TIMES* stencilled in white on its case. Jamie tried to slow down to the pace of the photographer. He didn't know what he was having his picture taken for, but he liked getting his picture taken—especially for a newspaper. Once when his class had visited the fire department, his picture had been in the paper at home. He had bought seven copies of the paper and used that page for book covers. When the book covers began to tear, he covered the covers with Saran wrap. They were still in his bookcase at home.

Claudia sensed danger. At least *she* remembered that they had run away from home, and she didn't want any New York paper advertising her whereabouts. Or Jamie's either. Especially if her parents happened to be looking for her. Someone in Greenwich was bound to read the *New York Times* and tell her folks. It would be more than a clue; it would be like booking anyone looking for them on a chartered bus ride straight to the hideaway. Wouldn't her brother ever learn inconspicuous? She shoved him.

He almost fell into the man in the coat. Jamie turned to Claudia and gave her an awful look. Claudia paid no attention, for now they reached what everyone was standing in line to see. A statue of an angel; her arms were folded, and she was looking holy. As Claudia passed by, she thought that that angel was the most beautiful, most graceful little statue she had ever seen; she wanted to stop and stare; she almost did, but the crowd wouldn't let her. As Jamie passed by, he thought that he would get even with Claudia for shoving him.

They followed the line to the end of the Renaissance Hall. When the velvet ropes that had guided the crowd by creating a narrow street within the room ended, they found themselves going down a staircase to the main floor. Claudia was lost in remembrance of the beautiful angel she had seen. Why did she seem so important; and why was she so special? Of course, she was beautiful. Graceful. Polished. But so were many other things at the museum. Her sarcophagus, for example, the one in which her violin case was hidden. And why was there all that commotion about her? The man had come to take pictures. There would be something about it in tomorrow's paper. They could find out from the newspapers.

She spoke to Jamie, "We'll have to buy a *New York Times* tomorrow to see the picture."

Jamie was still mad about that shove. Why would he want to buy the paper? He wouldn't be in the picture. He chose to fight Claudia with the one weapon he had—the power of the purse. He answered, "We can't afford a *New York Times.* It costs a dime."

"We've got to get one, Jamie. Don't you want to know what's so important about that statue? Why everyone is standing in line to see it?"

Jamie felt that letting Claudia know that she couldn't get away with shoving him in public was more important than his curiosity. "Well, perhaps, tomorrow you can push someone down and grab his paper while he's trying to get up. I'm afraid, though, that our budget won't allow this expense."

They walked for a short while before Claudia said, "I'll find out some way." She was determined about that.

She was also determined about learning; they wouldn't skip a lesson so easily. "Since we can't learn everything about the Italian Renaissance today, let's learn everything about the Egyptian rooms. That will be our lesson instead."

Jamie liked the mummies even if he didn't like lessons, so they walked together to the Egyptian wing. There they encountered a class that was also touring the halls. Each child in the class wore a round circle of blue construction paper on which was written in magic marker: Gr. 6, W.P.S. The class was seated on little rubber mats around a glass case within which was a mummy case within which was the mummy they were talking about. The teacher sat on a folding stool. Both Claudia and Jamie wandered over toward the class and soon became part of it—almost. They listened to the guide, a very pretty young lady who worked for the museum, and they learned a lot. They didn't even mind. They were surprised that they could actually learn something when they weren't in class. The guide told them how mummies were prepared and how Egypt's dry climate helped to preserve them. She told them about digging for tombs, and she told them about the beautiful princess Sit Hat-Hor Yunet whose jewelry they would see in another room. Before they left this room, however, she wanted to know if there were any questions. Since I'm sure this group was typical of all the school groups that I've observed at the museum, I can tell you what they were doing. At least twelve members of Gr. 6, W.P.S. were busy poking at each other. Twelve were wondering when they would eat; four were worried about how long it would be before they could get a drink of water.

Only Jamie had a question: "How much did it cost to become a mummy?"

The pretty guide thought he was part of the class; the teacher thought that he was planted in the audience to pep up the discussion; the class knew that he was an imposter. When they bothered to notice Claudia, they knew that she was one, also. But the class had the good manners that come with not caring; they would leave the imposters alone. The question, however, would have caused at least ten of them to stop poking at each other; six to forget about eating and three others to find the need for drink suddenly less urgent. It caused Claudia to want to embalm Jamie in a vat of mummy fluid right that minute. That would teach him *inconspicuous*.

The guide told Jamie that some people saved all their lives so that they could become mummies; it was indeed expensive.

One of the students called out, "You might even say it costs him his life."

Everyone laughed. Then they picked up their rubber mats and walked to the next room. Claudia was ready to pull Jamie out of line and make him learn another part of the museum today, but she got a glimpse of the room they were to go to next. It was filled with jewelry, case after case of it. So they followed the class into that hall. After a short talk there, the guide bid them good-bye and mentioned that they might enjoy buying some of the museum pamphlets on Egypt. Jamie asked if *they* were expensive.

The guide answered, "Some are as inexpensive as a copy of the Sunday *New York Times*. Others cost much more."

Jamie looked over at Claudia; he shouldn't have. Claudia looked as satisfied as the bronze statue of the Egyptian cat she was standing near. The only real difference between them was that the cat wore tiny golden earrings and looked a trifle less smug.

They got the *New York Times* the next day. Neither Claudia nor Jamie bought it. The man who left it on the counter while he was looking at the reproductions of antique jewelry bought it. The Kincaids stole it from him. They left the museum immediately thereafter.

Claudia read the paper while they ate breakfast at Horn and Hardart's. That morning she didn't eat breakfast food for breakfast. Crackers and roasted chestnuts in bed at night satisfied only a small corner

of her hunger. Being hungry was the most inconvenient part of running away. She meant to eat heartily for every cent Jamie gave her. She bought macaroni and cheese casserole, baked beans, and coffee that morning. Jamie got the same.

The information they wanted was on the first page of the second section of the *Times*. The headline said: RECORD CROWD VIEWS MUSEUM "BARGAIN." There were three pictures: one of the record crowd standing in line; one of the statue itself; and one of the director of the museum with an assistant. The article was as follows: (Saxonberg you can find an original of the newspaper in my files. It's in one of the seventeen cabinets that line the north wall of my office.)

> Officials of the Metropolitan Museum of Art report that 100,000 people climbed the great stairway to catch a glimpse of one of its newest acquisitions, a twenty-four-inch statue called "Angel." Interest in the marble piece arises from the unusual circumstances attending its acquisition by the museum and from the belief that it may be the work of the Italian Renaissance master, Michelangelo. If proof is found that it is an early work of Michelangelo, the museum will have purchased the greatest bargain in art history; it was

purchased at an auction last year for $225.00. Considering that recently Prince Franz Josef II accepted an offer of $5 million for a small painting by Leonardo da Vinci, an artist of the same period and of similar merit, will give some idea of how great a bargain this is.

The museum purchased the statue last year when one of its curators spotted it during a preview showing of works to be auctioned by the Parke-Bernet Galleries. His initial suspicion that it might be the work of Michelangelo was confirmed by several other museum officials, all of whom kept their thoughts quiet in a successful effort to keep the bidding from being driven higher. The statue has been the subject of exhaustive tests and study by the museum staff as well as art experts from abroad. Most believe it to have been done about 470 years ago when Michelangelo was in his early twenties.

The statue was acquired by the Parke-Bernet Galleries from the collection of Mrs. Basil E. Frankweiler. She claims to have purchased it from a dealer in Bologna, Italy before World War II. Mrs. Frankweiler's residence on East 63rd Street was long a Manhattan showplace for what many considered one of the finest private collections of art in the

Western Hemisphere. Others considered it a gigantic hodgepodge of the great and the mediocre. Mrs. Frankweiler closed her Manhattan residence three years ago; important pieces from its contents have found their way to various auctions and galleries since that time.

Mr. Frankweiler amassed a fortune from the corn oil industry and from developing many corn products. He died in 1947. Mrs. Frankweiler now lives on her country estate in Farmington, Connecticut. Her home, which at one time was open to the greats in the worlds of art, business, and politics, is now closed to all but her staff, her advisors, and a few close friends. The Frankweilers had no children.

A museum spokesman said yesterday, "Whether or not conclusive proof will be found that this was the work of Michelangelo, we are pleased with our purchase." Although Michelangelo Buonarroti is perhaps best known for his paintings of the Sistine Chapel in Rome, he always considered himself a sculptor, and primarily a sculptor of marble. The question of whether the museum has acquired one of his lesser known masterpieces still awaits a final answer."

If Claudia's interests had been a little broader, if she had started with the national news on page one and had then read the continuations on page twenty-eight, she might have noticed a small article on that page, one column wide, that would have interested her. The date line was Greenwich, Connecticut, and it stated that two children of Mr. and Mrs. Steven C. Kincaid, Sr. had been missing since Wednesday. The article didn't mention any clues like Claudia's letter. It said that the children were last seen wearing nylon quilted ski jackets. Small help. Fourteen out of fifteen kids in the U.S.A. wear those. It went on to describe Claudia as brunette and pretty and Jamie as brunette and brown eyed. Police in the neighboring towns of Darien and Stamford in Connecticut and Port Chester, New York, had been alerted. (You see, Saxonberg, Claudia had found the article about the statue too easily. She didn't even look at the first section of the paper. I keep telling you that often the search proves more profitable than the goal. Keep that in mind when you're looking for something in my files.)

Claudia and Jamie read about the statue with great interest. Claudia read the article twice so that she could memorize it all. She decided that the statue was not only the most beautiful in the world but also the most mysterious.

Jamie said, "I don't think $225 is cheap. I've never had that much money in my whole life. Totaling up all my birthday and Christmas presents since I was born nine long years ago wouldn't make $225.

Claudia said, "You wouldn't consider two and a quarter cents very much, would you?"

Jamie answered, "I might."

"That's right. *You* might, but most people wouldn't. Well, if this statue is by Michelangelo, it's worth about $2,250,000 instead of $225. That's the same as saying that suddenly two and a quarter cents is worth $225."

Jamie thought this over a minute. He was impressed. "When I grow up, I'm going to find a way to know for certain who did a statue."

This was all Claudia needed. Something that had been smoldering inside her since she first saw the statue, that had been fed by the *Times* article, now flared into an idea.

"Jamie, let's do it now. Let's skip learning everything about everything in the museum. Let's concentrate on the statue."

"Can we still take class tours as we did yesterday?"

Claudia answered, "Of course. We don't have to skip learning *something* about everything. We just won't learn everything about everything. We'll concentrate on Michelangelo."

Jamie snapped his fingers. "I've got it!" he exclaimed. He held up his hands for Claudia to see.

"What does that mean?"

"Fingerprints, silly. If Michelangelo worked on that statue, his fingerprints would be on it."

"Fingerprints? Almost five-hundred-year-old fingerprints? How would you know that they belonged to Michelangelo? He didn't have a police record. I don't suppose he did. As a matter of fact, I'm not sure people were fingerprinted in those days even if they did."

"But what if we were to find identical fingerprints on something they knew that he did? We could compare them."

Claudia kept looking at the picture of the statue as she finished eating her baked beans.

"Jamie," she said, "do you think the statue looks like anyone special?" She folded her arms and gazed into the distance.

"No one I know looks like an angel."

"Think a minute." She cleared her throat and lifted her chin slightly and gazed into the distance. "Don't think about the hair style or the clothes or anything. Just think about the face." She nudged the page of the *New York Times* closer under Jamie's nose and resumed her pose. Jamie looked at the picture.

"Nope," he said looking up.

"Can't you see any resemblance?"

"Nope." He looked at the picture again. "Who do you think it looks like?"

"Oh, I don't know," she stammered.

Jamie noticed Claudia blushing. "What's the matter? You getting a fever?"

"Don't be silly. I just feel that the statue looks like someone in our family."

"You sure you don't have a fever? You're talking out of your head."

Claudia unfolded her arms and lowered her distant gaze. "I wonder who posed for it," she said half aloud.

"Probably some fat old lady. Then the chisel slipped, so he made a skinny angel instead.

"Jamie, you have as much romance in you as the wolf in Little Red Riding Hood."

"Romance! Boloney! But I do like the mystery part."

"So do I!" Claudia answered. "But I like more than that about Angel."

"We going to look for fingerprints then?"

Claudia reconsidered, "Well, we might look for fingerprints. That's one way. For a start." She looked at Jamie and sniffed, "But I'm sure it won't work. We'll look tomorrow. Even though it won't work." And she looked some more at the picture.

On the second day the crowd going up the broad staircase to see the little Angel was even greater. The newspaper article had made people curious. Besides, it was a cloudy day, and museum attendance always improves in bad weather. Some people who had not been to the Metropolitan Museum for years came. Some people who had never been there ever, came; they got directions from maps, subway conductors, and police. (I'm surprised, Saxonberg, that seeing my name in the paper in connection with Michelangelo didn't bring even you to the museum. You would have profited more than you would have thought by that trip. Are photo albums of your grandchildren the only pictures you look at? Are you altogether unconscious of the magic of the name of Michelangelo? I truly believe that his name has magic even now; the best kind of magic because it comes from true greatness. Claudia sensed it as she again stood in line. The mystery only intrigued her; the magic trapped her.)

Both children were annoyed when the guards plus the push of the crowd hurried them past the Angel. How could they possibly look for fingerprints when they were so rushed? After this hurried visit to the statue, they decided to do their research when they had the statue and the museum to themselves. Claudia especially wanted to make herself important to the statue. She would solve its mystery; and it, in turn, would do something important to her, though what this was, she didn't quite know.

As they once again reached the back stairs, Claudia asked Jamie, "With whom shall we dine today, Sir James?"

Jamie answered, "Oh, I don't know, dear Lady

Claudia. Shall we find a good and proper group?"

"Yes, let us, Sir James."

Thereupon, Jamie held out his arm, Claudia rested the tips of her fingers on the top of his hand, and they descended the stairs. They proved to be as fussy in their selection as Goldilocks. This group was too old; that group, too young; this, too small; that, all girls. But they found a good and proper group in the American wing where they spent a lovely and informative hour and a half learning about the arts and crafts of colonial days. They dined with the group, staying always at the rear of the line, always slightly apart. Both Jamie and Claudia had acquired a talent for being near but never part of a group. (Some people, Saxonberg, never learn to do that all their lives, and some learn it all too well.)

5

THEY HAD BEEN GONE FROM HOME FOR THREE DAYS now. Claudia insisted on a fresh change of underwear every day. That was the way she had been brought up. She insisted for Jamie, too. No question about it; their laundry was becoming a problem. They had to get to a laundromat. That night they removed all their dirty clothes from their instrument cases and stuffed those that would fit into various pockets. Those that didn't fit, they wore. A double layer of clothes never hurts anyone in winter, as long as the clean ones are worn closest to the skin.

Saturday seemed a good day for housekeeping chores. There would be no school groups for them to join. Claudia suggested that they eat both meals outside the museum. Jamie agreed. Claudia next suggested a real sit-down restaurant with tablecloths on the tables and waiters to serve you. Jamie said "NO" with such force that Claudia didn't try to persuade him.

From breakfast at the automat they went to laundry at the laundromat. They emptied their pockets of underwear and removed the layer of soiled socks. No one stared. Someone before them had probably done the same thing some time that week. They bought soap from a machine for ten cents and deposited a quarter into the slot in the washer. Through the glass in the door they watched their assorted clothing spill and splash over and over and around and around. Drying cost ten cents for ten minutes, but it took twenty cents worth of minutes to dry everything. When all was done, they were disappointed; all of it looked dismally gray. Very unelegant. Claudia had thought that their white underwear should not have been washed with the red and navy blue socks, but she would not have considered asking for more money for anything as unglamorous as dirty socks.

"Oh, well," she moaned, "at least they smell clean."

Jamie said, "Let's go to the TV department of Bloomingdale's and watch TV."

"Not today. We've got to work on the mystery of the statue all morning tomorrow, because tomorrow the museum doesn't open until one o'clock. Today we must learn all about the Renaissance and Michelangelo to prepare ourselves. We'll do research at the big library at 42nd Street."

"How about the TV department of Macy's instead?"

"To the library, Sir James."

"Gimbels?"

"Library."

They packed their gray-looking laundry back into their pockets and walked to the door of the laundromat. At the door Claudia turned to Jamie and asked, "Can we . . .?"

Jamie didn't let her finish, "No, dear Lady Claudia. We have not the funds for taxis, buses, or subways. "Shall we walk?" He extended his arm. Claudia placed her gloved fingertips on top of Jamie's mittened ones. Thus they began their long walk to the library.

Once there, they asked the lady at the information booth where they could find books on Michelangelo. She directed them first to the children's room, but when the librarian there found out what they wanted to know, she advised them to go to the Donnell Branch Library on Fifty-third Street. Jamie hoped this would discourage Claudia, but it didn't. She didn't even seem to mind back-tracking up Fifth Avenue. Her determination convinced Jamie that Saturday should be spent just this way. Once at the library, they examined the directory which told what was available where and when the library was open. In the downstairs Art Room the librarian helped them find the books which Claudia selected from the card catalogue. She even brought them some others. Claudia liked that part. She always enjoyed being waited on.

Claudia began her studies never doubting that she could become an authority that morning. She had neither pencil nor paper to make notes. And she knew she wouldn't have a lot of time to read. So she decided that she would simply remember everything, absolutely everything she read. Her net profit, therefore, would be as great as that of someone who read a great deal but remembered very little.

Claudia showed the executive ability of a corporation president. She assigned to Jamie the task of looking through the books of photographs of Michelangelo's work to find pictures of Angel. She would do the reading. She glanced through several thick books with thin pages and tiny print. After reading twelve pages, she looked to the end to see how many more pages there were to go: more than two hundred. The book also had footnotes. She read a few more pages and then busied herself with studying some of Jamie's picture books.

"You're supposed to do the reading!"

"I'm just using these pictures for relief," Claudia whispered. "I have to rest my eyes sometime."

MICHELANGELO
ART

"Well, I don't see any pictures that look like that statue," Jamie sighed.

"Keep looking. I'll do some more reading."

A few minutes later Jamie interrupted her. "Here he is," he said.

"That doesn't look anything like the statue. That's not even a girl," Claudia said.

"Of course not. That's Michelangelo himself."

Claudia replied, "I knew that."

"Two minutes ago you didn't. You thought I was showing you a picture of the statue."

"Oh, I meant . . . I meant. Well . . . there's his broken nose." She pointed to the nose in the picture. "He got in a fight and had his nose broken when he was a teenager."

"Was he a juvenile delinquent? Maybe they do have his fingerprints on file."

"No, silly," Claudia said. "He was a hot-tempered genius. Did you know he was famous even when he was alive?"

"Is that so? I thought that artists don't become famous until after they're dead. Like mummies."

They studied a while longer before Jamie's next interruption. "You know, a lot of his works were lost. They say *lost* in parentheses under the picture."

"How can that be? A statue isn't something like an umbrella that you leave in a taxi and lose. That is, those people who actually ride taxis; something you wouldn't know about."

"Well, they weren't lost in taxis. They were lost track of."

"What kind of a sentence is that? Lost track of?"

"Oh, boloney! There are whole long books about the lost works of Michelangelo. Picture works and sculptor works that people lost track of."

Claudia softened. "Is the little angel one of them?"

"What's the difference between an angel and a cupid?" Jamie inquired.

"Why?" Claudia asked.

"Because there's a lost cupid for sure."

"Angels wear clothes and wings and are Christian. Cupids wear bows and arrows; they are naked and pagan."

"What's pagan?" Jamie asked. "Boy or girl?"

"How would I know?" Claudia answered.

"You said they are naked."

"Well, pagan has nothing to do with that. It means worshipping idols instead of God."

"Oh," Jamie nodded. "The statue in the museum is an angel. It's dressed in its altogether. I don't know yet if an angel was lost . . ." Then he glanced over at his sister and muttered, "track of."

Claudia had begun her research confident that a morning's study would make her completely an expert; but Michelangelo had humbled her, and humility was not an emotion with which she felt comfortable; she was irritable. Jamie ended his research where Claudia had begun: very confident and happy. He felt that his morning had been well spent; he had seen a lot of pictures and he had learned about pagan. He leaned back and yawned; he was becoming bored with pictures of David and Moses and the Sistine Ceiling; he wanted to find clues. Already he knew enough to tell if Michelangelo had sculptured the little angel. All he needed was a chance to investigate. Without the guards hurrying him. He would know, but would his opinion be accepted by the experts?

"I think we should find out how the experts decide whether or not the statue belongs to Michelangelo. That will be better than finding out about Michelangelo himself," Jamie said.

"I know how they find out. They gather evidence like sketches he did and diaries and records of sales. And they examine the statue to see what kind of tools were used and how they were used. Like no one living in the fifteenth century would use an electric drill. How come you didn't take art appreciation lessons with me?"

"The summer before last?"

"Yes. Before school started."

"Well, the summer before last, I had just finished the second half of first grade."

"So what?"

"So boloney! It was all I could do to sound out the name of Dick and Jane's dog."

Claudia had no answer for Jamie's logic. Besides, Jamie agreed with her, "I guess it is better to look for clues. After all, we're doing something that none of the experts can do."

Claudia's impatience surfaced. She had to pick a fight with Jamie. "Don't be silly. They can read all this stuff, too. There's certainly plenty of it."

"Oh, I don't mean that. I mean that we're living with the statue. You know what they always say: The only two ways to get to know someone are to live with him or play cards with him."

"Well, at least the little statue can't cheat at cards like someone else I know."

"Claudia, dear, I'm no angel. Statue or otherwise."

Claudia sighed, "O.K. Sir James, let's go." And they did.

As they were walking up the steps, Jamie spied a Hershey's almond bar still in its wrapper lying in the corner of the landing. He picked it up and tore open one corner.

"Was it bitten into?" asked Claudia.

"No," Jamie smiled. "Want half?"

"You better not touch it," Claudia warned. "It's probably poisoned or filled with marijuana, so you'll eat it and become either dead or a dope addict."

Jamie was irritated. "Couldn't it just happen that someone dropped it?"

"I doubt that. Who would drop a whole candy bar and not know it? That's like leaving a statue in a taxi. Someone put it there on purpose. Someone who pushes dope. I read once that they feed dope in chocolates to little kids, and then the kids become dope addicts. Then these people sell them dope at very high prices which they just can't help but buy because when you're addicted you have to have your dope. High prices and all. And Jamie, we don't have that kind of money."

Jamie said, "Oh, well, bottoms up." He took a big bite of the candy, chewed and swallowed. Then he closed his eyes, leaned against the wall and slid to the floor. Claudia stood with her mouth open, stunned. She was on the verge of screaming for help when Jamie opened his eyes and smiled. "It's delicious. Want a bite?"

Claudia not only refused the bite, she also refused to talk to Jamie until they got to the restaurant. Lunch cheered her. She suggested that they play in Central Park for a while, and they did. They bought peanuts, chestnuts, and pretzels from the vendor outside the museum. They knew that since the museum opened late on Sunday, they would accumulate a lot of hunger before they got out. Their bulging pockets were now full of the staples of life: food and clothing.

Jamie entered the men's room. He had arrived, as was his custom, shortly before the first bell rang, the bell that warned everyone that the museum would close in five minutes. He waited; the bell rang. He got into a booth. First bell, second bell, it was routine just as boarding the school bus had once been routine. After the first day, they had learned that the staff worked from nine A.M. until five P.M., a work schedule just like their father's. Routine, routine. The wait from nine when the staff came until ten when the public came seemed long. Claudia and Jamie had decided that the washrooms were good for the shorter evening wait when the help left at the same time as the visitors, but the washrooms were less satisfactory for the long morning wait . . . especially after Jamie's close call that first morning. So time from eight forty-five until some safe time after ten in the mornings was spent under various beds. They always checked for dust under the bed first. And for once Claudia's fussiness was not the reason. Reason was the reason. A dustless floor meant that it had been cleaned very recently, and they stood less chance of being caught by a mop.

Jamie stood on the toilet seat waiting. He leaned his head against the wall of the booth and braced himself for what would happen next. The guard would come in and make a quick check of his station. Jamie still felt a ping during that short inspection; that was the only part that still wasn't quite routine, and that's why he braced himself. Then the lights would be turned out. Jamie would wait twelve minutes (lag time, Claudia called it) and emerge from hiding.

Except.

Except the guard didn't come, and Jamie couldn't

relax until after he felt that final ping. And the lights stayed on, stayed on. Jamie checked his watch ten times within five minutes; he shook his arm and held the watch up to his ear. It was ticking slower than his heart and much more softly. What was wrong? They had caught Claudia! Now they would look for him! He'd pretend he didn't speak English. He wouldn't answer any questions.

Then he heard the door open. Footsteps. More footsteps than usual. What was happening? The hardest part was that every corpuscle of Jamie's nine-year-old self was throbbing with readiness to run, and he had to bind up all that energy into a quiet lump. It was like trying to wrap a loose peck of potatoes into a neat four-cornered package. But he managed to freeze. He heard the voices of two men talking over the sound of water running in the sink.

"I guess they expect even more people tomorrow."

"Yeah. Sundays are always jammed up anyway."

"It'll be easier to move the people in and out of the Great Hall."

"Yeah. Two feet of marble. What do you figure it weighs?"

"I dunno. Whatever it weighs, it has to be handled delicate. Like it was a real angel."

"C'mon. They probably have the new pedestal ready. We can start."

"Do you think they'll have as many people as they had for the Mona Lisa?"

"Naw! The Mona Lisa was here for a short time only. Besides it was the real McCoy."

"I think this one's . . ."

The men left, turning off the lights as they did so. Jamie heard the door close before he melted. Legs first. He sat down on the seat as he allowed the familiar darkness as well as new realization to fill him.

They were moving Angel. Did Claudia know? They wouldn't have women moving the statue. There would be no one in the ladies' room washing up. Who would give her the information? He would. By mental telepathy. He would think a message to Claudia. He folded his hands across his forehead and concentrated. "Stay put, Claudia, stay put. Stay put. Stay put. Claudia, stay put." He thought that Claudia would not approve of the grammar in his mental telegram; she would want him to think *stay in place*. But he didn't want to weaken his message by varying it one bit. He continued thinking STAY PUT.

He must have thought STAY PUT exactly hard enough, for Claudia did just that. They never knew exactly why she did, but she did. Perhaps she sensed some sounds that told her that the museum was not yet empty. Maybe she was just too tired from running around in Central Park. Maybe they were not meant to get caught. Maybe they were meant to make the discovery they made.

They waited for miles and miles of time before they came out of hiding. At last they met in their bedroom. Claudia was sorting the laundry when Jamie got there. In the dark, mostly by feel. Although there is no real difference between boys' stretch socks and girls', neither ever considered wearing the other's. Children who have always had separate bedrooms don't.

Claudia turned when she heard Jamie come up and said, "They moved the statue."

"How did you know? Did you get my message?"

"Message? I saw the statue on my way here. They have a dim light on it. I guess so that the night guard won't trip over it."

Jamie replied, "We're lucky we didn't get caught."

Claudia never thought very hard about the plus-luck she had; she concentrated on the minus-luck. "But they held us up terribly. I planned on our taking baths tonight. I really can't stand one night more without a bath."

"I don't mind," Jamie said.

"Come along, Sir James. To our bath. Bring your most elegant pajamas. The ones embroidered in gold with silver tassels will do."

"Where, dear Lady Claudia, dost thou expect to bathe?"

"In the fountain, Sir James. In the fountain."

Jamie extended his arm, which was draped with his striped flannel pajamas, and said, "Lady Claudia, I knew that sooner or later you would get me to that restaurant."

(It makes me furious to think that I must explain that restaurant to you, Saxonberg. I'm going to make you take me to lunch in there one day soon. I just this minute became determined to get you into the museum. You'll see later how I'm going to do it. Now about the restaurant. It is built around a gigantic fountain. Water in the fountain is sprayed from dolphins sculptured in bronze. The dolphins appear to be leaping out of the water. On their backs are figures representing the arts, figures that look like water sprites. It is a joy to sit around that wonderful fountain and to snack petit fours and sip expresso coffee. I'll bet that you'd even forget your blasted ulcer while you ate there.)

Lady Claudia and Sir James quietly walked to the entrance of the restaurant. They easily climbed under the velvet rope that meant that the restaurant was closed to the public. Of course they were not the public. They shed their clothes and waded into the fountain. Claudia had taken powdered soap from the restroom. She had ground it out into a paper towel that morning. Even though it was freezing cold, she enjoyed her bath. Jamie, too, enjoyed his bath. For a different reason.

When he got into the pool, he found bumps on the bottom; smooth bumps. When he reached down to feel one, he found that it moved! He could even pick it up. He felt its cool roundness and splashed his

way over to Claudia. "Income, Claudia, income!" he whispered.

Claudia understood immediately and began to scoop up bumps she had felt on the bottom of the fountain. The bumps were pennies and nickels people had pitched into the fountain to make a wish. At least four people had thrown in dimes and one had tossed in a quarter.

"Someone very rich must have tossed in this quarter," Jamie whispered.

"Someone very poor," Claudia corrected. "Rich people have only penny wishes."

Together they collected $2.87. They couldn't hold more in their hands. They were shivering when they got out. Drying themselves as best they could with paper towels (also taken from the restroom), they hurried into their pajamas and shoes.

They finished their preparations for the night, took a small snack and decided it was safe to wander back into the Great Hall to look again at their Angel.

"I wish I could hug her," Claudia whispered.

"They probably bugged her already. Maybe that light is part of the alarm. Better not touch. You'll set it off."

"I said 'hug' not 'bug!' Why would I want to bug her?"

"That makes more sense than to hug her."

"Silly. Shows how much you know. When you hug someone, you learn something else about them.

An important something else."

Jamie shrugged his shoulders.

Both looked at Angel a long time. "What do you think?" Jamie asked. "Did he or didn't he?"

Claudia answered, "A scientist doesn't make up his mind until he's examined all the evidence."

"You sure don't sound like a scientist. What kind of scientist would want to hug a statue?"

Claudia was embarrassed, so she spoke sternly, "We'll go to bed now, and we'll think about the statue very hard. Don't fall asleep until you've really thought about the statue and Michelangelo and the entire Italian Renaissance."

And so they went to bed. But lying in bed just before going to sleep is the worst time for *organized* thinking; it is the best time for free thinking. Ideas drift like clouds in an undecided breeze, taking first this direction and then that. It was very difficult for Jamie to control his thoughts when he was tired, sleepy, and lying on his back. He never liked to get involved just before falling asleep. But Claudia had planned on their thinking, and she was good at planning. So think he did. Clouds bearing thoughts of the Italian Renaissance drifted away. Thoughts of home, and more thoughts of home settled down.

"Do you miss home?" he asked Claudia.

"Not too much," she confessed. "I haven't thought about it much."

Jamie was quiet for a minute, then he said, "We

probably have no conscience. I think we ought to be homesick. Do you think Mom and Dad raised us wrong? They're not very mean, you know; don't you think that should make us miss them?"

Claudia was silent. Jamie waited. "Did you hear my question, Claude?"

"Yes. I heard your question. I'm thinking." She was quiet a while longer. Then she asked, "Have you ever been homesick?"

"Sure."

"When was the last time?"

"That day Dad dropped us off at Aunt Zell's when he took Mom to the hospital to get Kevin."

"Me, too. That day," Claudia admitted. "But, of course, I was much younger then."

"Why do you suppose we were homesick that day? We've been gone much longer than that now."

Claudia thought. "I guess we were worried. Boy, had I known then that she was going to end up with Kevin, I would have known why we were worried. I remember you sucked your thumb and carried around that old blanket the whole day. Aunt Zell kept trying to get the blanket away from you so that she could wash it. It stank."

Jamie giggled, "Yeah, I guess homesickness is like sucking your thumb. It's what happens when you're not very sure of yourself."

"Or not very well trained," Claudia added. "Heaven knows, we're well trained. Just look how nicely we've managed. It's really their fault if we're not homesick."

Jamie was satisfied. Claudia was more. "I'm glad you asked that about homesickness, Jamie. Somehow, I feel older now. But, of course, that's mostly because I've been the oldest child forever. And I'm extremely well adjusted."

They went to sleep then. Michelangelo, Angel, and the entire Italian Renaissance waited for them until morning.

6

It was still dark when they awoke the next morning, but it was later than usual. The museum wouldn't open until one. Claudia was up first. She was getting dressed when Jamie opened his eyes.

"You know," he said, "Sunday is still Sunday. It *feels* like Sunday. Even here."

Claudia answered, "I noticed that. Do you think we ought to try to go to church when we go out?"

Jamie thought a minute before answering, "Well, let's say a prayer in that little room of the Middle Ages. The part with the pretty stained glass window."

They dressed and walked to the little chapel and knelt and said *The Lord's Prayer*. Jamie reminded Claudia to say she was sorry for stealing the newspaper. That made it officially Sunday.

"C'mon," Claudia said as she was rising, "let's go to the statue."

They walked over to Angel and looked very closely. It was difficult to look for clues. Even after their research. They were accustomed to having all the clues neatly laid out on a diagram placed in front of the exhibit.

"I still say that it's too bad we can't touch her," Claudia complained.

"At least we're living with it. We're the only two people in the whole world who live with it."

"Mrs. Frankweiler did, too. She could touch . . ."

"And hug it," Jamie teased.

"I'll bet she knows for sure if Michelangelo did it."

"Sure she does," Jamie said. He then threw his arms around himself, leaned his head way back, closed his eyes, and murmured, "Every morning when she got up, Mrs. Frankweiler would throw her arms about the statue, peer into its eyes, and say, 'Speak to me, baby.' One morning the statue ans . . ."

Claudia was furious. "The men who moved it last night hugged it when they moved it. There's all kinds of hugging."

She refused to look at Jamie again and instead stared at the statue. The sound of footsteps broke the silence and her concentration. Footsteps from the Italian Renaissance were descending upon them! The guard was coming down the steps. Oh, boloney!

thought Jamie. There was just too much time before the museum opened on Sundays. They should have been in hiding already. Here they were out in the open with a light on!

Jamie grabbed Claudia's hand and pulled her behind the booth where they rent walkie-talkies for a tour of the museum. Even though they were well hidden by the dark as they squatted there, they felt as exposed as that great bare lady in the painting upstairs.

The footsteps stopped in front of Angel. Jamie sent another mental telegram: Get going, get going, get going. Of course it worked. The guard moved on toward the Egyptian wing to cover the rest of his tour. The two children wouldn't even allow themselves a sigh of relief. They were that well disciplined.

After ten minutes lag time, Jamie tugged the hem of Claudia's jacket, and they cautiously got up. Jamie led the way back up the great stairway. As he did so, his logic became clear to Claudia. Thank goodness Jamie thought so clearly so fast, and thank goodness for those twenty acres of floor space. It would take the watchman more than an hour before he passed that way again.

They stealthily climbed the wide stairway, staying close to the rail. Step, pause. Step, pause. All the way to the top until they found themselves in front of the pedestal on which Angel had stood just the day before. Claudia paused to look, partly from habit and partly because anything associated with Angel was precious. Jamie paused to catch his breath.

"Why do you think they changed the velvet under her from blue to gold?" Claudia whispered.

This blue probably got dirty. C'mon, let's hide."

Claudia looked again at the velvet. Light was beginning to seep into the museum. Something on top of the velvet caught her eye. "One of the workmen must have been drinking beer when he moved the statue."

"Most people drink beer," Jamie said. "What's so unusual about that?"

"They don't let visitors bring in beer," answered Claudia. "I wonder why they allow the workers to do it? What if he had spilled it on Angel? See where he must have put his beer can on that platform." She pointed to the blue velvet covering the pedestal. "See the rings where the pile of the velvet isn't crushed."

Jamie said, "Yeah, Ballantine beer. Those three rings." Then he began humming a commercial that he had heard during the baseball game on television last spring.

Claudia interrupted, "Those are the marks of the beer can itself. After all, the emblem on the can is flat against the can. It could have been any kind of beer. Schlitz, Rheingold."

Jamie stared at the blue velvet. "You're right, Claude. Except for one thing."

"What's that?" she asked.

"The rings the beer cans made would have crushed the plush of the velvet *down* . . . and the plush of this velvet is crushed *up*."

"What kind of a sentence is that? Crushed *up*!"

"Oh, boloney! You just go ahead and pick on my grammar. Go ahead pick on my grammar. But you can't pick on my logic. The weight of the statue crushed all the velvet down except where the marble was chipped away and the plush was crushed up. Claudia, there's a crushed-up W in one of those circles that is also crushed up."

"For goodness' sake, Jamie. That's not a W; that's an *M*." She looked at Jamie, and her eyes widened, "*M* for Michelangelo!"

Jamie was rubbing his eyes. "You know, Claude, I saw that symbol yesterday on the cover of one of the books I looked at."

"What was it, Jamie? What was it?"

"How should I know? You were supposed to be doing the reading! I was just supposed to be looking for pictures and clues."

"James Kincaid, you are *something*. You are *absolutely* something. As if it would have hurt you to read one little thing. Just one little thing!"

Jamie said, "Well, we have a clue."

"We could know already."

"We have an important clue. I'll bet they never even looked at the bottom of the statue."

"Now we have to go back to the library today to find out what that symbol means. But we can't! That library is closed on Sundays. Oh, Jamie, I've got to know."

"We'll check the museum bookshop. Don't worry, Claude; I'll recognize the book. Right now, we better hide."

Claudia glanced at her watch. "Where are we going to hide up here? There's no furniture. We can't risk going downstairs again."

Jamie picked up a corner of the blue velvet drape. "Be my guest," he said indicating the floor under the platform with an elegant sweep of his hand.

Jamie and Claudia squatted under the platform waiting. It was close quarters under there. Jamie needed only to point his fingers to poke his sister in the ribs. "I say, Lady Claudia, I do believe we're safe and onto something really great."

"Perhaps, Sir James, perhaps."

Claudia didn't think about their close calls. They were unimportant; they wouldn't matter in the end, the end having something to do with Michelangelo, Angel, history, and herself. She thought about the history test she had had on Monday at school. There had been a question on the test that she couldn't answer. She had studied hard and read the chapter thoroughly. She knew where the answer was—the second paragraph in the right hand column of page 157. In her mind she could actually see *where* the *answer* was, but she couldn't think of *what* it was.

Angel was that way. An answer to running away, and also to going home again, lay in Angel. She knew it was there, but she didn't know what it was. It was just escaping her as the answer to the question on the test had . . . except this was even harder, for she wasn't exactly certain of the question she was trying to answer. The question had something to do with why Angel had become more important than having run away or even being safe, at the museum. Oh! she was right back where she had started. It was too stuffy under that velvet. How could anyone think straight? No wonder her thinking came out in circles. She knew one thing for sure: maybe they had a clue.

A crowd formed in front of the museum before it opened. The guard who was to have removed the pedestal and drape was called outside to set up saw-horses and make orderly rows out of the mass of people. The museum couldn't spare Morris until after the police had sent help for the sidewalk traffic. When he finally moved the platform and drape and took them to the basement for storage, Claudia and Jamie had already left and were browsing around the crowded bookshop peeking under the dust jackets of books about Michelangelo.

They found the book with the mark on the cover! The crushed-up mark on the dark blue velvet was

Michelangelo's stonemason's mark. He had chipped it into the base of the marble to identify himself as owner, much as brands are burned into the hides of cattle to identify their owners.

They emerged from the bookshop feeling triumphant. And hungry.

"C'mon," Claudia shouted as soon as they got out, "Let's grab a taxi to the Automat."

"We'll walk," Jamie said.

"We have income now. All we have to do is take a bath whenever we need money."

Jamie thought a second. "O.K. I'll allow a bus."

Claudia smiled. "Thank you, Mr. Pinchpenny."

"You call me Pinchpenny, and I'll call you . . ."

"Call me a taxi," she laughed, running toward the bus stop in front of the museum.

Jamie was feeling so satisfied that he gave Claudia seventy-five cents for brunch. He allowed himself the same. As they ate, they discussed what they should do about the awesome information they had.

"Let's call the *New York Times*," Jamie suggested.

"All that publicity! They'll want to know how we found out."

"Let's call the head of the Metropolitan."

"*He'll* want to know how we found out."

"We'll tell him," Jamie said.

"Are you out of your mind?" Claudia asked. "Tell him we've been living there?"

"Don't you think we ought to tell the museum about the crushed-up mark on the velvet?"

"We owe it to them," Claudia answered. "We've been their guests all this time."

"Then you figure out how we can let them know without getting caught. I'll bet you already have it all worked out."

"As a matter of fact, I do." Claudia leaned across the table and spoke to Jamie in her best secret agent fashion. "We'll write them a letter and tell them to look at the base of the statue for an important clue."

"What if they can't figure out what the clue is?"

"We'll help them with that when they need help. We'll reveal ourselves then. And they'll be very happy to have been our hosts," Claudia said. She paused long enough for Jamie to begin to get impatient, but just begin. "Here's the plan: we rent a post office box in Grand Central. Like when you send in box tops, you always send them to P.O. Box Number So-and-so. We write a letter and tell them to answer us at the box number. After they tell us that they need help, we reveal ourselves. As heroes."

"Can't we go home and wait? That was rough last night and this morning. Besides, then we can be heroes twice. Once when we return home and once when we reveal ourselves."

"No!" Claudia screeched. "We have to know about Angel first. We have to be right."

"Wow! What's the matter with you, Claude? You know you planned on going home sometime."

"Yes," she answered, "sometime. But not just anytime." Her voice was becoming high pitched again.

"Anytime we come home—from a visit to Grandpa's or from summer camp—they're always glad to see us."

"But it never makes any difference. Going home without knowing about Angel for sure will be the same as going home from camp. It won't be any different. After one day, maybe two, we'll be back to the same old thing. And I didn't run away to come home the same."

"Well, this has been more fun than camp. Even the food's been better. There's that difference."

"But, Jamie, it's not enough."

"Yeah, I know, it's not enough. I'm hungry most of the time."

"I mean the difference is not enough. Like being born with perfect pitch, or being born very ordinary and then winning the Congressional Medal of Honor or getting an Academy Award. Those are differences that will last a lifetime. Finding out about Angel will be that kind of difference."

"I think you're different already, Claude."

"Do you?" she asked. She was smiling and her eyes were modestly lowered, ready for a compliment.

"Yes. We're all sane, and you're *in*sane."

"Jamie Kincaid!"

"O.K. O.K. I'm insane, too. I'll go along with you. Besides some of the complications are getting interesting, even though some are dull. How will you disguise your handwriting?"

"No need to do that. I'll use a typewriter." Claudia waited for Jamie's look of surprise.

She got it. "Where are you going to get a typewriter?"

"In front of the Olivetti place on Fifth Avenue. We passed it twice yesterday. Once when you made us walk from the laundromat. And again when we walked from library to library. It's bolted to a stand outside the building for everyone to use. You know, sort of a sample of their product. It's free."

Jamie smiled, "It's a good thing that I'm insane about walking. Otherwise, you would never have found that typewriter."

"And it's a good thing that I'm an excellent observer," Claudia added.

They marched up Fifth Avenue and were delighted to find a piece of paper already in the typewriter. Across the top of the page someone had typed: Now is the time for all good men to come to the aid of their party. Claudia didn't know that this sentence was a common one used in practice typing. She thought it appeared appropriate to their message and would add a proper note of mystery besides. (Here,

Saxonberg, is a copy of the letter Claudia typed. You can see that her typing needed a great deal of improvement.)

Now is the time for all good men to come to the aid of their party;

Dear Museum Head,

We think that you should examine the bottom of the statue for an importandt clue. The statue we mean is the oen you bought for $225.00. And the clue is that you will find Michelangelo's stone mason's markk on the bottom. If you need help about this clue, you may write to us at Grande Central Post Office. Box 847 in Manhanttan.

Sincerely,

Friends of the Museum

Pleased with their effort, they felt that they could take the rest of the day off. They wandered around Rockefeller Center and watched the skaters for a short while. They watched the crowd watching the skaters for a while longer. When they returned to the museum filled with satisfaction and with snacks for their supper, they saw a long line of Sunday people waiting to climb the museum steps. Knowing that everyone in that line would be shepherded in and out, in front of and past the statue in a matter of minutes, they decided to enter through the rear entrance instead. The guard at that door told them that they would have to use the Fifth Avenue entrance if they wished to see Angel.

"Oh, we've already seen that!" Jamie said.

The guard from friendliness, helpfulness or, perhaps, sheer loneliness (very few people had entered through his door that day) asked Jamie what he thought of it.

"Well, we need to do more research, but it seems to me that . . ."

Claudia pulled Jamie's arm. "Come along, *Albert*," she urged.

On their way to the rooms containing Greek vases, they again observed the enormous crowd passing by the statue.

"As I was about to tell that guard, it seems to me that they should try to get to the *bottom* of the mystery."

Claudia giggled; Jamie joined in. They spent exactly enough time among the vases of ancient Greece to be able to man their waiting stations and not be discovered.

7

When they left the museum on Monday morning, Claudia walked to the bus stop without even consulting Jamie.

"Don't you think we ought to get breakfast first?" he asked.

"Mail early in the day," Claudia answered. "Besides, we want them to get this letter as soon as possible."

"It will get there faster if we deliver it by hand," Jamie suggested.

"Good idea. We'll get our mailbox number, write it in, and then take it to the museum office."

Since Jamie was official treasurer of the team, it

was he who approached the man behind the cage window at the post office.

"I would like to rent a post office box," he declared.

"For how long?" the man inquired.

"For about two days."

"Sorry," the man said, "we rent them quarterly."

"All right, then. I'll take eight quarterlies. That makes two days."

"Quarter of a year," the man said. "That makes three months."

"Just a minute," Jamie said. He held a whispered conference with Claudia.

"Go ahead. Rent it," she urged.

"It'll cost a stack of money."

"Why don't you find out instead of arguing about it now?" Claudia's whisper began to sound like cold water hitting a hot frying pan.

"How much will a quarter of a year be?" he asked the postman.

"Four dollars and fifty cents."

Jamie scowled at Claudia. "See. I told you a stack."

Claudia shrugged her shoulders, "We'll take a long, long bath tonight."

The postman hardly looked puzzled. People working at the Grand Central Post Office grow used to strange remarks. They hear so many. They never stop hearing them; they simply stop sending the messages to their brains. Like talking into a telephone with no one on the receiver end. "Do you or don't you want it?" he asked.

"I'll take it."

Jamie paid the rent, signed a form using the name Angelo Michaels and gave his address as Marblehead, Massachusetts. He received a key to Box Number 847. Jamie-Angelo-Kincaid-Michaels felt important having a key to his own mailbox. He found his box and opened the little door.

"You know," he remarked to Claudia, "it's a lot like Horn and Hardart's. Except that we could have a complete spaghetti dinner for both of us coming out of the little door instead of just empty, empty space.

Paying four dollars and fifty cents for empty space had been hard on Jamie. Claudia knew they wouldn't take a bus back to the museum. They didn't.

Both Claudia and Jamie wanted to deliver the letter, but neither thought he should. Too risky. They decided to ask someone to deliver it for them. Someone with a bad memory for faces. Someone their own age would be best; someone who might be nosey but who wouldn't really care about them. It would be easiest to find a school group and select their messenger. They began their search for the group of the day by looking in the usual places: Arms and Armor, the Costume Institute, and Egyptian Art. As they approached the Egyptian wing, they heard the shuffling of feet and a sound they recognized as the folding of chairs and the gathering up of rubber mats. They weren't anxious to hear the talk about mummies again; they never watched repeats on television, either. But they decided to look the group over. So they waited inside the tomb.

(Now, Saxonberg, I must tell you about that Egyptian tomb called a mastaba. It is not a whole one; it is the beginning of one. You can walk into it. You can spend a lot of time in it, or you can spend very little time in it. You can try to read the picture writing on the walls. Or you can read nothing at all. Whether you read or not, whether you spend a lot of time or a little in that piece of Ancient Egypt, you will have changed climate for at least that part of your day. It is not a hard place to wait in at all.)

The group was moving past the entrance. Claudia and Jamie were relaxed and waiting—wrapped up in the vacuum of time created by those warm stone walls. Puffs of conversation broke the silence of their tomb.

"Sarah looks like pharaoh. Pass it on."

"When are we gonna eat?"

"Man, what a lot of walking."

The conversation rained in softly and comfortably and told the two stowaways that they had the correct age group. That was the way kids in their classes always talked. Words continued to drizzle into their shelter.

"Hey, Rube, look at this."

"C'mon, Bruce, let me borrow it."

Something else now showered down upon them. Something much less comfortable. *Familiarity!* The names, Sarah, Bruce, Rube, were familiar . . . Ages ago, in time well outside the mastaba, they had heard these names—in a classroom, on a school bus . . .

Closer, louder, the sounds poured in. Then one small cloud burst right outside their door.

"Hey, let's go back in here."

Jamie's eyes caught Claudia's. He opened his mouth. Claudia didn't wait to discover whether he opened it in surprise or to say something. She clamped her hand over his mouth as fast as she could.

An adult voice urged, "Come on, boys. We have to stay with the group."

Claudia took her hand from Jamie's mouth. She looked at him solemnly and nodded *yes*. The "come-on-boys" voice belonged to Miss Clendennan, Jamie's third grade teacher. Rube was Reuben Hearst, and Bruce was Bruce Lansing. Sarah was Sarah Sawhill, and unfortunately, she did look a great deal like pharaoh. Believe it or not, the mountain had come to Mohammed; their school had come to them. At least, Jamie's class had.

Jamie was furious. Why had Claudia muzzled him? Did she think he had no sense at all? He pulled his eyebrows down and made his best possible scowl. Claudia held her finger up to her lips and signaled

him to stay quiet yet. The sounds of third grade shuffling and third grade jostling faded from their shelter. The quiet of the ages returned to the tomb.

But not to Jamie. He couldn't contain himself another minute. He could still feel the pressure of Claudia's hand over his mouth. "I have half a mind to join that group and go back with them and just be mysterious about where I came from."

"If you do that, it'll show that you have half a mind. Exactly half. Only half. Something I've suspected for a long time. You can't even see that this is perfect."

"How perfect?"

Claudia slowed down. "You go to the museum office. Deliver the letter. Tell them you are in the third grade group that is visiting from Greenwich and someone asked you to deliver the letter. The teacher said it would be O.K. If they ask you your name, say Bruce Lansing. But only if they ask."

"You know, Claude, when I'm not wishing I could give you a sock right in the nose, I'm glad you're on my team. You're smart even if you're hard to live with."

"You'll do it then?" Claudia asked.

"Yeah, I'll do it. It *is* perfect."

"Let's hurry before they come back."

Jamie entered the museum office, and Claudia stood guard outside the door. She intended to step inside the office if she spotted the class returning.

Jamie wasn't gone long. Everything had gone well, and they hadn't asked his name. Claudia grabbed his arm as he came out. All the energy of Jamie's wound-up nerves let loose. He collapsed as hard as if Claudia had suddenly jumped off the down end of a teeter-totter while he was still sitting on the up end.

"Yikes!" he yelled. Claudia was tempted to muzzle him again, but didn't. Instead she led him out the door into the Fifth Avenue crowd and began walking uptown with him as fast as she could go.

8

On Tuesday they again did their laundry. The product of their efforts this time looked only slightly grayer than it had the time before. Claudia's sweater was considerably shrunken.

They knew that it was too early to get an answer to their letter, but they couldn't resist starting down to Grand Central Post Office to take a look anyway. It was noon by the time they stopped and ate breakfast at a Chock Full O'Nuts on Madison Avenue. They dragged it out beyond the patience of the people who were standing waiting to occupy their seats. Both Claudia and Jamie almost didn't want to look at their box in the post office. As long as they didn't look, they still had hopes that they could find a letter there.

They didn't. They strolled along the streets and

found themselves near the United Nations building. Claudia suggested to Jamie that they take the guided tour she had read about when she was studying the Tourguide Book of the American Automobile Association.

"Today we can learn everything about the U.N."

Jamie's first question was, "How much?"

Claudia challenged him to walk in and find out. Fifty cents. Each. They could go if Claudia was willing to skip dessert that afternoon.

Jamie added, "You know, you can't have your cake and take tours, too."

"How about having tours and hot fudge sundaes, too?" Claudia asked.

They stood in line and got tickets for a tour. The girl selling tickets smiled down at them. "No school today?" she asked casually.

"No," Jamie answered. "The boiler on the furnace broke. No heat. They had to dismiss school. You should have heard the explosion! All the windows rattled. We thought it was an earthquake. Fourteen kids got cuts and abrasions, and their parents are suing the school to pay for their medical expenses. Well, it was about ten in the morning. We had just finished our spelling lesson when . . ."

The man behind Jamie who was dressed in a derby hat and who looked more as if he belonged in the U.N. than visiting it said, "I say, what's holding up this line? *I repeat, what* is *holding* up this line?"

The girl gave Jamie the two tickets. As she did so, the man in the derby hat was already pushing his money onto the counter. The girl looked after Jamie and Claudia as they were leaving and said, "Where is . . ."

She couldn't finish her question. The man in the derby hat was scolding the girl. "No wonder it takes the U.N. forever to get something done. I've never seen a line move more slowly." He only looked as if he belonged; he certainly didn't act it.

The girl blushed as she gave the man his ticket. "I hope you enjoy your tour, sir." She acted as if she belonged.

Jamie and Claudia sat with other ticket holders waiting for their numbers to be called.

Claudia spoke softly to Jamie, "You sure are a fast thinker. Where did you cook up that story about the furnace?"

"I've had it ready and waiting ever since we left home. First chance I've had to use it," he answered.

"I thought I had thought of everything," Claudia said.

"That's O.K."

"You're quite a kid."

"Thanks." Jamie smiled.

The guide who was calling the numbers finally said, "Will the people holding tickets number 106 to 121 please go to the double doors on the wall opposite this desk. There your guide will begin your tour."

Jamie and Claudia went. Their guide was an Indian girl who wore a sari and whose long hair was bound into a single braid that hung down her back to well below her waist. With one hand she lifted the folds of her sari; her walk was flavored by her costume: her steps were short and light and there appeared to be great movement around her knees. Claudia looked at her guide's skin and thought of smoky topaz: November, her mother's birthstone. She listened to her guide's accent and formed the sounds in her mind without listening to what the sounds said.

Thus, when the tour was finished, Claudia was no expert on the United Nations, but she had discovered something: saris are a way of being different. She could do two things, she decided. When she was grown, she could stay the way she was and move to some place like India where no one dressed as she did, or she could dress like someone else—the Indian guide even—and still live in an ordinary place like Greenwich.

"How did you like those ear phones where you can tune in almost any old language at all?" Jamie asked his sister. "Pretty keen, huh?"

Claudia seemed to have a far away look in her eye.

"Yes," she answered. It sounded like "yah-ess." Jamie inspected Claudia closely. She was holding one arm crooked and the other pressed against her stomach. Her steps seemed shorter than usual and lighter than usual, and there appeared to be great movement around her knees.

"What's the matter with you?" he asked. "You got stomach cramps or something?"

Claudia lowered her eyes to him and said, "Jamie, you know, you could go clear around the world and still come home wondering if the tuna fish sandwiches at Chock Full O'Nuts still cost thirty-five cents."

"Is that what gave you stomach cramps?" he asked.

"Oh, just skip it! Just skip it." Claudia knew she would have to discover some other way to be different. Angel *would* help her somehow.

Her hopes centered more than ever on Box 847 in the post office, and the following day when they peeked through its little window, they saw an envelope. Claudia was prepared to be the discoverer of great truths, Greenwich's own heroine of the statue—and only twelve years old. Jamie was so excited that he could hardly get the key into the lock to open the box. Claudia waited while he opened it and the envelope, too. He held the letter unfolded and off-center so that they could read it together. In silence.

Saxonberg, I have here attached a copy of the actual letter which I have in my files:

Dear Friends of the Museum:

We sincerely thank you for your interest in trying to help us solve the mystery of the statue. We have long known of the clue you mention; in fact, that clue remains our strongest one in attributing this work to the master, Michelangelo Buonarroti. Other evidence, however, is necessary, for it is known that Michelangelo did not carve all the marble blocks which were quarried for him and which bore his mark. We cannot ignore the possibility that the work may have been done by someone else, or that someone counterfeited the mark into the stone much later. We summarize the possibilities as follows:

1. *The work was designed and done by Michelangelo himself.*
2. *The work was designed by Michelangelo but done by someone else.*
3. *The work was neither designed nor done by Michelangelo.*

Our hope, of course, is to find evidence to support the first of these three possibilities.

Neither Condivi nor Vasari, Michelangelo's biographers who knew him personally mention the master carving this little angel; they mention only the angel carved for the altar in Siena. However, in a letter he wrote to his father from Rome on August 19, 1497, Michelangelo mentions ". . . I bought a piece of marble . . . I keep to myself, and I am sculpturing an image for my own pleasure." In the past experts have believed the image which he sculptured for his own pleasure to be a cupid. Now, we must examine the possibility that it was an angel.

The problem of Angel has now become a matter for consensus. Four Americans, two Englishmen, and one German, all of whom are experts on the techniques of Michelangelo have thus far examined the statue. We are presently awaiting the arrival of two more experts from Florence, Italy. After all of these experts have examined the statue, we will write a summary of their opinions which we will release to the press.

We greatly appreciate your interest and would enjoy your disclosing further clues to us if you find them.

Sincerely,

Harold C. Lowery
Public Relations,
The Metropolitan Museum of Art

Claudia and Jamie walked from the post office to

Grand Central Terminal and sat down in the waiting room. They sat perfectly quiet. Disappointed beyond words. Claudia would have felt better if the letter had not been so polite. A nasty letter or a sarcastic one can make you righteously angry, but what can you do about a polite letter of rejection? Nothing, really, except cry. So she did.

Jamie let her cry for a while. He sat there and fidgeted and counted the number of benches. She still cried; he counted the number of people on the benches. She was still at it; he calculated the number of people per bench.

After the big blobs of tears stopped, he said, "At least they treated us like grown-ups. That letter is full of big words and all."

"Big deal," Claudia sobbed. "For all they know, we *are* grown-ups." She was trying to find a corner of her shredded Kleenex that she could use.

Jamie let her sniff some, then he quietly asked, "What do we do now? Go home?"

"What? Go home now? We haven't even got our clothes. And your radio is in the violin case. We'd have to go home absolutely empty handed."

"We could leave our clothes; they're all gray anyway."

"But we never even used your radio. How can we face them at home? Without the radio and all. With nothing." She paused for a minute and repeated, "With nothing. We've accomplished nothing."

"We accomplished having fun," Jamie suggested. "Wasn't that what you wanted when we started out, Claude? I always thought it was."

Claudia began big tears again. "But that was then," she sobbed.

"You said you'd go home after you knew about Angel. Now you know."

"That's it," she sobbed. "I do not know."

"You know that you don't know. Just as the people at the museum don't know. C'mon," he pleaded, "we'll enjoy telling them about how we lived in the museum. The violin case can be evidence. Do you realize that we've lived there a whole week?"

"Yes," Claudia sighed. "Just a week. I feel as if I jumped into a lake to rescue a boy, and what I thought was a boy turned out to be a wet, fat log. Some heroine that makes. All wet for nothing." The tears flowed again.

"You sure are getting wet. You started this adventure just running away. Comfortably. Then the day before yesterday you decided you had to be a hero, too."

"Heroine. And how should I have known that I wanted to be a heroine when I had no idea I wanted to be a heroine? The statue just gave me a chance . . . almost gave me a chance. We need to make more of a discovery."

"So do the people at the museum. What more of

a discovery do you think that you, Claudia Kincaid, girl runaway, can make? A tape recording of Michelangelo saying, 'I did it?' Well, I'll clue you in. They didn't have tape recorders 470 years ago."

"I know that. But if we make a real discovery, I'll know *how* to go back to Greenwich."

"You take the New Haven, silly. Same way as we got here." Jamie was losing patience.

"That's not what I mean. I want to know how to go back to Greenwich different."

Jamie shook his head. "If you want to go different, you can take a subway to 125th Street and then take the train."

"I didn't say *differently*, I said *different*. I want to go back different. I, Claudia Kincaid, want to be different when I go back. Like being a heroine is being different."

"Claudia, I'll tell you one thing you can do different . . ."

"Differently," Claudia interrupted.

"Oh, boloney, Claude. That's exactly it. You can stop ending every single discussion with an argument about grammar."

"I'll try," Claudia said quietly.

Jamie was surprised at her quiet manner, but he continued to be businesslike, "Now about this discovery."

"Jamie, I want to know if Michelangelo did it.

I can't explain why exactly. But I feel that I've got to know. For sure. One way or the other. A real discovery is going to help me."

"If the experts don't know for sure, I don't mind not knowing. Let's get tickets for home." Jamie started toward the New Haven ticket window. Claudia stayed behind. Jamie realized that she was not following, returned to her, and lectured, "You're never satisfied, Claude. If you get all A's, you wonder where are the pluses. You start out just running away, and you end up wanting to know everything. Wanting to be Joan of Arc, Clara Barton, and Florence Nightingown all in one."

"Nightingale," Claudia sighed. She got up then and followed slowly behind her brother. But she was feeling too low to go home. She couldn't. She just couldn't. It just wasn't right.

There were only two windows that didn't say, "*Closed.*" They waited a short while as the man in front of them purchased a red commuter's pass like the one that had brought them to Manhattan.

Jamie addressed the man behind the counter and said, "Two half-fare tickets for . . ."

"FARMINGTON, CONNECTICUT," Claudia broke in.

"To get to Farmington, you have to go to Hartford and take a bus," the ticket agent said.

Jamie nodded to the man and said, "Just a minute,

please." He stepped away from the window, grabbing Claudia's arm. He pulled her away.

Claudia whispered, "Mrs. Basil E. Frankweiler."

"What about Mrs. Basil E. Frankweiler?"

"She lives in Farmington."

"So what?" Jamie said. "The paper said that her house was closed."

"Her New York house was closed. Can't you read anything right?"

"You talk that way, Claude, and . . ."

"All right, Jamie. All right. I shouldn't talk that way. But, please let's go to Farmington. Jamie, please. Can't you see how badly I need to find out about Angel? I just have a hunch she'll see us and that she knows."

"I've never known you to have a hunch before, Claude. You usually plan everything."

"I have, too, had a hunch before."

"When?"

"That night they moved the statue and I stayed in the washroom and didn't get caught. That was a hunch. Even if I didn't know it was a hunch at the time."

"O.K. We'll go to Farmington," Jamie said. He marched to the ticket window and bought passage to Hartford.

They were waiting at track twenty-seven when Claudia said to Jamie, "That's a first for you, too."

"What is?" he asked.

"Buying something without asking the price first."

"Oh, I must have done that before now," he answered.

"When? Name one time."

"I can't think of it right now." He thought a minute then said, "I haven't been a tightwad all my life, have I?"

"As long as I've known you," Claudia answered.

"Well, you've known me for as long as I've known me," he said smiling.

"Yes," Claudia said, "I've been the oldest child since before you were born."

They enjoyed the train ride. A large portion of it went over track they had never before seen. Claudia arrived in Hartford feeling much happier than she had since they received the morning's mail. Her self-assurance had returned to her.

The Hartford station was on Farmington Avenue. Claudia reasoned that they could not be far from Farmington itself. Why take a bus and worry about which stop to get off? Without consulting Jamie she hailed a cab. When it stopped, she got in; Jamie followed. Claudia told the driver to take them to the house of Mrs. Basil E. Frankweiler in Farmington, Connecticut. Claudia sat back. In a taxi at last.

(And that, Saxonberg, is how I enter the story. Claudia and Jamie Kincaid came to see me about Angel.)

9

Up the entire length of my long, wide, tree-lined road they came.

"Do you suppose that Mrs. Frankweiler owns the highway?" Jamie asked.

The taxi driver answered, "This ain't no highway. It's all her propitty. I tell ya, this dame's loaded. In front of the house this here begins to resemble wattcha call a *normal* driveway."

Claudia discovered that indeed it does. My tree-lined avenue circles in front of my house. Jamie looked up at my house and said, "Another museum."

Claudia answered, "Then we should feel very much at home."

Jamie paid the taxi driver. Claudia pulled his arm and whispered, "Tip him."

Jamie shrugged his shoulders and gave the driver some money. The driver smiled, took off his hat, bowed from the waist, and said, "Thank you, sir."

After he drove away Claudia asked, "How much did you give him?"

Jamie answered, "All I had."

"That was stupid," Claudia said. "Now, how are we going to get back?"

Jamie sighed, "I gave him seventeen cents. So it wasn't such a great tip. Also, it would never be enough to get us back. We're broke. How do you feel about that, Miss Taxi Rider?"

"Pretty uncomfortable," she murmured. "There's something nice and safe about having money."

"Well, Claude, we just traded safety for adventure. Come along, Lady Claudia."

"You can't call me Lady Claudia anymore. We're paupers now."

They ascended the low, wide steps of my porch. Jamie rang the bell. Parks, my butler, answered.

"We'd like to see Mrs. Basil E. Frankweiler," Jamie told him.

"Whom shall I say is calling?"

Claudia cleared her throat, "Claudia and James Kincaid."

"Just one moment, please."

They were left standing in the reception hall more than "one-moment-please" before Parks returned.

"Mrs. Frankweiler says she doesn't know you."

"We would like her to," Claudia insisted.

"What is the nature of your business?" he asked. Parks always asks that.

Both hesitated. Jamie decided on an answer first, "Please tell Mrs. Basil E. Frankweiler that we are seeking information about the Italian Renaissance."

Parks was gone a full ten minutes before his second return. "Follow me," he commanded. "Mrs. Frankweiler will see you in her office."

Jamie winked at Claudia. He felt certain that mentioning the Italian Renaissance had intrigued me.

They walked behind Parks through my living room, drawing room, and library. Rooms so filled with antique furniture, Oriental rugs, and heavy chandeliers that you complain that they are also filled with antique air. Well, when a house is as old as mine, you can expect everything in it to be thickened by time. Even the air. My office surprised them after all this. It surprises everyone. (You once told me, Saxonberg, that my office looks more like a laboratory than an office. That's why I call what I do there *research.*) I suppose it does look like a lab furnished as it is with steel, Formica, vinyl and lit by fluorescence. You must admit though that there's one feature of the room that looks like an office. That's the rows and rows of filing cabinets that line the walls.

I was sitting at one of the tables wearing my customary white lab coat and my baroque pearl necklace when the children were brought in.

"Claudia and James Kincaid," Parks announced.

I allowed them to wait a good long while. Parks had cleared his throat at least six times before I turned around. (Of course, Saxonberg, you know that I hadn't wasted the time between Park's announcement that Claudia and James Kincaid wanted to see me and the time they appeared at the office. I was busy doing research. That was also when I called you. You sounded like anything but a lawyer when I called. Disgusting!) I could hear the children shuffling back and forth impatiently. The importance of Parks's manner is what kept them from interrupting me. They shuffled and scratched, and Jamie even emitted two very false sneezes to attract my attention. It's particularly easy for me to ignore fake sneezes, and I went on with my research.

I don't like to waste time, so when I at last turned around, I did so abruptly and asked directly, "Are you the children who have been missing from Greenwich for a week?" (You must admit, Saxonberg, that when the need arises, I have a finely developed sense of theatrics.)

They had become so used to not being discovered that they had entirely forgotten that they were runaways. Now their reaction was one of amazement. They both looked as if their hearts had been pushed through funnels.

"All right," I said. "You don't have to tell me. I know the answer."

"How did you know about us?" Jamie asked.

"Did you call the police?" Claudia asked at the same time.

"From the newspapers," I replied, pointing to Jamie. "And no," I replied pointing to Claudia. "Now both of you sit down here and talk about the Italian Renaissance."

Jamie glanced at the newspapers I had been researching. "We're in the newspapers?" He seemed pleased.

"Even your pictures," I nodded.

"I'd like to see that," Claudia said. "I haven't had a decent picture taken since I've been able to walk."

"Here you are." I held out several papers. "Two days before yesterday you were on the fifth page in Hartford, the second page in Stamford and the front page in Greenwich."

"The front page in Greenwich?" Claudia asked.

"That's my school picture from the first grade!" Jamie exclaimed. "See, I don't have one of my front teeth."

"Goodness! This picture of me is three years old. Mother never even bought my school pictures the last two years." Claudia held her picture up for Jamie to see. "Do you think I still look like this?"

"Enough!" I said. "Now, what do you want to tell me about the Italian Renaissance?"

"Is your butler calling the police while you stall us here?" Jamie asked.

"No," I answered. "And I refuse to keep reassuring you. If you keep on with this kind of talk, I shall find you so dull that I shall call your parents as well as the police to get rid of you. Is that clear, young man?"

"Yes," Jamie muttered.

"Young lady?"

Claudia nodded yes. They both stood with bowed heads. Then I asked Jamie, "Do I frighten you, young man?"

Jamie looked up. "No, ma'am. I'm quite used to frightening things. And you're really not so bad looking."

"So bad looking? I wasn't referring to the way I look." Actually, I never think much about that any more. I rang for Parks. When he arrived I told him to please bring me a mirror. Everyone waited in silence until Parks returned with the mirror. Silence continued as I picked it up and began a very long and close inspection of my face.

It's not a bad face except that lately my nose seems to have grown longer, and my upper lip appears to have collapsed against my teeth. These things happen when people get older. And I am getting just that. I ought to do something about my hair besides have Parks cut it for me. It's altogether white now and looks like frayed nylon thread. Maybe, I'll take time out and get a permanent wave, except that I hate beauty parlors.

"My nose has gotten longer. Like Pinocchio. But not for the same reason. Well, not most of the time," I said as I put down the mirror. Claudia gasped, and I laughed. "Oh, so you were thinking the same thing? No matter. I never really look past my eyes. That way I always feel pretty. Windows of the soul, you know."

Claudia took a step closer to me. "You really do have beautiful eyes. They're like looking into a kaleidoscope—the way those golden flecks in them keep catching the light."

She was quite close to me now and actually peering into my face. It was uncomfortable. I put a stop to that.

"Do you spend much time looking in mirrors, Claudia?"

"Some days I do. Some days I don't."

"Would you care to look now?"

"No, thank you," she said.

"Well, then," I said, "we'll continue. Parks, please return this mirror. We want to talk about the Italian Renaissance. James, you haven't said one word since you told me that I look frightening. Speak now."

"We want to know about the statue," Jamie stammered.

"Speak up, boy," I commanded. "What statue?"

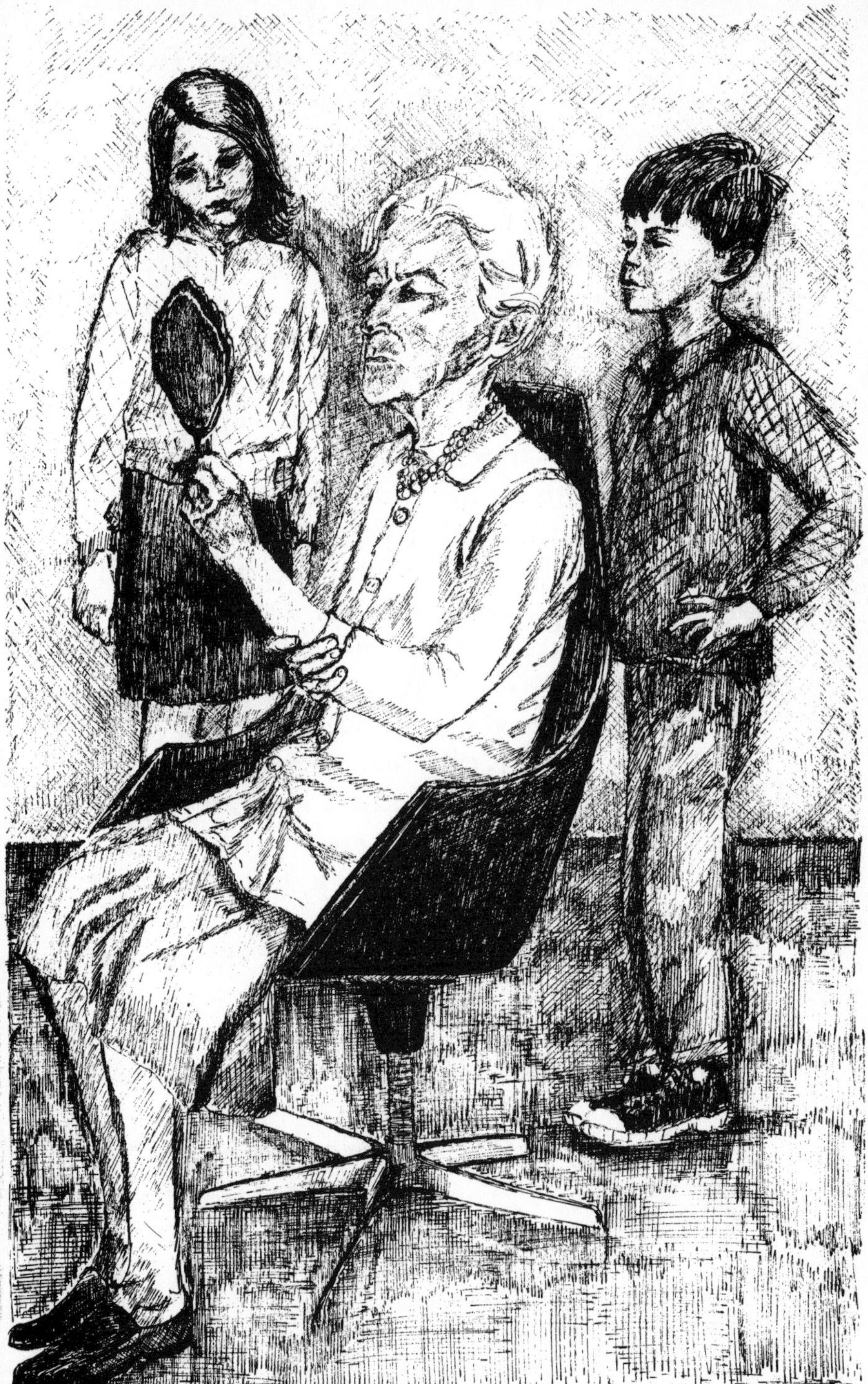

"The statue in the Metropolitan Museum in New York City. In Manhattan. The one of the angel."

"The one you sold for $225," Claudia added.

I walked over to my files of newspaper clippings and pulled out a manilla folder, the one which has all the newspaper clippings about the auction and the museum buying the statue. It also contains the article about the crowds going to see the statue.

"Why did you sell her?" Claudia asked pointing to the picture of Angel.

"Because I don't like to donate things."

"If I owned such a lovely statue, I'd never sell it. Or donate it either. I'd cherish it like a member of my own family," Claudia preached.

"Considering all the trouble you've caused your family, that isn't saying very much."

"Have they been worried?" she asked.

"If you hadn't been so busy looking at your picture in the paper, you could have read that they are nearly frantic."

Claudia blushed. "But I wrote them a letter. I told them not to worry."

"Evidently your letter didn't work. Everyone is worried."

"I told them not to," she repeated. "We're going home anyway as soon as you tell us if Michelangelo carved Angel. Did he do it?"

"That's my secret," I answered. "Where have you been all week?"

"That's our secret," Claudia answered, lifting her chin high.

"Good for you!" I cheered. Now I was certain that I liked these two children. "Let's go to lunch." Examining the two of them in that bright light I saw that they looked wrinkled, dusty, and gray. I instructed them to wash up while I told the cook to prepare for two more.

Parks led Jamie to one bathroom; my maid, Hortense, led Claudia to another. Apparently, Claudia had never enjoyed washing up so much. She took forever doing it. She spent a great deal of time looking into all the mirrors. Examining her eyes very carefully, she decided that she, too, was beautiful. But mostly her thoughts were about the beautiful black marble bathtub in that bathroom.

(Even in this very elegant house of mine, that bathroom is especially grand. All the walls are black marble except for one that is mirrored entirely. The faucets are gold, and the spigot is shaped like a dragon's head. The tub looks like a black marble swimming pool sunken into the floor; there are two steps down to the bottom.)

There was nothing she wanted more than to take a bath in that tub. She examined her eyes a little longer and then spoke to her image in the mirror, "You'll never have a better chance, Lady Claudia. Go ahead. Do it." So she did. She opened the taps and began undressing as the tub was filling up.

Meanwhile, Jamie had done his customary job of washing up. That is, he had washed the palms but not backs of his hands, his mouth but not the rest of his face. He emerged from the bathroom long before Claudia and growing impatient, began wandering through rooms until he found Hortense and asked her the whereabouts of his sister. He followed directions to Claudia's bathroom where he heard the water still running. It takes a lot of water to fill that tub.

"Suicide!" he thought. "She's going to drown herself because we're caught." He tried the door; it was locked.

"Claudia," he yelled, "is anything the matter?"

"No," she answered. "I'll be right there."

"What's taking you so long?"

"I'm taking a bath," she called.

"Oh, boloney," Jamie answered. He walked away to find me. I was waiting in the dining room. I'm accustomed to eating on time, and I was hungry.

"That nutty sister of mine is taking a bath. Don't mind her. She even takes baths when she comes in from swimming. She even made us take baths while we were hiding at the Metropolitan Museum. I think we should start without her."

I smiled, "I think, James, that you already have."

I rang for Parks, and he appeared with the salad and began serving.

"How did Claudia manage to take a bath in the museum?" I asked casually.

"In the fountain. It was cold, but I didn't mind when we found . . . Uh oh. Uuuuh. Ooooh. I did it. I told. I did it." He rested his elbow on the table and his chin on his hand. He slowly shook his head. "Sometimes I stink at keeping secrets. Don't tell Claudia I told. Please."

"I'm curious to know how you managed." I *was* curious, and you know that I can be absolutely charming when I want information.

"Let Claude tell you all that. She did the planning. I managed the money. She's big on ideas, but she's also big on spending money. I managed fine until today. Now we're broke. Not one cent left to get back to Greenwich."

"You can walk or hitchhike."

"Try telling that to Claude."

"Or you can turn yourselves in. The police will take you back, or your parents will come and get you."

"Maybe that will appeal to Claudia, but I doubt it. Even though she sure doesn't approve of making herself walk."

"Perhaps we can work out a deal. You give me some details, and I'll give you a ride back."

Jamie shook his head. "You'll have to work that out with Claude. The only kind of deal I can make concerns money, and we don't have any more of that."

"You are poor, indeed, if that's the only kind of a deal you can make."

Jamie brightened. "Would you like a game of cards?"

"Which game?" I asked.

"War."

"I assume you cheat."

"Yeah." he sighed.

"I may decide to play after lunch anyway."

"Can we start eating now?" Jamie asked.

"You don't worry about manners too much do you?"

"Oh," he replied, "I don't worry about them too much when I'm this hungry."

"You're honest about some things."

Jamie shrugged his shoulders. "You might say that I'm honest about everything except cards. For some reason I'm helpless about cheating at cards."

"Let's eat," I said. I was anxious, for I do enjoy a good game of cards, and Jamie promised to provide just that.

Claudia appeared as we were finishing our soup. I saw that she was annoyed that we had not waited for her. She was all bound up in concern for good manners, and she wanted very much to let us know that she was annoyed and why. She acted cool. I pretended I didn't notice. Jamie didn't pretend; he simply did not notice.

"I'll skip the soup," Claudia announced.

"It's good," Jamie said. "Sure you don't want to try it?"

"No, thank you," Claudia said. Still cool.

I summoned Parks; he appeared bearing a silver casserole.

"What's that?" Jamie asked.

"*Nouilles et fromage en casserole,*" Parks answered.

Claudia showed interest. "I'll have some, please. Sounds like something special."

Parks served. Claudia looked down at her plate, looked up at me and moaned, "Why, it's nothing but macaroni and cheese."

"You see," I laughed, "under the fancy trappings, I'm just a plain lady."

Claudia laughed then. We all did, and we began enjoying our lunch. I asked Claudia what she would like to do while Jamie and I played cards. She said that she would like to just watch us and think.

"Think about what?"

"About how we're going to get back home."

"Call up your family," I suggested. "They'll come for you."

"Oh, it's so hard to explain over the phone. It will cause so much commotion."

I was astounded. "You still don't think you've caused any commotion so far?"

"I haven't really thought about it very hard. I've been so busy worrying about Michelangelo and avoiding getting caught. If only you'd tell me if the statue was done by Michelangelo. Then I would feel that I could go home again."

"Why would that make a difference?" I asked.

"It would because . . . because . . ."

"Because you found that running away from home didn't make a real difference? You were still the same Greenwich Claudia, planning and washing and keeping things in order?"

"I guess that's right," Claudia said quietly.

"Then why did you run away?"

Claudia's words came slowly; she was forming thoughts into the shape of words for the first time in a long time. "I got the idea because I was mad at my parents. That was getting the idea. Then I started planning it. I thought that I had to think of everything, and I thought of an awful lot. Didn't I, Jamie?" She looked over at her brother, and he nodded. "I enjoyed the planning. Without anyone knowing that I was doing it. I am very good at planning."

"And the more plans you made, the more it became like living at home away from home," I interrupted.

"That's true," she said. "But we did enjoy living away from home in a mild kind of way."

(Notice that Claudia is still being very careful not to reveal to me where she and Jamie stayed. I wasn't ready to push yet. I felt I had to help the child. Don't laugh as you read this, Saxonberg; I do have some charity in me.)

"What part of living away from home did you like the best?"

Jamie answered first. "Not having a schedule."

Claudia became impatient. "But, Jamie, we did have a schedule. Sort of. The best that I could manage under the circumstances. *That* wasn't the most fun part of running away."

"What was the most fun part for you, Claudia?"

"First, it was hiding. Not being discovered. And after hiding became easy, there was Angel. Somehow, Angel became more important than running away."

"How did Angel become involved with your running away?" I purred.

"I won't tell you," Claudia answered.

I put on my surprised look and asked, "Why not?"

"Because if I tell you how Angel got involved, it will be telling you too much else."

"Like telling me where you've been all week?"

"Maybe," she answered coolly.

"Why don't you want to tell me that?"

"I told you before; that's *our* secret."

"Oho! You don't want to lose your bargaining weapon," I crowed. "Is that why you're not telling me where you stayed?"

"That's part of the reason," she said. "The other part is—I think the other part is—that if I tell, then I know for sure that my adventure is over. And I don't want it to be over until I'm sure I've had enough."

"The adventure is over. Everything gets over, and

nothing is ever enough. Except the part you carry with you. It's the same as going on a vacation. Some people spend all their time on a vacation taking pictures so that when they get home they can show their friends evidence that they had a good time. They don't pause to let the vacation enter inside of them and take that home."

"Well, I don't really want to tell you where we've been."

"I know," I answered.

Claudia looked at me. "Do you know I don't want to tell you, or do you know where we've been? Which do you mean?"

"Both," I told her quietly. I resumed eating *nouilles et fromage en casserole.*

Claudia looked over at Jamie. Jamie had slipped down in his seat and had thrown his napkin over his face. Claudia jumped up from her seat, grabbed the napkin off Jamie's face. Jamie quickly threw his forearms where the napkin had been.

"It slipped, Claude; it slipped out." Jamie's voice was muted since his forearms were protecting his mouth.

"Jamie! Jamie! That was all I had. All we had. The only thing we had left."

"I just forgot, Claude. It's been so long since I've had a conversation with anyone but you."

"You shouldn't have told her. You heard me say

to her that that was our secret. Twice. Now everything is lost. How can I get her to tell? You had to go and blab it all. Blabbermouth!"

Jamie looked at me for sympathy. "She does get emotional."

"Claudia," I said, "be seated."

She obeyed. I continued. "All is not lost. I'm going to make a bargain with you. Both of you. First of all, stop referring to me as *her*. I am Mrs. Basil E. Frankweiler. Then if you give me all the details of your running away, if you tell me everything—*everything*—I'll give you a ride home. I'll have Sheldon, my chauffeur, drive you home."

Claudia nodded "no."

"A Rolls Royce, Claudia. And a chauffeur. That's a very fine offer," I teased.

Jamie said, "How about it, Claude? It beats walking."

Claudia squinted her eyes and crossed her arms over her chest. "It's not enough. I want to know about Angel."

I was glad that I wasn't dealing with a stupid child. I admired her spirit; but more, I wanted to help her see the value of her adventure. She still saw it as buying her something: appreciation first, information now. Nevertheless, Claudia was tiptoeing into the grown-up world. And I decided to give her a little shove. "Claudia. James. Both of you. Come with me."

We walked single file through several rooms to my office. For a minute I thought I was leader in a game of follow-the-leader.

Jamie caught up with me and said, "For an old lady you sure can walk fast."

Claudia then caught up with Jamie and kicked him.

We arrived at my office, and I motioned for them to sit down.

"Do you see those filing cabinets along that wall?" I asked pointing to the south wall. "Those are my secrets. In one of them is the secret of Michelangelo's Angel. I'll share that secret with you as the rest of my bargain. But now my information is more important than yours. So you must have a handicap. The handicap is that you must find the secret file yourselves, and you have one hour to do it in." I turned to leave, then remembered, "And I don't want my files messed up or placed out of order. They're in a special order that makes sense only to me. If you move things around, I won't be able to find anything. And our whole arrangement will be off."

Jamie spoke, "You sure know how to nervous a guy."

I laughed and left the room. I tiptoed into the large closet I have next to my office. From there I watched and listened to all they did.

Jamie got up immediately and began opening file drawers. Claudia shouted, "STOP!" He did.

"What's the matter with you, Claude? We have only one hour."

"Five minutes of planning are worth fifteen minutes of just looking. Quick, give me the pencil and note pad from that table." Jamie ran to get them. Claudia immediately began making a list. "Here's what we'll look up. I'll take the odd numbers; you take the even."

"I want odd."

"For goodness' sake, Jamie, take odds then."

Here's the list Claudia wrote:

1. Michelangelo
2. Buonarroti
3. Angel
4. Parke Bernet Galleries
5. Metropolitan Museum of Art
6. Italian Renaissance
7. Auctions
8. Sculptor
9. Marble
10. Florence, Italy
11. Rome, Italy

Jamie looked over the list. "I changed my mind. I'll take evens. There's one less."

"Talk about wasting time!" Claudia screamed. "Take evens then, but get to it."

They began to work very rapidly. Claudia once or

twice cautioned Jamie not to make a mess. They had exhausted the list, odds as well as evens. There were folders on most of the categories they looked up, but upon examining them, they found not one hint of Angel. Claudia was feeling depressed. She looked at the clock. Six minutes to go.

"Think, Jamie, think. What else can we look up?"

Jamie squinted his eyes, a sign that he was thinking hard. "Look him up under . . ."

"What kind of language is that? Look him *up under* . . ."

"Oh, boloney, Claude. Why do you always pick on my gra . . ."

"Boloney, boloney! That's it, Jamie. She bought Angel in Bologna, Italy. The paper said so. Look up Bologna." Both ran back to the files and pulled out a file folder fat with papers and documents. It was labeled: BOLOGNA, ITALY. They knew even before opening it that it was the right one. I knew, too. They had found the file that held the secret.

Claudia was no longer in a hurry; she sauntered over to a table, carefully laid down the file, smoothed her skirt under her, and sat in a chair. Jamie was jumping up and down, "Hurry up, Claude. The hour is almost over."

Claudia was not to be hurried. She carefully opened the folder, almost afraid of what she would find. The evidence was sealed between two sheets of glass. The evidence was a very special, very old piece of paper. On one side was written a poem, a sonnet. Since it was written in Italian, neither Claudia nor Jamie could read it. But they could see that the handwriting was angular and beautiful, in itself almost a work of art. And there was a signature: Michelangelo. The other side of the paper needed no translation. For there, in the midst of sketches of hands and torsos, was a sketch of someone they knew: Angel. There were the first lines of a thought that was to become a museum mystery 470 years later. There on that piece of old paper was the idea just as it had come from Michelangelo's head to his hand, and he had jotted it down.

Claudia looked at the sketch until its image became blurred. She was crying. At first she said nothing. She simply sat on the chair with tears slowly streaming down her face, hugging the glass frame and shaking her head back and forth. When at last she found her voice, it was a hushed voice, the voice she used for church. "Just think, Jamie, Michelangelo himself touched this. Over four hundred years ago."

Jamie was looking through the rest of the folder. "The glass," he said. "I'll bet he didn't touch the glass. Are his fingerprints on it?" He didn't wait for an answer before asking something else. "What do you suppose the rest of these papers are?"

"They are my research on Angel," I answered as I emerged from my hiding place in the closet. "He did it in Rome, you know. I just file it under *B* for Bologna to make it hard."

Both children looked up at me startled. Just as they had lost all their feelings of urgency, they had also lost all thoughts of me. Finding a secret can make everything else unimportant, you know.

Claudia said nothing and nothing and nothing. She continued clutching the drawing to her chest and rocking it back and forth. She appeared to be in a trance. Jamie and I stared at her until she felt our eyes focused on her like four laser beams. She looked up at us then and smiled.

"Michelangelo did sculpture the statue, didn't he, Mrs. Frankweiler?"

"Of course. I've known for a long time that he did. Ever since I got that sketch."

"How did you get the sketch?" Jamie asked.

"I got it after the war. . . ."

"Which war?" Jamie interrupted.

"World War II. Which war did you think I meant? The American Revolution?"

"Are you that old?" Jamie asked.

"I'm not even going to answer that."

Claudia said, "Hush, Jamie. Let her tell us." But she couldn't hush either. She rushed in with an explanation, "I'll bet you helped some rich Italian nobleman or some descendant of Michelangelo's to escape, and he gave you the sketch out of his undying gratitude."

"That's one explanation. But not the correct one. There was a rich Italian nobleman involved. That part is right."

"Did he sell it to you?" Jamie asked.

Claudia rushed in again with another explanation, "He had this beautiful daughter and she needed this operation very badly and you . . ."

Jamie interrupted. "Hush, Claudia." Then he asked me, "Why did he give it to you?"

"Because he was a very, very bad poker player, and I am a very good one."

"You won it at cards?" I could see admiration grow in Jamie's eyes.

"Yes I did."

"Did you cheat?" he asked.

"Jamie, when the stakes are high, I never cheat. I consider myself too important to do that."

Jamie asked, "How come you don't sell the sketch? You could get quite a boodle for it. Being that it matches up with the statue and all."

"I need having the secret more than I need the money," I told him.

I knew that Claudia understood. Jamie looked puzzled.

"Thank you for sharing your secret with us," Claudia whispered.

"How do you know that we'll keep your secret?" Jamie asked.

"Now, now, a boy who cheats at cards should be able to answer that."

Jamie's face broke into a huge grin. "Bribery!" he exclaimed. "You're going to bribe us. Hallelujah! Tell me. I'm ready. What's the deal?"

I laughed. "The deal is this: you give me the details of your running away, and I'll give you the sketch."

Jamie gasped. "That doesn't sound like bribery. That doesn't even sound like you, Mrs. Frankweiler. You're smarter than that. How do you know that I won't slip about your secret as I did about the museum?"

That boy really amused me. "You're right, Jamie. I am smarter than that. I've got a method to keep you slip-proof about the sketch."

"What's that?"

"I'm not going to give you the sketch outright. I'm going to leave it to you in my will. You won't tell my secret because if you do, I'll write you out of my will. You would lose all that money. You said that the sketch was worth quite a boodle. So you're going to be very good about keeping this secret. Claudia will keep quiet for a different reason. Her reason happens to be the same as mine."

"Which is what?" Jamie asked.

"Simply because it is a secret. It will enable her to return to Greenwich *different*."

Claudia looked at Jamie and nodded. Something I had just said made sense.

I continued, "Returning with a secret is what she really wants. Angel had a secret and that made her exciting, important. Claudia doesn't want adventure. She likes baths and feeling comfortable too much for that kind of thing. Secrets are the kind of adventure she needs. Secrets are safe, and they do much to make you different. On the inside where it counts. I won't actually be getting a secret from you; I'll be getting details. I'm a collector of all kinds of things besides art," I said pointing to my files.

"If all those files are secrets, and if secrets make you different on the inside, then your insides, Mrs. Frankweiler, must be the most mixed-up, the most different insides I've ever seen. Or any doctor has ever seen, either."

I grinned. "There's a lifetime of secrets in those files. But there's also just a lot of newspaper clippings. Junk. It's a hodgepodge. Like my art collection. Now, you'll tell me all about your running away, and I'll add that to my files."

Whereas Jamie's excitement bubbled out of him in grins and spurts of jittering around the room, Claudia's excitement flowed not bubbled. I could see that she was a little surprised. She had known that Angel would have the answer, but she had expected it to be a loud bang, not a quiet soaking in. Of course secrets make a difference. That was why planning the runaway had been such fun; it was a secret. And hiding in the museum had been a secret. But they weren't permanent; they had to come to an end. Angel wouldn't. She could carry the secret of Angel inside her for twenty years just as I had. Now she wouldn't have to be a heroine when she returned home . . . except to herself. And now she knew something about secrets that she hadn't known before.

I could tell that she felt happy. Happiness is excitement that has found a settling down place, but there is always a little corner that keeps flapping around. Claudia could have kept her doubts to herself, but she was an honest child, an honorable child.

"Mrs. Frankweiler," she said swallowing hard, "I really love the sketch. I really do. I love it. Just love, love, love it. But don't you think you ought to give it to the museum. They're just dying to find out whether the statue is real or not."

"Nonsense! What a conscience you suddenly have. I want to give it to you. In exchange. If you and Jamie want to give it to the museum after you inherit it, then you give it to the museum. I won't let the museum people near here. If I could keep them out of Connecticut altogether, I would. I don't want them to have it while I'm alive."

Claudia wiped her forehead with the sleeve of her sweater and asked, "Why not?"

"I've thought about that for a long time, and I've decided 'why not?' What they'll do is start investigating the authenticity of the sketch. They'll call in authorities from all over the world. They'll analyze the ink. And the paper. They'll research all his illustrated notes and compare, compare, compare. In short, they'll make a science of it. Some will say 'yes.' Some will say 'no.' Scholars will debate about it. They'll poll all the authorities, and probably the majority will agree that the note and the statue are really the work of Michelangelo. At least that's what they should conclude. But some stubborn ones won't agree, and thereafter the statue and the sketch will appear in books with a big question mark. The experts don't believe in coincidence as much as I do, and I don't want them to throw doubt on something that I've felt always, and actually known for about twenty years."

Claudia's eyes widened, "But, Mrs. Frankweiler, if there is the slightest doubt that either the statue or the sketch is a forgery, don't you want to know? Don't you want the last little bit of doubt cleared up?"

"No," I answered abruptly.

"Why not?"

"Because I'm eighty-two years old. That's why. There now, Jamie, you see, I slip too. Now I've told you how old I am."

Jamie looked at his sister and asked, "What's that got to do with anything, Claude?" Claudia shrugged.

"I'll tell you what it's got to do with it," I said. "I'm satisfied with my own research on the subject. I'm not in the mood to learn anything new."

Claudia said, "But, Mrs. Frankweiler, you should want to learn one new thing every day. We did even at the museum."

"No," I answered, "I don't agree with that. I think you should learn, of course, and some days you must learn a great deal. But you should also have days when you allow what is already in you to swell up inside of you until it touches everything. And you can feel it inside you. If you never take time out to let that happen, then you just accumulate facts, and they begin to rattle around inside of you. You can make noise with them, but never really feel anything with them. It's hollow."

Both children were quiet, and I continued. "I've gathered a lot of facts about Michelangelo and Angel. And I've let them grow inside me for a long time. Now I feel that I know. That's enough for that. But there is one new thing that I'd like to experience. Not know. Experience. And that one thing is impossible."

"Nothing is impossible," Claudia said. She sounded to me exactly like a bad actress in a bad play—unreal.

"Claudia," I said patiently, "When one is eighty-two years old, one doesn't have to learn one new thing every day, and one knows that some things are impossible."

"What would you like to experience that is impossible?" Jamie asked.

"Right now, I'd like to know how your mother feels."

"You keep saying that she's frantic. Why do you want to feel frantic?" This came from Claudia. Now she sounded like the real Claudia Kincaid.

"It's an experience I would like to have because it's part of a bigger experience I want."

Claudia said, "You mean you'd like to be a mother?"

Jamie leaned toward Claudia and whispered in the loudest, wettest whisper I have ever heard, "Of course that's impossible. Her husband is dead. You can't be a mother without a husband."

Claudia poked Jamie, "Never call people *dead*; it makes others feel bad. Say 'deceased' or 'passed away.' "

"Come now, children. Put away the file. You must tell me all about your adventure. All, all, all about it. What you thought and what you said and how you managed to carry off the whole crazy caper."

10

I KEPT THE CHILDREN UP LATE GETTING THE DETAILS. Jamie and I played war while Claudia talked into the tape recorder. Jamie ended up with two aces and twelve cards more than I; the game cost me thirty-four cents. I still don't know how he does it. It was my deck of cards; but I was somewhat preoccupied listening to Claudia and interrupting her with questions. And then there was that telephone call from the children's parents. I knew you'd tell them, Saxonberg. I knew it! What a combination you are: soft heart and hard head. It was all I could do to persuade them to stay home and let me deliver the children in the morning. Mrs. Kincaid kept asking if they were bruised or maimed. I think she has read too many accounts of lost children in the newspapers. You realize now why I insisted that they stay overnight. I wanted all sides of the bargain kept, and I had to get my information. Besides I had promised them a ride home in the Rolls Royce, and I never cheat when the stakes are high.

When it came to be Jamie's turn to talk into the tape recorder, I thought that I would never get him to quit fussing with the switches. He enjoyed saying something and then erasing it. Finally, I scolded him, "You're not Sir Lawrence Olivier playing Hamlet, you know. All I want are the facts and how you felt. Not a theatrical production."

"You want me to be accurate, don't you?"

"Yes, but I also want you to finish."

Claudia asked for a tour of the house while Jamie told his story. She asked about everything. We rode the elevator up to the third floor, and she went from one room to the next. I hadn't been through the entire house for a long time, so I enjoyed the tour, too. We talked; we both enjoyed that also. Claudia told me about her routine at home. When we came back to the black marble bathroom, she told me how she came to take a bath there earlier. I allowed her to pick the bedroom where she would sleep that night.

Very early the next morning I had Sheldon drive them to Greenwich. I'm enclosing a copy of his report for your amusement, Saxonberg; you ought to be in a mood to laugh now.

The boy, madam, spent the first five minutes of the trip pushing every button in the back seat. I transported them in the Rolls Royce as you requested. He pushed some buttons at least twelve times; others I stopped counting at five. He seemed to regard the button panel, madam, as some sort of typewriter or piano or I.B.M. computer. Without realizing it he pushed the button to the intercom *on* and neglected to push it *off*. In this way I overheard all their conversation; they thought they were privately sealed behind the glass screen that divides the front seat from the back. The girl was quiet while the other tested things. Everything, I might add.

Finally, the girl remarked to the other, "Why do you suppose she sold Angel in the first place? Why didn't she just donate it to the museum?"

"Because she's tight. That's why. She said so," the boy answered.

"That's not the reason. If she were tight, and she knew it was worth so much, she would never have sold it for $225."

Thank goodness the girl interested him in conversation. He stopped pushing buttons. Besides neglecting to turn off the intercom, he also neglected to turn off the windshield wipers on the rear window. I might add, madam, that it was not raining.

"Well, she sold it at auction, silly. At an auction you have to sell it to the highest bidder. No one bid higher than $225. It's that simple."

The girl replied, "She didn't sell it for the money. She would have shown her evidence if she really wanted a big price. She sold it for the fun of it. For excitement."

"Maybe she didn't have room for it anymore."

"In that museum of a house? There're rooms upstairs that . . . oh! Jamie, the statue is only two feet tall. She could have tucked it into any corner."

"Why do *you* think she sold it?"

The girl thought a minute. (I was hoping she would answer soon, madam. Before the boy got interested in the buttons again.) "Because after a time having a secret and nobody knowing you have a secret is no fun. And although you don't want others to know what the secret is, you want them to at least know you have one."

I observed from the rear view mirror, madam, that the little boy grew quiet. He looked at the girl and said, "You know, Claude, I'm going to save my money and my winnings, and I'm going to visit Mrs. Frankweiler again." A long pause, then, "There's something about our running away that I forgot to say into the tape recorder."

The girl said nothing.

"Wanna come, Claude? We won't tell anyone."

"How much did you win last night?" the girl asked.

"Only thirty-four cents. She's a lot sharper than Bruce."

"Maybe my twenty-five cents from the cornflakes came already. That would make fifty-nine." The girl was silent for a few minutes before she asked, "Do you think she meant that stuff about motherhood?"

The boy shrugged his shoulders. "Let's visit her every time we save enough money. We won't tell anyone. We won't stay overnight. We'll just tell Mom and Dad that we're going bowling or something, and we'll take a train up instead."

"We'll adopt her," the girl suggested. "We'll become her kids, sort of."

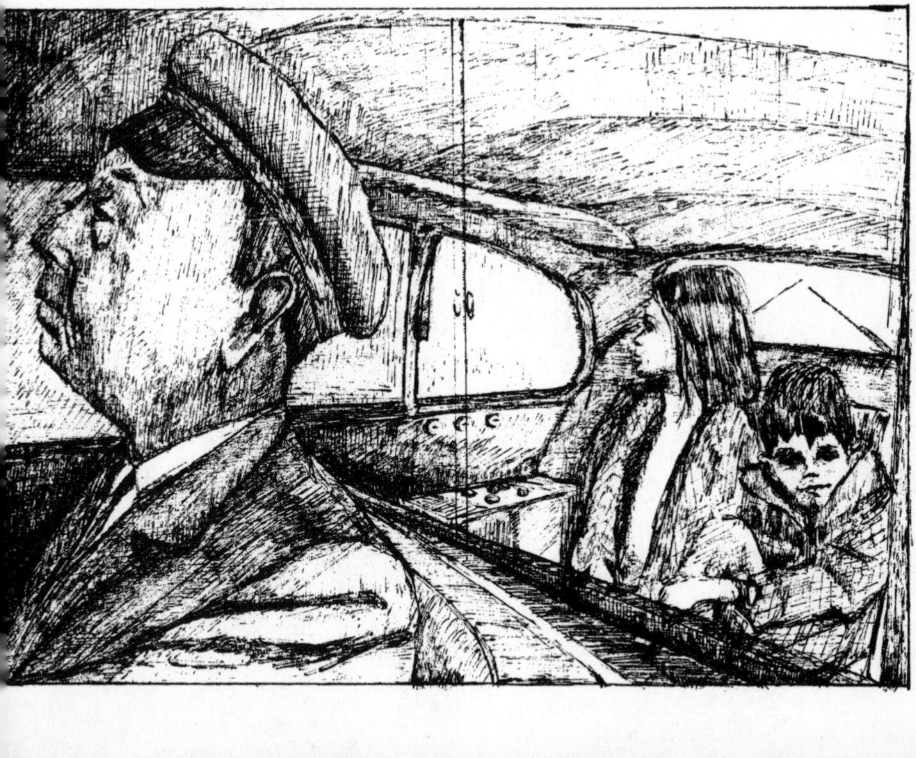

"She's too old to be a mother. She said so herself. Besides, we already have one."

"She'll become our grandmother, then, since ours are deceased."

"And that will be our secret that we won't even share with her. She'll be the only woman in the world to become a grandmother with never becoming a mother first."

I drove the car to the address they gave me, madam. The shades were up, and I could see a quite handsome man and a young matron watching by the window. I also thought I saw our own Mr. Saxonberg. The boy had opened the doors even before I had completely stopped. That is a very dangerous thing to do. A much younger creature, also a boy, came running out of the house immediately ahead of the others. As I drove away, this younger one was saying, "Boy! what a car. Hey, Claude, I'll be your *sponsibility* the rest of . . ."

The children, madam, neglected to say thank you.

Well, Saxonberg, that's why I'm leaving the drawing of Angel to Claudia and Jamie Kincaid, your two lost grandchildren that you were so worried about. Since they intend to make me their grandmother, and you already are their grandfather, that makes us—oh, well, I won't even think about that. You're not that good a poker player.

Rewrite my will with a clause about my bequeathing the drawing to them. Also put in a clause about that bed I mentioned, too. I guess I ought to donate it to the Metropolitan Museum. I haven't really begun to like donating things. You'll notice that everyone is getting these things after I'm dead. I should say *passed away*. After you have all those things written into my will, I'll sign the new version. Sheldon and Parks can be witnesses. The signing of the will will take place in the restaurant of the Metropolitan Museum of Art in New York City. You'll come there with me, dear Saxonberg, or lose me, your best client.

I wonder if Claudia and Jamie will come visit me again. I wouldn't mind if they did. You see, I still have an edge; I know one bit more of a secret than they do. They don't know that their grandfather has been my lawyer for forty-one years. (And I recommend that for your own good, you not tell them, Saxonberg.)

By the way I heard a radio interview by the new Commissioner of Parks in New York City. He said that his budget had been cut. When asked by a reporter where the money that should have been spent for the parks was going, the commissioner replied that most of it was going towards increased security for the Metropolitan Museum. Suspecting that something special had prompted this move, I asked Sheldon to call his friend, Morris the guard, to find out if anything unusual had been discovered lately.

Morris reported that a violin case was found in a sarcophagus last week. A trumpet case was found two days later. Morris says that guards who have worked at the museum for a year have seen everything; those who have worked there for six months have seen half of everything. They once discovered a set of false teeth on the seat of an Etruscan chariot. They sent the children's cases to Lost and Found. They are still there. Full of gray-washed underwear and a cheap transistor radio. No one has claimed them yet.

Jennifer,
Hecate,
Macbeth,
William McKinley,
and Me,
Elizabeth

To Paul, Laurie, and Ross
for loving a witch

jennifer,
  hecate,
macbeth,
  william mckinley,
        and me,
        elizabeth

1

I FIRST MET JENNIFER ON MY WAY TO school. It was Halloween, and she was sitting in a tree. I was going back to school from lunch. This particular lunch hour was only a little different from usual because of Halloween. We were told to dress in costume for the school Halloween parade. I was dressed as a Pilgrim.

I always walked the back road to school, and I always walked alone. We had moved to the apartment house in town in September just before school started, and I walked alone because I didn't have anyone to walk with. I walked the back way because it passed through a little woods that I liked. Jennifer was sitting in one of the trees in this woods.

Our apartment house had grown on a farm about ten years before. There was still a small farm across the street; it included a big white house, a greenhouse, a caretaker's house, and a pump painted green without a handle. The greenhouse had clean windows; they shone in the sun. I could see only the roof windows from our second floor apartment. The rest were hidden by trees and shrubs. My mother never called the place a farm; she always called it THE ESTATE. It was old; the lady who owned it was old. She had given part of her land to the town for a park, and the town named the park after her: Samellson Park. THE ESTATE gave us a beautiful view from our apartment. My mother liked trees.

Our new town was not full of apartments. Almost everyone else lived in houses. There were only three apartment buildings as big as ours. All three sat on the top of the hill from the train station. Hundreds of men rode the train to New York City every morning and rode it home every night. My father did. In the mornings the elevators would be full of kids going to school and fathers going to the train. The kids left the building by the back door and ran down one side of the hill to the school. The fathers left the building by the front door and ran down the other side of the hill to the station.

Other kids from the apartment chose to walk to school through the little woods. The footsteps of all of them for ten years had worn away the soil so that the roots of the trees were bare and made steps for walking up and down the steep slope. The little woods made better company than the sidewalks. I liked the smells of the trees and the colors of the trees. I liked to walk with my head way up, practically hanging over my back. Then I could see the patterns the leaves formed against the blue sky.

I had my head way back and was watching the leaves when I first saw Jennifer up in the tree. She was dressed as a Pilgrim, too. I saw her feet first. She was sitting on one of the lower branches of the tree swinging her feet. That's how I happened to see her feet first. They were just about the boniest feet I had ever seen. Swinging right in front of my eyes as if I were sitting in the first row at Cinerama. They wore real Pilgrim shoes made of buckles and cracked old leather. The heel part flapped up and down because the shoes were so big that only the toe part could stay attached. Those shoes looked as if they were going to fall off any minute.

I grabbed the heel of the shoe and shoved it back onto the heel of that bony foot. Then I wiped my hands on my Pilgrim apron and looked up at Jennifer. I didn't know yet that she was Jennifer. She was not smiling, and I was embarrassed.

I said in a loud voice, which I hoped would sound stout red but which came out sounding thin blue, "You're going to lose that shoe."

The first thing Jennifer ever said to me was, "Witches never lose anything."

"But you're not a witch," I said. "You're a Pilgrim, and look, so am I."

"I won't argue with you," she said. "Witches convince; they never argue. But I'll tell you this much. Real witches are Pilgrims, and just because I don't have on a silly black costume and carry a silly broom and wear a silly black hat, doesn't mean that I'm not a witch. I'm a witch all the time and not just on Halloween."

I didn't know what to say, so I said what my mother always says when she can't answer one of my questions. I said, "You better hurry up now, or you'll be late for school."

"Witches are never late," she said.

"But witches have to go to school." I wished I had said something clever.

"I just go to school because I'm putting the teacher under a spell," she said.

"Which teacher?" I asked. "Get it? *Witch*

teacher?" I laughed. I was pleased that now I had said something clever.

Jennifer neither laughed nor answered. But I was sure she'd got it. She looked at me hard and said, "Give me those three chocolate chip cookies, and I'll come down and tell you my name, and I'll walk the rest of the way to school with you."

I wasn't particularly hungry for the cookies, but I was hungry for company, so I said, "Okay," and reached out my hand holding the cookies. I wondered how she could tell that they were chocolate chips. They were in a bag.

As she began to swing down from the branches, I caught a glimpse of her underwear. I expected that it would look dusty, and it did. But that was not why it was not like any underwear I had ever seen. It was old fashioned. There were buttons and no elastic. She also had on yards and yards of petticoats. Her Pilgrim dress looked older than mine. Much older. Much, much older. Hers looked ancient. Of course, my Pilgrim costume was not new either. I had worn it the year before, but then I had been in a different grade in a different school. My cousin had worn the costume before that. I hadn't grown much during the year. My dress was only a little short, and only a little tight, and only a little scratchy where it was pinned, and it was only absolutely uncomfortable. In other words, my costume was a hand-me-down, but Jennifer's was a genuine antique.

After Jennifer touched the ground, I saw that she was taller than I. Everybody was. I was the shortest kid in my class. I was always the shortest kid in my class. She was thin. Skinny is what she really was. She came toward my hand and looked hard at the bag of cookies.

"Are you sure you didn't bite any of them?" she demanded.

"Sure I'm sure," I said. I was getting mad, but a bargain's a bargain.

"Well," she said, taking one cookie out of the bag, "My name is Jennifer. Now let's get going." As she said "going," she grabbed the bag with the other two cookies and started to walk.

"Wait up," I yelled. "A bargain's a bargain. Don't you want to know my name?"

"I told you witches are never late, but I can't be responsible for you yet . . . Elizabeth."

She knew my name already! She walked so fast that I was almost convinced that she was a witch; she was practically flying. We got to school just as the tardy bell began to ring. Jennifer's room was a fifth grade just off the corridor near the entrance, and she slipped into her classroom while the bell was still buzzing. My room was four doors further down the hall, and I got to my room *after* the bell had stopped.

She had said that witches are never late. Being

late felt as uncomfortable as my tight Pilgrim dress. No Pilgrim had ever suffered as much as I did. Walking to my seat while everyone stared at me was awful. My desk was in the back of the room; it was a long, long walk. The whole class had time to see that I was a blushing Pilgrim. I knew that I was ready to cry. The whole class didn't have to know that too, so I didn't raise my eyes until I was seated and felt sure that they wouldn't leak. When I looked up, I saw that there were six Pilgrims: three other Pilgrim girls and two Pilgrim boys. That's a lot of Pilgrims for a class of twenty. But none of them could be witches, I thought. After checking over their costumes and shoes, I decided that at least three of them had cousins who had been Pilgrims the year before.

Miss Hazen announced that she would postpone my detention until the next day because of the Halloween parade. Detention was a school rule; if you were late coming to school, you stayed after school that day. The kids called it "staying after." I didn't feel grateful for the postponement. She could have skipped my "staying after" altogether.

Our lesson that afternoon was short, and I didn't perform too well. I had to tug on my dress a lot and scratch under my Pilgrim hat a lot. I would have scratched other places where the costume itched, but they weren't polite.

At last we were all lined up in the hall. Each

class was to march to the auditorium and be seated. Then one class at a time would walk across the stage before the judges. The rest of the classes would be the audience. The classes at the end of the hall marched to the auditorium first.

There were classes on both sides of the hall near my room, and the space for the marchers was narrow. Some of the children had large cardboard cartons over them and were supposed to be packages of cigarettes or sports cars. These costumes had

trouble getting through. Then there was Jennifer. She was last in line. She looked neither to the right nor to the left but slightly up toward the ceiling. I kept my eye on her hoping she'd say "Hi" so that I wouldn't feel so alone standing there. She didn't. Instead, well, I almost didn't believe what I actually saw her do.

But before I tell what I saw her do, I have to tell about Cynthia. Every grown-up in the whole U.S. of A. thinks that Cynthia is perfect. She is

pretty and neat and smart. I guess that makes perfect to almost any grown-up. Since she lives in the same apartment house as we do, and since my mother is a grown-up, and since my mother thinks that she is perfect, my mother had tried hard to have us become friends since we first moved to town. My mother would drop hints. HINT: Why don't you call Cynthia and ask her if she would like to show you where the library is? Then you can both eat lunch here. Or HINT: Why don't you run over and play with Cynthia while I unpack the groceries?

It didn't take me long to discover that what Cynthia was, was not perfect. The word for what Cynthia was, was *mean*.

Here's an example of mean. There was a little boy in our building who had moved in about a month before we did. His name was Johann; that's German for John. He moved from Germany and didn't speak English yet. He loved Cynthia. Because she was so pretty, I guess. He followed her around and said, "Cynsssia, Cynsssia." Cynthia always made fun of him. She would stick her tongue between her teeth and say, "Th, th, th, th, th. My name is Cyn-*th*-ia not Cyn-*sss*-ia." Johann would smile and say, "Cyn-*sss*-ia." Cynthia would stick out her tongue and say, "Th, th, th, th, th." And then she'd walk away from him. I liked Johann. I wished he would follow me around. I would have taught him English, and I would never even have minded if he called me Elizabessss. Another word for what Cynthia was, was *two-faced*. Because every time some grown-up was around, she was sweet to Johann. She'd smile at him and pat his head . . . only until the grown-up left.

And another thing: Cynthia certainly didn't need me for a friend. She had a very good friend called Dolores who also lived in the apartment house. They told secrets and giggled together whenever I got into the elevator with them. So I got into the habit of leaving for school before they did. Sometimes, on weekends, they'd be in the elevator when I got on; I'd act as if they weren't there. I had to get off the elevator before they did because I lived on the second floor, and they lived on the sixth. Before I'd get off the elevator, I'd take my fists, and fast and furious, I'd push every floor button just the second before I got out. I'd step out of the elevator and watch the dial stopping at every floor on the way up. Then I'd skip home to our apartment.

For Halloween Cynthia wore everything real ballerinas wear: leotards and tights and ballet slippers and a tutu. A tutu is a little short skirt that ballerinas wear somewhere around their waists. Hers looked like a nylon net doughnut floating around her middle. Besides all the equipment I listed above, Cynthia wore rouge and eye make-up and lipstick and a tiara. She looked glamorous, but I could tell that she felt plenty chilly in that costume. Her teeth were chattering. She wouldn't put on a sweater.

As we were standing in the hall waiting for our turn to go to the auditorium, and as Jennifer's class passed, Cynthia was turned around talking to Dolores. Dolores was dressed as a Pilgrim. They were both whispering and giggling. Probably about Jennifer.

Here's what Jennifer did. As she passed Cynthia, she reached out and quicker than a blink unsnapped the tutu. I happened to be watching her closely, but even I didn't believe that she had really done it. Jennifer clop-clopped along in the line with her eyes still up toward the ceiling and passed me a note almost without my knowing. She did it so fast that I wasn't even sure she did it until I felt the note in my hand and crunched it beneath my apron to hide it. Jennifer never took her eyes off the ceiling or broke out of line for even half a step.

I wanted to make sure that everyone saw Cynthia with her tutu down, so I pointed my finger at her and said, "O-o-o-oh!" I said it loud. Of course, that made everyone on both sides of the aisle notice her and start to giggle.

Cynthia didn't have sense enough to be embarrassed. She loved attention so much that she didn't care if her tutu had fallen. She stepped out of it, picked it up, shook it out, floated it over her head, and anchored it back around her waist. She touched her hands to her hair, giving it little pushes the way women do who have just come out of the beauty parlor. I hoped she was itchy.

Finally, our class got to the auditorium. After I sat down, I opened the note, holding both my hands under my Pilgrim apron. I slowly slipped my hands out and glanced at the note. I was amazed at what I saw. Jennifer's note looked like this:

Meet for Trick or Treat
at
Half after ſix P.M. o'clock
of thiſ evening.
By the ſame tree.
Bring two (2) bagſ.
Thoſe were good cookieſ

I studied the note a long time. I thought about the note as I watched the Halloween parade; I wondered if Jennifer used a quill pen. You can guess that I didn't win any prizes for my costume. Neither did Cynthia. Neither did Jennifer (even though I thought she should have). We all marched across the stage wearing our masks and stopped for a curtsy or bow (depending on whether you were a girl or a boy) in front of the judges who were sitting at a table in the middle of the stage. Some of the girls who were disguised as boys forgot themselves and curtsied. Then we marched off. Our class was still seated when Jennifer clop-clopped across the stage in those crazy Pilgrim slippers. She didn't wear a mask at all. She wore a big brown paper bag over her head and *there were no holes cut out for her eyes*. Yet, she walked up the stairs, across the stage, stopped and curtsied, and walked off without tripping or falling or walking out of those gigantic shoes.

2

OUR FAMILY RUSHED THROUGH SUPPER that night. But the trick or treaters started coming even before we finished. Most of the early ones were bitsy kids who had to bring their mothers to reach the door bells for them.

I didn't tell my parents about Jennifer. I mentioned to my mother that I was meeting a friend at 6:30, and we were going to trick or treat together. Mom just asked, "Someone from school?" and I just said, "Yes."

The days start getting short, and the evenings start getting cool in late October. So I had to wear my old ski jacket over my costume. I looked like a Pilgrim who had made a bad trade with the Indians. Jennifer was waiting. She was leaning against the tree. She had put on stockings. They were long, black, cotton stockings, and she wore a huge black shawl. She smelled a little bit like moth balls, but I happen to especially like that smell in autumn.

"Hi," I said.

"I'll take the bigger bag," she replied.

She didn't say "please."

I held out the bags. She took the bigger one. She didn't say "thank you." Her manners were unusual. I guessed that witches never said "please" and never said "thank you." All my life my mother had taught me a politeness vocabulary. I didn't mind. I thought that "please" and "thank you" made conversation prettier, just as bows and lace make dresses prettier. I was full of admiration for how easily Jennifer managed without bows or lace or "please" or "thank you."

She opened her bag, stuck her head way down inside, and said:

"Bag, sack, parcel post,
Fill thyself
With goodies most."

She lifted her head out of the bag and tightened her shawl. "We can go now," she said.

"Don't you mean 'Bag, sack, parcel, *poke?*' " I asked. "Parcel *post* is the mail; *poke* is a name for a bag."

Jennifer was walking with her head up, eyes up. She shrugged her shoulders and said, "Poetic license. *Poke* doesn't rhyme."

I shrugged my shoulders and started walking

with her. Jennifer disappeared behind a tree. No master spirit had taken her away. She reappeared in a minute, pulling a wagon. It was the usual kind of child's wagon, but to make the sides taller, she had stretched a piece of chicken wire all along the inner rim. Jennifer pulled the wagon, carried her bag, clutched her shawl, and clop-clopped toward the first house. I walked.

I had been trick or treating for a number of years. I began as a bitsy kid, and my mother rang the door bells for me, as other mothers were ringing them for those other bitsy kids that night. I had been a nurse, a mouse (I had worn my sleepers with the feet in), and other things. I had been a Pilgrim before, too. I mentioned that I had been a Pilgrim the year before. All I mean to say is that I'd been trick or treating for years and years and years, and I'd seen lots of trick or treaters come to our house, but I'd never, never, never seen a performance like Jennifer's.

This is the way Jennifer operated: 1. She left the wagon outside the door of the house and out of sight of her victim. 2. She rang the bell. 3. Instead of smiling and saying "trick or treat," she said nothing when the people came to the door. 4. She half fell against the door post and said, "I would like just a drink of water." 5. She breathed hard. 6. The lady or man who answered would say, "Of course," and would bring her a drink of water. 7. As she reached out to get the water, she dropped her big, empty bag. 8. The lady or man noticed how empty it was and said, "Don't you want just a little something?" 9. The lady or man poured stuff into Jennifer's bag. 10. The lady or man put a little something in my bag, too. 11. Jennifer and I left the house. 12. Jennifer dumped the treats into the wagon. 13. Jennifer clop-clopped to the next house with the bag empty again. 14. I walked.

Jennifer did this at every house. She always drank a glass of water. She always managed to drop her empty bag. I asked her how she could drink so much water. She must have had about twenty-four glasses. She didn't answer. She shrugged her shoulders and walked with her head up, eyes up. I sort of remembered something about a water test for witches. But I also sort of remembered that it was something about witches being able to float on water that was outside their bodies, not water that was inside their bodies.

I asked Jennifer why she didn't wear a mask. She answered that one disguise was enough. She told me that all year long she was a witch, disguised as a perfectly normal girl; on Halloween she became undisguised. She may be a witch, I thought, and, of course, she was a girl. But perfect never! And normal never!

I can say that Jennifer collected more treats on that Halloween than I had in all my years put together including the time I was a mouse in my sleepers with the feet in. Because I was with Jennifer each time she went into her act, I managed to collect more treats on that Halloween than I ever had before but not nearly as many as Jennifer. My bag was heavy, though.

Jennifer and I parted about a block from my apartment house. My bag was so heavy that I could hardly hold it with one hand as I pushed the button for the elevator. I put the bag on the floor while I waited. When the elevator arrived, I leaned over to pick up my bundle and heard my Pilgrim dress go *r-r-r-r-r-r-i-p*. I arrived at our apartment, tired and torn, but happy. Happy because I had had a successful Halloween; happy because I had not met Cynthia on the elevator; and happy because my costume had ripped. I wouldn't have to be an itchy Pilgrim another Halloween.

3

School went very well the next day. We played dodge ball in gym; I got Cynthia out. I aimed a good one right at the back of her legs; it almost knocked her over. It wasn't much fun getting after Cynthia in front of the teacher, though. Since the teacher was a grown-up, Cynthia acted sweet. She smiled when she got called out and pretended that it was the nicest thing that had ever happened to her.

I didn't mind "staying after" that day. It was cloudy and chilly. There was nothing special to do during the afternoon, and no one special to do it with. Miss Hazen made me write "I will not be tardy" one hundred times. I used a lot of time doing it. I practiced all different kinds of printing and all different kinds of writing. A couple of times I tried to write as Jennifer did but decided that I would need something more special than a ball point pen. I numbered the lines in Roman numerals, and that took a lot of time. I had to figure out whether 49 should be XXXXIX or XLIX or IL. I'm sure I enjoyed my punishment much more than Miss Hazen did. Maybe she wished she had made me write it only fifty times. She would say things like, "You'll just have to go faster," or "Are you almost ready?" or "You work much faster than this usually."

I finished. Walking home alone seemed less lonely when there weren't a lot of other kids walking in two's and three's. Even the cop who guards the school crossing had gone off duty. I was walking calmly and patiently; that's the way I was feeling. Miss Hazen zoomed past me in her car. She didn't notice when I waved to her. When you're driving that fast, I guess you have to concentrate on steering. I'll bet she was glad that the cop was gone. The little woods said November now; maybe because it was cloudy.

A little way into the woods I spotted a note tacked to the Jennifer tree. For me! For me! I knew it was for me. It was written on brownish paper in Jennifer's peculiar handwriting. It said:

Library Reading Room
Saturday 10:00 A. M. o'clock
of the morning

I folded the note and left the tack in the tree. Then I zoomed the rest of the way home wishing that it could be Saturday in five minutes.

The rest of that week seemed to have a month's worth of days, but Saturday came. It was a golden day full of the smells of autumn. I told my parents that I'd skip going grocery shopping with them. I told them that I had some work to do at the library. No argument. I was usually a nag for them to take to the A & P. I wasn't very popular at the A & P either. Once I had rammed the cart into a big mountain of cracker boxes. Avalanche! I told the manager that I'd pick them all up, and I did. I arranged them very artistically; the aisle was blocked for forty-five minutes. I hadn't been very popular at that A & P since.

When I got to the library reading room, I knew Jennifer was already there. Her wagon was parked by the encyclopedias. She was looking at a big book of maps when I came in. Libraries are for whispering, and I soon discovered that Jennifer whispered beautifully, with many nice ssssssssssss sounds coming out like steam out of a kettle.

I whispered, "Hi."

She whispered back, "Did you bring something to eat?"

"No," I said. "A & P day. The cupboard was bare."

She closed the atlas and looked at me for what seemed like a very long time. Leaning way over and in such a quiet voice that it was almost zero, she said, "I've decided to make you an apprentice witch."

"What do I have to do?" I asked.

"Answer 'yes' or 'no.' " I must have looked worried. She didn't let me waste time; she came across soft but fast. "If you really want to be a witch, nothing you have to do will seem like too much. If you don't really want to be witch, everything will seem like too much. Answer 'yes' or 'no.' "

I answered, "Yes."

"We'll start today," she said and got down from her chair. She replaced the huge book of maps on its proper shelf before pulling the wagon toward the check-out table. The wagon was loaded with seven heavy, large books. She handed these up to the librarian one at a time and then replaced each one in the wagon after it had been checked out.

The librarian said to Jennifer, "Did you finish last week's supply?" I guessed that Jennifer was well known at the library.

Jennifer sighed and said, "Of course." She grabbed the handle of the wagon and pulled it out the door and down the steps to the street. Those steps are steep. But not a single book fell out of Jennifer's wagon on the bumpity way down.

That Saturday Jennifer was dressed as she was

usually dressed for school. That is, she wore a skirt. I later learned that she never wore jeans or shorts. She always wore a skirt. It was always an ordinary skirt. There was one thing about the way she was dressed that Saturday that was unordinary. Around her neck she had a gigantic key. She had it hanging from an old yo-yo string. The wagon was heavy with her books. Jennifer had to pull it with both hands behind her, and she had to lean way over to make the wagon move. That made the key hang very low; it would clung the sidewalk every now and then.

We headed for Samellson Park. We didn't talk much on the way. I didn't ask Jennifer where she lived and whether she had any brothers and sisters and where her father worked. She didn't ask me either. I suspected she knew everything about me anyway. There wasn't too much to know. I am an only child.

When we got to the park, we walked toward the fountain. First, Jennifer took a drink. I'd never seen anyone love water the way Jennifer did. Then we sat down on one of the benches nearby. The water fountain was in the center of a cement circle. There were paths leading to it from four different sides of the park. I'd guess that the circle was about nine feet across. I soon learned that much as she loved water, Jennifer was more interested in the cement circle than she was in the fountain.

"Now, if you're ready," she said, "we'll begin."

I would have been more ready if Jennifer had not seemed so serious. She was as serious as a doctor ready to give me a DPT booster shot. A witch doctor, I thought. When I answered, I tried to sound firm and a little bit annoyed, the way Jennifer did with the librarian. I said, "Of course." Jennifer could not be imitated. My voice came out loud Elizabeth instead of cool Jennifer.

Jennifer took a piece of chalk out of her pocket and made a chalk mark all around the edge of the concrete circle. That crazy key kept scraping along the concrete as she bent over. I hoped that after I became a witch's apprentice, I wouldn't get goose pimples from that noise any more. After the whole circle was completed, Jennifer took a candle from her pocket. She lit it and stuck the candle onto the concrete near the bottom of the fountain by dripping some of the wax first. After standing there with her eyes wide open, staring at the big sky, she marched out of the circle straight over to me.

"Watch me," she said. "When I'm ready, I'll point to you. When I point to you, you may enter the magic circle. But be quiet. Don't sneeze, burp, or breathe loud. Also, don't talk."

Then Jennifer walked back to as near center as she could get without actually standing inside the fountain. She closed her eyes and spun around three times, holding her hands straight down at her sides. As she spun around, she chanted:

"Xilka, Xilka, Besa, Besa;
Xilka, Xilka, Besa, Besa;
Xilka, Xilka, Besa, Besa."

On the third spin, and with her eyes still closed, she pointed right at me. I walked into the magic circle, scared, shaking, and certainly not talking.

Jennifer took the big key from around her neck, twirled it over her head, and laid it on the ground near the center of the circle. Next she took a pin out of her pocket. She pricked her finger; and without even asking permission, she pricked mine, too. Holding her hand over mine, she placed both our hands on the key. Each of our fingers dripped a drop of blood onto it. Jennifer picked it up, spit on it, and handed it to me. So I spit on it, too. She held the key over the candle to dry the spit and the blood. The candle made cackle sounds as she did this. When the key was dry she put it back down on the concrete and blew out the candle. Then she took her forefinger that had been pricked and hooked it to my forefinger that had been pricked. We marched around the key three times before she stopped and picked it up. Holding it out by the yo-yo string, she chanted:

"So thee and me shall never part,
Wear this key around thy heart."

Jennifer put the key around my neck. The yo-yo string was so long that the key hung not around "thy heart" but around "thy knees." Looking me hard in the eyes she stuck out her pricked forefinger. I stuck out mine. We hooked our fingers together and shook them up and down three times and did another marching around the magic circle.

I was so impressed with the ceremony that I still didn't want to say anything to break the magic spell. The big key kept clunging me on the knees. I waited until we walked out of the magic circle and were standing back at the bench before I said, "Don't you think this string is a little long? Unless now that I'm an apprentice my heart has slipped down

to my knees." I laughed at my little joke. Jennifer didn't laugh.

She said, "I got it from a very tall witch."

"May I shorten it some?" I asked.

She replied, "You can tie it up, but don't cut it."

I lost no time tying it up so that it hung over my heart. My knees already felt black and blue.

Then Jennifer said, "For the first week of your apprenticeship you must eat a raw egg every day. And you must bring me an egg every day. Make mine hard boiled. And you must read this book about witchcraft; it tells about some of my famous relatives. They were hanged in Salem, Massachusetts."

I said, "A *raw* egg?"

She said, "I knew you'd ask that. R-A-W. Leave my egg by the tree. See you next week."

And that's the way Jennifer and I parted that first Saturday. We walked in opposite directions. I looked back after I had taken only a few steps. I couldn't see either Jennifer or her wagon. They had disappeared.

All the way home I thought about my friend, Jennifer, the witch. I also thought that I had gone out an ordinary girl and had come back a witch's apprentice. I didn't feel different except that I felt like throwing up every time I thought of eating a raw egg. Every day! *For a week!*

4

HOW I MANAGED TO EAT A RAW EGG every day the next week was less of a mystery than what happened to the hard boiled eggs I left for Jennifer. I left the egg every morning on my way to school. On two mornings I left our apartment so late that I was almost tardy for school again. But when I walked home at noon, the egg was always gone. There was always a little brown piece of paper with the words:

Received one (1) egg

I wondered how she managed to pick up the egg and still get to school on time. I never saw her that week.

Here's how I solved the problem of the raw egg: milkshakes, that's how. My mother didn't usually make milkshakes because I am what is known as a fussy eater. Such as I won't eat anything cooked with tomato sauce. I won't eat the crusts of bread, and I won't even taste anything with mayonnaise. I never eat eggs. Even when I was a little baby before I knew better, I knew better. I never ate eggs then either. Poached or boiled, scrambled or broiled, I never eat eggs.

Every day that week I asked for a milkshake. My mother would say "no." Then I'd say that I'd like her to break an egg into it. She'd be delighted at that. I'd drink my milkshake and hardly know I was drinking a raw egg.

I'd boil the egg for Jennifer the night before and keep it in my underwear drawer until morning. I read parts of *The Black Book of Witchcraft,* but I couldn't finish it. It was an encyclopedia. I read about the Pilgrim witches in Salem, Massachusetts. One of them was Captain John Alden, who was the son of Priscilla and speak-for-yourself John. Some of them were little kids. Just like Jennifer; just like me. Some of them were hanged.

The weather was getting colder, and I was ordered to add layer after layer of clothes. I didn't mind. If my mother said to put on ear muffs, I put on ear muffs. If my mother said to put on knee socks, I put on knee socks. Each trip to and from school had become an adventure. Dressing for that adventure became exciting, too. My mother was amazed; she said that I was acting like a different child. Of course, I was a different child. She thought the eggs were responsible.

On Friday I found two notes. One was about the egg, and one was about meeting in the reading room of the library again. So it happened that we got to meeting in the library every Saturday morning "at 10:00 A.M. o'clock of the morning," as Jennifer said. We'd check out our books. I usually took out one book besides renewing *The Black Book of Witchcraft.* Jennifer always took out seven books. I could tell that the librarian liked Jennifer even though Jennifer never said "hello" or "good-bye" or "please" or "thank you." Librarians love good readers, and Jennifer was that. In fact, Jennifer wasn't just a good reader, Jennifer was a *serious* reader.

After we'd checked out our books, we would dump them into Jennifer's wagon. Both of us would pull the wagon to the magic circle in the park. She always parked the wagon near the bench outside the magic circle. Then Jennifer and I would hook our forefingers together and silently march around three times; the first time slowly, the second time mediumly, and the third time rapidly. We talked about witches in colonial days and the man who liked to hang witches in colonial days: Cotton Mather. We talked about plants that eat insects: insectivorous. We talked about the painter who cut off his ear: Van Gogh. We talked about the guillotine in France, about being shipwrecked on an island without water, about lice and the bubonic plague, and other interesting things.

Every week I ate a different special food and left some kind of food by the Jennifer tree. I didn't always leave the same food for Jennifer. Apprentice witches have much stricter diets than master witches. One week I had to drink black coffee every day; Jennifer said hers would spill, so we settled on coffee cake for Jennifer. Other foods I had to eat every day were:

¼ cup uncooked oatmeal; Jennifer got ¼ cup sugar frosted flakes.
1 raw hot dog; Jennifer got the same.

My mother was not always too patient about my food habits. She couldn't understand why I wanted a hot dog for lunch every day, especially an uncooked one. But I had this reputation for being a fussy eater. Besides, I was an only child; besides, I was a nag.

Soon it was Thanksgiving weekend. It was on Thanksgiving Saturday that Jennifer decided we should make a magic ointment. There were three main kinds of ointments:

Ointments that make you fly
Ointments that change you into an animal
Ointments that kill people

"Let's not kill anyone," I said.

"Okay," Jennifer answered.

"Let's make the ointment that will change us into another animal," I said. "I'd enjoy changing into a giraffe. I'd be tall, and I'd have beautiful brown eyes."

"They can't make any noise. They don't have a larynx, which is a voice box," Jennifer said. "If I'm going to be an animal, I'm going to be a noisy one. Or else a fast one. I'll be a panther; they're fast."

"But all the panthers and all the giraffes in the whole U.S. of A. live in zoos. We'd be caged! Do you suppose we should become loose animals?"

Jennifer thought a minute and said, "I'll be a cougar."

"What's that?" I asked.

"A western wildcat," she answered.

I thought a minute and said, "I'll take a French poodle; they're smart dogs, and I've always wanted curly hair."

Jennifer gave me a sharp look and said, "If I'm a wildcat and you're a poodle, we're going to fight like cat and dog."

"Okay," I said, "you change."

She answered, "I said cougar before you said French poodle."

"But I said change first." Jennifer said nothing. I waited, then I said, "Besides, being first doesn't make you right." Jennifer said nothing; so I continued, "People first believed that the world was flat; being first didn't make them right. It doesn't make you right either." Jennifer still said nothing. I waited.

She looked straight ahead. At last she spoke. She said, "Cougar."

I said, "Poodle."

She said, "Cougar."

I said, "Poodle."

Then she said nothing. And I said nothing. She wouldn't argue. She began to read the *Black Book.* We were just *thinking* about changing into cougar and poodle, and we were fighting. Imagine how unfriendly we'd be when we actually changed! I was ready to admit that I should become a Siamese cat. Before I said so, Jennifer looked up from the *Black Book* and said, "There's no way we can pick which animal we'll be. Suppose we both become mosquitoes."

"I know who I'll bite first," I said looking straight at her.

Jennifer didn't notice. She was still looking at the *Black Book*. "We could both easily lose our lives to DDT or even a fly-swatter. Let's make the flying ointment."

"Fine with me," I said. We turned the pages of the book to find out how to make the ointment. The witches didn't ever give the exact ingredients. So Jennifer gave me a new assignment. I was to read the *Black Book* very carefully and make a list of all the possible ingredients that could go into a flying ointment. She said that she would find out what chants to chant when we spread the ointment on ourselves.

"Where are you going to find out?" I asked. Jennifer didn't answer. She shrugged her shoulders and looked up. I got mad. Some days I got really mad at Jennifer. Some days I really didn't like being her apprentice. But I was always a little bit worried that she would choose another apprentice. Sometimes when I got angry like this, I'd say to myself, "Who does she think she is, anyway?" And I'd answer, "She's Jennifer."

Before I'd got Jennifer, I'd had no one. In the days before Jennifer, I would talk to Tony, the janitor in our building. He was a very usual kind of person; he'd always say something about the weather first. "Cold today." "Cheely again." "Wew! itsa hota one." Then he'd say something about his work. "Them boys oughta getta boot for dirting up thisa place." After talking to Tony only a couple of times I knew everything. Such as how many kids he had and which ones were "gooda boys." I knew even before September was over. He liked questions and answered all of them as long as I stayed polite. Imagine Jennifer doing that!

I could ask her questions until I was indigo in the face. (Indigo is deeper than blue.) She still wouldn't tell me. I knew she wouldn't tell me, so actually I never tried very hard.

After all, she had chosen me because she knew that I had all the makings of a fine witch. That must have been why she chose me. And I knew that she was a fine witch already. When you understand something that important about someone, you don't have to know a lot of other stuff. Like does she have to dry the dishes after supper, and what kind of house does she live in. Besides, even if I did find out all this usual, Tony kind of stuff and discovered that Jennifer lived in an ordinary house and did ordinary things, I would know that it was a disguise.

So I got mad, but I didn't stay mad. Every time I thought I couldn't eat one more apprentice food, I would eat it. I wanted to be a witch so bad that I would eat it. There was a lot I didn't find out about her and a lot I gave in to. But it was worth it. Being an apprentice witch was worth it. Besides, I thought how nice it would be to fly.

The next week, Jennifer said I was to eat a raw onion every day. I was to leave her a raw carrot, peeled, wrapped in Saran, and slightly salted.

5

THE MINUTE WE GOT BACK FROM Thanksgiving weekend, the whole school started getting ready for Christmas and the Christmas play. Especially our grade. This year the fifth grade was to put on the play. The play is always presented twice; once for the whole school and once for the Parent and Teachers Association meeting at night. There are three fifth grade classes in William McKinley Elementary School; that's my school. Three fifth grades adds up to about sixty kids. All the other classes of William McKinley Elementary School were to sing carols and recite poems.

That first Monday afternoon after Thanksgiving all the fifth graders met in the auditorium. Each classroom teacher had read the play in the morning. Mrs. Stuyvestant would direct the play; Mrs. Stuyvestant would choose the cast for the play; Mrs. Stuyvestant had written the play. The play was long. It had to be long so that all sixty kids could get a chance to act. Our school was democratic about Christmas. Here's the play:

There is a king who lives once upon a time (of course). He has a beautiful daughter (of course). He loves his beautiful daughter very much (of course). She is very unhappy. No one knows why she is very unhappy. The king wants to make her happy, so he asks her what can he give her for Christmas. She doesn't know (of course). The king goes to Santa's workshop, and he asks Santa what can he give his beautiful, unhappy daughter for Christmas. Santa's workshop is full of merry elves who all love the princess like crazy. They are all hammering and sawing and carrying on. Santa holds up all these dolls and things, but the king doesn't think they will make the princess smile. He shakes his head and walks away. Then the king goes to the queen's chamber, and he asks the queen what can he give their beautiful, unhappy daughter for Christmas. The queen's chamber is full of beautiful ladies-in-waiting who all love the princess like crazy. They are all singing and dancing and carrying on. The queen holds up all these clothes and things, but the king doesn't think they will make the princess smile. He shakes his head and walks away. Then the king goes to the kitchen, and he asks the chef what can he give his beautiful, unhappy daughter for Christmas. The kitchen is full of cook's helpers who all love the princess like crazy. They are all stirring big pots and being jolly and carrying on. The chef holds up all these cakes and cookies and things, but the king doesn't think they will make the princess smile. He shakes his head and walks away. He walks to his throne room. He sits down to think. He thinks and thinks. He thinks he has a real problem. Soon an old scrub woman comes in. She looks so happy scrubbing that the king thinks she has an answer to unhappiness. He asks her what can he give his beautiful, unhappy daughter for Christmas. She tells him that he should give the beautiful, unhappy princess a puppy because to be happy you have to love and take care of someone as well as be loved and be taken care of. She tells him that that is one of the lessons of Christmas. The king thinks this is a great idea. He gets his beautiful, unhappy princess a puppy (of course). She smiles happily (of course), and the play is over (at last).

Guess who was the beautiful princess? Cynthia (of course). Guess who was the little puppy? The smallest kid in the class. Me (of course). Jennifer was a lady-in-waiting. I couldn't tell whether she enjoyed being a lady or not. She kept her eyes up the whole time Mrs. Stuyvestant was choosing the cast. No one knew that Jennifer and I had made a pact sealed in blood. No one knew that we were witch and apprentice or that we even knew each other. Witchcraft is a private affair. Very private. It's secret.

Remember that my apprentice food that week was one raw onion per day. It was no problem because I love onion sandwiches. I loved onion sandwiches even before I was a witch's apprentice . . . when I was an ordinary, fussy eater. Here is my recipe for onion sandwiches: toast the bread, butter it, slice the onions, salt them, place them on the buttered slice of toast and cover with an unbuttered slice, cut off the crusts (of course) and eat. Delicious. On Sunday I had announced to my mother that I would be having an onion sandwich for lunch every day the next week.

"*Every* day?" my mother asked.

"Yes, *every* day," I answered.

"Hot dogs last week; onions this week. There must be some special reason," she said.

"There is," I answered. My voice was trailing because I was stalling for time to think of a reason.

"Tell me," my mother said. I could tell her patience was small because her voice was very slow and very patient. My father was home. That was the way she talked when she was angry if my father was home.

I thought fast. "I am conducting an experiment. I think I can keep from catching a cold for a whole year if I eat one onion a day for a whole week before winter officially begins."

"Well," my mother said, "you'll surely keep from catching cold for the week if not for the whole year. No one will be able to get close enough to give you any germs." Her voice was still slow and low.

"Please, may I try it?" I asked.

"Thank goodness you don't know about asafetida," she said.

"What's asafetida?" I asked.

"I'll never tell," she answered.

I believe that if you like onions, you should love onions. Nice people love onions. If you love onions, you should find the odor of onions on someone's breath very pleasant.

Our first full rehearsal for the Christmas play was on Friday afternoon. It was a long rehearsal. All the teachers except Mrs. Stuyvestant took coffee breaks. Everyone had to be prompted. Everyone stood in the wrong places. Mrs. Stuyvestant would bounce up on stage and move the people around. She made chalk marks on the stage where they were to stand. By the end of that first rehearsal the floor looked like our classroom blackboard just after Miss Hazen explained long division by the New Math. Mrs. Stuyvestant was the tallest woman I have ever seen. Everyone called her Mrs. Sky-high-vestant.

My part was toward the end of the play. The king brings me (the puppy) to Cynthia (the princess). I didn't have any lines to memorize. My role meant putting on an old doggie costume and crawling around on all fours. And making bow-wow sounds. When the king gives me (the puppy) to Cynthia (the princess), Mrs. Stuyvestant said that I was to stand up on my hind legs and put my hands (paws) on Cynthia's lap, look up at her face, stick out my tongue, and pant. "Pant with excitement," Mrs. Stuyvestant said. "Frolic around," Mrs. Stuyvestant said. I was afraid that Mrs. Stuyvestant would ask me to wag my tail. Cynthia (the princess) was to snuggle her head up to mine and smile. Then everyone from Santa's workshop, from the Queen's chamber, and from the royal kitchen was to come back on stage and sing and dance and carry on.

Even though this was not a dress rehearsal for anyone else, I had to be in costume to get used to walking on all fours. Mrs. Stuyvestant said that, too. The puppy costume was made of some fuzzy black orlon stuff that was thick, heavy, and hot. Inside, it smelled like a small glue factory. We rehearsed the elves and the ladies-in-waiting and the cooks. Long before I had to walk onstage, I was so hot inside the costume that I was sure I was going to commit spontaneous combustion. But I had heard that the show must go on. Mrs. Stuyvestant said that. The only thing I did, the only thing I could do, was to unzip the head part of my costume and fling it back like a hood. I got some relief. Since this was only a rehearsal and no one else was in costume, I figured that it didn't make any difference.

Cynthia had been on stage almost the whole rehearsal. The king keeps visiting her during the play to see if she is smiling yet. She smiled the whole time she was on stage. She was supposed to be unhappy, but she was grinning. She wasn't laughing. Just grinning. Like the Mona Lisa. Mrs. Stuyvestant would say, "Be unhappy." Cynthia would frown; but soon the grin would creep back over her face. She was grinning when the king brought me in.

The king announced, "Princess, it is Christmas now, and it was Christmas then . . . when you last smiled. Here is our gift. We give you this puppy with our love for you to love." Then the king took me (the puppy) up to the princess. I put my hands (paws) on her lap. I stuck out my tongue. I panted. Cynthia, who had been grinning when she was not supposed to, was now supposed to smile very large. Large enough for the audience in the back rows to see, Mrs. Stuyvestant said. Cynthia took a deep breath and began to snuggle her head up to mine. Instead of sighing and smiling, she stopped the sigh and the smile and puffed out her cheeks like the old North Wind and clamped her hands over her nose and mouth and ran from the stage. Mrs. Stuyvestant ran after her. I don't know what they discussed off stage, but Mrs. Stuyvestant came back to me and sniffed me and asked me to kindly take the puppy costume home and have my mother kindly launder it, and she asked me to kindly not eat raw onions be-

fore rehearsals. Since this was Friday, the end of my onion week, I kindly agreed.

Jennifer was off stage. As I walked away, I saw a Mona Lisa smile on *her* face. She winked. No one saw that but me.

We had rehearsals every gym period, every music period, and every art period. They didn't call it "rehearsal" during art period because we stayed in the art room and painted the sets and made cardboard crowns (covered with aluminum foil, glued and sprinkled with glitter dust). For the kitchen scene we made a stove out of big cardboard cartons that we painted black. It looked nice from the back rows where the audience sat. It looked nicest from the very last row. Mrs. Stuyvestant asked each of us to bring in a cookie sheet or a pan or a kettle or a stirring spoon. We were to be sure to put our names on what we brought in so that we could get it back when the play was over. I brought in two cupcake pans and put one letter of my name on the inside of each cupcake hole. It looked like this:

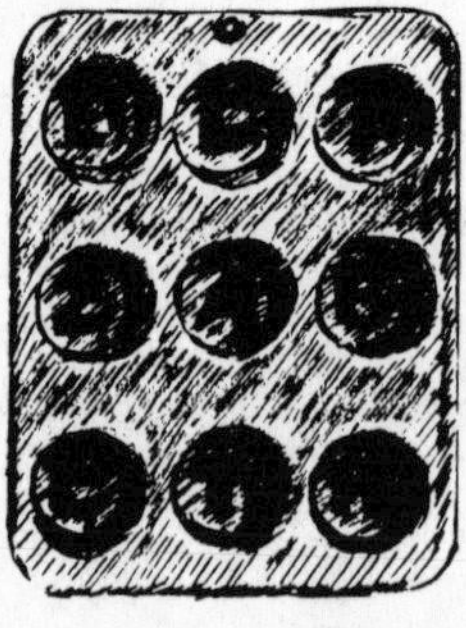

I hoped that the whole audience, even the very last row would see. Mrs. Stuyvestant asked me to kindly wash it off and kindly Scotch tape my name on the bottom—very small. She said, "In the theater one does not get top billing just because one can write one's name very large. One gets top billing because one has earned stardom." One always knew when Mrs. Stuyvestant was scolding because she always called you *one* instead of your name.

Cynthia brought in her mother's electric mixer. She knew that she was the only kid in the whole U.S. of A. whose mother would let her carry the family's electric mixer to school. Mrs. Stuyvestant told her that it was very generous of her mother to lend it, and it was very generous of her to have carried it all the way from home. (I knew that Cynthia's mother had driven her to school that day, but Cynthia didn't mention it. Another example of the way Cynthia was: two-faced.) But Mrs. Stuyvestant didn't consider the mixer picturesque enough. In other words, in the days when there were kings and princesses, there just weren't any electric mixers. Cynthia didn't even have sense enough to be insulted. She sighed sadly and told Mrs. Stuyvestant that she would manage to get the mixer home, somehow, even though it was heavy.

Jennifer caused a small sensation. She brought in a huge black three-legged pot. It would hold about twenty quarts of water. A little kid could swim in it almost. Jennifer didn't have to write her name on that pot to identify it. No one else had ever seen anything like it except in a museum. I happened to know that it was the pot we were going to cook our flying ointment in.

Mrs. Stuyvestant was overjoyed. She put her hands on her waist (with her elbows pointing out and her toes pointing out, too, she looked like a long, tall, five-pointed star) and exclaimed, "Oh, Jenny, how *won*-derful! It's *too* cute! A *three*-legged kettle!"

If you ever want to make Jennifer angry, call her what Mrs. Stuyvestant did. Call her Jenny instead of Jennifer, her rightful name.

Jennifer looked up, way up at Mrs. Sky-high-vestant and said, "That makes one, two, three, doesn't it?"

Mrs. Stuyvestant looked down, way down at Jennifer and said, "What do you mean, Jennifer?"

Jennifer answered, "*Won*-derful, *too* cute, *three*-legged. That's one, two, three." Jennifer didn't smile.

Mrs. Stuyvestant said, "I had no idea you were so clever." She smiled. I could tell that Jennifer wished that Mrs. Stuyvestant had not smiled. She wanted her to notice how angry she was at being called Jenny instead of Jennifer.

Everyone was a little surprised at how clever Jennifer was. She almost never spoke in class or during rehearsals. She never spoke to me; she would just slip me a note every now and then. I was worried that everyone would find out how clever Jennifer was. It feels wonderful to have a secret. Sometimes I thought I wanted our secret to be discovered accidentally, but I didn't want to share Jennifer with the entire fifth grade. It was lucky, the kids of William McKinley Elementary School weren't ready to make the discovery. They were no longer paying any attention. Mrs. Stuyvestant walked all around the pot, pleased and smiling. She smiled over at Jennifer and asked, "By the way, Jenny, how did you get it here?" She was still feeling cozy toward Jennifer.

Jennifer pretended that she didn't hear the question. She was making herself very busy shaking a can of spray paint, and that little ball inside the can was rattling away. Mrs. Stuyvestant said, "Jenny. Oh, Jenny!" No answer from you-know-who. "Jenny. Oh, Jenny!" No answer from you-know-who again. Mrs. Stuyvestant started walking toward Jennifer and said, "Jenny. Oh, Jennifer!" The minute she said *Jennifer,* you-know-who looked up.

"Yes?" asked Jennifer.

"I was wondering," Mrs. Stuyvestant said, "how you got that heavy kettle to school."

"Brought it in my wagon," answered Jennifer.

"Then your wagon is parked at school?" asked Mrs. Stuyvestant.

"Yes," answered Jennifer.

"Do you think that you can lend it to Cynthia to

help her get her mixer home?"

Jennifer asked, "You want me to put the mixer in my wagon?"

Mrs. Stuyvestant said, almost sarcastically, "That's what I had in mind."

Jennifer replied, "I'll be happy to."

Mrs. Stuyvestant said, "Thank you." She smiled pleasantly at Jennifer and began to turn around.

Before she was completely turned around, Jennifer said, "Do you think I should tie my wagon to the bumper?"

Mrs. Stuyvestant spun around. "The bumper? Bumper? The bumper of what?"

Jennifer answered, "The bumper of their car."

Mrs. Stuyvestant was too puzzled to get angry. She merely asked, "Why do that?"

Jennifer answered, "Because Cynthia brought the mixer here in their car, so I guessed that that was the way she would get it home, too." Somehow, Jennifer managed to look innocent.

Mrs. Stuyvestant looked at Jennifer. Mrs. Stuyvestant looked at Cynthia. Of course, Jennifer's conversation had been just one shade on the safe side of fresh. But Cynthia's conversation had been just one shade on the safe side of lying. Mrs. Stuyvestant looked from Jennifer to Cynthia and then back again. She threw her arms in the air, turned around and walked out of the room. Cynthia glared at Jennifer. Jennifer kept shaking the spray paint and kept looking up at the ceiling.

"Oh, Jennifer," I thought to myself, "how strong you are. Nerves of steel and the heart of a witch!"

No one noticed when Jennifer passed me a note later in the period. I was painting hinges on one of the oven doors. The note had only one word on it. It said:

Ugh!!!

I knew what Jennifer meant, and I put my head inside the oven and laughed and laughed.

We got through the two performances of the play. They seemed short. Like standing over a stove all day long cooking up some very elegant soup, adding hundreds of special ingredients, stirring and stirring, and then having everyone gulp it down in five minutes.

The performance in front of the school wasn't as glamorous as the one for the Parent and Teachers Association at night. For one thing, the auditorium wouldn't get dark. For another thing, some of the kindergarten kids and the first graders who had sisters or brothers in the play would yell out, "Hi, Johnny," or "Hello, Sis." Only Richard yelled back. He was a cook in the kitchen scene; he stood on stage and shook a wooden spoon at his little brother in the audience and yelled, "Mom told you not to call me." Mrs. Stuyvestant talked to all of us after this performance. She told us about how in the theater one never lets the audience know how one feels. One always acts as if the world begins and ends at the edge of the stage. She talked on some more about *one* and *the theater,* but Richard just sat there and bit his nails. He didn't know which *one* she meant.

The evening performance for the P. and T.A. went much better. Richard's little brother stayed home. I saw Jennifer's mother sitting in the audience. I knew it was Jennifer's mother because she was the only Black mother there. She looked as normal as mine. Maybe she wasn't a witch.

Maybe witchery skipped generations as blue eyes do. All of a sudden blue eyes can pop up. That is like my brown-eyed uncle who married my brown-eyed aunt and who had a blue-eyed daughter named Emma. Maybe a normal mother and a normal father can give birth to a witch daughter named Jennifer. Of course, I didn't see her father since fathers almost never come to P. and T.A. meetings. Maybe Jennifer inherited being a witch from her father. Maybe Jennifer's father was a wizard, which is a boy witch.

6

THIS WAS MY FIRST CHRISTMAS VACATION living in our apartment; it was pretty dull. No fireplace. No chimney. A lot of relatives came visiting and pinching. They always pinched my cheek and hugged me and kissed me and asked, "Don't you have a kiss for your Aunt Buzzie? You remember how you used to always call me Aunt Buzzie because you couldn't pronounce Beatrice?" They thought that I was still small because I was still little. They didn't realize that although my size hadn't caught up with my age, my brain had. Still I always had a kiss for Aunt So and So who asked. And I always stayed still for the hugging, but I escaped a lot of cheek pinching that year. Just as they would lift their hands to pinch me, I'd blow my cheeks up with air, and their fingers would slip.

Jennifer and I still met on Saturdays. We always walked to the magic circle. Sometimes it was snow-ing and sometimes it was slushy, but Jennifer always brought her wagon. Sometimes now we talked about nonwitch stuff. Jennifer knew a lot about a lot of things. Partly her being a witch and partly her reading so much. For example, one week my apprentice food was five uncooked spaghettis every day. She told me all about how spaghetti was really Chinese but Marco Polo brought it home to Italy where it was a real success. She told me about how it was manufactured and how much it cost to buy stock in some famous macaroni company on the New York Stock Exchange.

We were really working on the flying ointment. Some of the ingredients were going to take a long time to collect, so Jennifer decided that we had to start immediately. For example, she decided that we needed about two teaspoonfuls of fingernail parings —one teaspoon from each of us. It takes a lot of parings to fill a spoon. I had to quit biting my nails, which made my mother the happiest woman in the whole U.S. of A. I figured that toenails and fingernails were all pretty much the same, so I also saved toenail cuttings. I saved them all in an old BAND-AID box, which I kept in my underwear drawer along with the key and Jennifer's notes. I wore the key only on Saturdays.

Jennifer said that Christmas was a dangerous time of year for witches because everyone acted happy and tried to be good; Christmas week required special precautions. She said that instead of eating a special food, we were to give up a special food, and it wouldn't count to give up any old food. It had be a food you especially loved. I thought a long time, trying to make up my mind whether to give up candy or give up cake. I loved candy more, and so to prove myself absolutely honest, I said to Jennifer, "I'll give up candy."

Jennifer said, "I'll give up watermelon."

"For how long?" I asked.

"Until New Year's Day, January the 1st, at 7:00 P.M. o'clock of the evening," she answered.

"I know P.M. is the evening, Jennifer," I answered.

"Agreed?" she asked.

"I even know that A.M. is of the morning, Jennifer," I answered.

"Agreed?" she asked.

"I even know that New Year's Day is January the 1st, Jennifer." I was getting tired of her telling me everything twice. Like New Year's Day and January the 1st; like P.M. and of the evening. But she still wouldn't argue.

"Agreed?" she asked.

"Agreed," I answered.

Then we hooked our fingers together and marched around the magic circle. Jennifer said that our chants must be especially powerful this time. We had to be careful to face inward in the circle so that our heels and not our toes made prints in the outer rim of the circle. Like when your mother makes a pie crust, and she presses the crust around the rim of the pan with a fork. Always in the same direction.

As we marched around, toes always pointing inward, Jennifer kept repeating this chant:

"Hecate, Hecate, Dock,
Around this circle we walk.
Within one hour make candy sour
And melon hard as a rock."

Then she carefully stepped out of the magic circle and motioned for me to do the same. I did. She sat down on the park bench closest to the circle and removed her boots. She motioned for me to do the same. I did. She put her socks inside her shoes, which were inside her boots, and stood up. She motioned for me to do the same. I did. She started walking toward the magic circle. She motioned for me to do the same. I didn't. My feet were frozen. She turned around and motioned for me again. She looked cross. I followed.

We walked around the magic circle again making certain that we never stepped out of the footprints we made the first time. As we walked around, we both chanted:

"Hecate, Hecate, Dock,
Around this circle we walk.
Within one hour make candy sour
And melon hard as a rock."

Then we both stepped out of the circle being careful to not make any new footprints. Jennifer walked, but I ran. My feet were numb from the cold. We dried our feet with our socks and put on our shoes without socks, then put on our boots. I stuffed my socks into my jacket pocket, and Jennifer dumped hers into the wagon. We walked back and looked at the beautiful pattern we had made in the snow. Our circle looked extra magical then.

Jennifer reached down and dug the snow out of two of the footprints. It was pressed down and a little bit dirty. She rolled two snowballs and gave one to me.

"We'll need this for our flying ointment," she said. "Save it in your deep freezer."

Jennifer dumped her snowball into her wagon. I held mine in my hands. I had forgotten my mittens. My hands were freezing; my feet were freezing. I took my socks out of my pocket and put them on my hands. That helped a little.

Then Jennifer said, "On New Year's Day at 7:00 P.M. o'clock of the evening, you'll find a note pinned to the tree. Read the note. Do as it says. No F.F. until then. The note will tell when we'll meet again."

"F.F.?" I asked.

"Forbidden Food," she answered.

Without another word she tilted her head upward, her eyes upward, and started home. I didn't dare wish her a Merry Christmas. That would not have been witching.

I walked home. Rather fast. I thought as I walked that I really loved watermelon, too. Maybe I should have made that my F.F. instead of candy. I was almost at our apartment door before I realized that I had never, absolutely never, heard of *anyone* having watermelon for Christmas. Maybe they did in Australia or New Zealand where they were below the equator and where everything was upside down, but I never heard of watermelon at Christmas in the whole U.S. of A.

That week we had staying guests: Aunt Drusilla and Uncle Frank. They are really my father's aunt and uncle, which makes them my great-aunt and great-uncle. The only thing great about them I could see was their ages. Together they were 133 years old. They had never had any children, and they thought that kids were pets who talked. I never sat near them. If I did, they would stroke my hair and pat my arm all the time. They were great cheek-pinchers. They would smile at me and say, "Does our Lizzie want an ice cream?" Everything they said turned out to be a question. Instead of "Good morning" they always said, "Isn't it a good morning?" They said things like, "My, isn't she a handsome girlie?" Something else about them was that they had the most peculiar food habits I have ever seen.

They ate something called Health Foods, which they brought with them in big cardboard boxes from a special Health Food store in Manhattan. They had boxes called *Lion's Milk* and all kinds of seeds and several kinds of honey and strange juices like sauerkraut juice and celery syrup. My mother would put our supper on the table and then spread out all these crazy seeds and stuff for the Greats. You can imagine how my mother looked when they first came and my father carried in all that stuff. She waited until they were in the bedroom unpacking their clothes. Then she came over to me. She bent to my ear and said in a low, slow voice, "If - you - dare - to - ask - for - one - crazy - food - this - week - I'm - moving - into - a - hotel - and - no - one - will - hear - from - me - until - after - the - 4th - of - July."

So I had been relieved when Jennifer said that for my apprenticeship this week, I had to give up something special instead of eat something special.

I walked in with my socks on my hands, dripping this dirty snowball across the rug, trying to get to the freezer. The Greats spotted me. Great-aunt Drusilla got up from the couch and said, "What are we doing, dearie?"

I knew that I had time to think of an answer because Great-uncle Frank always repeated what Great-aunt Drusilla said. She always returned the courtesy; she repeated what he said.

Great-uncle Frank did not disappoint me; he asked, "What are we doing, dearie?"

I said, "Putting this in the freezer."

Great-uncle Frank said, "And why are we doing that?"

Great-aunt Drusilla said, "And why are we doing that?"

I said, "To keep it frozen."

Great-aunt Drusilla said, "And why are we keeping it frozen?"

Great-uncle Frank said, "And why are we keeping it frozen?"

I said, "For an experiment."

G.A. Drusilla said, "And is this for school, sweetie?"

G.U. Frank said, "And is this for school, sweetie?"

I said, "Science class."

G.A. Drusilla said, "Oh?"

G.U. Frank said, "Oh?"

I said, "Yes?" and marched to the freezer. The puddle on the living room rug wasn't too big.

My mother came out of the bedroom just as I was closing the freezer. She took only a quick look at

me and only a quick look at the puddle and said, "Take off those boots." I sat down on a kitchen chair and did. I forgot that my socks were on my hands and not on my feet. My mother noticed. When I had removed only the left shoe, she didn't quite believe that I had actually put on shoes and boots without socks. She waited until I took off the right shoe, too, to make sure. Then she said, "Do you really believe that you're not going to catch a cold all winter because of that onion business weeks ago?"

I shook my head, "Yes."

She said, "Have you ever thought that most people wear their socks on their feet, not on their hands?"

I shook my head, "Yes."

She said, "Will you repeat after me: socks are for feet; mittens are for hands."

I said, "Socks are for feet; mittens are for hands."

She said, "Say it again."

I said, "Socks are for feet; mittens are for hands."

She said, "Now please tell me, where are your mittens?"

I said, "In my sock drawer."

She threw up her hands, "Just get those socks off your hands and set the table."

As usual the Greats helped me set the table. They were very accurate about where the fork and knife went. Everything about food except how it tasted interested them. They cared about the vitamins it had in it and about what order it was served in and how fast it was eaten. They ate very slowly. They believed in chewing. "Proper mastication is essential to proper digestion," they said. Each said it for each meal. That makes two Greats times three meals a day or six times a day I heard it. On the third day, I looked up *mastication.* It means *chewing.* I thought that after they left, I'd send their slogan in for a toothpaste commercial.

The Greats nibbled their seeds and sipped their sauerkraut juice. I couldn't decide whether they loved to eat or hated to eat. Maybe they ate slowly so that the meal wouldn't end. Maybe they ate slowly because everything tasted so bad that they had to eat slowly to get it down.

I began to snitch samples of all their foods. I wrapped them in waxed paper and pinned a label on them. After all, I figured, not many apprentice witches could get Lion's Milk for their flying ointment. Even in Africa where there are plenty of witches called witch doctors and plenty of lions, not many witches get lion's milk. I thought it would be a useful ingredient; lions can leap great distances. Lion's Milk, I thought, could be lift-off juice. Except that Lion's Milk was a powder. I kept all these little packages in my underwear drawer near the key and the notes and the fingernails. My underwear drawer was getting lumpy.

On New Year's Eve my mother and father went to a party. It was the first party they had gone to in a long time. My mother was anxious to go, but she worried about it for a week. My mother worried about manners. Since the Greats were our house guests, she thought that it wouldn't be polite to go to the party without them. Since she didn't know the hostess very well, she didn't want to ask her to ask the Greats. She thought that it would be impolite to not go to the party after she had already said yes.

One night my mother was telling her politeness worries to my father. She was saying, "Maybe I should tell them that this invitation came at the very last minute and that it is important to your work to accept, and then ask them to please help out in this *emergency*."

The reason I know all this is because I had to sleep on a cot in their room while the Greats were visiting. My father was dozing. I guess when he heard *emergency,* he became wide awake.

"Emergency!" he said.

"Sh, sh, sh," my mother said.

"What is this? A *quiet* emergency?" my father asked.

"No, no, no," my mother answered. "I just thought that if we tell Aunt Drusilla and Uncle Frank that this *emergency* invitation came, and we just *have* to accept, they won't mind sitting with Elizabeth on New Year's Eve."

"Are you still worrying about that?" my father

asked. "Why don't you tell them the truth?"

"The truth! The truth!" my mother answered. "How can I tell them the truth?"

"Is the truth so bad?" my father asked. I could tell he was sleepy. "Maybe I don't understand the facts. What *is* the truth?"

"Simply that we were invited and they weren't," my mother answered.

My father gave a tiny laugh and said, "Sounds terrible. I'll handle it in the morning."

I started to laugh, too, but quickly buried my head in my pillow. My mother realized for the first time that I was awake.

"Elizabeth," she called.

I didn't answer.

"Elizabeth," she called. "I know you're awake, and if you utter one word of this to your aunt and uncle, you'll sleep in the bath tub for the rest of their visit." I didn't utter a sound.

My father "handled" it in the morning. He simply told his aunt and uncle that he and mother would be going out on New Year's Eve.

Great-aunt Drusilla said, "Isn't it wonderful to be young and to go out to parties?"

Great-uncle Frank said, "Isn't it wonderful to be young and to go out to parties?"

I don't know why they said that Mom and Dad were young. I know for a fact that each was well over twice my age.

Father then said, "I know you'll enjoy staying with Elizabeth."

Great-uncle Frank said, "Will we be baby-sitters?"

Great-aunt Drusilla said, "Will we be baby-sitters?"

Father said, "Yes."

Great-aunt Drusilla said, "Isn't that wonderful, Frankie?"

Great-uncle Frank said, "Isn't that wonderful Frankie . . . er . . . ah . . . I mean, Drusie?"

They could hardly wait for Mom and Dad to go to the party. My parents got all dressed up. I could tell that my mother was excited about going out. She combed her hair front and back. She usually didn't check the back of her hair by holding up a small mirror in front of the big mirror, but she did for New Year's Eve. Actually, they didn't look too old when they were all dressed up; they just looked mature.

I have never been so well baby-sat. The Greats laid out my pajamas and folded down the covers of my cot. They filled the bathtub for me and checked the temperature of the water. Great-uncle Frank called it "drawing my bath." Great-aunt Drusilla even put the toothpaste on my toothbrush for me. After I got to bed, both of them came into the bedroom every half hour to check me. It was almost impossible to go to sleep. They kept covering me.

Every part of me was covered except those parts I needed for breathing.

New Year's Day was cloudy and cold. My father slept through the first breakfast of the new year. My mother got up and kept smiling and yawning and thanking the Greats for baby-sitting. At five minutes before 7:00 P.M. I went to the Jennifer tree. I carried a flashlight; it was very dark out. It was also very cold. I got to the tree, and there was the note in Jennifer's own writing. It said:

Near the rootſ
You'll find a treaſure
Eat it up
At your pleaſure
But ſave the ſeedſ
Everyone
They'll be uſed
Before we're done.

Saturday. Library.
Half after 2:00 P.M. o'clock
of the afternoon

I bent down toward the roots of the tree. The flashlight shone on something small and round. I picked it up. It was the roundest, cutest watermelon I had ever seen in my whole, entire life. I carried it home, cradled it in my arms like a baby. When I walked into the living room, I put it in the middle of the floor and asked, "Watermelon, anyone?"

Everyone asked the same question at the same time, "Where did you get that?" I answered that I found it under a tree. I held it high over my head and led the parade to the kitchen. Even the Greats dug in and enjoyed it.

"Save the seeds!" I yelled.

Everyone was so busy eating, no one even asked me why.

7

The last Saturday of our winter vacation was a lazy day. I got up late and didn't do much until just before 2:00 P.M. except watch Great-aunt Drusilla and Great-uncle Frank pack for their trip home. They weren't leaving until after supper, but they began packing after breakfast. I think they would have stayed longer, but they were almost out of Health Foods. They wanted to get back to Manhattan for a fresh supply.

My mother breathed a sigh of relief when I told her that I was going to the library. I think she was exhausted from vacuuming; she had to vacuum three times a day because the Greats scattered so many seeds after each meal. I suggested to my mother that we get a parakeet instead of vacuuming. She hit me.

When I got to the library, I saw Jennifer's wagon outside the reference room. Jennifer was reading the encyclopedia, volume Vase-Zygote. I had not seen her for over a week. I was anxious to find out how she had spent her vacation. When she saw me walking in she looked up and whispered, "Did you bring anything to eat?"

"Some nuts," I answered.

"What kind?" she asked.

"Brazil nuts," I answered.

"Hard to crack," she said. She got up from the table and checked out her books. We piled our reading supply into Jennifer's wagon. Then we started toward the park. As we walked, we took turns pulling the wagon. I said, "Thanks for the watermelon. Where did you get it this time of year."

"Same place you did," she answered.

"But I just picked it off the ground," I said, and she answered, "That's where they grow." She gave me a sideways look and then marched on with her chin up, eyes up toward the sky. She never looked down as we walked. Even when we were going up and down curbs. She never fell or bumped into anything. Sometimes in school, I would see her walking down the hall reading a book. She could turn corners in the corridor, and she could open doors while she was still reading her book. She never tripped or fell. Reading and walking were her two best subjects, you might say.

Our magic circle was a mess. It was all gray and slushy and full of crumbs someone had thrown out for the squirrels and the birds. Jennifer looked at it and said, "Isn't it beautiful?" I looked at it and shrugged my shoulders. We hooked our fingers together and marched around as we always did to start. Then we sat down on the bench and began cracking and eating the Brazil nuts. Jennifer reached into her wagon and brought out a big box of salt . . . as if she had been certain that I would bring nuts or something that needed salt. Before salting each nut she licked it a little so that the salt would stick.

As we were eating our nuts, Cynthia and Dolores walked through the park. They were going ice skating. Both of them had ice skates over their shoulders. Dolores was sensibly dressed. She had on ski pants, a jacket, mittens, boots, stocking cap, and earmuffs. That was just the top layer. That was all I could see. That was what my mother called sensibly dressed. Cynthia was *in*-sensibly dressed. She had on one of those short skirts that flare out when you twirl, if you know how to twirl on ice. I hoped she was cold.

I had been an apprentice for a couple of months now. I thought that if I could just make Cynthia trip and fall down, all my apprenticeship would be worth it. As they walked past me, I followed them silently with my eyes and chanted to myself, "Trip and fall. Trip and fall. Trip and fall. Trip and fall." As they passed, Cynthia tripped over the handle of Jennifer's wagon. Since she tripped but did not fall, I felt like a one hundred per cent successful *half* witch.

After we finished eating all the nuts, we got down to business. Jennifer asked if I had eaten any F.F. before New Year's Day. I replied that I was insulted that she should even ask. Then I described the seeds and the Lion's Milk I had collected from the Greats. She looked pleased. I told her about how they always said everything as if it were a question. She looked pleased, so I imitated how Great-aunt Drusilla and Great-uncle Frank always repeated what each other said. For a minute I thought Jennifer was going to laugh. She didn't; she looked pleased, though.

Next Jennifer surprised me. She gave me a promotion. I was graduated from apprentice witch to journeyman witch. Now I was no longer to eat special foods. Instead, I was to take very careful precautions. She went over these precautions one by one. She called them taboos.

Taboo 1: Never lie on a pillow when I sleep.

Taboo 2: Never cut my hair. (I saw some problems there. I was already playing hide and seek through my bangs. My mother kept saying that she would cut them as soon as she had a minute free from vacuuming.)

Taboo 3: Never eat after 7:30 P.M. o'clock of the evening.

Taboo 4: Never make a call on the telephone. I asked Jennifer if I had permission to answer the phone if someone called me. Jennifer said, "Of course." She continued with the list.

Taboo 5: Never wear shoes in the house on Sundays.

Taboo 6: Never use red ink.

Taboo 7: Never light a match.

Taboo 8: Never touch straight pins or needles.

Taboo 9: Never dance at a wedding.

Taboo 10: Never get into bed without walking around it three times. (Another problem: my bed was in a corner pushed against the wall. Either I would have to convince my mother to change my room around, or I'd have to pull it out at night.)

Taboo 11: Never walk on the same side of the street as a hospital.

Taboo 12: Never sing before breakfast.

Taboo 13: Never cry before supper.

Some of these taboos seemed pretty hard. I told Jennifer that I didn't think some of them made any sense. She told me that if I were looking for things to make sense, perhaps I wasn't yet ready for promotion. I asked Jennifer if she always obeyed the taboos. She said that she always did—except that now she was allowed to light matches. I remembered that she had had to light a candle when I first became her apprentice. I was convinced that I could, I would, obey. I asked Jennifer for a list of the taboos so that I wouldn't disobey by mistake. She said that witches don't rely on lists. The list might get lost and fall into the hands of some good person and that would mean trouble for witches all over. She said that I must memorize the list before school started the next day. She was afraid that back at school my mind would be all cluttered up with school stuff. Right then I had to learn them all; Jennifer checked me. She stood up and said to me, "You have reached the end of your apprenticeship. You are now a journeyman witch."

I was pleased. I asked, "What comes next?"

"A master witch," she answered.

"Are you a master?" I asked.

"Of course," she replied. "Only masters can train new witches."

"What can a journeyman witch do?" I asked.

"You can cast short spells. Like making people trip."

I smiled happily. I had already done that; I began to feel full of electricity. "When will I become a master witch?" I asked.

"After we've successfully made the ointment and successfully used it," she answered.

I was so happy that I almost flew up to our apartment. I stopped short at the door and took off my shoes. I wanted to practice for Sundays.

School is very dull in January and February. No holidays, nothing to do but learn until Washington's birthday on February 22nd. Sometimes it snowed and sometimes it slushed, but we always met on Saturdays. I saved up everything that happened to me during the week to tell Jennifer. She seemed to enjoy all the details of life in the apartment house. She told me things, too. Not things about her other life, though. She talked about her *interests*. She was interested in weaving. She wanted to weave cloth so that it could have a pattern in it. The pattern would be seen only if the cloth was held in a special way. And the pattern she wanted to weave in was people's names . . . people she didn't like and sometimes people she liked. Then, if she folded the cloth, the person whose name was almost-invisibly-woven would double over with cramps; if she snipped a few of the pattern threads, the person whose name was almost-invisibly-woven would get a slight cut. She let me imagine what other things could happen to the cloth. The people she liked whose names were almost-invisibly-woven would stay smooth and clean and well aired. Jennifer was also interested in cryptography. We tried to talk in a couple of the codes she made up, but it took awfully long to say anything, and, after all, we had only our Saturdays together.

One Saturday in February we didn't meet. I'll tell about that one now.

Cynthia had a birthday party, and she invited me. I was amazed when I got the invitation. It came in the mail. *R.S.V.P.* was printed at the bottom. My mother said that *R.S.V.P.* meant that I had to let her know if I would come or not. I told my mother that I guessed I couldn't make it. She asked me why not. I told her that I was busy on Saturday.

"Doing what?" she asked.

"Going to the library," I answered.

"Can't you do that work some other time?" she asked. At this point I have to admit that I had never yet told my mother about Jennifer. She thought that I went to the library every Saturday to do schoolwork. At first I didn't tell her because she didn't ask. Later I didn't tell her because I didn't want to. Because Jennifer was a witch. And my mother always liked me to have cousins and proper friends. Besides, witchcraft is a private affair.

My mother was worried about what she called my "social development." That means that she thought I should make some friends.

I had heard my mother and father discussing me one night when they thought that I was asleep. My mother told my father that she didn't think it was *normal* for me to be happy without friends. My father told her that a usual body temperature was 98.6 degrees, but some people were healthy with a body temperature of only 98.4 degrees. That was *normal* for them. "So who's to say exactly what *normal* is?" my father said. My mother seemed to understand. For a while after this, she didn't bother me about my "social development." Until Cynthia's invitation came. Immediately, my mother began believing again that *normal* must be 98.6 degrees.

"Go to the library after school on weekdays and finish up your work. Then you'll be able to go to the party. I think it's very nice of Cynthia to invite you."

"Her mother made her do it," I said.

"That's a mean thing to say. It shows you don't think much of Cynthia, and it shows that you think even less of yourself." She paused a minute, pointed a finger at me and said, "You're going. Call Cynthia now." With that, she took the receiver from the telephone and held it out for me. How could I tell my mother that I wouldn't go and also tell her that I wouldn't use the phone? I hadn't yet broken a single taboo. I didn't want anything as foolish as Cynthia's party to make me break one.

I thought fast; I talked fast. "I won't bother to telephone. I'll run upstairs with my message."

"That's the spirit," my mother answered.

I went upstairs, knocked on Cynthia's door and

R.S.V.P.'d, "Yes."

Cynthia said that she was delighted that I could come and that she was sorry she couldn't invite me in right then, but she was busy. Her good manners didn't impress me. They just told me that her mother was within hearing distance. Her good manners always got me mad.

Now I was faced with a real problem: letting Jennifer know that I couldn't meet her on Saturday. I wrote her a note explaining the situation. I pinned it to the Jennifer tree on my way to school the next morning. When school was dismissed at lunch, I checked the tree and saw that she had put a note in its place. Jennifer had answered:

Give Heed!!

While at the party
Be on awareſ.
Do not eat cake
Or play muſical chairſ.

After I had told Cynthia "yes" and after I had received this permission from Jennifer, I was glad that I was going to the party. I enjoyed getting mad at Cynthia. I also thought that it would be fun to tell Jennifer all about how ordinary girls act at a party; normal girls who had a temperature of 98.6 degrees.

From the first moment I awakened on the Saturday of the party, things did not go well. Not at all. In the first place it was a butterscotch day; I was never in a good mood on butterscotch days. There was a candy factory in our town. On different days they made different flavors. In our part of town, we breathed flavored air. Orange was pleasant; cherry and lime were hardly noticeable; mint was delicious (I could pretend that I was smoking a menthol cigarette). But butterscotch was a hard flavor to breathe.

In the second place, my mother looked at my hair and decided that I couldn't go to the party without a trim. Especially my bangs. She said something about my head looking like a pot of spaghetti that had boiled over. She ran to get the scissors. I ran to get my bathing cap.

"Get that thing off your head," she said. "All I want to do is trim your bangs."

"I want them to grow out. Please," I answered.

"How can you possibly look neat for the party?" she asked.

"I'll shampoo it and pin it back," I answered. "After all, it is my hair."

"I never doubt that it's yours," my mother said, "but I sometimes doubt that it's hair. Okay, go wash it."

I worked hard on the shampoo job, and I used about fifty thousand bobby pins to hold it back. If someone had held a magnet anywhere near my head, I feel certain that it would have lifted me five feet off the floor.

My party dress was also a problem; it was two years old. I always grew, but every year I grew less than most people. If I had grown a great deal, my mother would have bought me a new dress, but everything always *almost* fitted, and so we managed to get another year's wear out of it. That was what had happened with the Pilgrim costume, too. I was very uncomfortable. With my hair pinned back tight and my dress so tight, I felt as if I wouldn't be able to move unless someone pulled my arms and legs with strings the way you pull a marionette. I was in no party mood.

My mother wrapped the gift she had gotten for Cynthia. Two days before, she had asked me what I thought Cynthia would like; I had answered, "A pet boa constrictor." My mother didn't think that was very funny. She bought her a pair of stretch gloves, since we didn't know her size.

I went up to Cynthia's apartment and rang the

bell. When she opened the door and greeted me, all I could see was pink. She was wearing a pink dress. Pink balloons were hanging from the ceiling; the table was set with pink paper cups and pink paper dishes. In the middle of the table was a pinkly frosted cake.

I limped in. I had planned a limp right after Jennifer's note. I needed an excuse to not play musical chairs, so I invented a sore leg. Most of the girls were late for the party. All were in the fifth grade at William McKinley Elementary School, but I hadn't been to a party with them before. They were either surprised to see me there or else they didn't recognize me with my hair pinned back. They would look over at me and say "Hi," then look again and say "Oh, hi, I didn't recognize you at first." I wasn't being a great social success at the party. The party wasn't being a great social success with me.

Instead of turning a record player or radio on and off for musical chairs, Cynthia played the piano. I hoped the neighbors on the fifth floor who lived under her would call up and complain about the noise. They didn't. Cynthia probably had them enchanted. To what Cynthia could do, there was no end; to what I, Elizabeth, the journeyman witch, could do, there was no start.

I couldn't play pin the tail on the donkey (there was a pink donkey and pink tails, imagine!) because I could not touch pins: Taboo Number 8. I couldn't play musical chairs; I couldn't eat cake: Jennifer's warning. I was so miserable about my hair and musical chairs and my dress that I tried hard to accidentally forget the taboos. I tried to make a slight mistake that couldn't possibly be my fault; but the harder I tried, the harder it was to forget that I was

a journeyman witch. Then I thought that, perhaps, this party was one of the torture trials I had read about in the *Black Book*. So I decided instead to enjoy being odd. And I did.

After pin the tail and musical chairs, everyone played treasure hunt. The treasure was the prize.

I found the treasure with no trouble at all. As soon as the treasure hunt was announced, I walked straight to it. It was under the sofa pillow. I had sat on it during musical chairs and pin the tail. I had been too polite to mention the lump in the sofa. All the girls said, "Oh, how did you?" I just shrugged my shoulders and gave them a Jennifer-type look. The treasure was a little box of chocolates. Squashed chocolates.

The next and last game was dropping clothes pins into a milk bottle. I got nine in. I won. Sometimes being short was nice. My prize was a package of hair ribbons. Four of them were pink. When I opened it and saw what it was, I said, "Well, it looks as if I have this prize all tied up." Everyone looked at me and smiled. I didn't smile back.

Then we all sat at the pinkly-pinkly table. Maria and Helen sat on either side of me and didn't seem to mind sitting there at all. First, Cynthia opened her presents. She said, "Oh, how lovely!" every single time. It was disgusting. Before she opened each gift she held it up and said, "I wonder who this is from?" She was just asking; she didn't want an answer. I answered. I said, "Maria," or "Dolores," or whoever the correct person was. I had been the first one at the party, and it was easy to remember who brought what. But when they asked, "Elizabeth, how do you do it?" I gave them another Jennifer-type look.

Finally, Cynthia's mother lit the candles on the cake and everyone sang "Happy Birthday to You." I didn't sing. I know everyone wondered why. They didn't ask. I didn't explain. I couldn't explain. I couldn't tell them that I was enjoying being different.

It was even no trouble to not eat cake. No trouble at all.

Cynthia stood by the door and said, "Good-bye and thank you for coming" to everyone. She said it to me, too, but she didn't mean it. She said it because her mother was standing there, behind her back. That's the only reason. I know that's the only reason because as she said it, she screwed up her face and stuck out her tongue.

I said, "Good-bye, and thank you for inviting me." I said it loud enough for her mother to hear. Then I stepped on Cynthia's foot as hard as I could. With my "sore" leg. Just once. I left without looking back. I could bet that my normal temperature was not 98.6 degrees.

When I got back to our apartment, my mother asked, "Did you thank for the party?"

I answered, "Of course." The whole day had changed. The wind had changed and the air wasn't butterscotch. It was freshly baked bread. There was also a bread factory in our town.

8

I SHARED WITH JENNIFER MY PRIZES FROM the party. I told her all about how pink everything was, and I told her how I won the treasure, and I told her about calling out the names on the gifts. I described these tricks with pride. Jennifer allowed me to finish before she made me feel dumb, "You must be careful never to show your witchcraft in public. Don't be tempted into showing off."

"But, Jennifer," I said, "you can hardly call those tricks *witchcraft*. I just memorized those gifts, and I happened to accidentally sit on the treasure."

Jennifer looked serious. She said, "Why do you think it was so easy to memorize those names?"

"Because I was the first one at the party?" I answered.

"Why do you think you were the first one at the party?" she asked.

"Because my mother sent me up there early?" I answered.

Jennifer paused a minute to let me think. Then she said, "Why do you think you sat on the treasure?"

"Because you said that I couldn't play musical chairs?"

"Why do you think I said you couldn't play musical chairs?" she asked.

"Because . . . because . . . because I don't know." I answered.

She said no more about the party, so I said no more. I felt disappointed because I had saved up much more gossip. Watching normal girls and collecting things to tell her about how they acted had helped me during the party. I couldn't understand why Jennifer didn't want to hear about normal girls.

We returned to business. We began as usual by hooking our fingers together and marching around the magic circle. It took me a little while to want to talk witch talk; I was still in a party mood. But the magic of our circle worked. We discussed our plans for the flying ointment.

I had completed my first responsibility. I had listed all the ingredients. Most of the recipes needed plants like foxglove, cowbane, and my very favorite, deadly nightshade. I had felt certain that every witch would put witch hazel on the list; not one did. Jennifer called the items from these famous recipes, *general ingredients.* Everyone needed the general ingredients, but everyone also needed special ingredients. Everyone could use the same general parts, but each witch must use some particular things that were different from all the other witches' things. That's why we had our particular fingernails and our particular snowball footprints.

The way we divided the work was that Jennifer learned the chants and got the general stuff. I got my own special stuff, some of hers, the charcoal for the fire, and the three-pound can of Crisco. We needed the Crisco as a base for the ointment so that it would really stick. We had thought about using Vaseline, but we decided that it would be hard to get three pounds of Vaseline. When I took the Crisco, I planned to tell my mother that it was for the needy. I was the needy.

I was worried about getting foxglove, cowbane, and deadly nightshade. Jennifer told me to not worry. "Where will you get them?" I asked.

"From my father."

I was amazed. "Is your father a wizard?"

"Some people say that he is a plant wizard," she muttered.

"Honest?" I said. "A real wizard!"

"I said *plant* wizard," she answered.

"Oh, Jennifer," I gasped. "How wonderful! My father is only a commuter."

Then Jennifer said, "Maybe we should make a flying potion instead."

"What's the difference between a flying ointment and a flying potion?" I inquired.

"You drink a potion; it works from the inside. You salve a flying ointment all over yourself; it works from the outside."

"Drink it?" I asked.

"Yes. There's a plant that grows in South America called *ayahuasco*. We could use that. Maybe some jungle witch could fly it here."

"Drink it?" I squealed.

"Yes," she repeated.

"I vote for the ointment."

Jennifer sighed, "It does seem a shame to waste all of our research. We'll have all our general ingredients ready for spring vacation." I somehow knew that Jennifer was relieved that I voted for the ointment. I somehow knew that she mentioned the potion just to stop me from thinking about her father. I enjoyed knowing without letting her know that I knew.

The weather in March is a lot like me. Nice for one day and then nasty for two. In March I'm always waiting for warm days, and when they come, I wonder why I waited. My mother never admits that it can be warm in March. She always insists that I wear an undershirt and my heavy winter coat until May. She never has my heavy winter coat cleaned in March. She waits to clean it for summer storage. Neither my mother nor the weather can decide whether winter isn't quite over or whether winter is almost over. So I spend the warm days of March in my heavy, itchy, dirty winter coat. And in my undershirt. I spend the warm days of March uncomfortably. But I wait for them.

When we met on Saturdays in March, Jennifer always brought Hilary Ezra with her. Hilary Ezra was our toad. Around New York most people don't have toads in March. Around New York most people don't have toads in March or watermelons in January. Jennifer was not most people. She came to the park the first Saturday in March and said, "Today I brought the toad." She held him out in her hand. He wasn't very big. For a minute I thought

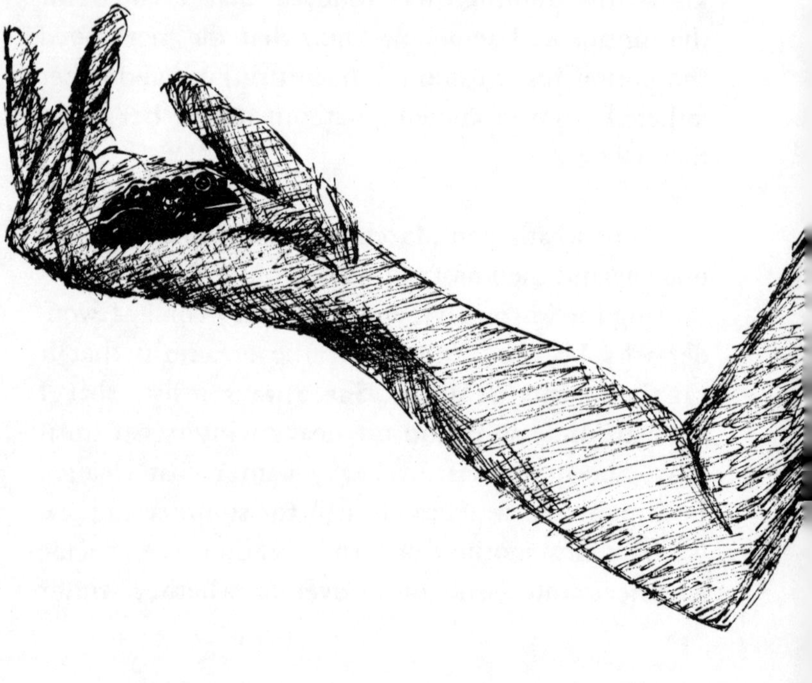

he was the plastic kind that you buy in kits. The kind that are stuck on a cardboard under one big plastic bubble. Sometimes they are glued on a card under separate little plastic bubbles, and the card says "Farmyard Friends," or "Dinosaurs—Great and Small." The toad moved. I jumped. Jennifer closed her hand.

"Where did you get him?" I asked.

"Witches always have toads," she answered. "Toads are the first ingredient." She paused a second, looked up toward the sky and said, "What's the matter, didn't you ever read *Macbeth?*"

"Well, no," I said, "I've *heard* about *Macbeth.*"

"Every modern witch ought to read *Macbeth,*" Jennifer said. "Those witches cooked up a wonderful brew. Not flying ointment brew. Trouble brew. And the first ingredient to go in was a toad." Then Jennifer stared at me and recited:

> "Round about the cauldron go:
> In the poison'd entrails throw.
> Toad, that under cold stone
> Days and nights has thirty one
> Swelter'd venom sleeping got,
> Boil thou first i' the charmèd pot."

She stared at me the whole time she was reciting.

"Did Macbeth say that?"

"Of course not," she scolded. "Macbeth wasn't

a witch. The witches say that as they stir their brew of trouble. Notice they boiled the toad first in the pot."

"What are the witches' names in *Macbeth?*" I asked.

"First witch, second witch, third witch," she answered, "and Hecate, the queen of the witches is in it, too."

"What kind of trouble was in the pot?" I asked.

"They gave him a warning," she replied.

I thought a minute and said, "It doesn't sound mean to warn someone. That doesn't sound like trouble. Sounds rather nice, as a matter of fact."

"It wasn't nice," Jennifer insisted. "How can you be a witch and be good, too? The two just don't go together."

"What did they warn him of?"

"The truth."

I couldn't understand what could be so awful about the truth. I had heard grown-ups talk about the *awful truth,* but I couldn't understand what they meant. So I asked, "What's so bad about the truth?"

"They told him the truth in such a way that he got to feeling too sure of himself. He became careless and brought about his doom."

"What did they tell him?" I asked.

"I won't tell. You have to read *Macbeth.* Every modern witch should. Those witches were wonderful."

"Give me an example," I begged. "Please?"

"I'll give you an example of the *kind* of thing they did." She thought a long minute before beginning. "Suppose they said to you first, 'Elizabeth, beware of . . . beware of the toad. The toad will cause you pain.' You think to yourself that you like the toad. Besides, you can't imagine how any toad with no sharp claws and no sharp teeth can cause you pain. But since the witches warned you–you will beware."

"Yes," I said, "I would listen. They might mean that I'll get a wart and need to have it burned off."

Jennifer nodded. "Next they tell you that no animal born where rain can fall will harm you. Then you think to yourself... toads are always born out of doors in a pond or a lake where rain can fall. So you don't have to worry much about the toad or about most animals."

I silently agreed. Then Jennifer continued, "Next they tell you that you'll have no pain until the home of the toad comes to you. You think . . . how can a lake or a pond or a park come to me? So after the first warning, which you are perfectly willing to believe, you end up feeling pretty sure of yourself."

"What's wrong with feeling pretty sure of yourself?" I asked.

"Pretty sure is okay. But *too* sure isn't okay. Imagine being so sure of yourself for a test that you never even open the book."

"Oh, I'm never that sure." I was watching the toad and wanting to pet him.

Jennifer was still concentrating on *Macbeth.* "In *Macbeth,* Hecate says:

> 'And you all know, security
> Is mortals' chiefest enemy.' "

"Is man a mortal?" I asked.

"Of course," Jennifer answered.

"Then, is that Hecate's way of saying the story of the tortoise and the hare? You know, that fable about the rabbit being so sure of winning the race that he wasn't even careful. He didn't try very hard to win."

"Yes," Jennifer explained. "Except that they didn't make Macbeth sure of winning . . . they made him sure he'd never lose."

"Never lose what?" I demanded.

"His life," she croaked. She looked at me hard. I swallowed hard.

"Jennifer," I asked, "what do you ever do besides read?"

She looked up at the sky and sighed and said very seriously, "I think." She continued looking up at the sky and added, "Now do you absolutely understand about the witches' warning?"

"Macbeth's witches?" I asked.

"Any witches."

I nodded. For just a minute the idea crossed my mind that Jennifer actually was warning me. Then I thought, "Oh, well, how can a lovely little toad cause me pain?"

"May I hold him?" I asked.

"Of course." She handed him to me.

"Jennifer, do witches ever name their toads?"

"Never," she answered.

"I think we should," I said.

"We shouldn't," she said.

"I think we should call him *Hilary*. *Hilary* means cheerful. And he is bright-eyed and cheerful."

"Witches don't name toads," she said.

"Yep, Hilary is a fine name."

"Witches don't name toads," she repeated.

"*Hilary* means cheerful, and you are cheery, dearie," I murmured. To the toad . . . not to Jennifer.

"He should be called *Ezra* if he's called anything at all," she replied.

"Why Ezra?" I demanded.

"Because *Ezra* means *help* . . . and he'll help us make the flying ointment."

"*Hilary* is better," I insisted.

"Ezra," she said.

"How about Hilary Ezra?" I asked.

"Agreed," she answered.

I think I grew to love Hilary Ezra from that very second. Naming him was the first argument I ever won from Jennifer. For once *I* had convinced *her*. I thought.

We both loved Hilary Ezra. We always called him by his entire, complete name. We enjoyed catching insects for him to eat. We would bring a ruler to the park to see how far he would jump. We marked down the date. We would calculate his average jump for the day, his longest jump, his lifetime average, and his lifetime record. He was wonderful company for being such a dumb animal. He always wore a prize ribbon. Not first prize or second prize. One of my ribbons I had won at Cynthia's party.

Each of us tried to be kinder to Hilary Ezra than the other. We would argue about whose turn it was to pull him in the wagon. We placed an old window screen over the top of the wagon so that he couldn't jump out. He was not a grateful animal; he would try to jump out every time we took the screen away. It was easily true that each of us loved Hilary Ezra more than he loved us. Sometimes it almost seemed true that we loved Hilary Ezra more than we loved each other. Hilary Ezra became the one thing that made me jealous of Jennifer. I admired the way she could read. I admired the way she could walk looking up at the sky. I admired the cool way she could ignore someone (even me) if she wanted to. I admired all these things. I always felt grateful when she shared her talents with me even if sharing them made her bossy. But I didn't feel grateful when she shared Hilary Ezra. I felt jealous because I wished that I could have him all the time. He had pretty eyes.

One day Jennifer brought Hilary Ezra to school in her pocket. It was warm that day and all the fifth grades were out on the playground playing kick ball. Hilary Ezra hopped out of Jennifer's pocket as she was guarding first base. The first person to notice was Tommy Schmidt. He had just kicked the ball and was on his way to first when he spotted Hilary Ezra. Everyone was yelling, "Go, Tom, go. Run, Tom, run." Tom did not go. Tom did not run. Tom stopped dead. Jennifer was looking up at the sky as usual. There was sudden quiet when Tom stopped. Jennifer reached down, picked up Hilary Ezra and put him back in her pocket. She buttoned her pocket closed. No one said a word. I smiled to myself. A very small smile. I couldn't let anyone know that he was mine, too.

During March I was practicing casting small journeyman witch spells. Sometimes I was successful. Here is a list of my successful spells:

1. Cynthia got sick and missed eight days of school. Miss Hazen made me take her homework to her every day. Besides, being only a journeyman witch, I couldn't make her terribly sick.
2. Miss Hazen didn't call for our arith-

metic homework the day I didn't do it.

3. It rained on the day of the class trip to the zoo. Everyone got sick. Two kids threw up. The bus smelled awful from all the fumes and wet raincoats and all. The zoo didn't smell too good, either. I loved it.
4. Cynthia and Dolores had a fight. It lasted only a short while. I could still cast only short spells.

All in all, I was feeling very competent.

9

SPRING VACATION CAME. IT WAS THE middle of April. Jennifer and I had invested all of our Saturdays in witchcraft. We had invested bicycling time, movie time, roller-skating time, lounging-around-the-house-in-your-pajamas time. Now we would see if it had been worth it.

We arranged to meet at the park at 7:00 A.M. o'clock of the morning. The first Monday of vacation. This meant that I had to be up at 6:30 A.M. o'clock of the morning. My mother heard me getting up and getting dressed. She came into my bedroom, glanced at the clock, said, "I don't believe it," and went back to bed. That saved my having to answer a lot of questions. I was nervous. I couldn't eat breakfast, partly because I wanted to be lighter for our flight.

I had written a list the night before. I checked off the items one by one. My fingernails, the watermelon seeds, the frozen snowball in an old milk carton, the foods the Greats had donated, the three pound can of Crisco, a spatula to get the Crisco out of the can, charcoal briquets and fluid to light them. I put everything into a large shopping bag from Bloomingdale's and carried it to the park.

Jennifer was already at the park when I got there. She had brought her big kettle somehow. Her whole wagon was filled with potted plants. With the screen over it, it looked like a tiny greenhouse on wheels. Maybe Jennifer had made two trips. Inside the kettle were the matches, her fingernails, and her snowball, now melted in an old herring jar. Her fingernails were saved in a match box. I could tell that she had just added to the supply because her fingernails were very short right then. Both of us had chanted for a windy day; we got one. It was warm, too. We decided that we had enough proper ingredients, the proper chants, and a good proper wind. We were ready to fly.

We knew exactly what we were supposed to do. We transferred the ingredients from the kettle to my Bloomingdale's shopping bag. Then we carried the kettle, the shopping bag and the wagon to near the center of our magic circle where we placed them on the ground around the bottom of the water fountain. That done, we silently marched around the circle seven times. Each time around we went faster and faster. Then we went to the picnicking part of the park where there are barbecue grilles for people if they want to use them. I placed the charcoal on the grille and doused it with lighter fluid. Jennifer lit the match since she no longer had to obey Taboo 7. Together we lifted the huge cauldron to the top of the grille.

First we opened the can of Crisco and emptied it into the cauldron. Then Jennifer threw in the key that opened the can. We marched around and marched around the cauldron. We marched around and marched around. It seemed to take awful long for three pounds of Crisco to melt. We kept *silence* the whole time. The Crisco melted; then we added the other ingredients. She chanted, and I stirred after each addition. In went the deadly nightshade. "Xilka, Xilka," stir, stir. The snowballs; the Crisco steamed and cackled. "Besa, Besa," stir, stir. Next the foxglove. "Xilka, Xilka," stir, stir. Then the Lion's Milk. "Besa, Besa," stir, stir. The watermelon seeds. Chant and stir. The fingernails. Chant and stir. The food of the Greats. Chant and stir. All went into the pot. "Xilka, Xilka, Besa, Besa," stir, stir, stir.

Then Jennifer lifted the screen from the wagon and slowly withdrew Hilary Ezra from his home. She didn't look at me. She kept chanting as she reached up and dangled my lovely pet by one leg over the cauldron.

I gasped. I had forgotten that Hilary Ezra was a

proper ingredient. Jennifer heard my gasp and saw the look of horror on my face. She gave me a cross look in return. We were not supposed to speak until we finished all our chanting. She was chanting and dangling my beautiful Hilary Ezra over the pot. I couldn't stand it one second longer. I yelled, "STOP," grabbed her wrist, and shook her hand until she dropped Hilary Ezra to the ground. He hopped away from us forever.

Jennifer said nothing. She picked up the empty Crisco can and walked to the magic circle water fountain. There she filled the can with water. She threw the water on the fire.

"What are you doing?" I asked.

"Putting out the fire," she answered.

"I know that. I mean *why* are you doing it?"

"Ask what you mean," she answered.

"All right," I said. "Then why are you doing it?"

"Because the spell is over. You'll never make a proper witch. You still want too many reasons *and* you are too sentimental."

"And you, Jennifer, are too hard-hearted. You never even hesitated."

"You are dismissed," she said. She didn't even look up at me.

"You . . . " I screamed, trying hard to think of something awful to call her. "You . . . you . . . you . . . you, JENNY!" I yelled and I walked away. I

waited until I was out of the park before I began to cry.

I cried at first because I had lost Jennifer, Hilary Ezra, and the flying ointment. I cared in that order. I cried because I was angry with myself. Like flunking a test because you didn't study and there's no excuse. I had flunked the flying ointment test. We had worked hard on it. As I got closer to home, I began to think about Hilary Ezra. Then I got mad at Jennifer. Not hurt feelings. Good mad feelings. That had been the first time I had ever disobeyed. I thought that Jennifer was mean. She was mean to Hilary Ezra, and she was mean to me. And I kept saying "mean" to myself, but by the time I reached our apartment building, I realized something else. Jennifer was not being mean to Hilary Ezra. She wanted me to stop her from boiling him in oil. I remembered about the witches in *Macbeth;* the toad was supposed to be the first ingredient. She had told me that. She had purposely kept him until last. She had purposely dangled him over the pot so long. She always found a way to not get mad at herself but to get mad at me instead. I was sure if I hadn't stopped her, she would have stopped herself. By the time the elevator came, I was crying with rage.

When I walked into our apartment, my mother looked at me and said, "What in the world happened to you?"

"I had a fight," I answered.

"With whom?" she asked.

"Jennifer," I replied.

"And who is Jennifer?" she asked.

"Some old witch," I yelled and ran to my room and slammed the door.

10

If Jennifer hadn't told me that I was no longer a journeyman witch, I would have known anyway. The spell was over. The next morning, I came down with a cold. Not only did I have a virus, but my mother said that I probably got it from Cynthia. I had the same symptoms as she had had. I had picked up Cynthia's nasty germs. And they got ripe during vacation. I didn't even have a chance to miss school.

I cried a lot during that vacation. My mother thought it was mostly because I was sick and because my temperature really was not 98.6; it was higher. But, of course, it was only partly that. I got mad a lot, too. Like when I remembered that no one, absolutely no one, would notice when I snubbed Jennifer at school. No one at school knew that we even knew each other.

I was well enough to return to school on schedule. We began right where we left off, New

Math and all. I didn't enjoy it too much. I still walked to school alone, of course. But for the first time since Halloween it seemed lonely. Thoughts of Jennifer had been good company. Looking for notes and leaving notes on the Jennifer tree had made each trip to school a tiny adventure. For a couple of days I tried walking to school by the sidewalk route. I didn't enjoy that any more. The men from the road department were shoveling the sand out of the gutters. In the winter they had thrown the sand out to keep the cars from slipping in the snow. Their shovels scraped along the sidewalk and gave me chills. My days as a witch were truly over.

I went back to walking through the woods. The ground was soft and moist; even the most sheltered snow had melted.

On Friday I searched the Jennifer tree during each of my four trips. I didn't find a note any time. On Saturday my mother started getting ready to go to the A & P. I yelled, "Wait a minute; I'm coming, too."

She looked surprised and said, "I thought you'd be going to the library as usual."

"Oh," I said, "that project is finished."

"Did you get an *A* on it?" my mother asked.

"Not exactly," I answered.

"For all the work you did on that project, I thought you'd not only get an *A*, you'd get a medal."

"Well," I said, "sometimes you work real hard

on something and all you get for it is a stupid virus."

"What does that mean?" my mother asked.

"Oh, I don't know," I answered. I began to cry.

"It's that virus," my mother said. "You still haven't recovered. It must be the virus; you cried on and off that whole week you were in bed. I think it's one of the symptoms."

Of course I was crying! Of course I had been crying! Jennifer had made the witches' warning come true. Hilary Ezra did cause me deep pain. Even though I couldn't explain the rest of that warning.

My mother was looking at me. She came over to me and put her hand under my chin and tilted my head upward. She said very gently, "Maybe you ought to stay in the apartment while Dad and I go to the store. Or maybe you'd like to invite Cynthia over."

The thought of spending a morning with Cynthia while my spirits were so low made me stop crying. "I'll stay. I'll stay alone," I said. I said it loud, and I said it fast.

"I'll never understand why you don't like Cynthia," my mother said. "I think she's charming."

"Mother," I said, "if you really want to know, I'll tell you why. Cynthia is a phony. I've known for a long time that she's a phony. And worse than that, she doesn't know she's a phony. She believes in Cynthia. She's a serious phony. And the only way

I can stand her is to absolutely ignore her."

"All right. All right," my mother said. "Stay here and don't let anyone in the apartment without finding out who it is. Peek through the peek hole." She meant the eye-sized hole in the door that most apartments have. It has a tiny one-way mirror in it, and you can see out without the outsiders seeing in.

After Mom and Dad had been gone about twenty or twenty-five minutes, I was beginning to feel like the loneliest girl in the whole U.S. of A. I made myself a glass of chocolate milk using enough syrup for three normal glasses. I also made myself four peanut butter crackers. Then I walked out the living room door to our terrace.

The trees were coming! New green was all over . . . green so new that it was kissing yellow. The windows of the greenhouse on THE ESTATE caught the sun and winked it back to me. As the shadows of the branches waved across the windows, the light seemed to blink on and off. A private kind of Morse code, I thought. I sat there staring at the roof of the greenhouse. It was pleasant on our terrace. I was happy that my mother had washed away the soot of winter and bought the porch furniture. The view from the terrace was far nicer than from anywhere else in the apartment. We hadn't really used the terrace since we moved in. In September we hadn't had porch furniture yet, and in October it had been so cold that we kept the terrace door locked. Then in April, right after Mom got it all ready, I got my virus.

THE ESTATE was the prettiest view we could see from our terrace. Looking in the other direction, we could see down Providence Street, but it was not nearly so peaceful. My eye kept wandering back to the greenhouse. The sun kept splashing on the windows. Blink. Blink. I decided that someday when I was rich and famous, I'd have a greenhouse. I'd have flowers all year round. I'd have fresh grown onions in winter, and I'd have watermelon in January.

WATERMELON IN JANUARY! Of course! TOADS IN MARCH! Of course! A place where no rain falls! Of course! The greenhouse was where Hilary Ezra had been born. And Jennifer's father was the plant wizard who grew the watermelon and the deadly nightshade. And Hilary Ezra's home did come to me that awful day in the park. Jennifer carried the greenhouse plants to the park in her wagon. There was a message in that Morse code of the windows. I was brilliant. I was a genius!

I was so pleased with my brilliance that I was angry that there was no one to tell about it. At least Jennifer would know I knew. I'd send her a special delivery letter in care of the Samellson Estate, and when she had to sign for the special delivery, she'd know that I had found her out. Or maybe I'd write her mysterious notes and leave them on the Jennifer tree . . . but then I couldn't be certain she'd get them. I'd call her on the phone except that I couldn't use the phone. No, of course I could use the phone. I had been dismissed. I'd get the phone book down and look up Mrs. Samellson's number. Wouldn't Jennifer be surprised when she heard my voice. She'd wonder how I knew where to reach her.

I was growing more brilliant by the minute. Mrs. Samellson was famous for her antiques. She would have a big three-legged kettle, and she would have a genuine Pilgrim dress. It had been easy for Jennifer to get my notes. Jennifer and I were neighbors! I was pacing the floor and eating salted cashew nuts, which I don't even like. I had to tell someone. I absolutely had to tell someone! I would cast a small spell. My mother would come home. I'd tell her! I'd test to see if I had any witchcraft left over. Then the doorbell rang. I pulled a chair over to the door so that I could look through the peek hole. I didn't

see anyone at first. Then I stood on tiptoes and looked way down at the floor. I saw a wagon. Jennifer's wagon! I jumped down from the chair and yanked the door wide open.

Jennifer walked into my house for the first time. Her eyes were up on the ceiling.

"Hi," I said.

"Do you have anything to eat?" she answered. I stood with my mouth open. How could anyone have such terrible manners?

Then I answered, "Oh, yes. What would you like? A raw egg? Or a raw onion? Perhaps you would like five uncooked spaghettis or some raw oatmeal? Which would you prefer?"

Jennifer looked at me and said, "I really want just a drink of water."

I laughed, "But look at your empty wagon. You must, absolutely must, let me fill it up with trick or treat."

Jennifer looked at me and smiled. First she smiled and then she laughed. Jennifer laughed. She really laughed and laughed and laughed. I also laughed. And then I laughed and laughed and laughed. For the first time we laughed together. We were laughing and playing together when my parents came home, and I introduced them to Jennifer. My mother smiled and said, "Hi, can you both give me a hand unloading these groceries?" We both did. Jennifer seemed to know where everything went.

Now we laugh together a lot. We walk to school together, too. Sometimes I play at her house, the caretaker's house on THE ESTATE. Sometimes we visit Mrs. Samellson who is even older than the Greats. She tells wonderful stories about her antiques. We don't even mind Cynthia too much. Neither of us is lonely any more. Sometimes we even play with Maria or Grace. But not too often. We don't have too much time to spare.

Neither of us pretends to be a witch any more. Now we mostly enjoy being what we really are . . . just Jennifer and just me . . . just good friends.

The View from Saturday

Thanks to Dr. Robert Stoll
for educating me about the life and times of Florida sea turtles.
—ELK

This is for David for beating the odds.

1

Mrs. Eva Marie Olinski always gave good answers. Whenever she was asked how she had selected her team for the Academic Bowl, she chose one of several good answers. Most often she said that the four members of her team had skills that balanced one another. That was reasonable. Sometimes she said that she knew her team would practice. That was accurate. To the district superintendent of schools, she gave a bad answer, but she did that only once, only to him, and if that answer was not good, her reason for giving it was.

The fact was that Mrs. Olinski did not know how she had chosen her team, and the further fact was that she didn't know that she didn't know until she did know. Of course, that is true of most things: you do not know up to and including the very last second before you do. And for Mrs. Olinski that was not until Bowl Day was over and so was the work of her four sixth graders.

They called themselves The Souls. They told Mrs. Olinski that they were The Souls long before they were a team, but she told them that they were a team as soon as they became The Souls. Then after a while, teacher and team agreed that they were arguing chicken-or-egg.

Whichever way it began—chicken-or-egg, team-or-The Souls—it definitely ended with an egg. Definitely, an egg.

People still remark about how extraordinary it was to have four sixth graders make it to the finals. There had been a few seventh graders scattered among the other teams, but all the rest of the middle school regional champs were eighth graders. Epiphany had never before won even the local championship, and there they were, up on stage, ready to compete for the state trophy. All four members of Maxwell, the other team in the final round, were in the eighth grade. Both of the Maxwell boys' voices had deepened, and the girls displayed lacy bra straps inside their T-shirt necklines. The fact that the necklines were outsized and that the two pairs of straps matched—they were apricot-colored—made Mrs. Olinski believe that they were not making a fashion statement as much as they were saying something. To her four sixth graders puberty was something they could spell and define but had yet to experience.

Unlike football bowls, there had been no season tallies for the academic teams. There had been no best-of-five. Each contest had been an elimination round. There were winners, and there were losers. From the start, the rule was: Lose one game, and you are out.

• • •

So it was on Bowl Day.

At the start of the day, there had been eight regional champs. Now there were two—Epiphany and Maxwell.

It was afternoon by the time they got to the last round, and Mrs. Olinski sat shivering in a windowless room in a building big enough and official enough to have its own zip code. This was Albany, the capital of the state of New York. This was the last Saturday in May, and some robot—human or electronic—had checked the calendar instead of the weather report and had turned on the air-conditioning. Like everyone else in the audience, Mrs. Olinski wore a short-sleeved T-shirt with her team's logo across the front. Maxwell's were navy; Epiphany's were red and were as loud as things were permitted to get in that large, cold room. The audience had been asked not to whistle, cheer, stomp, hold up signs, wave banners, or even applaud. They were reminded that this Bowl was for brains, not brawn, and decorum—something between chapel and classroom—was the order of the day.

Epiphany sat on one side of a long table; Maxwell, the other. At a lectern between them stood the commissioner of education of the state of New York. He smiled benevolently over the audience as he reached inside his inner breast pocket and withdrew a pair of reading glasses. With a flick of his wrist he opened them and put them on.

Mrs. Olinski hugged her upper arms and wondered if maybe it was nerves and not the quartering wind blowing from the ceiling vents that was causing her shivers. She watched with bated (and visible) breath as the commissioner placed his hand into a large clear glass bowl. His college class ring knocked bottom. (Had the room been two degrees colder, the glass would have shattered.) He withdrew a piece of paper, unfolded it, and read, "What is the meaning of the word *calligraphy* and from what language does it derive?"

A buzzer sounded.

Mrs. Olinski knew whose it was. She was sure of it. She leaned back and relaxed. She was not nervous. Excited, yes. Nervous, no.

The television lights glanced off Noah Gershom's glasses. He had been the first chosen.

• • •

Noah Writes a B & B Letter

My mother insisted that I write a B & B letter to my grandparents. I told her that I could not write a B & B letter, and she asked me why, and I told her that I did not know what a B & B letter was. She explained—not too patiently—that a B & B letter is a *bread and butter letter* you write to people to thank them for having you as their houseguest. I told her that I was taught never to use the word you are defining in its definition and that she ought to think of a substitute word for *letter* if she is defining it. Mother then made a remark about how Western Civilization was in a decline because people of my generation knew how to nitpick but not how to write a B & B letter.

I told her that, with all due respect, I did not think I owed Grandma and Grandpa a B & B. And then I stated my case. Fact: I was not just a houseguest, I was family; and fact: I had not been their houseguest by choice because fact: She had sent me to them because she had won a cruise for selling more houses in Epiphany than anyone else in the world and if she had shared her cruise with Joey and me instead of with her husband, my father, I would not have been sent to Florida in the first place and fact: She, not me, owed them thanks; and further fact: I had been such a wonderful help while I was there that Grandma and Grandpa would probably want to write me a B & B.

My brother Joey had been sent to my other set of grandparents, who live in a normal suburb in Connecticut. "Is Joey writing a B & B to Grandma and Grandpa Eberle?"

"Even as we speak," Mother replied.

"Well, maybe he has something to be thankful for," I said.

Mother drew in her breath as if she were about to say something else about what children of my generation were doing to Western Civilization, but instead, she said, "Write," and closed my bedroom door behind her. I opened the door and called out to her, "Can I use the computer?"

She said, "I know you can use the computer, Noah, but you *may* not." I was about to make a remark about who was nitpicking now, but Mother gave me such a negative look that I knew any thoughts I had had better be about bread and butter and not nitpicking.

I gazed at my closed bedroom door and then out the window. Door. Window. Door. Window. There was no escape.

I took a box of notepaper out of my desk drawer. The notes were bigger than postage stamps, but not by much. I took out a ballpoint pen and started pressing it against a piece of scrap paper, making dents in the paper but not making a mark. Ballpoint pens sometimes take a while to get started. When I was down in Florida, Tillie Nachman had said, "The ballpoint pen has been the biggest single factor in the decline of Western Civilization. It makes the written word cheap, fast, and totally without character." My mother and Tillie should get together. Between them, they have come up with the two major reasons why Western Civilization is about to collapse.

Not because I was trying to save Western Civilization but because I wanted to actually get my B & B letter written, I put the ballpoint pen back into the drawer and took out my calligraphy pen, the one that uses wet ink. I didn't fill it. I would fill it when I was ready to write. I also took out a sharpened pencil and a pad of Post-it notes to jot down any ideas that might come to mind.

I wrote *red wagon*. The red wagon had definitely been a gift—even though, under the circumstances, I didn't bring it back to Epiphany with me. I thought a while longer and wrote *tuxedo T-shirt*. It, too, had been a gift, but I didn't have that either. I wrote *calligraphy pen and bottle of ink*. A wet ink pen and a bottle of ink had been given to me, but the ones I took out of my desk drawer were ones I had bought myself. The calligraphy pen made me remember about the Post-it notes I had bought to correct the problem that had developed with the ink. Even though I had bought the Post-it notes myself, I added *Post-it notes* to my list. I peeled off the Post-it note containing my list and stuck it on the wall in front of my desk, and then, as my mother had commanded, I thought again.

Century Village where my Gershom grandparents live is not like any place I had ever been to. It is in Florida, but it is not exactly Disney World or Sea World or other regular destinations. It is like a theme park for old people. Almost everyone who lives there is retired from useful life. Grandma Sadie and Grandpa Nate fit in nicely.

It all started when Margaret Draper and Izzy Diamondstein decided to get married, and the citizens of Century Village called a meeting in the clubhouse to organize the wedding.

In their former lives, Grandma Sadie and Grandpa Nate had owned a small bakery right here in Epiphany, New York, so Grandma volunteered to do the wedding cake, and Grandpa Nate, whose chief hobby had always been violin playing, promised to arrange for the music.

My grandfather Gershom began practicing immediately and often. Grandma Sadie said, "Nathan, how can you stand playing the same piece over and over again?" And Grandpa Nate answered, "Why don't you ask me how I can stand making love to the same woman over and over again?" And even though she is the age she is, my grandmother blushed and said, *Sha! a shanda far die kinder*, a remark I had heard many times before Grandma and Grandpa moved to Century Village. Translated it means, "Hush up, it's a shame for the children," but what it really meant was that Grandpa was embarrassing Grandma.

Mr. Cantor, a retired postman from Pennsylvania, who was devoted to growing orchids, said that he would have enough blossoms for the corsages. And Mrs. Kerchmer said that she would lend her African violets for the centerpieces.

Tillie Nachman volunteered to do the invitations, and Rabbi Friedman, who was a rabbi in his former life, said he would perform the ceremony even though Margaret Draper was not Jewish and Izzy Diamondstein was. This was a late second marriage, and there wouldn't be any concern about what religion they should choose for their children since all their children were already grown up and chosen. Grandpa Nate later explained to me that unlike the average citizen of Century Village, rabbis don't have former lives. They are what they were; once a rabbi, always a rabbi.

Many citizens of Century Village were widows who had once been great family cooks, so they formed a committee to plan the wedding dinner. Everyone agreed to share the cost, and they made up a menu and a master shopping list.

After that first meeting, Grandpa Nate and I took Tillie Nachman, a former New York City person who had never learned to drive, to the stationery store so that she could buy the invitations. While she shopped for the invitations, Grandpa and I went to Wal-Mart to pick up Grandma's prescription, and that is when we saw the red wagon special. Grandpa bought it for me, and it's a good thing he did. It came in handy until Allen came along.

I checked my list. *Post-it notes.* I had bought them when we ran out of invitations. Of course, we didn't run out of invitations until Tillie's cat got its paws into the ink.

Tillie was filling in the *who-what-when-and-where* on the invitations when I noticed that she had the prettiest handwriting I had ever seen. "Calligraphy," she said. "It means beautiful writing," and she asked me if I would like to learn how to write like her. I said yes. She said she would give me lessons if I would help her address the envelopes. So Grandpa drove us to an art supply store where she bought me a calligraphy pen and a bottle of ink. It was while Tillie was trying out various pen points (called *nibs*) that she made the remark about the ballpoint pen being the biggest single factor in the decline of Western Civilization.

After choosing a nib Tillie said, "I hope in the future, Noah, that you will use a ballpoint pen only when you have to press hard to make multiple carbons."

I couldn't promise that. There were times in school

when a person had to do things fast, cheap, and without character.

Tillie said, "There are pens that come with ink in a cartridge, Noah, but I will have nothing to do with them." So when we were back at her condo, Tillie taught me how to fill a pen, or, as she said, "How to *properly* fill a pen."

One: Turn the filling plunger counterclockwise as far as it will go. Two: Dip the nib completely into the ink. Three: Turn the filling plunger clockwise until it stops. Four: Hold the nib above the ink bottle and turn the plunger counterclockwise again until three drops of ink fall back into the bottle. Five: Turn the plunger clockwise to stop the drops. Six: Wipe the excess ink completely from pen and nib.

When I told Tillie that six steps seemed a lot to have to do before you begin, she said, "You must think of those six steps not as preparation for the beginning but as the beginning itself."

I practiced my calligraphy. I practiced all twenty-six letters of the alphabet, including *X*, which was not part of any of the who-what-when-and-wheres or any of the addresses but is a very good letter to practice because fact: It is not easy.

When Tillie decided that I was good enough to help with the invitations, I sat on the floor of her living room and used her coffee table as my desk. She sat at the kitchen table. Fact: Many of the domiciles in Century Village do not have family rooms with desks.

There was a lot of writing to do because at the bottom of each and every one of those invitations, we wrote: Your presence but no presents. Tillie said that practically all the invitations that went out from Century Village said that.

"Besides," she said, "I think that making the wedding is enough of a present."

I was doing a wonderful job until Thomas Stearns, called T. S., Tillie's cat, pounced into my lap, and I jumped up and spilled the ink, and the cat walked through the spilled ink and onto a couple of the invitations I was addressing. A few—five altogether—now had cat's paws.

Tillie was pretty upset because she had not bought extras because she said, "I don't make mistakes." In her former life Tillie had been a bookkeeper. I heard her say, "I can add up a column of figures with the best of them." I didn't know if she meant the best of the computers or the best of the bookkeepers, and I didn't ask because I was afraid I already knew.

I told Tillie not to worry. I told her that I would think of something. And I did. That's when I bought the Post-it notes. I put a Post-it into each of the invitations that had a cat's paw mark. On the Post-it I wrote (in faultless calligraphy): Bring this specially marked invitation to the wedding and receive a surprise gift. When Tillie asked me what the surprise would be, I told her not to worry, that I would think of something. And I did. But fact: It wasn't easy.

On the day the groceries were to be purchased, the citizens of Century Village formed their version of the Home Shopping Network. They met in the clubhouse again. Everyone sat in rows, holding coupons they'd clipped since printing began. They asked me to be master of ceremonies.

I sat at a table in front of the clubhouse room and called out items from the master grocery list. It was a lot like a game of Go Fish. I said, "I need one Crisco, four margarines, *pareve*, and let's have all your paper towels." Everyone searched through their fistfuls of coupons and gave me the ones that were needed. Tillie circled the items we had coupons for.

Then we checked the newspaper for supermarket specials and made out lists for each of the stores, depending on which one had the best buy in a particular item. I wrote the Gershom list in calligraphy. It didn't slow things down too much, and the citizens of Century Village are accustomed to waiting.

Later that day, everyone returned to the clubhouse with the groceries and the store receipts. Tillie added, divided, and straightened out who owed and who was owed, and no one bothered to check because everyone knew that Tillie Nachman did not make mistakes. Then we had to check the grocery list against the menu and who was cooking what. I helped distribute the groceries to the proper households, using the new red wagon.

Fact: I did a wonderful job.

On the day of the wedding I was in great demand to take things over to the clubhouse in my wagon. The African violets alone took three trips, and the briskets took two. Next, Mr. Cantor and I delivered the orchid corsages to the bride and her maid of honor. In the real world, I had never met anyone who spent as much time with flowers as Mr. Cantor. Mrs. Draper's maid of honor was to be her daughter, Mrs. Potter. Mrs. Draper used to live in my hometown, which is Epiphany, New York, and her daughter, Mrs. Potter, still does. Mrs. Potter bought a new dress and flew down for the wedding, but we didn't fly down together. I had come weeks before—my first trip as an unaccompanied minor.

Mr. Cantor and I took flowers over to the groom and his best man to put in their buttonholes. Allen, who was Izzy Diamondstein's son, was to be best man. They both live in Florida and have the same last name.

Allen Diamondstein still lived in the real world because even though he was Izzy's child and even though he was full-grown, he was too young to live in Century Village. Fact: Allen Diamondstein was the most nervous human being I have ever seen in my entire life. Fact: His wife had left him. She had moved to Epiphany and taken a job with my father, who is the best dentist in town (fact).

Allen Diamondstein kept saying, "Isn't it ironic? My father is getting married just as I am getting divorced." This was not the greatest conversation starter in the world. No one knew what to say after he said it. Some cleared their throats and said nothing. Others cleared their throats and changed the subject.

I must have heard him say it a dozen times, and I never knew what to say either. At first I wondered if that was because I didn't know the meaning of *ironic*. So I looked it up.

The meaning that best fits (and does not use the same word in its definition) is "the contrast between what you expect to happen and what really happens." But after I looked it up, I couldn't figure out what was ironic about Allen Diamondstein's getting divorced and Izzy Diamondstein's getting married. The way Allen Diamondstein acted, I can tell you that divorce would be the only possible thing you could expect from marriage to him. And the way Izzy acted around Margaret, marriage would not only be expected, it would be necessary. *Sha! a shanda far die kinder*. They were embarrassing to watch, but not so embarrassing that I didn't.

Wedding cakes are not baked as much as they are built. In the real world, people don't build wedding cakes. They order in. If you are going to build it yourself, it is not done in a day. It takes three. On the first day, Grandma Sadie baked the layers. On the second, she constructed the cake, using cardboard bases and straws for supports, and made the basic icing to cover the layers. On the third day, she made the designer icing for the rosebuds and put the little bride and groom on top. Fact: The cake was beautiful.

Fortunately, Grandpa Nate took its picture right after she finished it, so Grandma Sadie can remember how it looked for a little while.

Allen Diamondstein would tell you that the red wagon was the problem, but I would say that it's ironic that he should say so. It definitely wasn't. He was. How else were we supposed to deliver the cake to the clubhouse? It was too tall to fit in the trunk of the car, and since on an average day the outside temperature in Century Village is body temperature, there would be a major meltdown before the cake got to the clubhouse where the wedding was to take place. That's when I got the idea to load up the wagon with ice, put a sheet of plastic over the ice, put the cake on top of that, and slowly wheel it over there, with me pulling and Grandpa checking the rear.

Grandpa Nate went to the Jiffy store and bought three bags of ice, and we loaded them into the wagon. Too much. Since we didn't want the bed of the wagon filled right up to the edge, we emptied some, dumping it out on the cement of the patio. That's where we were going to load the wagon so we wouldn't have to wheel the wagon down any steps to get it to the meeting room.

Just after we loaded the cake onto the wagon, Allen

Diamondstein came over to Grandma's. He said his father wanted him to pick up a prayer book, but I think his father sent him because he was making the groom nervous.

No one answered when he rang the front doorbell because we were all in the back loading the cake into the red wagon, so he walked around back to the patio. Unfortunately, he didn't see the wagon handle, so he tripped on it, slid on the wet concrete, fell in the puddle of melted ice and, unfortunately, toppled the wedding cake.

The little top layer was totally smashed; it fell in the same puddle as Allen, and the little bride and groom were seriously maimed.

So was Allen's ankle. Which fact I detected when he grabbed his foot and started to moan while still sitting in the puddle on the patio. Grandpa Nate called 911. Grandma Sadie returned to the kitchen to whip up a repair batch of icing. Grandpa Nate took the remains of the cake to the clubhouse, and I sat with Allen until the ambulance came. He was not good company.

The groom called to see what was taking Allen so long. I answered the phone, and I thought I would have to call 911 for him, too. "Don't panic," I said. "I'll be your best man."

I did not tell Izzy what had happened to the couple on top of the wedding cake because people get very superstitious at weddings and no one wants a wounded bride and groom sitting on top of the cake with which they are to start a happy marriage. I had seen that sort of thing often enough in the movies: A close-up of the shattered little bride and groom floating in a puddle of melted ice signifying the fate of the real bride and groom. So although I had to tell Izzy Diamondstein what had happened to Allen, I didn't say a word about the top of the wedding cake. I didn't think I could convince him that having the little bride and groom fall into a puddle was ironic.

He seemed to calm down when I volunteered to be best man, which was about the same time that we found out from the ambulance driver that Allen would be back at Century Village in time for the wedding even if he probably wouldn't be able to walk down the aisle.

As soon as the ambulance took Allen away, I ran over to Mr. Cantor's place and asked him to please, please find another orchid for the top of the cake although it would be better if he could find two since the second layer was now the top layer and was bigger. Mr. Cantor found two beautiful sprays of orchids, which Grandma Sadie artistically arranged around the new top layer.

Since I had promised to be best man, not having a tux was a problem. I couldn't fit in Allen's, not that I would have wanted to if I could. That's when Grandpa Nate called Bella Dubinsky.

In her former life, Bella had been an artist. She painted the pictures that went into the pattern books for people who sew their own clothes. In the real world I had never met anyone who sewed her own clothes, but in Century Village, I had met three. Bella had a supply of fabric paints, and within two hours, we had painted a T-shirt that looked like a tuxedo with a red bow tie. I say *we* because I helped color in the lines she drew. It's not easy filling in the lines on T-shirt material; it scrunches up under the weight of the brush, leaving skip marks. You have to go over it again and again. Fortunately, the paints dry fast, and by four o'clock, it was ready to wear.

Repaired, the wedding cake looked beautiful. If Allen had not told, no one would have guessed that those orchids didn't belong on top. But Allen told. He told everyone. He also apologized for my being best man. I didn't think that I was someone he had to apologize for. I had helped a lot, and I looked totally presentable in my tuxedo T-shirt, which was a real work of art.

Fact: Being best man is not hard. You walk down the aisle with the maid of honor. Who, in this case, was a matron of honor because she is married. I admit that having the son of the groom, Allen, as best man would have been a better match, size-wise, for the daughter of the bride even though one is married and the other divorced, but the essential fact is that I did a very good job. I stood beside the groom. Mrs. Potter stood beside the bride, and the four of us stood in front of the rabbi, and all five of us stood under the bridal canopy, which I know is called a *chupah* and which I think is spelled the way I spelled it. I didn't yawn, sneeze, or scratch any visible thing. I held the wedding ring until the rabbi nodded, and I handed it over.

I did an excellent job of being best man even though when I was under the chupah, I was under a lot of pressure trying to think of surprises for the cat's paw invitations. The idea came to me at the very moment Izzy smashed the glass and everyone yelled *mazel tov*. Even before Izzy stopped kissing the bride, I knew what I could do. (Fact: It was a very long and thorough kiss.)

It wouldn't be easy. It would mean giving up things I loved, but I had to do it.

When everyone except Allen was dancing the *hora*, I slipped out of the clubhouse and ran back to Grandma Sadie's. I took off my tuxedo T-shirt, folded it nicely, and put it in my red wagon. I found the package of Post-it notes, my calligraphy pen, and bottle of ink and after making sure that the ink was tightly closed, I put those in the wagon, too. When I returned to the wedding party, the dance was over, and everyone was sitting around looking exhausted. My moment had arrived.

I tapped a glass with a spoon as I had seen grown-ups do, and I said, "Ladies and gentlemen, will those lucky few who have the specially marked invitations, please come forward. It is time to choose your surprise gift." I saw them pick up their cat's-paw invitations and walk over to the band where I was standing beside my red wagon. "First," I said, "we have one hand-painted T-shirt, which is an original work of art done by Mrs. Bella Dubinsky. In addition, we have a calligraphy pen, almost new, and a bottle of ink, almost full. These are the perfect instruments for beautiful handwriting. We have one packet of Post-it notes, complete except for five." I swallowed hard and added, "And we have one red wagon."

Tillie Nachman, who could count precisely, said, "But that's only four gifts, and there were five cat's-paw invitations."

"Oh, yes," I said, "the fifth gift is the best gift of all."

Everyone asked at once, *Whatisit? Whatisit? Whatisit?*

I sucked in my breath until my lungs felt like twin dirigibles inside my ribs. "The best gift of all is . . . the very best . . . the very best gift of all is . . . to give up your gift."

A thick silence fell over the room. Then Tillie Nachman started clapping. Soon the others joined in, and I noticed Grandma Sadie and Grandpa Nate looking proud.

At first everyone who held a cat's-paw invitation wanted to be the one to give up his gift, but I did not want that. If they didn't take my presents, I would feel as if they didn't matter. Mr. Cantor stepped forward and took the Post-it notes. He said he could use them for labeling his plants. He said that he was donating an orchid plant as the fifth gift. Then Tillie promised calligraphy lessons to the person who took the pen and ink, and Bella promised fabric painting lessons to the person who took the tuxedo T-shirt. In that way each of my gifts kept on giving.

Four cat's-paw gifts were now taken.

Only the red wagon remained. Guess who had the fifth cat's-paw invitation?

Allen, the son of.

Allen said he didn't want the little red wagon. He said that he had no use for a wagon in the real world where he was an accountant.

When Izzy, the groom, rose from the table to make a toast, he lifted his glass of wine and said, "Margy and I want to thank all our friends in Century Village. We don't know if we can ever thank you enough for giving our life together this wonderful start. As you know, Margy and I have pooled our resources and bought a little condo on the ocean. Not exactly *on* the ocean. It is, after all, a high-rise. We will miss the community life here, but we don't want to miss our friends. We'll visit. We want you to visit us. Our welcome mat is out. Always. We leave many memories behind. And we are also leaving this little red wagon. Every time you use it, please think of this happy occasion."

Izzy started to sit down, but halfway he got up again and added, "Consider it a gift to everyone from the best man." He never said which best man he meant, but I'm pretty sure he meant me.

—

Now back in the real world, I sat at my desk and crossed every single item off the list. I didn't have the wagon, the Post-it notes, the T-shirt that Bella Dubinsky had designed, or the pen and ink that Tillie Nachman had bought me. I did have a new pad of Post-it notes and a new calligraphy pen—both of which I had bought with my own money when I got back to Epiphany.

I never had to write a B & B letter when we stayed at Disney World or Sea World. Of course, Century Village is not exactly Disney World or Sea World either. Century Village is not like any other place in Western Civilization. It is not like any other place in the entire world.

I picked up my pen and filled it *properly*, the six-step process that Tillie had taught me. She had said, "You must think of those six steps not as preparation for the beginning but as the beginning itself." I knew then that I had started my B & B. I let my pen drink up a whole plunger full of ink and then holding the pen over the bottle, I squeezed three drops back into the bottle.

And I thought—a B & B letter is giving just a few drops back to the bottle. I put away the tiny notepad and took out a full sheet of calligraphy paper and began,

Dear Grandma Sadie and Grandpa Nate,
Thank you for a vacation that was out of this world . . .

2

• • •

The contest had warmed up, and so had Mrs. Olinski. From her seat on the aisle she waited.

On her left sat Dr. Roy Clayton Rohmer, the District Superintendent for Clarion County. Both Dr. Rohmer and Mrs. Olinski paid strict attention to the commissioner, the man at the podium. There could be no mistake: This was the man of the hour, king for the day.

He wore a navy blue, precision fit pin-striped suit and a white-on-dazzling-white shirt. An edge of his French cuffs showed beneath his jacket sleeves. Mrs. Olinski was not sure how much the correct amount was, but she knew that if she put a spirit-level to his, they would be exactly right. The French cuffs were held together with onyx cuff links, and his collar was tied with a red-striped power necktie. The television lights beamed down on his crown of hair, which was tinted the color of peach pits. He was dressed, brushed, coiffed, and blow-dried not just to be seen but to be looked at.

Dr. Rohmer could not, would not take his eyes off the man at the podium, and Mrs. Olinski thought of *Alice in Wonderland*. "Don't look at me like that!" said the King to the Cheshire Cat. "A cat may look at a king," said Alice. Mrs. Olinski wanted to tell Dr. Rohmer that a cat may look at a king. But why bother? The audience was not permitted to speak.

• • •

After The Souls had won the Epiphany Middle School championship, Dr. Roy Clayton Rohmer paid a visit to Mrs. Olinski and asked—guess what?—why had she chosen this team. She still did not know (and wouldn't until after it was all over), but by that time the success of The Souls (even if she did not yet know that they were The Souls) had made Mrs. Olinski less timid.

Dr. Rohmer had announced that he had just completed a three-day workshop on multiculturalism for *ed-you-kay-toars*. Mrs. Olinski had always been amused by educators who called themselves *ed-you-kay-toars*. So, when he asked her how she had chosen the four members of her academic team, Mrs. Olinski knitted her brow and answered with hushed seriousness. "In the interest of diversity," she said, "I chose a brunette, a redhead, a blond, and a kid with hair as black as print on paper."

Dr. Rohmer was not amused. He gave Mrs. Olinski a capsule lecture on what multiculturalism really means.

"Oh," she said, "then we're still safe, Dr. Rohmer. You can tell the taxpayers that the Epiphany Middle School team has one Jew, one half-Jew, a WASP, and an Indian."

"Jews, half-Jews, and WASPs have nothing to do with

diversity, Mrs. Olinski. The Indian does. But we don't call them Indians anymore. We call them Native Americans."

"Not this one," she replied.

"Mrs. Olinski," Dr. Rohmer asked, "would you like it if people called you a cripple?"

Mrs. Olinski gave up. Everyone believed that she could be wounded by the word *cripple*. She could never explain to Dr. Rohmer, nor would she try to, that the word itself does not hurt, but the manner of its delivery can. For all of his training, Dr. Rohmer would never believe that cripples themselves are a diverse group, and some make jokes.

Nadia was the redhead of Mrs. Olinski's diverse group.

Had she been born five hundred years sooner, Raphael would have chosen her as a model for his cherubs. Tendrils of bright red hair framed her face, a spray of freckles powdered her nose, and she was as plump as a perfectly ripened peach. Raphael probably would have painted out the freckles, and that would have been a mistake. Like brushing the cinnamon off cinnamon toast.

For the first few weeks of the new school year, Nadia hardly spoke. All the sixth graders—like Mrs. Olinski herself—were new to Epiphany Middle School, but Nadia—like Mrs. Olinski herself—seemed most disconnected. Both were watchers and waiters, cautious about being friendly, about showing themselves.

Then on the middle Monday in October, Nadia Diamondstein arrived in class with a smile and addressed her teacher. "Don't you think, Mrs. Olinski, that autumn is the most glorious time of year?" Mrs. Olinski confessed that it was her favorite season and told Nadia that she sometimes felt guilty because she thought she ought to prefer spring, with its pledge to make the lilies bloom again.

Every morning thereafter, Nadia smiled as she entered class and greeted Mrs. Olinski with a word from her southern past. She said, "Hey."

Mrs. Olinski knew that Nadia Diamondstein was not only incandescently beautiful but was also a star.

• • •

The commissioner of education picked up the next question. Looking over the rims of his reading glasses, he slowly unfolded the paper. "This question has two parts," he said. "To receive credit, you must answer both parts." Lowering his eyes, he read, "What is the name given to that portion of the North Atlantic Ocean that is noted for its abundance of seaweed, and what is its importance to the ecology of our planet?"

Nadia Diamondstein rang in.

• • •

Nadia Tells of Turtle Love

My grandfather is a slim person of average height with heavy, heathery-gray eyebrows. He lives in a high-rise condominium on the beach in Florida. He lives there with his new wife whom he calls Margy. I was told to call her Margaret, not Aunt Margaret or Mrs. Diamondstein. It sounded disrespectful to me—calling a woman old enough to be my grandmother by her first name, but I did as I was told.

Last summer, just before my grandfather married Margaret, my mother and father got divorced, and Mother moved the two of us to upstate New York where she had grown up. She said that she needed some autumn in her life. I had never thought that I would see autumn in New York or anywhere else because even when we vacationed at a place that had one, we always had to return for school before it started. In Florida school starts before Labor Day. Whatever it says on the calendar, Florida has de facto summer.

Dividing up my time was part of the divorce settlement. I was to spend Thanksgiving, spring vacation, and one month over the summer with Dad. He left Christmas holidays for Mother because it is her holiday, not his. I am the product of a mixed marriage.

This first summer of their separation, Dad chose August for his visitation rights. He picked us up early Friday evening. *Us* means Ginger and me. Ginger is my dog. I do not know who was happier to see me at the airport—Dad or Ginger. The worst part of the trip had been checking Ginger into the baggage compartment.

Dad always was a nervous person, but since the divorce he had become terminally so. He was having a difficult time adjusting to being alone. He had sold the house that we lived in when we were a family and had moved into a swinging singles apartment complex, but my father could no more swing than a gate on rusty hinges.

For the first day and a half after I arrived, Dad hovered over me like the Goodyear blimp over the Orange Bowl. He did not enjoy the hovering, and I did not enjoy being hovered, but he did not know what to do with me, and I did not know what to tell him, except to tell him to stop hovering, which seemed to be the only thing he knew how to do.

On Sunday we went to see Grandpa Izzy and Margaret.

Grandpa Izzy was happy to see me. Under those bushy eyebrows of his, Grandpa Izzy's eyes are bright blue like the sudden underside of a bird wing. His eyes have always been the most alive part of him, but when Bubbe Frieda died, they seemed to die, too. Since he married Margaret though, they seem bright enough to give off light of their own. He is sixty-nine years old, and he is in love.

Margaret is a short blonde. She is very different from my bubbe but not very different from the thousands who make their home in South Florida. There are so many blond widows in the state of Florida, and they are all so much alike, they ought to have a kennel breed named and registered for them. Like all the others, Margaret dresses atrociously. She wears pastel-colored pantsuits with elastic waists or white slacks with overblouses of bright, bold prints. She carries her eyeglasses—blue-rimmed bifocals—on a gold metal chain around her neck. They all do. Margaret is not fat, but she certainly is not slim. She is thick around the middle, and when she wears her green polyester pantsuit, she looks like a Granny Smith apple. Grandpa Izzy would say Delicious.

Grandpa Izzy and Margaret are like Jack-Sprat-could-eat-no-fat and his wife-could-eat-no-lean. Grandpa Izzy says that Margaret is *zaftig,* which is Yiddish for pleasingly plump. Everything about her pleases him. He seems to find it difficult to keep himself from pinching her or pinching himself for having had the good fortune to find and marry her. Such public displays of affection can be embarrassing to a prepubescent girl like me who is not accustomed to being in the company of two married people who like each other.

On Sunday we went out for brunch at one of those mammoth places where the menu is small and the portions are large, and every senior citizen leaves with a Styrofoam box containing leftovers. We had to wait to be seated at the restaurant because Sunday brunch is a major social custom in Florida retirement communities. Dad twice asked the restaurant hostess how much longer we would have to wait. Grandpa Izzy and Margaret tried to tell Dad that they did not mind waiting since visiting with each other was part of the plan, and they did not mind doing it at the restaurant. But hovering at low altitudes seemed to be my father's new best thing.

When we were finally seated, we had a nice enough

time. Margaret had Belgian waffles and did not require a Styrofoam box for leftovers because there were none; she ate everything that was on her plate—strawberry preserves, pseudo whipped cream and all. She did not order decaf coffee but drank three cups of regular.

Margaret was not at all curious about me. I thought she would want to know how I liked our new home, which is in Epiphany, the very town she had lived in before she moved to Florida. Maybe she thought that I was not curious about her because I did not ask her about her wedding, which neither Mother nor I attended. But I believe that the grown-up should ask the questions first, and besides, Mother and I had gotten a full report on the wedding from Noah Gershom who, due to unforeseen circumstances, had been best man. I did not find Noah's account of the events surrounding his becoming best man quite as amusing as he did, but for several complicated reasons, I did not express my opinion.

One of the complications was that my mother works for Dr. Gershom, who is Noah's father. My mother is a dental hygienist by profession, and Dr. Gershom is a dentist. One of the reasons we moved to Epiphany was that Mother got a job there. My mother happens to be an excellent hygienist, and Dr. Gershom was lucky to get her, but nevertheless, I thought it best not to tell Noah Gershom that his account of my grandfather's wedding was not as amusing as he thought it was.

Dad's new apartment complex was miles away from our old neighborhood. I called two of my former friends, but getting together with them was not easy. Our schedules, which had once matched, seemed to be in different time zones now. Geography made the difference.

When we finally got together, I thought we would have fun. We did not. Either I had changed, or they had changed, or all of us had. I would not try again. I concluded that many friendships are born and maintained for purely geographical reasons. I preferred Ginger.

Work seemed to be the only thing that held Dad together, but leaving me alone that week while he went to the office made him feel guilty and ended up making him even more nervous, if such a thing were possible. I spent part of my time at the apartment complex pool, which was almost empty during the day. I read and watched talk shows and took Ginger on walks around the golf course that bordered the swinging singles complex. I enjoyed not having Dad hover over me, but I did not tell him so.

Grandpa Izzy called every day. He volunteered to come to swinging singles to pick me up after Dad left for work and after the morning rush-hour traffic. All the retirees in South Florida wait for the rush-hour traffic to be over, so that when they go out on the highways, they can create their own rush hour. But I declined. Then on Thursday, after I had had the unsatisfactory visit with my former friends, Grandpa Izzy called with a different suggestion. He asked Dad to drop me off at their place in the morning before he went to work. Margaret's grandson Ethan, who was my age, had arrived, and Grandpa Izzy thought a visit would be good for both of us. I thought he meant Ethan and me, but maybe he meant Dad and me because after he took the call, the look on my father's face was a new way to spell relief.

My only requirement was that I be allowed to bring Ginger. A lot of retirement high-rises have rules against dogs, visiting or otherwise, and I did not know Margaret's position on dogs. Grandpa Izzy said that Ginger would not be a problem. Of course, she never was. Ginger is a genius.

I did not know if I was developing an interest in boys, or if I would have washed my hair and put on my new blouse anyway. Perhaps, I was leaving prepubescence and was entering full pubescence or, perhaps, I was simply curious about Ethan. For example, why had Margaret said nothing about his coming when we had seen each other at Sunday's brunch? Margaret had mentioned having a grandson who was my age, but she said very little about him. Most grandmothers of her species carry a coffee-table-sized photo album in their tote-bag-sized pocketbooks. Either Margaret was a rare subspecies of grandmother or her grandson Ethan had done something strange to his hair. When grandmothers disapprove of grandsons, it is usually their hair. Their hair or their music. Or both. She must have known about his visit for at least two weeks because everybody I know has to buy airline tickets that far in advance to get the discount.

Grandpa Izzy's high-rise retirement condominium was three towns north of Dad's swinging singles apartment complex. The highway between them is bumper to bumper. Dad misjudged the time it would take to get there, so we did not arrive until after they had left for their morning walk. Dad gave me a key. I let myself in. There was a note on the refrigerator door saying that they had gone for their turtle walk and to make myself at home. The note was in Margaret's handwriting. No mistaking her *u*'s for *n*'s or her *i*'s for *e*'s. Margaret's handwriting was the smooth, round style used by the older generation of schoolteachers, which is exactly what Margaret was before she became an elementary school principal, which is what she was before she retired.

Ginger and I waited on the balcony and watched the three of them approach. Ethan appeared to be almost as tall as Margaret and almost as blond, but not for the same reason. From the distance of the balcony—it was the third floor—he appeared to be a healthy prepubescent. Of course, except for my father, appearances do not always tell much about a person's nervous condition.

The three of them were very excited when they returned.

Even though Ethan is Margaret's grandson, it was Grandpa who introduced me because Margaret did not. She went straight to the desk to dig a record book out of the drawer. "Ethan's lucky," Grandpa said. "Only his second day here, and this evening, we will be digging out one of our nests."

He was talking about turtle nests. Turtles had brought Grandpa and Margaret together.

The year after Bubbe Frieda had died, Grandpa Izzy sold their little house and moved to Century Village. For the next two years, early every morning, before the day got too hot, he drove to the beach where he took a walk. Many people from Century Village walked the beach where there was a sidewalk with markers for every half mile. A year ago last spring he noticed a blond zaftig woman who was returning about the same time he was leaving, so he began starting out earlier and earlier until, one day, they started out together. He introduced himself and asked her if she would like to take a walk with him. She replied by inviting him to join her on her turtle walk.

He accepted, not even knowing where or what it was.

And they have been doing it together ever since.

Margaret was checking in her record book. "We moved one hundred seven eggs," she said.

"We feel very protective of the nests we move," Grandpa explained to Ethan, who nodded as if he understood what Grandpa was talking about, leading me to believe that they had already explained turtles to him.

Sea turtles need beaches, of which Florida has many miles. All up and down the coastline, female turtles come out of the ocean and paddle their way across the sand, dig a hole, and lay eggs—about a hundred at a time. They use their flippers first to dig the hole and then to scoop the sand back over it before returning to the sea. The female will lay three to five clutches of eggs during a season, return to the water, and not come out of the water again for two or three years, when she is ready to lay again.

About fifty-five days after being laid, the eggs hatch.

From the first of May when the first eggs get laid until Halloween night when the last of them hatches, turtle patrols walk assigned stretches of beach. Members of a turtle patrol are trained to recognize the flipper marks that the mother turtles make.

About half the time the mother turtle lays her eggs in a dangerous place—where the eggs might get washed out because they are within the high tide line or where they might get trampled by people or run over by cars. Turtle eggs are a gourmet feast to birds, big fish, and especially raccoons. People approved by the Department of Environmental Protection are allowed to move the nests to safer ground. They post a stake with a sign over all the nests they find—the ones they move and the ones they do not—saying that it is against the law to disturb the nest. If you do, you can be fined up to $50,000 and/or go to jail for a year. The signs, which are bright yellow, make it very clear that it is an *and/or* situation.

Loggerheads are a threatened species. That means that they are not as seriously missing as endangered, but almost. Last year, encouraged by Grandpa Izzy, I did my science report on Florida turtles. We studied together. We accompanied Margaret on her turtle walks. (I called her Mrs. Draper then. I never guessed that only months later we would become almost related.) I got an A; Grandpa got permitted. Margaret had been permitted when they met.

I saved my report. I had begun it by asking, "Do you think it is harder to name Mr. Walter Disney's Seven Dwarfs or to name all five of the species of turtles that migrate off the coast of Florida?" My grandfather thought that was a wonderful way to begin a report. I had drawn a cover that showed all five kinds (loggerheads, greens, leatherbacks, hawksbill, and Kemp's ridley). My teacher commented on my cover, saying that it was exceptional. I saved the report because I thought I would draw a different cover—one showing a map of Florida beaches—and use it again in sixth grade when we were required to do a Florida history report. I did not know then that when I started sixth grade, I would be living in the state of divorce and New York.

Grandpa Izzy said, "Why don't you stay, Nadia? You've always enjoyed watching a nest being dug out. Ethan's coming." He looked over at Ethan, inviting him to reinforce the invitation. Ethan nodded slightly. "It'll be like old times," Grandpa said.

How could my Grandpa Izzy even begin to think that

our digging out a nest would be like old times? In old times, which were not so very long ago, I would have enjoyed—even been excited about—digging out a turtle nest. In old times Margaret would still be Mrs. Draper, and I would neither know nor care that she had a grandson Ethan.

"When will this happen?" I asked.

"After sunset, as usual," Grandpa replied, looking at me curiously, for he knew I knew.

"Oh, that is too bad," I said. "Dad is picking me up before supper, and he will be disappointed if I do not eat with him."

Grandpa said that he would call Dad at work and have him stop over so that he, too, could watch. And before I could tell them the real truth—that I would rather not attend at all—they had Dad on the telephone and everything was arranged. I was not angry, but I was seriously annoyed.

That afternoon the four of us went to the pool. I had to leave Ginger back at the apartment because dogs were not allowed at poolside. I had not brought my bathing suit, so I had to sit by the pool while the others swam. Margaret said that she was sorry that she did not have a bathing suit to lend me. "I don't think mine will fit," she said. I think she was attempting to make a joke because she smiled when she said it.

I do not know who, besides Margaret herself, any bathing suit of hers would fit. She had what the catalogs call "a mature figure," and she was not at all self-conscious about it or the starbursts of tiny blue veins on both her inner and outer thighs. Bubbe Frieda had never been *zaftig*, but she had had the good taste to wear what is called "a dressmaker bathing suit." It had a little skirt and a built-in bra. Of course, my bubbe's bathing suit never got wet, and Margaret did forty-two laps.

Ethan practiced a few dives. Grandpa coached him. Then they came and sat by me. I was curious to know if Ethan's trip had been planned long before they announced it. I asked him if he had changed planes in Atlanta. He said that he had. "On my flight out of Atlanta, there were seven unaccompanied minors," I said.

He smiled. "There were only five on mine. I guess I was a little late in the season."

"Did you have an advance reservation?" I asked.

"Yes," he replied. "Why do you ask?"

"I was just wondering," I said. I did not tell him what I was wondering about. "When you travel with a pet," I added, "you must plan in advance. The worst part of my trip was worrying about Ginger. She had to fly as baggage. We were advised to tranquilize her and put her in a dog carrier. Ginger had never been tranquilized before, and she has been dopey all week. She is just now getting back to her real self. I promised her that I will not do that again."

"How will you get her back?"

"I am going to talk to her and tell her to be quiet so that I do not have to tranquilize her."

"Maybe you just gave her too strong a dose."

"Maybe. But I do not care to experiment. She will make the trip just fine. Ginger is a genius."

"Someone has written a book about the intelligence of animals. Border collies are smartest."

"Ginger would not be listed. She is a mixed breed. Like me."

"What's your mix?"

"Half-Jewish; half-Protestant."

"That's good," he said. "Like corn. It's called hybrid vigor."

I took that as a compliment, but I did not thank him for it. "Are you a hybrid?" I asked.

"Not at all. The only claim my family has to hybridization is right there," he said, pointing to Margaret. "Grandma Draper is a thoroughbred Protestant, and Izzy is a thoroughbred Jew. But they don't plan on breeding."

I think I blushed.

Margaret was in charge of fifteen permitted volunteers. That meant that if she could not do the turtle patrol, one of them could. Permitted volunteers were licensed to move a nest or dig out a nest after the eggs had hatched, but they had to be supervised by her. All fifteen of Margaret's permitteds, plus friends and other interested parties showed up for the digging out. As soon as other beach walkers saw the hovering over the nest, they joined in. The audience was enthusiastic. They ooohed and aaahed, and at least once every three minutes, one way or another, someone said that nature was wonderful. Four people said, "Fascinating." Ethan did not oooh or aaah, and he did not say fascinating. He watched as patiently as a cameraman from *National Geographic*. My father hovered with the rest of them and said "fascinating" twice. Hovering had become his great recreational pastime.

Turtle patrols keep very close watch on all the nests on their stretches of beach, and they know when they are ripe for hatching, and sometimes they are lucky enough to be there when the turtle nests are emerging. That is what a hatching is called. When the turtles push their way out of the sand and start waddling toward the water's edge, they look like a bunch of wind-up toys escaped from Toys "R" Us. Watching a nest hatch is more interesting than digging one out after they've hatched, which is really only a matter of keeping inventory and making certain that everything that was or is living is cleared out. During old times, I had ooohed and aaahed at the digging out, but that evening it seemed as exciting as watching a red light change.

Like a proud parent, Margaret watched as Grandpa Izzy dug out the nest. Wearing a rubber glove on his hand, he reached down into the nest as far as his arm pit. He removed:

96 empty egg shells
4 unhatched whole eggs
1 dead hatchling
3 turtles that were half-in/half-out of the shell but were dead. Those are called dead-pipped.
1 turtle that was half-in/half-out of the shell but was alive. Those are called live-pipped.
2 live ones

Margaret took notes, counted again, and said at last that it all added up.

Grandpa released the two live turtles onto the sand. Everyone lined up on either side of them as they made their way to the water's edge.

Turtles almost always hatch at night, and after they do, they head toward the light. Normally, the light they head for is the horizon on the ocean. However, if a hotel or high-rise along the ocean leaves its lights on, the turtles will head toward the brighter light of civilization and never make it to the ocean. They do not find food, and they die. Turtles are not trainable animals. Their brains are in the range of mini to micro.

When the two hatchlings reached the water, everyone along the parade route applauded, and my father said fascinating for the third time.

Back at the nest, Margaret examined the live-pipped. She announced, "I've decided to keep it." Judge, jury, and defending attorney.

Dad asked what would happen to it, and Margaret explained, "It'll take a few days to straighten itself out. We'll give it a safe, cool, dark place in the utility room and release it after sunset when it's ready."

Dad could have asked me. I did get an A on that report.

When baby turtles come out of their shells, which are round—about the same size as a golf ball—they are squinched up into a round shape that fits inside the eggs. After they break through the shell, they spend three days down in the sand hole straightening themselves out. Sometimes they die before they make it out of the shell. Those are the dead-pipped. They are counted and discarded with the unhatched and the empties. A permitted person has to decide if the live-pipped are more alive than dead. If the decision is that they stand a good chance of surviving, they need care. They are lifted from the nest and taken home and given shelter until they straighten themselves out, and then they are released onto the sand.

"We never carry them to the water," Margaret explained. "They must walk across their native sand. We think that something registers in their brains that kicks in twenty-five years later because they return to the beach where they were born to lay their eggs."

As Margaret was explaining this, I thought about my mother's returning to New York. Her birthday is September 12, and I wondered if her need to return to autumn in New York had anything to do with some switch that had been turned on when she emerged.

Back at the condo, Grandpa carried the bucket containing the live-pipped into the utility room, and we all sat down to have milk and cookies. Oreos. Bubbe would have had homemade ruggelach. Margaret did not even know what ruggelach were until Grandpa Izzy took her to a kosher delicatessen and introduced her to them. She already knew about bagels because bagels have become popular even in places that never heard of them.

Margaret liked ruggelach, but I could tell she had no intention of learning how to make them. Grandpa Izzy, who had enjoyed ruggelach and bobka as much as anyone, had adjusted to Entenmann's and Oreos. I asked Ethan if he knew ruggelach. He did not. Knowing ruggelach is a hybrid advantage.

Before the evening was over, Grandpa Izzy suggested that Dad bring me back early enough so that I could take the morning turtle walk with him and Margaret and Ethan.

Then Margaret said, "Allen, why don't you come, too? The exercise will be good for your foot." Dad had broken his foot on the day of their wedding, and it had not yet healed. Margaret believed that a bad mental attitude had slowed it down. Much to my surprise, Dad agreed. "What about Ginger?" I asked.

"No problem," Grandpa Izzy said. "Just keep her on a leash like old times."

I started to say that Ginger has grown to hate the leash, but once again a look on Dad's face told me something, and I said nothing. So it was from a look of Dad's and a sentence left unspoken that the sequel to the turtle habit got started.

Dad and I would leave his apartment early, meet Margaret, Grandpa, and Ethan on the beach, and do our walk. Then Dad would return to Grandpa's and change into his business suit and leave for work. If time permitted, Dad would join us for breakfast. If not, the four of us would eat without him. We usually watched the rest of the *Today Show* before going for a swim.

Grandpa and Ethan got into an unofficial contest about how many laps they could do. I did not participate. I took a short swim, got out of the water, sat on the sidelines and read while Grandpa was teaching Ethan how to dive. He wanted to teach me, too, but I preferred not to.

One afternoon, we went to the movies. It was blazing hot and bright outside. We went into the movies where it was cool and dark, and then we came back out into the bright, hot sun. I felt as if I had sliced my afternoon into thirds, like a ribbon sandwich. Ethan, who never said much, had a lot to say about the camera angles and background music and described the star's performance as subtle. Never before in all my life had I heard a boy use the word subtle.

Dad had tickets for *The Phantom of the Opera.* This was the real Broadway show except that it was the road company. Not knowing that Ethan would be visiting, he had bought only four. As soon as he found out that Ethan would be in town, he started calling the ticket office to buy one more, but there were none to be had. He kindly volunteered to give up his ticket, but Grandpa Izzy and Margaret would not hear of it. Margaret said that she would stay home, and Grandpa Izzy said that he didn't want to go if she didn't.

I expected Ethan to do the polite thing and say that he would stay home. But he did not. Of course, Ethan usually said nothing. Even when it was appropriate to say something, Ethan could be counted on to say nothing. But on the subject of who should give up a ticket, Ethan was particularly silent, which was a subtle hint that he really wanted to go. At the very last minute, the problem was solved. One of Dad's clients mentioned that he had an extra ticket, and Dad bought it from him on the spot.

We met at the theater. Ethan had insisted upon taking the odd seat, saying that he would be fine. The odd seat was three rows in front of ours and closer to the center of the stage, but I do not think Ethan knew it at the time. I think he wanted to be alone, or, I should say, without us. At intermission, Ethan bought one of the ten-dollar souvenir programs, and after the show he thanked my father at least five times for getting him a ticket.

Dad was pleased with the way the evening had turned out. We went to the Rascal House for ice-cream sundaes after the show. Ethan could hardly keep himself from thumbing through his ten-dollar program. His head must have stayed back at the theater long after we left, for when the waitress asked for his order, he said, "They must have more trapdoors on that stage than a magic act."

My father actually hummed as he looked over the menu, and then right after we placed our orders, he dropped his bombshell.

He asked Margaret if he could be listed on her permit. He would like to be able to substitute for her or Grandpa Izzy. His apartment house was not far from a beach, he explained, and he would transfer to someone's permit there after I went back north. Then he would like to train so that he could head up a turtle patrol. His goal was to get licensed.

"Like father, like son," he said, patting Grandpa Izzy on the back.

Margaret said, "We'll get the process started tomorrow." She must have been quite proud of her loggerheads. They got her my grandpa, and now they got her my dad.

I did not care. I had Ginger. I preferred animals with fur and some measure of intelligence. Ginger had grown sleek and muscular with our long turtle walks. She was more affectionate than ever. For example, when we got back to the apartment after *The Phantom of the Opera*, she greeted me as if I were the best friend she had ever had.

Inside me there was a lot of best friendship that no one but Ginger was using.

The day after Dad dropped his bombshell, he and Ethan, Margaret and Grandpa walked the beach together, a tight, three-generation foursome. They got ahead of Ginger and me, and I made no effort to catch up. Instead, I slowed down and walked at the water's edge so that I could kick at the waves as they rolled ashore. Ginger and I fell farther and farther behind the others. I saw Ethan stop to wait for Ginger and me to catch up. He did not call to us, and I pretended that I did not notice. Ethan waited until Ginger and I were midway between Grandpa, Dad, and Margaret—until we were half-pipped—and then I slowed down even more. Dad stopped, called to Ethan—not to me —to catch up. Ethan looked toward Ginger and me, then toward Grandpa and Margaret, waited another second or two, and then walked fast-forward until he caught up with Dad, Grandpa, and Margaret.

On Tuesday evening we watched a nest hatch. It was one of theirs. "Theirs" means that it was one that Margaret had moved. Like the one on the first night of our turtle walks, this one also contained a hundred and seven eggs, but this time all one hundred seven turtles emerged. "One hundred percent," Grandpa cried, and he hugged Margaret. Then he congratulated Ethan and Dad. Ginger and I stayed on the fringe because I had to hold Ginger on a short leash so that she would not start chasing the baby turtles. Grandpa did not hug or congratulate me.

We all returned to Grandpa's apartment, and Dad insisted on taking us all out to the Dairy Queen to celebrate. Margaret ate a whole Peanut Buster Parfait without once mentioning cholesterol or calories.

I was sitting at poolside, reading. After doing our turtle walk, Margaret had gone to her volunteer duties at the garden club, and Grandpa Izzy had gone to his at the public library. Ethan and I were to let ourselves into their condo and start lunch. Ethan finished his laps and came out of the water. He sat at the deep end with his legs dangling into the water. I joined him at the pool's edge and put my feet into the water, too. I noticed that he had his key on an elastic cord around his ankle, and I also noticed that he had a key chain ornament that looked like a giant molar. As the daughter of a dental hygienist, I was interested in his key chain ornament and asked him where he got it.

"From your mother," he said.

I was not prepared for his answer. "My mother?" I asked in a voice that was too loud even for the out-of-doors.

"Well, yes. Your mother works for Dr. Gershom, doesn't she?"

"As a matter of fact, she does."

"She cleaned my teeth," he said.

There is not a worse feeling in this world than the feeling that someone knows something about you that he has known for almost a whole summer and has kept to himself. Even sharing what he knows about you with others is not as bad as knowing something and not telling you he knows. All you can think about is what he was really thinking the whole time he was speaking to you or walking the beach with you or swimming laps or playing fetch with your dog Ginger. I felt as if I had been spied on. I felt as if I had been stalked.

My heart was pumping gallons of blood up to my face. I could feel my neck throb. I controlled my voice so that it would not quiver. I said, "You should have told me that. You should have told me long before now. A person with good manners would have."

Ethan said, "I didn't think it was important."

I caught my breath and asked an intermediate question, "Does your mother also know Dr. Gershom?"

"He's our family dentist."

"And Margaret? Does she also know him?"

"I told you. He is our family dentist. Grandma Draper is part of our family. Before she moved to Florida, he was her dentist, too."

"Do not adopt that tone with me, Ethan Potter."

"What tone?"

"The tone of being patient and tolerant as if the questions I am asking are dumb questions. They are not dumb questions. I need to know what you know that I do not."

"I don't know what you don't know, so how can I know what I know and you don't?"

"Now, that is a dumb question. That is really a very stupid question."

"I don't think so."

"Just tell me what you knew about my mother and me and my father before we met."

"Okay. I'll tell you what I knew about you if you'll tell me what you knew about me."

"All right. You go first."

"When your mother said that she was divorcing your father and wanted to move to New York where she grew up, my grandmother set things up with Dr. Gershom."

"Margaret set what things up?"

"The job interview."

"Mother's job interview with Dr. Gershom?"

"I thought that was what we were talking about—your mother's job with Dr. Gershom."

"We are talking about what you know that I do not."

"And I am trying to tell you. Your mother told Izzy and Grandma Draper that she wanted to move to New York State, so Grandma set up a job interview with Dr. Gershom."

I had stayed in Florida with Dad while Mother had gone north to find a job and a house. No one—not Dad, not Mother, not Grandpa Izzy—no one had told me that Margaret had set up Mother's job interview with Dr. Gershom. Margaret could have. The others should have. No one seemed to think that it would matter to me where I lived. No one seemed to think that it would matter to me whether I spent my life in New York or Florida or commuting between the two.

My throat was dry. I took a deep breath of the chlorine-saturated pool air and asked, "Is there anything else you know about me that I don't know?"

Ethan shrugged. "Only that Noah was best man at Grandma and Izzy's wedding."

"The whole world knows that. I am asking you one last time. What do you know about me that I do not know you know?"

"Not much. Only that Noah never said what nice guys your dad and Izzy are."

"That is what you do not know. I was asking you what you do know." The pulse in my neck was about to break through the skin.

"I do know that you're pretty mad right now, and I think now you ought to tell me what you knew about me."

"Nothing."

"My grandma told you nothing about me?"

"That is correct. She said nothing about you. She did not even tell me that you were coming even though she had several opportunities to do so."

Ethan then asked a strange question. "Did she tell you anything about Luke?"

"Luke what? Luke warm?"

"My brother Lucas, called Luke. Did she tell you anything about him?"

"She did not."

Ethan smiled, more to himself than to me. "Well," he said, "we Potters make an art of silence."

"Your grandmother is a Draper."

"See?" he said, grinning. "It comes to me from both sides of my family."

I did not speak to him for the rest of the day, and when he left the pool to return to the condo for lunch, I did not go with him. I thought that it would do him good to know how it felt to be the recipient rather than the giver of silence.

It was obvious that it was Margaret who had made possible my mother's leaving my father. Margaret Diamondstein, formerly Draper, helped my mother move to New York. She moved turtles from one nest to another. She moved Grandpa Izzy out of Century Village. And now, she was helping my father get permitted. By next turtle season, she will be helping him move to the beach. Margaret Diamondstein, formerly Draper, was an interfering person.

I did not need Margaret interfering with my life. I would have nothing more to do with her. That meant no more walking on the beach. That meant no more swimming and breakfast. That meant no more turtle walks.

Never again a turtle walk. Never.

I would stop and never tell her why.

Never.

I was still at the pool when Dad came to pick me up. I went back to the condo while they all went down to the beach to check on a nest. After I showered and dressed, I watched from the balcony, staying back by the wall where I could not be seen. Ginger whimpered to let me know that she wanted to be down there, but I thought that at the very least, my dog ought to stay by—and on—my side.

I wanted to leave my father's house. I wanted to go home, to autumn.

That evening as we were driving back to swinging singles, I asked my father if he knew that Margaret had set up Mother's job interview.

"I did."

"I think you could have told me."

"I didn't think it was important."

"Why does everyone think they know what is important to me? This was important. This *is* important. Do you think it is right that you should know and Ethan should know, and I should not?"

All he said was, "I didn't know that Ethan knew." I waited for Dad to say something more, to apologize, or simply tell me that I was right, but he did not. Like Ethan, my father has a strong taste for silence. Mother always said, "Your father is not a communicator." She made that statement more than once. Sometimes more than once a day. I was glad that I had made the decision not to go on any more turtle walks and not to communicate with anyone about my decision.

The following morning when Dad knocked on my door, I was still undressed. He called through the closed door, "Better hurry. We'll be late." I said nothing. He opened the door a crack and said, "Nadia? Nadia, are you all right?"

"I am not going," I said.

"What's the matter? Don't you feel well?"

"I feel fine. I have decided to stay here."

"Why?"

"It is not important."

Dad waited by the door, waited for me to explain, but I said nothing. I wanted silence to make him as miserable as it had made me. He hesitated, then came into my room, sat on the edge of the bed, and said nothing. He hovered. I struggled with silence until I could not stand it another second, so I said, "Did you know that I did a report on turtles last year?"

"Yes. I knew that."

"You never seemed very interested in turtles when I did my report."

"I guess I had other things on my mind."

The pulse in my ears was so strong, I hardly heard him. "I guess it took an invitation from Margaret to get you interested."

"Partly that and partly that I had the time."

"Your child custody time," I said. Dad let out a long sigh and looked so embarrassed that I almost did not say what I was about to say, but I did. "I have decided not to spend your child custody time on turtle walks with Margaret and her grandson. Not today. Not tomorrow. Not ever. If you want to take turtle walks, you go ahead and take turtle walks. You can get permitted without me. All you need are turtles and Margaret." I had not only broken my silence, I was almost screaming.

Dad looked at his watch. If there is one thing I really detest, it is having someone look at his watch as he is talking to me. It says to me that time spent elsewhere is more important than time spent talking to me. "I have an appointment at the office in an hour." He glanced at his watch again.

"I am sure it is an important appointment," I said.

"Yes, it is," he replied.

Dad was so preoccupied with time that he did not even notice the sarcasm in my voice.

"Let me call Margaret to let her know we won't be there."

"You can go," I said. "You go. I would not want you to miss a turtle walk for my sake. It might interfere with your getting permitted."

"There's no way I can make it up there and back in time for my appointment."

"Are you trying to tell me that I have kept you from your turtle walk?"

"Well, no. But, yes." He looked confused. "What I meant to say is that, yes, this conversation has kept me from going on a turtle walk, but no, that is not what I am trying to tell you. You know that if it had not been for your unwillingness to go, I would have."

He glanced at his watch again. "Let me call Margaret. Then we'll have time for breakfast, and we'll talk about it." He started out the door, turned back and said, "I won't tell her why you're not coming."

"Tell her. I do not care. She knows every other thing about me. Tell her," I said. "And do not count on me for breakfast. I do not want any." I turned my back to him and my face to the pillow.

The telephone rang in the middle of the morning. I let the recorder get it. It was Margaret, telling me that she would come pick me up if I would call. I did not. Instead, I took Ginger for a walk around the golf course that borders swinging singles. When we returned, I saw that there was a message on the machine. I played it. It was Grandpa Izzy asking me to please call. I erased the message. I sat out by the pool for a while and read, came back to the apartment for lunch, and that is when I ate the breakfast cereal that my dad had put out on the counter in the kitchen. He called while I was eating. I did not pick the phone up then either.

After lunch, I took Ginger for another walk, called the airline to see how much it would cost if I changed my ticket to go home early. Thirty-five dollars. I watched three talk shows on television. One was about teenagers whose mothers flirt with their boyfriends. They were pathetic. Another was about men who said they lost their jobs because they refused to cut off their ponytails. They were pathetic. The third was about people who pierce weird body parts: One girl had a silver nail run through her bellybutton, and another one had a diamond stud put in her tongue. One exposed her bellybutton, and the other stuck out her tongue. They were disgusting. The phone rang twice. It was my dad again, sounding worried that I was not answering. Then it was Margaret again, saying that she hoped we would come over since another nest was due to hatch.

I erased all the messages.

Not answering the phone but hearing what people on the other end were saying was a little bit like spying. I enjoyed it.

Dad walked into the apartment looking frazzled. He was looking very much like the unstrung self who had picked me up from the airport. "Where were you?" he demanded. "I have been calling every twenty minutes."

"I noticed," I said. When he asked me why I had not returned his calls, I said that I did not think they were important.

"I'm taking tomorrow off," he said.

"What are you going to do?" I asked. "Hover?"

"What do you mean?"

"Nothing." *Nothing* is a mean answer, but sometimes nothing works. Sometimes nothing else does.

"I thought we might go up to Disney World. You used to like Epcot."

"What will I do with Ginger?" I asked.

"Well, let me find out what accommodations they have for dogs. . . ."

Just then the phone rang. Dad picked it up. I could tell by the way he was speaking that it was Grandpa Izzy asking if he would be coming over for the evening's turtle walk. When he hung up, Dad asked me if I would like to invite Ethan to come to Disney World with us. I could not believe he was asking me that question. I just stared at him.

"Well," he said, "he seemed to enjoy *The Phantom of the Opera* so much, I thought he might enjoy . . ." I continued to stare at my father and say nothing. He cleared his throat. "If you don't like the idea of asking Ethan, would you like to ask one of your friends from the old neighborhood?" He was practically pleading with me to ask someone. Without turtles my father did not know what to do with me.

Even though Disney World was only a two hours' drive from his apartment, Dad had decided that it might be more fun if we stayed overnight at one of Disney's theme hotels. He called and got us reservations, and we went to our rooms to pack our overnight bags.

That evening a northeaster hit the coast. The winds were thirty-five miles an hour with gales up to fifty. There was coastal flooding, which meant that the low lying highways and many side roads and ramps would be closed. That meant that the interstates that were normally bumper to bumper but moving would be bumper to bumper and not moving. Before we went to bed, Dad suggested that we avoid rush hour by starting out late in the morning instead of early.

The phone rang at midnight. Dad called in to me and said that I should pick up the phone. It was Grandpa Izzy.

"It's an emergency," he said, pleading. "Our hatchlings will be swept ashore by the winds. We have to harvest them early tomorrow before daylight. Before the birds get them. Margaret and I think you ought to drive up here now so that we can get an early start. Traffic will be impossible in the morning."

Grandpa was so sincere, so concerned about the turtles, so convinced that we would answer his 911 that it was obvious Dad had never told him that I had canceled all future turtle walks. I waited to see how Dad would turn him down. Dad did his best thing; he remained silent.

Grandpa said, "Nadia, are you there? Are you on the line, darling?"

"I am here, Grandpa. . . ."

"You know what will happen if we don't gather them up. Can't you come?"

"Dad and I had plans . . ."

"What plans, darling? You don't want the baby turtles to be blown ashore and die, do you? These are babies, Nadia. They need help."

"Dad and I were going to Epcot . . ."

"Why do you want to go there to see Mr. Walter Disney's Version of the World when you can see Mother Nature's real thing?" I had to smile. Grandpa Izzy always called Disney World *Mr. Walter Disney's Version of the World*. Then he said, "Margaret and I need your help, Nadia. So do the turtles. Sometimes one species has to help another get settled." Grandpa was apologizing for not telling me about Margaret's meddling. I did not know what to say.

Dad finally spoke up, "Let Mother Nature worry about the turtles. They can take care of themselves."

But I knew that they could not. I said, "Let me talk to Dad, Grandpa. I will call you back."

After I hung up, I went into the living room. Dad was in his pajamas. Striped. I had never seen Dad sitting in the living room in striped pajamas. He said, "Don't worry about the turtles, Nadia."

I explained, "The turtles will be easy to spot—so out of place, washed up on shore. The birds will eat them."

"They couldn't possibly eat them all."

"Those that do not get eaten will be lost."

"But, surely, the tide will come back and carry the seaweed—and the turtles along with it—back out." He smiled again. "What comes ashore always washes back out. That's not a philosophical statement, Nadia. It's a fact."

"They will be lost at sea."

"Lost at sea? The sea is their home."

"They will be lost at sea," I repeated.

"Nadia," Dad said, "how can that happen?"

"You have to understand turtles to understand how that will happen."

"I don't think I do."

"I told Grandpa I would talk to you."

My father sat on the sofa, looking out of place in his striped pajamas. He nodded, a slow, thoughtful nod, and I knew that he would pay close attention, and I knew that I could explain it all.

"It all starts," I said, "the minute the new hatchlings scamper over the sand toward the light of the horizon. Once they reach the water, they begin a swimming frenzy. They do not eat. They just swim and swim until they reach the Sargasso Sea. That is when they stop, and that is when

Mother Nature turns off the swimming-frenzy switch and turns on a graze-and-grow switch. For the next five to ten years, they will stay in the Sargasso Sea, feeding off the small sea animals that live in the floating mats of sargasso grass. Tonight when the wind blows that seaweed ashore, there will be a lot of immature turtles in it—swept along with the sea grass they have called home."

I paused in my narrative. I focused hard on Dad, and he focused hard on me. "Are you with me?" I asked. My father nodded, so I continued. "Here is the tragic part. Even if the tide does wash them back into the water, they will not be able to get back home because once the swimming-frenzy switch is turned off, it is turned off forever. Turtles do not have an emergency power pack or a safety switch to turn it on. So, there they are, once again at the water's edge, but this time they are without a mechanism for swimming east. And that is why they will be lost at sea. They will want to graze. They will have an appetite, but they will not be where they can satisfy it, and they will not know how to get there because they cannot turn back their internal clock. They will not find home. They will not find food. They will starve and grow weak and be eaten."

My father did not once look at his watch or the clock on the table by the sofa. His listen-and-learn switch had been turned on, and his own internal clock was ticking. I studied my father, sitting on the pale gray living room sofa in his blue striped pajamas. The storm in our private lives had picked him up and put him out of place. Me, too. I, too, had been picked up from one place and set down in another. I, too, had been stranded. We both needed help resettling.

"When Grandpa says that we must harvest the turtles, he means that we must gather them up and save them in buckets. Then we take them to Marineland. When the seas calm down, they will be taken fifty miles offshore and placed in the Sargasso Sea."

Dad smiled. "They need a lift."

Ginger rubbed herself against my legs. I stroked her back. "Yes," I said, "they do."

Without another word, we returned to our rooms, Dad and I. We got dressed. When we ran out to the car, the rain was coming down in sheets, and the wind was blowing so hard that umbrellas were useless. I held the back door open for Ginger, and she hopped in. Dad and I got pretty wet just from that short run to the car, and Ginger sat on the back seat, panting and smelling like the great wet dog she was.

The rain battered the car, and the wipers danced back and forth, never really clearing the windshield. There were only a few cars on the road. We didn't pass any of them not only because it was dangerous to do so but also because we welcomed their red tail lights as a guide. Cars coming the other way made spray that splashed over the hood. Dad's hands were clenched on the steering wheel.

These northeasters dump rain in squalls that last for miles, and then they let up briefly. During one of the few lulls in the storm, Dad leaned back slightly and asked, "What do the turtles do after they've finished their five to ten years in the Sargasso Sea?"

"They go to the Azores and become bottom feeders for a few years."

"And then?"

"And then they grow up. When they are about twenty-five, they mate. The females come ashore and lay their eggs—on the same shore where they were born—and immediately return to the sea, not coming ashore again for two or maybe three years when they are again ready to lay eggs. The males never return to shore."

Dad said, "You've left something out, Nadia. They are ten when they leave the Sargasso Sea, and they are twenty-five when they mate and lay eggs. What happens during the fifteen years between leaving the Azores and mating?"

Realization hit me. I laughed out loud. We were riding into a squall again, and Dad was concentrating so hard on driving that I was not sure he was even waiting for my answer. "What is it?" he asked.

"Another switch," I said.

He took his eyes off the road long enough to demand, "Tell me, what do they do?"

"In the years between leaving their second home and their return to their native beaches, they commute. Year after year, all up and down the Atlantic, turtles swim north in the summer and south in the winter. Did you already know that?"

"I didn't know for sure, but I had my suspicions."

I had to smile. "And did you have your suspicions about me?"

"For a while," he said. Then he took his eyes off the road long enough to return my smile. "But not now."

"Of course," I said, "I will be doing the same but opposite. I will commute north in the winter and south in the summer."

"Yep," he said. "And there will be times when you or I will need a lift between switches."

"Yes," I replied, "there will be times."

3

Mrs. Olinski's very first teaching job had been in an elementary school whose principal required sixth graders to memorize at least fourteen lines of poetry each month, insisted that fifth graders know their multiplication tables up through twelve times twelve, and permitted no one to exchange valentines unless the names on the envelopes were written neatly and spelled correctly. There was no graffiti on the walls; no gum chewing, running, or shoving in the halls. There was locker inspection once a month, and everyone who used the bathroom, flushed.

That principal's name was Margaret Draper.

Two years before Margaret Draper retired, the district reorganized its school system and sent sixth graders to middle school instead of elementary. Sixth had once been the top grade in elementary school, and was now the bottom grade in middle school. But it was still the place where kids had mastered enough skills to be able to do something with them. It was still the place where kids could add, subtract, multiply and divide, and read. Mostly, they could read—really read. Sixth grade still meant that kids could begin to get inside the print and to the meaning.

Mrs. Margaret Draper, who had never called herself an

ed-you-kay-toar, had always been a superb teacher and principal, but between the time she had started as an elementary school teacher and the time she had retired as a middle school principal, sixth grade had changed, but sixth graders had changed more. Sixth graders had stopped asking "Now what?" and had started asking "So what?" She had not been sorry to retire when she did.

That very first summer after Margaret Draper retired was when Eva Marie Olinski left teaching. That was the summer of her automobile accident. For all the many months following the accident, Mrs. Draper stayed in touch with the young Mrs. Olinski. They were both widows now, and they saw each other on a regular basis.

After Margaret moved to Florida they continued to stay in touch in a Christmas card/life-milestone way. So Mrs. Olinski knew the major facts of Margy's life. Her move to Century Village, her marriage to Izzy Diamondstein, her trips, her turtles.

Mrs. Olinski also knew that Ethan Potter was Margaret Draper's grandson even though Margy never had much to say about him. When Eva Marie saw that Ethan Potter was assigned to her homeroom, she refrained from asking Margy about him or Ethan about her. She wanted to discover Ethan all by herself, so she watched him closely. Probably more closely than she watched the others.

Ethan was smart, yes; he had a certain independence of mind, yes, and he still asked "Now what?" instead of "So what?"

When Mrs. Olinski decided that Ethan should be a member of her team, she did not tell Margy or, for that matter, anyone else either.

• • •

The commissioner of education of the state of New York smiled as he read the next question. "The following places in New York State are associated with women famous in American history. I shall name the place; you are required to tell me why it is important and name the woman associated with that place. You may choose three of the four places. If you answer all four, you will receive an extra two-point credit. If you choose to answer only three, the other team will have an opportunity to answer the fourth, and if correct, will receive one point.

"The place names are: Seneca Falls, Homer, Rochester, and Auburn."

Ethan rang in as the last syllable sounded.

Yes.

Ethan Potter would know all four parts.

Yes, yes, yes, and yes.

• • •

Ethan Explains the B and B Inn

I am always the longest rider. I live farther from school than anyone else on my route. I board the bus first and get off last. I always have. The bus ride is the worst part of the school day. It always has been. Going is bad; coming home is worse.

On the first day of the new school year, I boarded the bus as usual, nodded to Mrs. Korshak, the driver, and walked to the back of the bus. All the way to the back. It was an unwritten rule that the seat you chose the first day became your assignment—unless you were so unruly that Mrs. Korshak made you change. I chose the last double seat on the side opposite the driver. I placed my backpack on the seat next to me, and as nonchalantly as I could, placed my leg over that. If luck held—as it had for the past two years—when the other kids boarded, they would choose seats that appeared to be less occupied, and I would not have to share my seat for the rest of the school year.

I knew every stop along the route. I knew every house, every tree and shrub, every pothole in the road. My father is proud of the fact that there have been Potters in Clarion County since before Epiphany was a town.

There is a fuzzy, faded picture of my great-great-great-grandmother in the Clarion County Museum. The museum is located in the main room of an old schoolhouse that the local historical society saved from the wrecker's ball by having it declared an historical landmark. My ancestor is marching behind Susan B. Anthony who is leading a group to the polls in Rochester. In the picture, my ancestor is wearing bloomers, which was what they called the trousers that were invented by Amelia Jenks Bloomer of Homer, New York, and suffragette is what they called the women who were fighting for a woman's right to vote. Instead of getting to vote, my triple-great-grandmother got arrested.

There is no picture of her at the first convention for women's rights, but she was there. In the family archive, which my Grandmother Draper passed on to my mother when she moved to Florida, there is a letter from her, postmarked Seneca Falls and dated 1848.

There have been farmers and educators on both sides of my family ever since there have been tractors and blackboards, and there have been strong women on my mother's side for just as long.

Last August when I was visiting my grandmother Draper in Florida, notice came that my homeroom teacher for grade six would be Mrs. Olinski. Unless she proved to be someone who had changed her name because of marriage or some other legal procedure, she would be new to Epiphany Middle School. I hoped she was. Having a teacher who didn't know I had an older brother would be a welcome change.

There is nothing wrong with Lucas, and that is what is wrong with him. He is a genius, a star athlete, and is always doing something wonderful and/or record setting. Half the population of Epiphany is convinced that Luke Potter will become so famous that his name will become a noun like Kleenex or Coke. The other half is convinced that Luke Potter will become a verb like Xerox or fax. And if someday, someone says, "*Luke* me that information, please," that information will be organized, memorized, and set to music.

Luke is six years older than I. He is in college now, but that has not put an end to his reputation. He has become a myth like Paul Bunyan or Davy Crockett. Because my name is Potter but not Lucas, I have been a disappointment to every one of my teachers during my previous six years—kindergarten counts.

The bus swung through the winding streets of The Farm, the subdivision that was made out of the Sillington place. The last of the Sillington sisters died and left their land to Clarion College. The college didn't want a farm, so it sold all the surrounding land to a developer who put in roads, sidewalks, and sewers, divided it up into lots, and sold it to builders. Every subdivision has a name. They named this one The Farm. It is no more a farm than the Aquarium at Epcot is the Atlantic.

None of the historical residents of Epiphany liked the idea of having the Sillington place parceled off for a subdivision. My parents, for example, hated it. My mother says that if people want to live in a place where every tree and shrub is put in place by a landscape architect, why don't they go live in a theme park? Mother avoids the subdivision as if it were a toxic waste dump. She refers to the people who live in The Farm as *them*. In her mind, there is a big difference between *them* and *us*, between living *on* a farm and living *in* The Farm. To *them* farming is a lifestyle not a livelihood. The fact that milk comes from cows has probably occurred to *them*, but *they* prefer to think of it as recycled grass.

The way I see it, the difference between farmers and suburbanites is the difference in the way we feel about dirt. To *them*, the earth is something to be respected and preserved, but dirt gets no respect. A farmer likes dirt. Suburbanites like to get rid of it. Dirt is the working layer of earth, and dealing with dirt is as much a part of farm life as dealing with manure: Neither is user-friendly but both are necessary.

When the bus picked up the last passengers from the last stop in The Farm, I lifted my leg off my backpack. My foot had fallen asleep, and it felt heavy as I lowered it. I rested it on the floor and allowed the pinpricks of blood to tease their way back up my leg. I shook my leg a little—not wanting to draw attention to myself—and turned my back to the aisle and gazed out the window. I am very good at gazing. I am also very good at listening. Gazing and listening are all right for church, but they sure kill a lot of conversations.

Instead of making its way back to the state road that parallels the lake, the bus took a left turn and started down Gramercy Road, the road that borders The Farm and the last within the two-mile radius that allows free bus transportation. Was I the only one who noticed that the bus was making an unscheduled stop? The only house there is the Sillington place. No one lives there. The house, which was given to the college along with the farm, was in a state of disrepair, and the college wanted to tear it down, but since it was the oldest farmhouse in Clarion County, it was saved by that same group that saved the schoolhouse. It is a huge old farmhouse that has had so many add-ons it looks like a cluster of second thoughts. About a hundred years ago, someone added a wraparound porch with enough gingerbread trim to look like a lace collar. The main feature of the first floor is the dining room, which stretches from the front of the house to the back because in the days when the Sillington place was a working farm, Mrs. Sillington used to feed all the itinerant farmhands breakfast and supper. They ate at long trestle tables that stretched the length of the room. There is a picture in the museum. When the Sillingtons first settled in Clarion County, before there was a state road parallel to the lake, they owned all the land down to the water's edge. The house itself is perched atop a knoll, and from the upstairs windows you get a good view of the lake.

I continued to stare out the window as the bus rolled down Gramercy Road. The Sillington house came into view. Standing at the edge of the drive was a man and a kid. The man was wearing a long navy blue apron and a white turban. A turban. A white turban. Like an illustration from *The Arabian Nights*. Equally strange: The kid was wearing shorts and knee socks. No one in Epiphany wears shorts on the first day of school. Even if it is ninety-five degrees in the shade—and sometimes it is—no one wears shorts on the first day of school. And no one—ever—wears knee socks with shorts. No one. Ever.

The kid was holding a leather book bag. Ever since backpacks were invented, no one—ever—in the entire school system, grades K through twelve, carries a book bag, especially a leather one.

The kid boarded the bus, the dark man wearing the long apron waved, and the kid stopped at the top of the steps and waved back. Even first graders on the first day of school don't do that.

The kid started making his way to the back of the bus.

Before I could resume my seat-occupied sprawl, the kid was standing in the aisle next to my seat.

"Is this seat occupied?" he asked.

No one ever asks. They just stand in the aisle until you move and make room for them. Even if he had asked if the seat was *taken* instead of asking if it was *occupied*, I could have told that he had a British accent. He didn't look British. His skin was the color of strong coffee with skim milk—not cream—added; the undertones were decidedly gray. His lips were the color of a day-old bruise. He had more hair than you would think a single skull could hold. His hair—blue-black, thick and straight—did not have the hard sheen of the hair of a Chinese or Japanese but had the soft look of fabric.

"Julian Singh," he said, extending his hand. No one (a) introduces himself and then (b) extends his hand to be shaken while (c) wearing shorts and (d) knee socks and (e) holding a genuine leather book bag on (f) the first day of school.

I extended my hand. "Ethan Potter," I said. I did not smile. How could I? For a single moment of neglect, I would be stuck with having this kid as a bus partner for the rest of the school year.

I didn't want to set up any expectations. I wanted to ignore Julian Singh for the rest of the ride, and I managed to say nothing until the bus had turned left off Gramercy and was back on Highway 32, but then curiosity got the best of me. "Did you buy the Sillington house?" I asked.

"Yes," Julian replied. "The purchase was completed several weeks ago. There were quite a few delays in arranging the permits."

"Permits?" I asked.

"Yes. Permits. Father is converting Sillington House into a B and B."

"A *B and B*?"

"Yes. A bed and breakfast inn. Rather like a small hotel. Except we will not be responsible for dinners, and thus we will support only a limited menu. Actually, the kitchen in Sillington House is quite remarkable. It is as large as many full-service restaurant kitchens. We must make Sillington House handicap accessible before we are ready for occupancy. Mrs. Gershom was most helpful in getting permits for the conversion."

"I'll bet she was," I said. "Is your father a cook?"

"Yes." Julian smiled. "A chef. He was chef on board the *Skylark*, the cruise ship. Father decided that we needed to settle down. He has always wanted to own an inn, so he purchased Sillington House. That is what we will call it."

"That is what it has always been called."

"Yes. So Mrs. Gershom informed us. Father believes that with the college nearby, many visiting parents will welcome such a place."

"Indeed," I said. I don't think I ever said that word before. What is there about an English accent that makes people seem more intelligent than they maybe are? And was it catchy?

I turned to the window and rested my forehead against the pane. How did he come by his English accent? Where did he go to school before? Was he really unaware of being weird? How did he get to be so weird? But enough was enough. If I didn't pocket my curiosity, I would be giving away more than a bus seat.

When the bus stopped, in a feeble attempt to postpone

the inevitable, I pretended to be looking for something. Mrs. Korshak waited, watching in her rearview mirror. At last after everyone else had left, I walked the length of the aisle and stood for a second at the top of the steps.

There was Julian Singh waiting for me.

I knew he would be.

Julian said, "I am assigned to Mrs. Olinski, Room Twelve. Are you nearby?"

"I guess so," I replied, holding up my room assignment notice.

"What a stroke of luck," Julian said.

"Indeed," I replied.

Mrs. Olinski was the first teacher Epiphany ever had who taught from a wheelchair.

She sat, waiting, until we were all seated. Then she introduced herself. "I am Mrs. Olinski. I am one of those people who gets to use all those good parking spaces at the mall." She turned toward the blackboard and wrote in big, block letters:

MRS. OLINSKI
PARAPLEGIC

As she wrote *paraplegic*, Mrs. Olinski spelled it out, "P-A-R-A-P-L-E-G-I-C. It means that I am paralyzed from the waist down." Her voice was steady, but I noticed that her hands were not. The O of Olinski was not round or smooth but nervous. I don't know what made me look at Julian Singh at that moment, but I did. He sat upright in his chair, not looking at Mrs. Olinski or the blackboard but staring into the middle distance, as if looking at the word *paraplegic* or the paraplegic herself was too painful.

Mrs. Olinski told us that she had become paralyzed in an automobile accident. Confined to a wheelchair as she was, she could not reach the top portion of the blackboard, so, stretch though she would, the words were written in the middle of the board—eye level for most standing sixth graders.

Hamilton Knapp, who had taken a seat in the very last row, farthest from the door, stood up and said, "Excuse me, Mrs. Olinski, but I can't see what you've written. Could you write a little higher on the blackboard, please?"

Mrs. Olinski smiled. "Not at the moment," she said.

Ham sat down and said, "Sorry." She didn't mean that smile, and Ham Knapp didn't mean that "sorry."

The remainder of the morning was taken up with bookkeeping matters such as passing out supplies and assigning seats. We were seated in alphabetical order, and as luck would have it, Ham Knapp ended up way back in the room, in the very seat he had chosen for himself.

Nadia Diamondstein was seated three rows over and two rows forward. I could see her red hair. Nadia and I were almost related. This past summer, her grandfather had married my grandmother. In August when I visited them, Nadia was visiting her father. We often walked the beach together. And one day after a storm, we rescued a batch of hatchling turtles and took them out to sea.

The light from the window shone on Nadia's side of the room. When she moved her head, the morning light caught in her hair the way the sun had when she turned her back to the ocean. Fringes of her hair framed her face in a halo. Whenever that halo effect happened, I wanted to stare at her until the sunlight stopped, but my heart stopped before the light did. Then there was a period during my vacation when Nadia chose not to walk with her father and me. I waited for her to catch up, and when I did, she slowed down, and I missed seeing the light in her hair. I never told Nadia how much I liked seeing the halo the sunlight made of her hair. Sometimes silence is a habit that hurts.

Noah Gershom sat in back of Michael Froelich and in front of Hamilton Knapp. His father is our family dentist. His mother sells houses—a lot of them in The Farm—and for reasons too complicated to tell, Noah Gershom was best man at my grandmother Draper's wedding early last summer. It was pretty funny the way it happened, but my mother, who was maid of honor, was not amused. She cannot forgive Mrs. Gershom for selling houses at The Farm. I think she would change dentists if there were another one as good in Epiphany. Potters have always taken good care of their land and their teeth.

Julian Singh sat in the row to my right and two seats back.

At lunchtime, I sat on the end of the bench. Noah took a seat next to me. Nadia came from the food line carrying her tray and found no vacant seat at any of the girls' tables, so she sat next to Noah. Julian, who had brought his lunch, was seated at a table at the far end of the room, all alone. He finished eating and left the cafeteria without waiting for the bell or asking permission. When Mrs. Olinski saw him leave, she followed. She must have wanted to tell him the rules without calling him out to embarrass him. It took her a while to maneuver her wheelchair between the tables, so Julian had a head start. Shortly after Mrs. Olinski made her way through the door, the bell did ring, and we all left, and were just behind Mrs. Olinski as she made her way down the hall.

When we entered the classroom, we saw that someone had erased PARAPLEGIC and written CRIPPLE instead. Julian was the only person in the room. He was facing the blackboard, holding an eraser. He turned around, looking startled when he saw us file in, led by Mrs. Olinski in her wheelchair.

Mrs. Olinski approached him wordlessly. She held out her hand, and Julian silently handed over the eraser. Mrs. Olinski turned from him to the blackboard and slowly and deliberately erased the word CRIPPLE.

The question was: Had Julian erased PARAPLEGIC, or was he in the process of erasing CRIPPLE? I glanced back at Hamilton Knapp and saw him exchange a look and a slight smile with Michael Froelich, and I knew the answer.

Julian Singh quickly took the trophy for being the strangest person to ride the bus. It took only two days for the other kids to make his life miserable. They stuck their feet into the aisle of the bus to trip him as he made his way toward the back, but even though he seemed to have his eyes focused straight ahead, he managed to stop just short of the protruding feet and say in his perfect British accent, "Beg your pardon. Would you mind?" And he would patiently wait in the aisle until they pulled their legs in. They had to pull their legs in because Mrs. Korshak would not start the bus rolling until everyone was seated. When they tried again, they met with the same result. Again. The same.

No normal person would continue to be cheerful and wear short pants.

I knew what they would do next. And sure as God made green apples, they did.

Their next form of torment was to repeat whatever Julian said in an exaggerated imitation of his accent. They tossed *I say* and *beg your pahdon* front to back and across the aisle. Julian knew that he was the butt of their jokes, and I could tell that he cared, for I could see his cheeks glow red. But he said nothing, and kept his distance, or whatever distance he could manage on a crowded bus.

I still looked out the window during the ride to and from school and never spoke beyond answering "Hi" to his cheerful "Good morning." I always managed to delay getting off the bus long enough so that I would be last. I stood at the top of the stairs long enough to spot Julian waiting for me but not long enough to irritate Mrs. Korshak. It took a full week before Julian took the hint that I did not choose to walk with him from the bus to the building.

About the third day that Julian started off for class without waiting for me, I stood at the top of the stairs of the bus, checking to see if he was gone and spotted Michael Froelich waiting just inside the schoolyard fence by the side of the gate where we entered. As soon as Julian was clear of the other kids, I saw Froelich get into a crouch and I knew what was coming.

I ran down the bus steps and hooked my arm through Julian's and began walking rapidly toward the school. Julian hardly had time to react before we were at the gate. I held onto Julian, blocking him from Michael Froelich.

From the foot of the schoolhouse stairs, Hamilton Knapp came barreling toward us. He grabbed Julian's book bag and ran with it to a tree beyond the school fence. My saving him from Froelich had slowed his chasing Knapp. He disentangled his arm and started toward Ham, but now his way was blocked by Michael, running backward, waving his arms like a guard in a game of basketball.

Julian didn't call for help. He didn't call out at all. Not even with a begging look in his eyes did he ask for help. Julian, who proved to be stronger and quicker than I would have guessed, escaped, ran to Ham, and managed to retrieve his book bag after a serious tug-of-war, but not before Ham Knapp had managed to write "I am a ass" with a black felt tip pen.

No one said anything about the incident. During the day, Julian put his book bag with the written side against the wall of his cubby, and on the way home that evening, he kept the written side of his book bag against his leg. I knew that the pen Ham used would leave permanent marks on leather.

The following morning Julian waited at the bus stop, still wearing short pants and knee socks. It was really the knee socks that did it. Short pants, tube socks, and Reeboks would have been a little off-center but not weird. He boarded the bus, waved to his father, and said "Good morning" as he took his seat.

Between *a* and *ass*, he had squeezed in a *p*. And in the space beneath that, he had changed the message. His book bag now read:

I am a passenger
on Spaceship Earth

A lightened ring in the leather around the first four syllables where someone had made several attempts to erase the writing looked like a halo.

I admired that halo. I guess I like halos.

Following the book bag incident, things on the bus cooled down, and so did the weather. Julian began to wear long pants—corduroys. I wondered if he even owned a pair of jeans.

The time of year had come when the after-school hours were growing shorter and shorter, and I had pumpkins to attend to. Every Saturday morning from June until mid-November, I went with Mother to the Farmers' Market and helped her sell her fresh produce and free range eggs. In September and October we sold a lot of pumpkins. Mother paid me, and I saved almost all of it.

I was the son who was scheduled to inherit the farm because Luke was scheduled for greater things. I knew that as soon as I announced to my family what I wanted to do, I would have to be prepared to pay my own way.

There was no one in Epiphany to whom I could tell my plans. No one in Epiphany would believe that Ethan Potter wanted to go to New York City to work in the theater. I didn't want to be an actor. I wanted to design costumes or stage sets, but I could not tell anyone. In mental mileage, Epiphany, New York, is farther from New York City, New York, than the road mileage from New York to Hollywood.

Last summer Nadia Diamondstein's father took us to see *The Phantom of the Opera*. I had seen high school plays and plays that Clarion U. had put on, but I had never seen something like that. When that chandelier came down from the ceiling, my throat went dry. No one I knew was sitting by me, and I squeezed the arms of my chair to keep myself from getting up to cheer. I had seen football fans act the way I felt. I dream about that show. I bought a souvenir booklet that cost ten dollars, and I had looked at it so often that I was wearing the gloss off its pages. Someday I'm going to design costumes for a show like that.

But first I had to harvest pumpkins.

On the third Saturday after school began, Julian and his father appeared at market. I saw them first from a distance. They did not stand out in that crowd because the Clarion County Farmers' Market attracts a lot of people from the college, and the college in turn attracts a lot of dark-skinned people. Julian's father was carrying a basket over his arm. A lot of the college people and suburbanites believe it is the ecological thing to do. I saw Julian pointing me out to his father before they made their way to our booth.

Julian introduced his father to both Mother and me. Mr. Singh sang the praises of the quality of the goods at the market. (Everyone does. There is a rule that you cannot sell anything at the market that you do not grow or make yourself.) He said that as soon as his B and B opened for business, he would become a regular customer.

When they left, Mother asked about them. She had never before expressed a friendly interest in the fate of the Sillington house. I told her as much as I knew.

On the following Saturday, Julian and his father came to our booth again. Mr. Singh took forever to select four pumpkins from the $2.50 pile. They were not very big, but they were so similar in shape and size that they looked like clones. Julian handed me a ten-dollar bill. I hated that. I don't know why I hate taking money from someone my age even though it isn't charity. I took the money, which was folded in half, and said, "Thank you." A lot of the booth operators say, "Have a nice day." I never do. Mother never does either. Sometimes she'll say, "Enjoy," but never "Have a nice day." Except for Uncle Lew who was in politics, Potters are famous for not saying anything they don't mean.

I waited until Julian and his father were on the far side of the next booth before I unfolded the ten-dollar bill. A small Post-it note was attached inside the fold. I glanced at it, couldn't understand it, looked at it harder, and decided to pocket the money with the note instead of putting it in the cashbox. I'd make it up with Mother.

Business was brisk the entire morning, and that was good. It meant that there would be fewer pumpkins to reload. I didn't have a chance to give Julian's note a second glance or a second thought. Well, maybe I did give it a second thought but not a third and not for long.

At home I waited until I was alone in my room before taking the ten-dollar bill from my pocket. I peeled the Post-it from inside the fold.

Alice's Adventures in Wonderland
Chapter VII Title

I found the book on the shelf in the living room and carried it upstairs. I closed my bedroom door, sat on the edge of my bed, and turned the pages until I came to Chapter VII, the chapter called "A Mad Tea Party."

This was obviously an invitation. The strangest I had ever received. I not only had never been invited to a tea party before but had never before been invited to a party where I was not told the time and the place. Either the mystery would clear up, or it wouldn't. Either way, I wouldn't give it a second thought or discuss it with anyone.

Including Julian Singh.

Having established my habit of not speaking to Julian

on the bus, it was easy to avoid talking about the message in the ten-dollar bill. And, to his credit, Julian gave no hint—no secret smiles or glances out of the corner of his eye—to indicate that he was waiting for a response. Instead, he boarded the bus, walked to the back, said "Good morning" just as he always did and said nothing for the rest of the way. And he did not wait for me at the foot of the bus steps.

I once again managed to be the last one off the bus. As I picked up my backpack, I found a Post-it note attached to the underside of the left shoulder strap. I pulled it off and read it.

Tea Time is always 4:00 P.M.
World Atlas
Map 4: D–16

I put it in my shirt pocket.

Our class would be in the school media center after lunch. We were allowed to browse for the first fifteen minutes. I found the atlas. Map 4 was New York State. D–16 of Map 4 was Clarion County. On the page facing Map 4 was a drawing of a house with a lacy wraparound porch. The address, 9424 Gramercy Road, was written beneath it. I took the drawing from the book and put it in my shirt pocket with the other two notes. I now knew the what, the where, and part of the when. I still didn't know the date.

As I returned to my study table, I passed Nadia Diamondstein among the stacks. She was in the fiction section, removing a book from the D's. *D for Dodgson*, Lewis Carroll's real name. I watched Nadia quickly leaf through the book she held in her hand, then go check it out. It was *Alice's Adventures in Wonderland*.

That evening as I was undressing, I removed the notes

from my shirt pocket. Behind the Post-its and the small sketch of the Sillington House there was a fourth piece of paper: a small page from a pocket calendar. The month of October. The fourteenth was circled. Now I knew everything I needed to know except how Julian had slipped that into my pocket.

For the first time since I started school—no, even longer than that—for the first time ever, I was looking forward to a party. And I knew that part of the reason I was looking forward to it was because Julian had not made it public. Whenever someone makes out a guest list, the people not on it become officially uninvited, and that makes them the enemies of the invited. Guest lists are just a way of choosing sides. The way Julian had done the inviting, I didn't know who else was coming—although I strongly suspected that Nadia Diamondstein would be, and that thought did not displease me.

I wondered if I should bring a gift. It was always better to bring something. I didn't know what. I suspected that sports equipment was out. Books: He probably had as many books as the library. Video game? Wrong. Clothes: NO! Then, when I was in the shower, a word dropped from the showerhead. *Puzzle*. That was it. That was exactly it. A puzzle would be the perfect present for Julian Singh. The video store at the mall had dozens of different puzzles that were not electronic. I had seen three-dimensional puzzles and jigsaw puzzles that had a different picture printed on either side.

I didn't want to tell anyone that I was going to a party. A *tea* party of all things. I hardly believed it myself. I needed a way to get to the mall, so on the Saturday of the party, I asked Mother to please drop me off at the mall on the way home from market. She asked why, as I knew she would, and I told her that I had to buy a present for a party I was going to later that afternoon. Mother was not pleased. She liked to get home right after market so that we could unload the truck and straighten out the accounts. She said all right—not gladly—and told me that she would wait in the truck while I made my purchase.

Why couldn't she come into the mall and browse like a normal woman? Why? Because she knew there was no better way to get me to hurry.

I hopped down from the truck and ran to the video game store. As luck would have it, no salesperson pounced on me the minute I entered. If I had been there to browse, not buy, they would have. Now, I had to practically beg for attention. High on top of the shelves stocked with closed cartons of games of every sort was a display of jigsaw puzzles. There were picture puzzles of waterfalls, 1,000 pieces. There was another one that was a painting of water lilies done in a very loose way. Still another had a picture of a waterfall on one side and a picture of a koala bear on the other. One was a totally white circle. That would be tough because there would be no pattern to help a person line up the pieces. I decided on that one. Two salesclerks were standing at one end of the counter talking. I walked toward them and had to say "Excuse me" twice. I pointed to the puzzle I wanted and said I would like it gift wrapped.

"That's number four-sixty-two. We're all out."

"Then why do you have it on display?"

"It's very popular. We're expecting another shipment next week."

"I need it today," I said. "It's all right with me if you sell me the sample."

"I can't."

"Why? I don't need a discount or anything just because it's the display. I'll pay full price."

The clerk said, "The models are glued together, see, and pasted on a board. So how else do you think they stay up?"

I looked around. "Then I'll take the one that has two different pictures. The one next to the all-white one."

"We're out of that one, too."

"Could you please check your stock in the back?"

"I checked this morning. We don't have it. We have the heart-shaped one in stock."

I looked it over. Instead of a circle, it was shaped like a heart. It was all pink except for a small red heart within the large pink one. Although it wouldn't be quite as difficult as the all-white circle, it, too, would be hard. But it was pink. Pink! Even on Valentine's Day, for a Valentine's Day party, I wouldn't consider giving a pink heart to another guy. "I'll take the water lilies then."

"That's one of our most popular puzzles," the clerk said. "It's a reproduction of a famous painting by an impressionistic French artist who was famous."

"Does that mean you are out of it, too?"

"'Fraid so."

I thought of Mother waiting in the truck. "Okay," I said, "give me the heart-shaped one. And gift wrap it, please." How could a store that seemed so un-busy be sold out of all the good stuff?

"That will take a while," the clerk said.

"Can you hurry? Please?"

"Not if you want me to do a good job."

"Medium," I said. "Can you do a medium job in a hurry?"

The salesclerk smiled and called to her fellow worker.

She asked him to do the gift wrap as she rang up the sale. Then while we both waited, she asked, "Is that a present for your girlfriend?"

I knew it. I knew it. My choice was not half wrong; it was all wrong. I was on the verge of asking her to take it back and give me a refund when the clerk emerged from the back room carrying the puzzle box all wrapped in pink paper. I thought I would die. Then I thought of Mother waiting in the truck and asked for a bag to carry it in.

Mother folded the newspaper she was reading. She turned the key in the ignition even before she asked, "What did you get?"

"A puzzle."

"Good idea," she replied.

"Yeah, about twenty minutes ago, I thought so, too."

"By the way, where is this party?"

"The Sillington house."

"Well," Mother said, "I'll bet you'll have good food. I hear that Mr. Singh is a wonderful cook."

"I don't guess I'll be finding that out. I'm only going for tea."

"For tea?" Mother asked, a broad smile breaking across her face. *"Tea?"* she repeated.

I wished I could bite off my tongue. How in the world had I let that piece of information escape? "Yes," I said. "For tea. It's a tea party, and tea is always at four."

It would be a good walk—a mile and a half. I could cover three miles in forty-five minutes, so I guessed that I would need a half hour to make it to the Sillington House without a sweat. I was not about to ask Mother to drive me there. I put on a plaid flannel shirt and my best sweater. At the last minute, I put on a necktie. I don't know why I did, and I didn't want to think about it.

Nadia and Julian were on the front porch. They were bending over a small ball of fur. It was a puppy.

"She is Ginger's child," Nadia explained.

"Neat," I replied. I hated saying *Neat*. Nadia's red hair in the autumn light made me forget not to say it.

Mr. Singh came out onto the porch, and Julian made a formal introduction. We shook hands. "How do you like Julian's present from Nadia?" he asked.

I said "awesome" and immediately wished I hadn't.

Mr. Singh held his hand over his brow to make a sunshade and looked into the distance. "That looks like our other guest. Let us welcome him." Then he turned to me and Nadia and asked if we would please excuse him and Julian for a minute.

Nadia and I stood there on the front porch and said nothing to each other. No one would guess that we were almost relatives. We watched Noah Gershom get out of the car and start walking up the brick path to the house. In one hand he held a beautifully wrapped present. I watched Mr. Singh with his white turban and long blue apron over his trousers and Julian at his side walk down the path to greet him. Silhouetted against the sky, they looked like a travel poster for a distant land.

Mr. Singh stepped aside to allow Julian and Noah to precede him up the walk.

Julian took Noah's gift and said, "I believe you know everyone here except Alice."

"Who's Alice?" Noah asked.

Nadia answered. "She is Ginger's daughter. Ginger is my dog, and I have given Julian one of her puppies."

"Did you ask if Julian can have a pet?" Noah asked.

"No," she replied.

"I've never heard of someone giving someone a pet for a present without permission."

"I could not believe that anyone would not want one of Ginger's puppies."

"What if Julian has an allergy?"

"If Julian had an allergy—which he does not—he would still want one of Ginger's pups. Ginger is a genius." She looked at me and added, "She is a hybrid genius of unknown I.Q.," and I knew that she was acknowledging our conversation of last summer.

"Oh," Noah said. He hit his forehead with the palm of his hand. "Of course. Of course. I almost forgot. Ginger is the dog that invented $E = mc^2$."

"$E = mc^2$ was not invented. It was discovered, and Einstein discovered it. Ginger is a genius of her genus. She is the best there is of *Canis familiaris*, and Alice is the best of her litter."

"Alice," Noah repeated. "Who named her that?"

"I did," Nadia said. "I thought Julian would like the name because he sent me the invitation to tea in the book, *Alice's Adventures in Wonderland*."

"I've never heard of someone giving someone a pet for a present without permission and then choosing that pet's name without even asking."

Nadia said, "Well, Noah, now you have. In a single afternoon you have heard of both."

The large center hall of the Sillington house had a staircase that curved upward like a stretch of DNA. To the right of the hall was a living room that had a huge fireplace on the end wall; there was no furniture in the room, and the wallpaper was peeling from the walls. On the left of the center hall was the long dining room. I did not remember its having a fireplace, but it did. I was drawn into the room by the large, framed poster hanging over the fireplace mantel.

EXTRAORDINAIRE
SIMONETTA
Chanteuse

Taking up most of the space in the poster was a full-length picture of a smiling, dark-haired woman in a green satin gown. At the bottom was the information:

Appearing Nightly
November 14–29
The Stardust Room

Julian came up behind me. "That is my mother," he said.

"Your mother is a chanteuse?"

"Yes, she was a chanteuse," he said, pronouncing it *shawn-tewz*.

"What does a shawn-tewz do?"

"She sings."

"I saw *The Phantom of the Opera* last summer. There was a wonderful chanteuse in that show."

Julian smiled but said nothing.

"Has she retired?" I asked.

"No," he said. "She died."

"Oh," I said, embarrassed. "I'm sorry."

Julian looked up at the poster. "That poster is quite old.

From before my birth. The Stardust Room mentioned there is on a cruise ship. Mother performed there and on other cruise ships. Before it was necessary for me to start school, I used to travel with Mother and Father. Then I went to boarding school in the north of England in the fall and winter and traveled with them during one of the summer months. Until this year."

"Are you an alien?" I asked.

"Actually, no," he said. "Mother was an American by birth; Father is by naturalization. I was born on the high seas. That makes me American."

"As American as apple pie," I said.

Julian smiled. "Not quite," he said. "Let us say that I am as American as pizza pie. I did not originate here, but I am here to stay." He extended his arm in the direction of Nadia and Noah and took a small step back so that I could pass in front of him. "I think we must join our other guests," he said. "Please," he said. I crossed in front of him, and as I did so, I felt that I was crossing from stage right to stage left and wearing a tuxedo, and I did not mind the feeling at all.

The long trestle tables that are in the picture in the history museum were gone. The dining room was now furnished with two tables-for-two, three tables-for-four, and one larger table at the far end toward the back of the house. Around the tables were an assortment of chairs, none of which matched but seemed to.

The tea was very hot, so we could not gulp it down. We sat at the four sides of a table-for-four and slowly began not to hurry. We sipped the tea and ate small sandwiches that Mr. Singh brought out on a large round tray. Later he brought a three-tiered tray of small pastries. They were delicious, and after finishing hers, Nadia licked her forefinger and with it, picked up the crumbs from her plate. She licked her finger clean so delicately that not even Miss Manners would call it bad.

I, who always preferred silence to speaking, actually started the talking. I asked, "How many eighth graders does it take to screw in a lightbulb?"

Noah replied, "How many?"

I answered, "Only one. They all know how to screw up."

Everyone laughed.

Noah asked, "Where did you hear that one?"

"I made it up," I confessed. I had made that joke up when lightbulb jokes were popular, but I had never told it to anyone before. I was so pleased with their response to a joke I made up that I told them one I had thought of the day Ham Knapp and Mike Froelich had attacked Julian's book bag.

"What is the difference between a pig sty and the sixth grade?" I asked.

Julian said, "I don't know. What is the difference?"

"In a pig sty an ass is a ham."

Julian quietly said thank you, and no one asked why.

After the tea was gone and the cakes were eaten, Julian opened his presents. Noah's first. A bottle of black, black ink, a pen and a pad of paper marked with double and single lines, and a paperback book.

"For calligraphy," Noah explained. "The ink is called India ink. I thought that would be appropriate."

Julian laughed. "Yes, indeed it is." (Indeed again.) "Calligraphy is a skill I have always wanted to acquire."

"I can teach you," Noah said.

Julian flashed his most dazzling smile at Noah. "I would appreciate that very much," he said.

"Consider it done," Noah replied.

Nadia said, "I have always wanted to write like that. You can teach me, too."

"Do you have the pen?" he asked.

"I will get one." Nadia looked over at me. "Ethan, I think you will feel very left out if you do not get one, too."

"I will make each of you a list of what you need. I'll make the list in calligraphy. Watch me, and it will be your first lesson." Noah filled the pen. It was a very long process. "Filling the pen is not what you do before you begin. It is the beginning," he said. "Learn to make a plus sign so that both the vertical and horizontal strokes are the same thickness. That is your second lesson. You can practice as soon as you buy your materials." We waited and watched as Noah wrote out the two lists.

Before Julian opened up my gift, I knew that it was going to be just right. And it was. "A puzzle!" Julian exclaimed. "I love puzzles. Let's do it now."

So without bothering to clear away our cups and saucers, we took seats at the larger table toward the back of the room. As we began to spread out the pieces of the puzzle, Nadia said, "Just like the Mad Hatter's Tea Party—we all moved one place on."

We worked on the puzzle, each one allowing himself a section of the table and the necessary quiet. Then when all the pieces were used up, we brought our sections together, pushing them left-to-right or right-to-left until they fit together. One piece was missing. We looked on the floor and around the legs of our chairs but didn't find it. I was annoyed with the people who had sold me the puzzle. "They've got their nerve selling defective puzzles," I said.

"But the box was sealed," Noah said.

Julian said, "I think Nadia has it in her hair."

"Do not be ridiculous," Nadia said. "I do not."

"Oh, yes, you do. I see it. Can you see it?" he asked me and Noah. Before we could answer, Julian reached across the table and pulled the last piece of puzzle from Nadia's hair. He held it up between his thumb and forefinger and said, "Dear friends, may I present you with the final solution?" He reached down as if to place the piece of puzzle in the small lake of brown tabletop near the center of the puzzle. But when he opened his hand, out fell three red-and-white-striped mints. "Ah, yes," he said, "I almost forgot our after-tea mints. Please help yourselves." We each picked up a mint, and Julian said, "I think it's time to wrap this up. Ethan," he said, "would you please see if that pesky piece is still in the box?"

I reached down on the floor, opened the box, and there it was—the last piece of puzzle. I took it from the box, put it in place and said, "I'm impressed."

And I was. And so were we all.

The party broke up when Mrs. Gershom arrived to take Noah home. As Noah stood at the front door saying his thank you's, Julian said, "Same time next week. But, please, your presence but not presents."

Noah said, "I've heard that before. As a matter of fact, I've put it in writing."

I left shortly after Noah. The days were getting short, and it was dark when I left Sillington House. Mrs. Gershom had offered to drive me home, but I wanted to walk. I wanted to walk the road between Sillington House and mine. I wanted to mark the distance slowly. Something had happened at Sillington House. Something made me pull sounds out of my silence the way that Julian pulled puzzle pieces out of Nadia's hair.

Had I gained something at Sillington House? Or had I lost something there? The answer was yes.

The Monday morning following our tea, Julian boarded the bus and said "Good morning" exactly the way he had said it every other day. We did not speak again, and when the bus came to its final stop, we did not wait for each other or walk together into Mrs. Olinski's classroom. That was the way I wanted it. And that was the way it remained.

On Saturday Mother asked me where I was going. I told her. She asked me why, and I said we were working on a project, and that turned out to be the truth.

Mr. Singh was stripping old paper off the walls of one of the bedrooms, and all of us got involved. Mr. Singh had a steamer to loosen the paper from the walls. Noah made a contest out of seeing who could pull off the longest strip. Working quietly on one side of the window, easing the paper off inch by inch, Nadia ended up with a piece that was almost as long as the room was tall. She won.

"What will be my prize?" she asked.

"Ask Noah," I said. "He has a proven talent for thinking of prizes."

"When will I know my prize?" Nadia asked.

"Before our meeting is over," Noah said. "I think I need some tea to think."

When we sat down to our afternoon tea, Nadia proposed that we give ourselves a name.

I thought it was a good idea and suggested, "The Gang of IV. *I, V,* the Roman numerals."

Noah said, "No. Nadia gets to choose the name. And that is her prize for pulling off the longest strip of wallpaper. Besides, I think she already has something in mind."

"As a matter of fact, I do," she said. "And swear that as my prize, you will accept my choice."

We said we would.

"Good," she said. "Then it is settled. We are *The Souls*."

"I agree," I said immediately.

Noah cocked his head to one side. "I . . . like . . . it . . . but . . . I think it ought to be The Sillington Souls."

"I did not say that, Noah. I said *The Souls*. Besides, 'Less is more.'"

"What does that mean?" Noah asked. "Less is more. Less is more what? Or less what is more? What does it mean? Less is more."

"Think about it," Nadia said. "If someone hands you a card that says that she is President, Clarion National Bank, it means more than if she hands you a card that says she is First Vice President, Loan Department, Clarion National Bank, Epiphany Branch. If you say *Michelangelo*, it means more than Michelangelo Smith, and just plain *Leonardo* means more than Leonardo Jones."

Noah said, "I don't think you can say *just plain* and apply it to Leonardo."

Nadia said to Noah, "Noah Gershom, you may be smart beyond your years, but you are not wise."

"All right. All right," Noah said. "The Souls." He smiled. "I like it."

"Good," I said, looking over at Julian. "What about you?"

"I agree. We will be The Souls. Let us shake on it."

We rested our elbows on the table's edge and reached toward the center of the table until our hands clutched. "We are now The Souls," Nadia said. When we released our hands, each of us was holding a shiny new penny.

"Ah, yes," Julian said. "If you'll check the date on the coin, you will see they are new—minted in the year The Souls was born."

One Saturday afternoon, shortly after The Souls was born, as we sat around the table-for-four where we had had our tea, I broke the silence by asking—I really don't know why—except that it was something I had been thinking about, "If you could live one day of your life all over again, what day would it be? And why?"

Nadia said, "I would like to live over the morning my father and I helped my grandfather and Margaret rescue the turtles that had been blown ashore by the northeaster." She explained about the turtles, their life cycle, and our walks along the beach up until the morning after the storm. "It was like a scavenger hunt. Ethan was there. Do you remember, Ethan?" I nodded. "For two whole days, we kept them safe in buckets, all covered with wet seaweed. And then Margaret, Grandpa Izzy and my dad, Ethan and I drove to Marineland. Ethan and I kept the buckets between us in the back seat, and the three adults crowded together in the front seat. We were crowded, wet, and messy, and it was fun." She looked over at me, and smiled. "Even your grandmother laughed at the sight of us as we got out of the car." I nodded again. "The marine biologist took us out to the Sargasso Sea, and allowed us to empty the buckets over the edge of the boat. We gave the turtles a lift, and we made it possible for them to continue that phase of their life. It was a most wonderful day. Remember, Ethan?"

I remembered.

Noah said, "I would like to live over the day I was best man at a wedding in Century Village that involved four grandparents—two of mine and one each of two other Souls."

Noah had a knack for telling a story, and all of us laughed, even the two of us who already knew the details. Nadia, who had not found the details funny before, found them funny now.

Julian, ever polite, asked, "Is it now my turn?"

Nadia said, "Please."

Julian picked up a deck of cards. He spoke as he shuffled. "If I could repeat one day of my life," he said, pushing the cards across the table to Noah. "Cut them, please." Noah did, and Julian nodded. "I would choose the time we were sailing back to England," he said as he began to deal the cards, going round and round. "All during the journey from the Mediterranean, Gopal, who did close-up magic, had been teaching me how to play poker." Julian looked over the table and counted the cards—three—at each place. Then he slowly dealt another round as he continued talking. "Finally on the day we docked at Southampton, the very day before I was to start boarding school . . ." Julian smiled, laid the remaining deck of cards in the middle of the table, and said, "Would you mind turning over your cards?"

We did. I, who was on Julian's left had four two's; Noah, who was next had four three's; Nadia had four four's. Julian said, "On the day we docked at Southampton, Gopal said something to me . . ." Julian turned over two of the top cards from the remaining deck: Aces. "On the day we docked, Gopal said that I had chops." Julian turned over the next two cards: Two more aces. "That day when Gopal told me that I had chops, that is the day I would like to live over."

We applauded.

"What are chops?" Noah asked.

"Chops," Julian said, "is to magic what doing scales is to a chanteuse. Without it you cannot be a magician, with it alone you cannot be an artist."

Something in Sillington House gave me permission to do things I had never done before. Never even thought of doing. Something there triggered the unfolding of those parts that had been incubating. Things that had lain inside me, curled up like the turtle hatchlings newly emerged from their eggs, taking time in the dark of their nest to unfurl themselves. I told jokes I had never told before. I asked questions I had never asked before. When it was my turn to tell what day I would like to live over, after Nadia had finished, after Noah and Julian had, too, I told mine.

The Souls listened and were not embarrassed to hear, and I was not embarrassed to say, "I would like to live over the day of our first tea party. And, look," I added, "every Saturday since, I get to do just that."

4

Mrs. Olinski sat, waiting, until all the members of her class were seated. Then she introduced herself. "I am Mrs. Olinski. I am one of those people who gets to use all those good parking spaces at the mall." She turned toward the blackboard and wrote in big, block letters:

MRS. OLINSKI
PARAPLEGIC

As she wrote *paraplegic,* Mrs. Olinski spelled it out, "P-A-R-A-P-L-E-G-I-C. It means that I am paralyzed from the waist down."

Mrs. Olinski had thought about what she would say to this, her first sixth-grade class in ten years. She wrote it all down, revised, memorized, and rehearsed until she could deliver her lines with a light touch. Her voice held steady, but her hands did not, and the O of Olinski was the rough shape of an oil spill.

Then a student in the back—Hamilton Knapp—stood up. "Excuse me, Mrs. Olinski," he said, hesitating slightly, mispronouncing her name. "I can't see what you've written. Could you write a little higher on the blackboard, please?"

Mrs. Olinski replied, "Not at the moment," and managed an embarrassed smile. The rest of her prepared remarks flew out of her head. She thought she had thought of everything. But here she was with a problem about sight lines to the blackboard. Given time, she would figure it out, but she wished it had not come up on the very first hour of her very first day back.

After Hamilton Knapp sat down, she laughed nervously. "I was about to tell you that being a paraplegic does not mean that there is anything wrong with my hearing or my eyesight, but I guess we'll have to figure out what to do about the eyesight of those of you who will be seated in the back of the room."

Mrs. Olinski decided that she would write nothing more on the blackboard for the rest of the morning but would leave what she had already written right there so that she could check it out after lunch. She would return before the rest of the class, wheel herself to the back of the room while it was still empty, and check out the sight lines.

She took the roll, checking on the spelling and pronunciation of each child's name, and passed out general supplies and the books for the social studies she would be teaching. Finally, she assigned seats in alphabetical order, last names first.

The year of her accident, Mrs. Olinski had had two Jennifers in her class. This semester, Jennifer was out of fashion, and J-names for boys were in. She had J-names from Jared to Julian, including two Jasons. When she returned from lunch and saw CRIPPLE written on the blackboard, she knew more than the names had changed. Sixth graders had changed.

• • •

Ethan finished answering the four-part question about the history of the state of New York. ". . . the first women's rights convention organized by Elizabeth Cady Stanton. Auburn was the home of Harriet Tubman who ran the underground railroad."

"That registers six points for the Epiphany Team," the commissioner said. There was a spontaneous burst of applause from their side of the aisle that was immediately suppressed by the commissioner. "I must admonish the audience not to applaud. It is distracting to both teams."

Mrs. Olinski remembered the day that rude applause had distracted a performance. Her fourth choice had been causing her problems, but it had been on the very day when rude applause interrupted a play that she had made the fourth and final choice for her team.

• • •

It was the Saturday afternoon after they became The Souls, sometime after they had finished their four o'clock tea, when Julian had said, "We must have a project," and Noah had asked, "Isn't peeling wallpaper enough?"

Julian grinned and said no. He took a small object from his pants pocket and kept it hidden in his fist. He rested his hands lightly on the edge of the table.

"And the calligraphy lessons. Aren't they enough?" Julian said no again, and Noah asked, "Now what?"

Nadia said, "I think Julian already has something in mind."

"Indeed I do." Julian turned his fist over and opened his hand. There within his palm was a small ivory monkey, only two inches high. He laid it on the table and waited until each of The Souls had inspected it thoroughly before saying, "Gopal gave me this little sculpture. It can do tricks." Julian then stood the little figure first on one foot, then the other; one arm, then the other. "You see, this monkey can balance on any one of its four limbs."

Noah asked, "What is that supposed to mean?"

Ethan replied, "I think it has something to do with Mrs. Olinski."

Julian smiled broadly. "Indeed it does."

"Mrs. Olinski?" Noah repeated. "Mrs. Olinski? What?"

"I think that Julian wants us to help her," Ethan explained.

"Help her do what?" Noah asked.

Nadia said, "Stand on her own two feet. Have you never heard that expression, Noah?"

"Of course, I have heard that expression, but fact: Mrs. Olinski cannot stand on her own two feet and further fact: she obviously . . ." Noah's voice trailed off as he understood. "I get it," he said. "I get it. It is scary trying to stand on your own two feet especially when you don't have a leg to stand on, so to speak."

Julian rubbed the little ivory monkey. "There are some in the school who try to get her off balance. Some are in our homeroom."

"We can give her some support," Ethan said.

"Better than that," Nadia said, "we can give her a lift."

They all turned to Noah. "What do you suggest?" they asked, knowing Noah would have an answer. And he did.

• • •

The commissioner reached into the bowl again. He allowed his hand to touch bottom before spreading his fingers to pick up the next question.

"An acronym is defined as a word formed from the initial letters of a series of words. For example, RADAR is an acronym for RAdio Detecting And Ranging. R-A from *radio;* D from *detecting;* A from *and;* and R from *ranging.* Can you give me two more examples of acronyms that have entered our language as words?"

Julian Singh's buzzer went off. "Posh and tip," he called out.

• • •

Julian Narrates
When Ginger Played Annie's Sandy

It was the Saturday of Thanksgiving weekend that Ethan Potter suggested to Nadia Diamondstein that she have Ginger play Annie's Sandy. I had no idea what he was talking about. I knew, of course, that Ginger referred to Nadia's beloved and talented dog, so I thought that perhaps *Annie's Sandy* was a video game played by the canine orders. However, the word *play* referred to playing a part in a musical show about an orphan named Annie in a show called *Annie,* and Sandy was the name of the dog belonging to the title character. Epiphany High School was putting on the play for The Holiday Season. Until we moved to Epiphany, I had no idea how busy Americans are between Thanksgiving and New Year's Day, the time they refer to as The Holiday Season. Everyone asks, "Are you ready for the holidays?" And then afterward, they ask, "How were your holidays?" During the holidays themselves, no one asks about them.

When Ethan suggested that Nadia have Ginger try out, Nadia said, "Ginger does not do Arf." Another remark I did not understand. I did not intend to ask. I knew that if I waited, an explanation would come. It did.

The play, *Annie,* is based on an American comic strip

called "Little Orphan Annie," and when Annie's Sandy speaks, in the balloon over his head is written *Arf!* Everyone had already been cast for the high school production but not the dog Sandy, and Mrs. Reynolds, the play's director, had put a notice on the bulletin board that anyone with a well-trained dog could try out.

Ethan said, "They call that a 'cattle call.'"

Noah said, "Why would they call it a cattle call, if they are asking for dogs?"

Ethan said, "It's a theatrical saying. It means an open audition. Even if they mean people, they call it a cattle call."

"Then what do they call a cattle call?" Noah asked.

Ethan replied, "A round-up, I guess." He turned to Nadia and said, "Ginger's bark will do very well. Besides, she looks a lot like Sandy except that her eyeballs aren't blank." (In time I came to understand that remark, too. The artist who drew the comic strip never drew irises on the eyes of people or dogs.)

Noah said, "There is one other thing."

Nadia ignored Noah. She said to Ethan, "If I do have Ginger try out, she will get the part. Ginger is a genius."

Noah said, "There is one other thing."

Nadia turned to Noah and said, "Ginger is a genius. She will get the part."

"Nadia, my dear," Noah insisted, "Sandy is a male, and fact: Ginger is a—if you'll excuse the expression—a bitch. From everything I've ever learned in health education, genes, not genius, determine—if you'll excuse the expression—sex. Fact: Unless Ginger visits a plastic surgeon, she won't fit the part."

Nadia said, "Noah, is there any subject in this whole world that you do not know more about than every other being on this planet?"

Noah shrugged. "Not every other being on the planet. Let's just say, 'Every other being in this room.' "

"Do you have a dog?" she asked.

"No, but . . ."

"Just answer the question. Do you have a dog?"

"No, but . . ."

"Just answer the question. Have you ever had a dog?"

"No, but . . ."

"Just answer the question. Have you ever had a dog?"

"No."

Nadia said, "I rest my case."

Noah would not give up. "Have you ever had allergies that kept you from having a dog?" he asked.

"No."

"Have you ever had a brother who had allergies that kept you from having a dog?"

"No, I have not and neither have you."

"Have you ever had a brother?"

"No."

"I . . . "

Ethan interrupted. "Getting back to Ginger. You ought to let her try out."

Nadia said, "I shall. She will get the part, and they will consider themselves lucky, which they should, because Ginger is a genius."

The bickering between Nadia and Noah no longer made me uncomfortable. As a matter of fact, I had begun to enjoy it. And so had we all, including Noah and Nadia.

Once Nadia made her decision to have Ginger try out for the part, I told them that in the days when I had traveled with my parents on the cruise line, I saw a number of animal acts. There were not many, for keeping animals on board ship is not easy. I explained that wild animals were out of the question as were the larger varieties of domestic animal such as cow or horse. There was a monkey, once, but it was a terrible thief. The monkey whose name was Sapphire (his hind quarters were bright blue) would swing down from a flagpole or a railing and steal shiny objects like pens or barrettes or, even worse, jewelry. Sapphire always would drink anything that was left unattended in a cup or a glass. As a result Sapphire was often drunk and incapable of bladder control. Most passengers were not amused, and the captain had Sapphire and his owner put off the ship at the next port.

"Most of the animal acts on board ship involved dogs," I explained. "From watching them I learned what trainers do."

So it was that even before the cattle call, The Souls began the intensive training of Ginger.

I taught each of The Souls how to palm a treat so that no one in the audience would notice. First, we taught Ginger to respond to Nadia, and then Nadia fused with Ethan and then Ethan with Noah, then Noah with me until at last Ginger would respond to the treat and not the person. We trained Ginger to accept the treat without excessive salivating. Most people who are not dog owners, and even many who are, do not care very much for a tongue bath.

Ethan got a copy of the script. In the play, the policeman asks, "Is that your dog, little girl?" and Sandy is supposed to bark. We taught Ginger to bark on cue, and the more she did it, the more it sounded like *Arf!*

Ginger had learned her lines. Ginger had learned her cues. Ginger was a genius.

Eight dogs, their owners, the entire cast of the play, and The Souls attended the dog try-outs. I had thought about bringing Alice, but Papa advised against it. He said that a daughter should not be in competition with her mother, but I think he would have missed her during the times she would be at rehearsals. Alice and Papa kept each other company when I was at school. Alice had become our early-warning system. Every time someone started up the path to Sillington House, Alice barked to let us know. We were a little concerned that when we had paying guests, which would be soon, this might be a problem.

One of the eight dogs was quickly eliminated on grounds of disobedience. The second had a problem with his plumbing, and Mrs. Reynolds was not amused by the snickers in the audience or the mess on stage. The next two were small, nervous creatures that looked like battery-operated plush toys. They did not run in a straight line but zigzagged and yipped their way across the stage. Numbers five and six were male and did embarrassing things to legs, any legs—male or female—that happened to be onstage. The two remaining contenders were Ginger and Michael Froelich's dog, Arnold. Arnold, a well-behaved yellow Labrador retriever, was larger than Ginger and was—quite decidedly and obviously—male.

I wanted Ginger to get the part, not only because she belonged to Nadia and not only because she was Alice's mother but also because I did not want Michael Froelich to have the honor. Since those first weeks at school, I had done my best to avoid both Michael Froelich and his friend, Hamilton Knapp.

Arnold tried out before Ginger. The girl who was to play Annie stood center stage, clapped her hands upon her thighs, and Arnold leaped across the stage, placed his paws upon Annie's shoulders, and caused her to lean backward.

She almost fell. Froelich ran across the stage and quickly hooked a leash to Arnold's collar and said to Stage-Annie, "I promise you that won't happen again, but it will help if you dig your heels in a little."

Mrs. Reynolds, the drama teacher, said, "Next."

It was Ginger's turn, and Stage-Annie once again clapped her hands on her knees. Nadia quietly whispered, "Go, Ginger," gave her a little push on her rump and quickly crossed to the other side of the stage behind the backdrop and stood in the wings on the opposite side of the stage where no one in the audience could see her, but Ginger could. In between stood Stage-Annie, holding a treat.

Privately, before try-outs began, I had slipped backstage and taught Stage-Annie how to palm a treat and pass it off so that no one in the audience could see. Ginger walked across the stage with enthusiasm and dignity and quietly nuzzled Stage-Annie's hand before sitting at her feet.

Ginger was in every way clearly superior to every other dog there. Even her mixed-breed looks better suited the part than Arnold's purebred sleekness. Ginger was first rate. Ginger had star quality. Ginger got the part.

Mrs. Reynolds, the drama coach who was director of the play, said, "Ginger will be Annie's Sandy, and Arnold will be Ginger's understudy."

We Souls, sitting in the audience, applauded, and Ethan stood and yelled, "Bravo! Mrs. Reynolds. Bravo!" Ethan had always wanted to stand up in a theater and yell *Bravo!*

Mrs. Reynolds said, "Who is doing that yelling?"

Ethan waved his hand and called out, "It's me, Mrs. Reynolds. Me. Here. Ethan Potter."

Mrs. Reynolds shielded her eyes from the footlights to see out over the audience. "Ethan Potter?" Still screening her eyes, she smiled. "Ethan Potter. I didn't recognize you." I believe that she did not recognize him, for the person yelling *Bravo!* was Ethan, The Soul—not Ethan, the silent. Then she asked, "How is your grandmother, Ethan?"

"She's fine, Mrs. Reynolds. She got married last summer."

"I heard," Mrs. Reynolds replied. "And how is that big brother of yours? How's Lucas?"

"He's fine, Mrs. Reynolds."

"Will you tell him I said hello?"

"Yes, I will."

"When will you see him again?"

"He'll be home for Christmas."

"I hope he'll come see the play," she said. "Will you tell him?"

"Yes, I will."

Ethan did not say another word until we left the auditorium that day.

Ginger learned to bark Arf! on cue and quickly won the hearts of the entire cast as well as Mrs. Reynolds. Nadia was beaming.

Nadia had kindly passed along training information to Froelich and to Stage-Annie, and Arnold's performance improved to within a shade of Ginger's. It would have been better if Arnold had been eliminated altogether. Second best can be worse than not-in-the-running. Who knew what was happening inside Froelich's head as he trained Arnold. Who knew what was happening inside Froelich's head when he attended rehearsals—he had to attend them all—and had nothing to do except to wait backstage and watch admiration and affection be heaped on Ginger. That amounted to a lot of work for little glory. During the actual performances he and Arnold were to stay backstage and out of sight—unless something happened to Ginger. Did having Arnold as understudy make Froelich feel like an underdog?

I was not without worry.

The main performance was to be on Saturday evening before the winter recess. That was when friends and family would attend. This event was exciting for Papa and me not only because Alice's mother was about to make her dramatic debut but also because Sillington House was, too. Mr. and Mrs. Diamondstein were flying up from Florida to celebrate Christmas with the Potters and would be our first paying guests. They planned to arrive in time to see Ginger play Annie's Sandy.

Papa had only one of the guest bedrooms ready, but he was quite proud of it, and so was I. He hung the bed linen out on a clothesline he strung across the backyard so that everything would smell of the sweet air that blew off the lake. He purchased a beautiful cut glass carafe and matching drinking glass and put them on the nightstand by the bed. He purchased a poinsettia and put it on the dresser. In the closet were the heavy hangers of polished wood—not those permanently attached things that you find in cheap motels nor the weak wire ones you get from the dry cleaners—that Papa had bought in England. We had them all facing the same way so that their shadows on the wall looked like a computer rendering of an architectural cross section. The sink and tub were scrubbed until their whiteness could snow-blind. The faucets shone bright enough to use as mirrors.

The Diamondsteins arrived on the Friday afternoon before the official start of the school holiday. That was the afternoon that I and all the other members of the elementary and middle schools of Epiphany were to attend a special matinee performance of *Annie*. For the cast it would be something more than a full dress rehearsal because of a full live audience.

Everyone at Epiphany Middle School was to be transported to the high school by bus. That meant walkers and car-poolers were all going by bus so that our usual seating arrangement was not in order. I had a window seat.

Jared Lord had the window seat two rows in front of me. Ham Knapp took the seat next to him. Ever since the first few weeks of school, when I could not avoid Knapp and his friends, I did my best to ignore them. But I was never unaware of them. Since I had become a Soul and since Froelich had started attending rehearsals, I had become less concerned about him, but Ham was another matter. I was never, never unaware of him or any of his friends. Whenever Knapp was anywhere nearby, all my senses were on alert.

Even though it was late December, the sun, pouring in through the windows of the bus as it waited in the car park, had heated it up like a greenhouse. We were dressed in woolens, so we opened the windows before sitting down for the ride to the high school. I mention all of this because as soon as the bus started out of the car park, the wind coming through the open windows of the bus caused a peculiar warp in the sound.

The first word I heard was *tranquilizer*. It flowed out of one window and back in through mine as clearly as if Ham Knapp were sitting in the seat next to me.

I rested my head against the window post and began to listen intently. The woof of wind produced by cars approaching in the opposite direction caused some blanks in the conversation, but I heard enough.

. . . tranquilizer and laxative . . .

How did you . . .

. . . sent biscuits . . . doggie treats . . . for the star dog.

. . . laxative and tranquilizers and those four little legs will buckle, and those little bowels won't hold . . . There followed some laughter and some mumbling.

Nadia had told The Souls about Ginger's bad reaction to tranquilizers during her trip to Florida last August. She could very well have told this to everyone including Froelich. Froelich could have told Knapp, or Knapp could have heard it himself, for Nadia enjoyed talking about Ginger.

Tranquilizers and *laxatives . . . Pass out like a mop. Instant coma.*

What's the point? She'll pass out backstage.

. . . point is that star dog Ginger is out and buddy dog Arnold is in.

It was clear Ham meant harm to Ginger.

No problem . . . Mother keeps a supply . . .

Why would his mother keep a supply of animal tranquilizers at home?

. . . easy . . . gave them to Nadia . . . gift from my mother . . .

Of course! Knapp's mother was a veterinarian, the owner and operator of Vet in a Van. On several occasions I had seen the van bring Ham to school. The van was painted with the Vet in a Van logo and beneath it was written: Pat Knapp, DVM. I had assumed that Dr. Pat Knapp was a man and that his mother had borrowed the car. It had not occurred to me that his mother was the vet in the van.

It took no great leap of intelligence to realize that Hamilton Knapp had laced Ginger's dog treats with tranquilizers and laxatives so that she would do one, possibly two, embarrassing things on stage. He gave Nadia the drugged treats and told her that they were a gift from Dr. Knapp, who was Ginger's veterinarian. I could easily picture Hamilton Knapp telling Nadia that Dr. Knapp wanted Ginger to have these special treats for her performance. Nadia was so crazy about Ginger that she would believe that anyone who met her wanted to give her gifts.

As soon as the bus stopped, I made my way forward and slipped a Year-of-the-Souls penny into Noah's hand. In the crush at the bus door, I had time to whisper, "Backstage emergency. Cover for me." For reasons we had not spoken of, yet each of us understood, none of us was ready to reveal our association. I watched Noah make his way toward Ethan and pass a Soul penny to him. He had understood. I knew he would.

Just inside the auditorium, Noah bent down to tie his shoe, and Ethan tripped over him. They caused enough confusion for me to slip back outside and run around toward the back of the building and enter the auditorium through the stage door.

I was backstage.

I stayed in the shadow of the wings for a minute until I could get my bearings. The cast was jabbering, tugging at their clothes, too excited about themselves to pay attention to anyone else.

The first time Ginger appears onstage, she is running in front of the dog catcher. She is supposed to be a stray, and her fur must look matted and dirty. Nadia accomplished this by wetting portions of Ginger's fur and tamping them down. From the audience, the wet spots look dark and dirty. For Ginger's second appearance, she wears a rope leash, and for her final appearance, a scene in which Ginger and Annie have taken up residence at the mansion of the wealthy Daddy Warbucks, Ginger-as-Sandy appears clean and brushed and wears a rhinestone collar and red ribbon around her neck. Between acts Nadia has time to dry Ginger's fur and brush her until her coat glistens.

Backstage between the wings stood the prop table where Nadia kept the big red bow and rhinestone collar, the hair dryer, the rope, and the treats that Stage-Annie uses to entice Ginger. I saw the table and worked my way invisibly through the backstage crowd, a technique I had learned from Gopal when I helped him with his act on board the cruise ship.

The treats were already laid out on the props table. I saw the rope. I also saw a fancy collar, but it was wider than Ginger's, and the red bow was different. I examined the treats. They, too, were different. They were shaped like strips of bacon. Ginger's usual treats were shaped like small bones. I was sure that these were drugged. I edged my way over to the table to pick up the dog biscuits and throw them away. I would destroy these treats, and then, if time and opportunity allowed, I would find Nadia's supply and substitute good ones for the drugged ones.

If time and opportunity did not allow, then Ginger would have to go into her act without a bribe. I would count on Ginger's genius.

Before I had a chance to scoop up the bacon-shaped treats from the table, I saw Froelich and Arnold coming out of the boys' dressing room. Arnold was wet down and not wearing his collar or dog tags. Mrs. Reynolds was waiting outside the boys' dressing room. She smiled and said something to Froelich and then called, "Places, everyone."

As the backstage crowd started breaking up, I saw Nadia. She was holding Ginger's leash and carrying the shopping bag where she kept her props. Ginger was still wearing her regular collar and dog tags.

Had something already happened to Ginger?

It was only minutes to curtain. I changed directions and slipped back into the shadow of the wings. I waited until Nadia came within a few feet of where I stood. I came forward, slipped a Year-of-the-Souls penny into her hand, and immediately returned to the shadows. Nadia gave no indication that she had the penny, but she was at my side in less than a minute.

"Is Ginger all right?" I asked.

"She is fine," she said, shortening her leash and laying the shopping bag down on the floor. She reached down to pet Ginger. "Ginger is having a day off. It was Mrs. Reynolds's idea. Mike Froelich has been so good about coming to rehearsals, and Arnold has become so well trained that Mrs. Reynolds decided to let him play Sandy at this performance."

"Oh," I said, "when did you find out?"

"Just this morning. Do not worry. Arnold is only a substitute. Ginger will appear at all of the evening performances."

"So the treats on the props table are Arnold's, not Ginger's?"

"In a manner of speaking. Our vet sent them over for Ginger, but since Arnold is performing today, I gave him some. We both use the same vet."

The treats awaiting Arnold were drugged. Neither Michael nor Nadia knew it. And Hamilton Knapp did not know that Arnold, not Ginger, was about to consume them.

I could save Arnold from the poisoned treats, let him go on, and let Knapp think that his dirty trick had worked. One for the price of two. Or I could let Arnold eat the drugged treats, embarrass Froelich, and let Ginger go on. Two for the price of one.

There they were, waiting on the prop table. There they were, waiting for my decision.

"Why are you here, Julian?" Nadia asked.

"To wish you 'Break a leg,'" I said. "'Break a leg' is what you say to theater people instead of good luck."

"And what do you say to theater dogs?" she asked.

"You double it. You say, 'Break two legs.'"

Nadia laughed. "Really?" she asked.

"Really," I replied.

Nadia laid her shopping bag down at my feet and tugged at Ginger's leash. "Come along, Ginger," she said, "let us go wish some people to break some legs."

I watched them walk away.

I made my decision.

I waited in the dark of the wing until the orchestra was well into playing the overture, for then I knew that the house lights would be lowered, and I could make my way to my seat unnoticed. Noah and Ethan had propped their jackets and backpacks on an aisle seat so that the shadow cast in the darkened auditorium could easily be mistaken for a person. I slipped into the seat, nodded to both Noah and Ethan, and waited for Sandy's first appearance on stage.

The first time Sandy appeared, running across the stage being chased by the dog catcher, the audience broke into spontaneous applause. They were already in love. The second time, the policeman asked, "Is that your dog, little girl?" and Sandy walked across the stage and sat at Stage-Annie's feet, and once again the audience broke into applause. This time, however, when the applause was about to die down, Knapp and Lord exchanged a triumphant look and began barking, "Arf! Arf! Arf!" and clapping in rhythm. Soon all the other kids picked up on that, and the play could not continue.

Senior monitors started fanning down the aisles to locate the source of the trouble, but before the monitor was even with their row, Knapp's hands were folded in his lap; his lips, sealed.

When the play was finished and after all the players had taken a bow, Arnold-as-Sandy walked in front of all the actors and sat down, center stage. The red bow had slipped from the back of his neck to the side. He sat downstage, center, for only a second before glancing over his shoulder, getting up, and walking a few steps upstage to line up with the other players. Stage-Annie and Daddy Warbucks took a step to the right and to the left respectively to make room for him. Arnold looked out over the audience, sitting in a circle of light, and the audience went wild.

They stood, began clapping in rhythm to their chant, *SAN-dy, SAN-dy, SAN-dy*. Knapp and Lord picked up the beat and started an undertone of *Arf!Arf!Arf!*, and soon the audience became a two-part chorus with half the auditorium chanting SAN-dy, and the other half responding with ARF, ARF in a manner more suited to an athletic contest than musical theater. The curtain was dropped, the house lights came on, and the chanting softened, faded, and died. Knapp and Lord exchanged a satisfied look.

Mrs. Reynolds walked onstage and stood in front of the curtain. She held a microphone in her hand and hissed into it, "Sit-t-t-t down!"

THUMP-THUMP-THUMP-THUMP-THUMP-MP-MP-MP—the sound of hundreds of bottoms hitting hundreds of seats followed.

Mrs. Reynolds waited until an embarrassed silence fell over the auditorium. "Part of the theater experience is learning to be a good audience. You have not been a good audience. You have been a very bad one. I am sorry that you have not learned at home how to act in public. I am ashamed for you because I know you are not ashamed for yourselves. I would like you to leave. Now. You can start correcting your behavior by leaving this auditorium in a quiet and orderly fashion."

Suddenly senior monitors appeared at the end of every third row, and we quietly and slowly made our way toward the exit. The auditorium was almost empty by the time we reached the exit. Mrs. Olinski was sitting in her chair between the doors. She called my name. "Julian. Julian Singh," she called, "I would like to see you a minute."

Had she seen me slip backstage? Or did she think that I started that ruckus in the auditorium? My school days are over, I thought. I will be expelled, I thought. How will I break the news to Papa?

Mrs. Olinski said, "I understand you have guests at Sillington House."

"Yes, ma'am, we do. Mr. and Mrs. Diamondstein were due to arrive from Florida this afternoon."

"Mrs. Diamondstein is an old friend of mine. She asked me to stop by and meet her new husband. How would you like to ride home with me?" she asked.

I was so relieved that I could not speak. I answered by nodding my head like one of those nodding animals that Americans put on the rear ledge of their automobiles.

Ethan, who was just behind me, said, "May I come, too? Mrs. Diamondstein is my grandma Draper."

"Yes, so she is. I had almost forgotten. Of course, you may come."

"Let me go backstage and get Nadia," Ethan suggested. "Mr. Diamondstein is her grandfather."

Mrs. Olinski laughed. "It seems all of our sixth grade is one happy family. Go ahead," she said. "Go backstage and tell Nadia to meet us at my van."

A voice that was midway out the door called, "Can I come, too?"

"You, Noah? What reason do you have?" Mrs. Olinski asked.

"Me?" Noah asked. "You want to know what reason I have for coming along?"

Mrs. Olinski smiled patiently.

"Well, Mrs. Olinski, my reason is the best of all. Fact: I was best man at their wedding."

Mrs. Olinski laughed. "Were you really?"

"Yes, I was. I'll tell you about it. I'll spare no detail."

Mrs. Olinski laughed. "Then, by all means, Noah, you must come along."

Noah grinned. "I have always wanted to ride in a handicapped van. All my life, I have wanted to see how a disabled person like yourself applies the brakes and steps on the gas."

Mrs. Olinski said, "I don't exactly *step* on the gas."

"There you go!" Noah said. "This is precisely what I would like to see. I would precisely like to see exactly how you *apply* the gas."

Mrs. Olinski said, "That is either the most honest or the most dishonest answer I have ever heard. I must notify the bus driver that I'll be driving you four souls home."

Why did she say that? She was smiling. Did she know that we were The Souls? Did she know? Noah caught my eye and quickly changed the subject. "You'll have to take Ginger home, too, Mrs. Olinski. If you don't mind, of course. You don't have to have any special fittings in the van to transport animals. It's a good thing, too. Now, if Ginger were a seeing-eye dog . . ."

Mrs. Olinski interrupted. "Noah," she said, "run down to the bus and tell Mrs. Korshak that I will be along in a minute. I have a message for her."

"I'd be happy to give her that message, Mrs. Olinski."

"I'm sure you would, but the message involves permissions that I, not you, have the authority to give." Noah started down the row of yellow buses, and Mrs. Olinski followed.

There had been a moment backstage when I had been tempted to allow Arnold to eat the drugged treats. That had been the same moment that I thought it would be satisfying to get even with Froelich and Knapp. But then I was able mentally to separate Froelich from Knapp and Arnold from both of them, so I slipped over to the props table, scooped up all the poisoned treats, and put them in my right pocket. At the same time I substituted Ginger's wholesome treats—treats I had taken from Nadia's shopping bag—from my left pocket.

The drugged treats were still in my pocket.

Ethan, Nadia, and Ginger had not yet come out of the auditorium. Noah and Mrs. Olinski had gone to speak to Mrs. Korshak. I stood alone. There was something I wanted to do. When Knapp had started that ruckus, I had momentarily regretted my decision to save Arnold. I was still so angry that I was about to violate one of the cardinal rules that Gopal had taught me.

I walked out onto the street so that no one on the sidewalk would notice as I made my way down the line of buses waiting—headlight to taillight—by the curb. Beyond them was the line of cars waiting for pickups. Traffic could go only one way, and no one was allowed to make a U-turn, so even those cars that had already picked up their riders were stuck, waiting for the buses to load.

Gopal had taught me that magicians never reveal the secrets of their trade to laymen. Gopal always said that magicians who were interested in letting people know how clever they were were not really magicians. "Don't ever destroy the wonder," Gopal had said. "Let your magic show you off, not you show off your magic."

I knew that Hamilton Knapp would find out soon enough that Arnold, not Ginger, had been chosen for the afternoon's performance. He would find out soon enough that his trick had not worked. I knew that I should never reveal to Hamilton Knapp that I had saved Arnold from the fate he had meant for Ginger. I knew all of that. Yet I moved toward the Vet in a Van. Dr. Knapp was behind the wheel, waiting for her turn to pull out. I walked around the back of the van onto the sidewalk on the passenger's side. I tapped on the window and motioned for Ham to roll it down. I reached into the open window. He pulled away from me but said nothing.

"What's the matter?" his mother asked.

"Your son has something growing out of his head," I said as I pulled two bacon-shaped doggie treats from his ears. "I think these belong to you," I said as one by one I dropped the rest of the drugged biscuits on his lap. I turned and walked away.

I was glad that I had chops. Gopal would forgive me.

5

The deadline for choosing an academic team was the Tuesday following the winter holiday. The other homeroom teachers were ready by Thanksgiving. They had held mini contests in their classrooms and had selected the winners of those. They had ready answers for anyone who asked how they had chosen their teams. In the teachers' lounge, Mrs. Sharkey, who taught sixth grade math, accused Mrs. Olinski of being dictatorial, and Ms. Masolino, who taught music and who did not have a homeroom at all, hinted that she was lazy. Mrs. Olinski did not take kindly to these remarks. Her voice quavering, she answered her critics. "I have my reasons," she said, even though she knew she didn't. Something stronger than reason was having its way with her, and she didn't know what that was either.

Mrs. Laurencin, Epiphany Middle School principal, called Mrs. Olinski into the office one afternoon and quietly warned her that she better have a good answer for the parents of any high honor roll student who didn't make her team. Mrs. Olinski said, "By the time they get to sixth grade, honor roll students won't risk making a mistake, and sometimes to be successful, you have to risk making mistakes." Mrs. Laurencin agreed with her but warned her that that would not be a very popular reason. "Furthermore," Mrs. Olinski added, "sometimes we even have to risk making fools of ourselves." Mrs. Laurencin never approved of that answer either.

Even though Mrs. Olinski could not tell why, she could tell when she decided not to hold try-outs. It was on a Saturday in late October, some time after four o'clock. She had been correcting social studies papers and had just finished reading Noah Gershom's essay on the First Amendment when the thought flew into her head. She would appoint her team, the way the president appointed his cabinet. She made her decision. Just. Like. That.

She chose Noah right away, and almost immediately after, she thought of Nadia and Ethan. They looked like strong candidates. She would watch them and see.

In the weeks that followed, she became more convinced of their being right for the job. She had not yet officially notified any of them because she wanted to make all four appointments at the same time, and the fourth was causing problems.

She had been considering asking Hamilton Knapp—yes, *that* Hamilton Knapp. Although he was naughty, he was also smart, and bad boys had always held a certain charm for her. But each time something told her he was the right choice, something else told her he was wrong. So she held back.

While she waffled between asking Ham and not asking him, she never gave a thought to asking Julian Singh. He was smart (or else his English accent made him seem so).

And he was sophisticated (or else his English accent made him seem so). But Julian Singh was too far off the mainland. He was an island unto himself, definitely not a team player. Ham Knapp was a leader. Ham Knapp had friends. But Julian stood alone. Just as he had stood alone the first day of school at the blackboard in front of the word CRIPPLE.

On the day that Epiphany Middle School was invited to attend *Annie,* Mrs. Olinski had driven her van to the high school and had arrived ahead of the school bus. She waited at the foot of the steps as the kids filed out. She saw Julian Singh push his way forward and then scurry down the steps and out of sight. He had disappeared into thin air. She didn't want to call into thin air and look to all the world (and all the other teachers) as if she had no control of her class. Mrs. Olinski was annoyed with Julian Singh. Once inside the auditorium, she had looked for him again but had been unable to spot him before the house lights dimmed, and the show got under way.

Then Sandy appeared on stage, and the clapping and the chanting *Arf! Arf! Arf!* had started in the section of the auditorium where her class was seated. From where she had been sitting, in a handicapped space by the exit, she could not see who had started it, but she knew one of her students was responsible. She knew it, and she was angry. Mrs. Olinski had a great tolerance for mischief, but she had no patience for malice. This was not mischief. There is a playful quality to mischief. This was malice. There is a mean quality to malice. Someone in her class was terribly mean.

When the lights went on, and Mrs. Reynolds stormed on stage to scold the audience, Mrs. Olinski was able to wheel herself around to examine her students. With a sick feeling in her stomach, she scanned them one at a time. Like the cursor on a computer screen her eyes moved from the first row to the second, then stopped. Her pulse quickened. She knew. She had no proof, never would have proof. But she knew. She knew who had started the ruckus.

And she knew then that she would not, could not, ask Hamilton Knapp to be the fourth member of the team.

And that is when she went to tea at Sillington House.

Margaret Draper Diamondstein must have been waiting at the window. No sooner had Mrs. Olinski stopped her van than her old friend came rushing out the door. She was wearing a jogging suit but no coat. The wind was whipping off the lake, and she hugged her upper arms and stamped her feet as she waited for the door to open. Margy Diamondstein reached up into the van, and Eva Marie Olinski reached down out of it, and they hugged.

Then a voice said, "Hi, Grandma."

It was Ethan.

Margaret asked, "Ethan? Is that you?"

"Yeah. Me. Ethan."

"Come on down out of that van and let me see you," she said. Ethan stood in front of her, looking enchantingly awkward until Margaret pulled him to her. Eva Marie Olinski saw his arms hanging limply at his side, his wrists hanging below his cuffs like meter sticks showing how much he had grown since the jacket was new. Ethan slowly lifted his arms and fit them around his grandmother's waist as she rested her chin on the top of his head. She closed her eyes and absorbed the blond waxy smell of his hair before she stood him at arm's length. "You've grown since summer," she said.

"I have. I know," he answered, and shot his arms out of his sleeves showing several inches bare above the wrist bones. "Would you believe, only a month ago, these covered my fingertips?"

Margaret laughed and said, "No, Ethan, I would not believe."

"Just testing."

Nadia waited until they had backed away from each other before saying, "Hello, Margaret."

"Nadia!" Margaret said. "What a surprise. Is Eva Marie—Mrs. Olinski—your teacher, too?"

Nadia replied, "Yes, Margaret. Yes, she is."

At that moment a slender man with heavy gray eyebrows came out of Sillington House, holding his knuckles to his hips as he looked over the scene. He saw Nadia and sprinted over, calling, "Nadia! Nadia!" He hugged her close and then kissed the top of her head several times until Ginger wedged her way between them. "I had no idea I'd see you this afternoon."

Nadia said, "Ginger is a star, Grandpa. She is excellent."

Her grandfather replied, "I have no doubt about that. After all, Ginger is a genius. And we're going to see her tomorrow night. We're all going. We're going with your mother."

"I know," Nadia said, looking very pleased. "I know."

Eva Marie Olinski watched Margaret Draper Diamondstein hug her grandson. The new Mrs. Diamondstein was dressed in a jogging suit. A turquoise jogging suit. *Turquoise!* She had always regarded the color turquoise, like shocking pink and chartreuse, as the color equivalent of the word *ain't*: quaint when seldom used but vulgar in great doses. As she watched Margaret hug her grandchild and Izzy hug his, her mental censors and her customary good manners started shutting down. She could not stand it another minute. She was on the verge of screaming with pain and rage when she felt her wheelchair begin to move. She felt herself being pushed toward the front porch of Sillington House.

Eva Marie Olinski was so blinded by jealousy that she had not noticed Mr. Singh come out. From behind her chair his voice floated down upon her in soft waves. "I have prepared a tea," he said.

A tea? she thought. Yes, a tea. It was that time of day. It was four o'clock.

"The others will join us shortly." Eva Marie Olinski turned around and at eye level saw a long blue apron. Her eyes traveled upward and saw a black beard, a broad white smile, a pair of amber eyes, a white turban. Saved by a genie, she thought.

Mr. Singh maneuvered her wheelchair to a table in the back of the dining room. Without asking, he ceremoniously poured tea into a delicate china cup. *Cream?* No. *Sugar?* No. *Yes, it is best to drink tea without.* And she did. She drank unhurriedly. Before her cup was empty, she felt something lift from her shoulders. Was it jealousy or injury? Was it anger? Was it all of the above? She replaced her emptied cup in its saucer. She waited. She was calm.

Margy and Izzy joined her at the table, and she drank another cup of tea and ate a cucumber sandwich, taking four bites out of a patch of bread so trim she could have swallowed it whole. She hardly heard what Margaret and Izzy were saying. She did not interrupt, and soon she was listening, first out of politeness—for courtesy was the first of her civilized senses to return—and then out of interest, genuine interest.

She looked around the room and saw the four children, Ethan, Noah, Nadia, and Julian sitting at a table on the far side of the room. They were talking among themselves and drinking tea. They did not interrupt one another, Mrs. Olinski thought, how unusual. There were nods and smiles and obvious pleasure in one another's company. Mrs. Olinski thought, how unusual to find four sixth graders who listen to one another sympathetically, unselfishly. How curious. How *courteous*. Mrs. Olinski thought, when people come to tea, they are courteous. She thought, I believe in courtesy. It is the way we avoid hurting people's feelings. She thought that maybe—just maybe—Western Civilization was in a decline because people did not take time to take tea at four o'clock.

The Souls continued their animated conversation, when suddenly, as if on signal, the four of them looked back at Mrs. Olinski.

And that is when she knew.

That is the exact moment she knew that Julian Singh would be the fourth member of her team and that she would always give good answers when asked why she had chosen them. And then and there, she also knew that someday she would drink another cup of slow tea at Sillington House.

6

• • •

The commissioner looked over his list of possible answers. "Posh and tip?" he asked.

Julian quickly answered, "Posh means fashionable and is the acronym for Port Out, Starboard Home, referring to the time when India belonged to Britain, and the people traveling there wanted the shady side of the ship both going and coming. And tip, meaning the small sum of money given for services rendered, is the acronym for To Insure Promptness."

The commissioner laughed. "You may be a little ahead of us on that one, Epiphany. I don't have either of those acronyms on my list. We'll have to check with our advisory panel." He nodded to the three people sitting at a table on the far side of the room. One rapidly punched keys on a computer as the other two consulted large books. The three of them conferred briefly and passed a note to the commissioner.

"We can allow posh, but we do not find a reference for tip."

Julian said, "With all due respect, sir, I think you ought to check another source."

• • •

Their path to the state finals started with the sixth-grade championship. Mrs. Olinski had expected victory, for her team was quick and informed and worked together perfectly. No one had expected them to trounce the other two sixth grades, but they did. Their victory was so profound that the sixth-grade math teacher, Mrs. Sharkey, confided to the music teacher, Ms. Masolino, that for the first time in the history of Epiphany Middle School there was a chance—just a possibility, mind you—that a sixth-grade team might beat the seventh grade. Mrs. Sharkey said that, after all, she knew the current seventh grade, for she had taught them just last year, and in her opinion, when they were very, very good, they were mediocre.

The Souls practiced during activities hour—that portion of time between eleven-thirty and one o'clock that was not devoted to eating lunch. Mrs. Olinski read questions from note cards: one card; one question. She used three sets of questions.

The first was a series of questions required of everyone in a particular grade. Knowing that they would be competing with grade seven, she added their questions to her sixth grade set. The second set had been culled from previous contests. Some required only speed: How many quarters in twenty dollars? Some required cleverness: If one man could paint an eight foot by twelve foot wall in a half hour, how long would it take three men to paint a wall that was eight feet by twenty-four feet? The third set of questions were ones she had made up by weeding items from the news and connecting them to geography or history or both: A masterpiece by the artist Rembrandt was recently stolen from a museum in his native country. What is that country? What is its capital? Mrs. Olinski required that they find the country on a map, and then would ask them to name two other famous artists. Their countries? Their capital cities?

They beat grade seven, almost doubled their score. Fact: No sixth grade team had ever defeated a seventh grade team. They were scheduled to go up against grade eight. Further fact: No sixth grade had ever competed against the eighth because no sixth grade had ever gotten that far.

When word got out that Mrs. Olinski's homeroom had a chance of beating the eighth grade, kids from the other two sixth grades started signaling a thumbs-up sign when passing a team member in the hall. They raised their arms high overhead and lifted their thumbs like a forest of small apostrophes at the ends of their closed fists.

Excitement grew throughout the week. Mrs. Olinski's sixth graders were David versus the eighth grade Goliath, and the kids with the slingshots knew how to use them. Soon the vanquished seventh grade chose sides; they would cheer for grade six. On Thursday, the day before the showdown, kids from grades six and seven lined the halls between the cafeteria and Mrs. Olinski's room and gave her and The Souls a round of applause as they returned from lunch to practice. Mrs. Olinski smiled and said thank you, thank you as she wheeled herself between the flanks of honor guards.

Traces of her smile remained as the rest of the class filed

in for social studies. She sat at her desk and sorted out the papers that were due to be returned.

The room was quiet until a student in the back of the room let out an enormous belch and said, not too sincerely, "Sorry."

Mrs. Olinski continued sorting papers before looking up. "Hamilton Knapp?"

"Yes, ma'am," he answered.

"Would you please come to the front?"

He walked slowly, watching her, a half smile on his face. She let him take his time. Before he reached the front of the classroom, someone launched another belch. Its sound rocketed forward, and the laughter that followed traveled the same trajectory. Mrs. Olinski waited until Ham reached the front of the room before asking, "Jared Lord, would you please join Mr. Knapp?"

Jared also took his time, and Mrs. Olinski did not rush him either. As he ambled down his row toward the front of the room, smiling faces lifted and tilted toward him like the broad front faces of sunflowers as they follow the sun across heaven. Mrs. Olinski allowed that, too.

"Now, Mr. Knapp and Mr. Lord," she said, "I would like the two of you to teach the entire class how to belch on command. Please describe the process for all of us." She picked up a piece of chalk from the ledge. "Which one of you wants to take notes on the instructions we are about to receive?" Neither volunteered, so she thrust the chalk into Knapp's hand. "I think you enjoy writing on the blackboard, Mr. Knapp," she said. Ham took the chalk. The class registered its approval with body language that was the equivalent of silent applause.

The class waited. "I'll help you with the spelling," Mrs. Olinski said.

Ham began to clown around, rolling his eyes and saying, "Well, first you . . ."

The rest of the kids tightened their stomachs, opened their mouths, and tried to figure out how to explain a belch. Jared stood at the blackboard—empty-handed, awkward, uncomfortable—and he too, tried to figure it out. Knapp made another attempt. "Well, first you . . ." Then another long, awkward, uncomfortable wait. "Well, first you . . ."

Mrs. Olinski allowed them to stand there until three minutes seemed like thirty. Then she sent them back to their seats. "Since you cannot describe what you have done, I would call belching loudly to interrupt our class an *unspeakable act.* Unspeakable. And because you cannot explain how to do it, I would say that you cannot teach either." She paused, locked eyes first with Knapp and then with Lord before adding, "But I can. If I choose to, I can explain how to belch on command, and I could teach you. If I so choose." She looked at Knapp and Lord again, her nostrils flared slightly, then slowly turned her head to the class and added, "But I don't.

"The front of this classroom is privileged territory. There are only two reasons for you to be here. One, you are teaching something to the rest of the class or, two, you have been invited. From now on, the only tricks that I am willing to put up with are those that you can first explain and then teach."

She looked at Jared Lord and asked, "Do you understand, Mr. Lord?" Jared attempted a grin. His attempt failed, and he nodded yes. "Then let us have no more interruptions with unspeakable acts. No barking *Arf!* either. Do you understand me, Mr. Knapp?" Ham nodded yes. "Mr. Lord?" Jared said, "Yes, ma'am."

As he returned to his seat, no one smiled at Ham or even made eye contact with him.

Suddenly Nadia Diamondstein thrust her left leg straight out into the aisle. Noah Gershom, who was three seats in back of her, stuck out his right leg. Ethan Potter saw and raised his right arm in the air. As if on cue, Julian Singh raised his left fist. For a moment above and below eye level, all four limbs stuck out, and then, just as quickly, all four disappeared. It was quite a balancing act.

Mrs. Laurencin called a school assembly for the contest against the eighth grade. The principal herself asked the questions. If a team missed its question, the other team had an opportunity to answer. To break a tie, the last team to answer correctly had to correctly answer one additional question.

This was the question that the eighth grade could not answer and Noah could: Name all the parts of the human eye in the order that light reaches them.

This was the four-part question that they answered to win: Name the famous fathers of: Queen Elizabeth I of England. Esau and Jacob. Alexander the Great. Our country.

Mrs. Laurencin was impressed. The sixth grade was jubilant. Ms. Masolino said she knew it all along, and Mrs. Sharkey said they gave new meaning to the term "bottoms up."

The Souls were now the school's team. The next step was the contest against Knightsbridge for the district championship.

7

• • •

Any other team on spaceship Earth would have worried about Julian's defying an official of the sovereign state of New York. But not The Souls. They would let him risk whatever he wanted.

The commissioner was—to put it politely—annoyed. He looked at his seating chart. "Mr. Singh?" he asked. "Are you Julian Singh?"

"Yes, sir, I am."

"Well, Mr. Singh, we all agreed to stand by the ruling of the panel of experts."

"The panel's information is not complete, sir."

"Mr. Singh, we must stand by the ruling of the panel."

"Sir," Julian said, "long ago in England, pub owners used to place a box on the bar. They put a sign on the box that said To Insure Promptness, capitalizing each of the three words. People dropped coins . . ."

"I'll allow posh but not tip."

"With all due respect, sir, you are wrong."

At that point, the commissioner could have disqualified the entire Epiphany team—and maybe would have—except that he was rendered speechless.

• • •

To prepare for the contest with Knightsbridge, Mrs. Olinski continued to drill her team during activities hour. The week of the Knightsbridge contest, the five of them brown-bagged their lunches so that they could practice through lunch. Mrs. Olinski's packets of note cards grew. She drew questions at random from each of the three sets. The Souls had become so familiar with some of them that she had to ask only, "What did Martin Luther . . ." before four hands shot up in the air and four voices would shout out, "The Ninety-five Theses."

That would not do. Answering before a question was completed or having several kids answer at once were violations of the rules that would cost points. Mrs. Olinski reminded them that if they continued to do that, the penalties could easily add up to a loss. Her team seemed to communicate with a secret stealth language that slipped beneath thought. It took only one warning, and they stopped. Just. Like. That.

With the success of her team, Mrs. Olinski was asked more and more often how she had chosen them, and she continued to give several good answers, varying them as the need arose. They worked well together. They were willing to take time to drill. They understood the rules. They were quick. All of these answers were true, but not the whole truth. The whole truth was that Mrs. Olinski did not yet know the whole truth.

Then the day before the contest for the district championship Mr. Connor LeDue, the principal of Knightsbridge Middle School, found some pretext to visit Mrs. Olinski. He stood to one side of her wheelchair, leaned over, smiled, and said, "I heard a rumor that your team is expecting to blow mine out of the water." His smile was as genuine as a Xeroxed signature.

In order to make eye contact with someone standing where Mr. LeDue stood, Mrs. Olinski had to stretch her neck in two directions—up and to the side—and open her eyes wide. This made her look worshipful. She wasn't.

Mr. LeDue applied his smile again and said, "I told our coach that she could expect to be hung if she lets your sixth grade grunges beat us out."

"Well then," Mrs. Olinski replied, "much as I respect your coach, I recommend that you start buying rope." She shifted her head slightly and added, "By the way, Mr. LeDue, in our grunge neighborhood, we say *hanged*, not *hung*. Check it out."

Dr. Roy Clayton Rohmer, the district superintendent, was a worried man. Item one: He worried about his contract that was up for renewal. Item two: He worried about the district playoffs. Item three: He worried about Mr. Homer Fairbain, his deputy superintendent in charge of instruction. He worried because item three could affect item two, which could affect item one.

The previous year when Mr. Homer Fairbain had been

master of ceremonies for the district playoffs, the contest had been broadcast on educational TV. When he was to ask the question, *What is the native country of Pope John Paul II?* Mr. Fairbain asked, "What is the native country of Pope John Paul Eye Eye?" The day after the broadcast, there were five letters to the editor in the paper about Mr. Fairbain, none favorable.

Dr. Rohmer knew that this year's broadcast would have a larger than usual audience, partly because people were curious about having a sixth grade team be a contender for the district middle school championship but mostly because everyone would be waiting for Homer Fairbain to goof. Dr. Rohmer had to let Mr. Fairbain be master of ceremonies again. It would be his one chance to show the community that he had learned a thing or II.

Dr. Rohmer knew that if the names of any of the former Soviet Socialist Republics—Uzbekistan or Azerbaijan or, Heaven forbid! Kyrgyzstan—appeared in any of the questions, Homer would embarrass himself. If he had to read the names of the ministers of Japan or Zaire, or any name containing more consonants than vowels, or more vowels than consonants, he would embarrass himself. He would also embarrass Dr. Rohmer and make him worry a lot.

Mr. Fairbain, who was a humble man, saw no problem with requesting help from one of the reading teachers until Dr. Rohmer pointed out that the entire staff of remedial reading teachers came from the very department he was in charge of.

Dr. Rohmer, whose patience was as close to the end as his contract, arranged to give Mr. Fairbain the questions a week in advance, told him to practice reading them out loud, and strongly suggested that if he had any difficulty with them—anything at all—to see one of the school's speech therapists. (Therapists came from the department of student services, not curriculum.)

The Souls stayed after school late the Thursday before the Knightsbridge contest. Mrs. Laurencin sent in Cokes and pizza for the team. On Friday afternoon, she came into Mrs. Olinski's room and told the team that after this practice, she wanted everyone to go home and get a good night's sleep, and that win, lose, or draw, she couldn't be more proud of all of them tomorrow than she was at that moment.

For all the reasons given—an unprecedented sixth grade championship team, the snobbishness and arrogance of the Knightsbridge team, as well as waiting for Mr. Fairbain to make a fool of himself—the Knightsbridge cafetorium was filled to capacity. Small kids were perched on tabletops because there weren't enough chairs, and the Epiphany sixth graders stood like caryatids leaning against three of the four walls of the room.

Mr. Fairbain did well and actually seemed to be enjoying himself until syllabication did him in. The question was to name the tribe associated with each of the following Native American leaders and name a major accomplishment of one. The leaders' names were Sequoyah, Tecumseh, Osceola, and Geronimo. However, *Geronimo* was hyphenated at a line break, so *Gero* appeared on one line and *nimo* on the next, and unfortunately, Mr. Fairbain read it as Jair-oh-NEEM-oh.

Dr. Rohmer hoped that no one would notice, and no one on the Knightsbridge team did. Fact: They could not answer the question. Then it was The Soul's turn to answer, and Julian corrected Mr. Fairbain. "With all due respect, sir, I believe one of the men of whom you speak is Geronimo, a member of the Apache tribe."

Poor Mr. Fairbain. He looked down at the card, squinted, read it, and said, "Yes, indeed, you are right, young man. Good for you." He caught Dr. Rohmer's eye and knew he had done something wrong. He laughed nervously and said, "You look a bit like an Indian yourself."

Julian smiled. "I am a hybrid. I am in part what is called East Indian."

"Well, now, that is special," Mr. Fairbain said, smiling and looking out over the audience, and wanting to reinforce his compliment, asked, "What is your tribe?"

Dr. Rohmer paled to the point of translucence, and the audience gasped. Everyone—even those who had not had diversity training at taxpayer expense—knew that even though it was correct to recognize a person's ethnicity, it was not correct to comment upon it in public.

Mrs. Olinski thought Dr. Rohmer would have to be taken out on a stretcher. Mr. Fairbain noticed Dr. Rohmer's sudden anemia, and without knowing what he had done wrong, but knowing it was something, said, "That's all very interesting, young man, but I'm afraid we must move along. Can you answer the question or not?"

"I can, sir," Julian replied. And he did.

His answer put Epiphany ahead.

They had to answer one more question: What is the origin of the phrase, "to meet one's Waterloo" and what does it mean?

There was a clear, bright gleam in Ethan's eye as he concluded his answer with, ". . . *to meet one's Waterloo* means to suffer a crushing defeat." Crushing applause followed a nanosecond of crushing silence. Everyone clapped. But not the sixth-grade sentinels who lined the walls. Instead, upon a signal from Michael Froelich, they took from their pockets a piece of rope, which they pinned on their shirts in the place where a medal would go.

When The Souls came down off the stage, they stood four abreast behind Mrs. Olinski's wheelchair and pushed her toward the back of the room where the sixth graders converged and formed a phalanx that lifted her—wheelchair and all—onto their shoulders and carried her out of the building and into the parking lot.

Two of the boys stopped short of Mrs. Olinski's van. One was Michael Froelich. He hopped on top of the other fellow's shoulders and draped a noose over the antenna of Mrs. Olinski's van.

Ethan said, "Look, Ma, no hands," and Noah said, "Look, Ma, no legs," and Nadia thought, "Sometimes people need a lift between switches," and Julian said nothing but rubbed the little ivory monkey in his pocket.

Other victories followed, but none was sweeter.

8

After defeating Knightsbridge, The Souls started drilling for the regionals.

There were eight regions in the state. Each was named for a major body of water that touched the counties within its boundary. They were named for lakes, great and small; for rivers, flowing south or east, and one was named for a sound, Long Island Sound. Epiphany was in the region called Finger Lakes. Finger Lakes had never won the state championship. The Hudson River region, which included Maxwell Middle School, had won three out of the past four years.

The week before the regionals, Mrs. Olinski arranged with Mrs. Laurencin to have the school opened on Saturday afternoon so they could have an extra drill. Her team had always been willing—even eager—to practice, so she was surprised and disappointed when they refused.

Finally Noah spoke. "No disrespect intended, Mrs. Olinski, but we would prefer not to."

No disrespect, but. But what? But they prefer not to! "What happens on Saturday that is more important than an extra practice session?" she asked.

Noah answered, "We have tea. On Saturdays we all have tea."

"You have *tea?*" she asked.

"Yes," Noah said. "We have tea."

"At Sillington House," Nadia added.

"At four," Ethan added.

Then Julian said, "Tea is always at four, Mrs. Olinski."

Mr. Singh's teas at Sillington House were becoming well known in the community, and Mrs. Olinski remembered her half promise to herself after the matinee of *Annie*. She would have another cup of slow tea, and the children had just extended a half invitation. Two halves make a whole, she thought. She would go to tea at Sillington House at four o'clock on Saturday afternoon.

At precisely three forty-five Mrs. Olinski locked the door to her house, got in her van, and drove to Sillington House. She arrived at four and had hardly let herself down from her van when she saw the front door swing open and Mr. Singh come down the path to the curb. He insisted upon wheeling her up the ramp across the wide porch. He paused before they entered the front hall and said, "We are glad you have come, Mrs. Olinski."

"Why?" she asked.

"Because Sillington House is its own place, Mrs. Olinski. You will soon see." He wheeled her through the front hall and into the dining room where The Souls were standing behind a table in the back.

There were two other tables where paying guests were already seated. They smiled and nodded at her in the approving way people do when they see people in wheelchairs.

Mr. Singh wheeled her around to the side of the table opposite The Souls. They greeted her. Quietly. In unison.

One word. They said, "Welcome." A place had been set at the end on the side of the table away from the wall. Handicap parking, she thought.

Julian said, "We have not yet poured your tea, Mrs. Olinski. We did not want it to get cold."

Ethan poured. Mrs. Olinski lifted her cup in a silent toast and slowly sipped. Even before replacing her cup in its saucer, she once again felt something lift from her shoulders. She nibbled on the small sandwiches with no crust and soft fillings and ate the tiny tarts with bites as delicate as the tarts themselves. Mrs. Olinski felt—the sensation was so strange to her that she hardly remembered the word—relaxed. She could not remember a time since her accident—maybe even before it—when she had not forced herself not to notice people noticing her. Yet, the children watched her eat cake and drink tea, and she did not feel at all self-conscious. Mrs. Olinski finished the last of the miniature cream puffs, delicately touched her napkin to the corners of her mouth, folded it, laid it on the table alongside her saucer, lifted her eyes, and saw four smiles adorn the faces opposite her. She returned their smiles with a grin.

Other paying guests had arrived, and The Souls excused themselves as they made trips in and out of the kitchen bringing tea and tiered trays of tea sandwiches and cakes. They rejoined Mrs. Olinski at her table, and waited until the creased V between her eyes smoothed out and disappeared altogether. Then when the last of the paying guests had paid his check, Noah said, "We begin practice after we clear up."

There was a tip under the rim of the saucer on each of the tables of the paying guests. Whoever picked up the money put it into a box on the sideboard to which a small sign, written in calligraphy said, TO INSURE PROMPTNESS.

After The Souls had disappeared into the kitchen, Mr. Singh came out. He laid several packs of note cards on the table and sat across the table from Mrs. Olinski. He sat with his back as straight as his chair, and said, "They were getting worried, Mrs. Olinski."

"Who was?"

"The Souls, Mrs. Olinski."

"The Souls?" she repeated. "Who are The Souls?"

"It would be more proper to ask, *what* are The Souls."

"All right, then. *What* are The Souls?"

"The Souls, Mrs. Olinski, are what Noah, Nadia, Ethan, and Julian have become. Do you understand?"

"No, Mr. Singh, I'm afraid I don't. Is this some strange Indian philosophy, Mr. Singh? Reincarnation. That sort of thing?"

He smiled. His smile was as white as his turban and almost as broad. "An incarnation, perhaps. Not a reincarnation. Nadia chose the name."

"Why were they getting worried?"

"They worried, Mrs. Olinski, because you were on the verge of choosing another. Such a choice would have been disastrous."

Mrs. Olinski had never told anyone—*anyone*—that she had been on the verge of choosing another. She grew uneasy. Why was Mr. Singh destroying the wonderful relaxed feeling she had had only minutes ago? She nervously cleared her throat. "But I did not," she said defensively.

"Yes. It was most fortunate. They have been waiting, Mrs. Olinski."

She said, "I'm afraid I still don't understand. Waiting for what? What are you trying to tell me, Mr. Singh?"

He smiled. The white of his teeth made a dazzling underline to his turban. "Just think about this, will you? You have never been able to explain how you chose the members of your team. You have given answers but no explanations."

How did he know that?

"Think of the atom, Mrs. Olinski. There are energies within that tiny realm that are invisible but produce visible results." Mr. Singh shook his head slowly. "Do not feel uneasy, Mrs. Olinski. Hamilton Knapp would truly have been a terrible choice."

Mrs. Olinski had never told anyone—*anyone*—that she had been on the verge of choosing Hamilton Knapp. How could Mr. Singh tell her not to be uneasy when everything he said made her uneasy!

Mr. Singh stood. "Later," he said. "Later you will understand. But for now, we would like to express our gratitude for realizing that Julian was the necessary soul."

She nodded. "All right," she said. "Later."

He pushed the packets of cards in front of her. "Would you like to be quizmaster today?"

"I guess I would."

"I'll send them in. They are ready to begin."

She absentmindedly turned over the cards. There was one question per card, just like hers, but these were written, not typed. The writing was calligraphic, the paper white, the ink as black as Hecate's soul. She examined the questions—they were good ones—and hardly noticed when the children had come out of the kitchen and taken places at the table on the side opposite her.

"Who wrote these?" she asked.

Noah said, "We all did. I gave Julian a calligraphy kit for our first Saturday, and I taught them all."

"Who made up the questions?"

"You made up some," Julian said. "And the rest of us contributed others."

"You, too, Mr. Singh?"

Mr. Singh bowed slightly from the waist. "My specialties are languages and weights and measures. Cooks must know weights and measures."

Mrs. Olinski laughed. "Where did you come up with that category?"

"I'm a big fan of *Jeopardy!* on the television. When Julian and I lived on the cruise ship, they very often had quiz contests to amuse the patrons. This happened very often when the weather was bad." He bowed again. "If you will be quizmaster today, Mrs. Olinski, I shall return to my kitchen. I am trying out new recipes for bran muffins. Americans care very much for bran. I learned of this when I was on the cruise ship." He smiled. "We must talk again, Mrs. Olinski."

Noah was saying, "There are some holes we need to plug, Mrs. Olinski."

"What are they?" she asked.

Julian answered. "Music and the Bible."

Noah said, "I keep telling Julian that we can skip the Bible."

Julian said, "When I watch *Jeopardy!* with Papa, the Bible is very often a category. I think we need it."

Noah said, "Fact: This is New York. Not India, not England, and certainly not a cruise ship. This is New York. And fact: There is the law. There is no way anyone involved with teaching in a public school in the state of New York is going to quiz anyone who is in school at taxpayer expense on the Bible. They'd be slapped with fourteen lawsuits before the buzzer finished sounding. Don't you agree that's a fact, Mrs. Olinski?"

Mrs. Olinski was not thinking about facts. She was thinking about their name, The Souls. "I like it," she said out loud.

"You like the Bible?"

"Well, yes," she replied. "I like the Bible. As literature, as history, I'm comfortable with it as a category."

Noah sighed. "Does that mean the New Testament and the Old Testament?"

"Wouldn't hurt," Mrs. Olinski replied.

"And the Koran?"

"Wouldn't hurt," Mrs. Olinski replied.

"The Upanishads?" Julian asked.

"Those, too?" Noah asked.

"Wouldn't hurt," they all said in unison. And then they all laughed until Noah caught on and laughed, too.

It was dark when Mrs. Olinski left Sillington House, and she was glad. The dark wrapped the afternoon around her and kept it close. Sillington House was its own place. She lifted one hand from the steering wheel, whipped it off to one side, and snapped her fingers. She laughed. The Finger Lakes Regional Championship was in the bag.

9

• • •

The commissioner of education, recovered from the shock of having a contestant protest a ruling, cited Julian. He took away the two points he had been given for answering half of the question and gave Maxwell a chance to answer. The two acronyms they gave were MADD: Mothers Against Drunk Driving. Julian was about to protest that answer on the basis that MADD was not a true acronym because it was a word even before it became an acronym. But the word itself was spelled with one *d* not two, so Julian, who was patient beyond his years, said nothing and waited. Maxwell next came up with SONAR.

While waiting for them to decide what sonar stood for, one of the panel of experts looked up from a heavy volume and sent a signal to the commissioner. He walked over to her. When he returned to the lectern, he said, "We have an adjustment to make on the score. Tip is an acronym for To Insure Promptness.

We restore the five points we subtracted as penalty and add four for answering the question. Maxwell will be allowed to retain two points for MADD, but will not receive credit for SONAR."

Julian said, "Thank you, sir."

No one dared applaud, but everyone in the row to the left of Mrs. Olinski sported smiles that were very loud, and in the row behind her, Nate and Sadie, Izzy and Margy sat on their hands. Even Margy got that excited.

• • •

Between their regional championship and their trip to Albany, word had gotten out that something unusual was happening in Epiphany. Mrs. Laurencin had made a call to the local newspaper, and Mrs. Olinski and The Souls were featured above the fold on the first page of the metro section of the Epiphany *Times*.

That started the blitz of publicity to which Dr. Roy Clayton Rohmer happily surrendered. He hungered for "positive taxpayer feedback," so he called a press conference. After Holly Blackwell, the popular anchorwoman of Channel Three Eyewitness News, accepted his invitation, he invited Mrs. Olinski, The Souls, Mrs. Laurencin, and Mr. Homer Fairbain to attend.

While arranging The Souls behind Dr. Rohmer like a backdrop of the American flag, Holly Blackwell pointed the microphone at Nadia and, pitching her voice a full octave higher than her on-air voice, asked, "And * where * did * we * get * all * these * bee-YOU-tee-ful * red * curls?"

Nadia looked around. "We?" she asked. "Does someone

else have red hair?" Whereupon Holly Blackwell turned her back on all The Souls and instructed the cameraman to pan across their faces occasionally but to focus on Dr. Rohmer. Mrs. Olinski was not pleased. Here were four kids who could speak in complete sentences without a single *you-know* as filler, and Holly Blackwell asked them nothing. She asked Mrs. Olinski one question. Guess what it was. How did she choose her team? Mrs. Olinski gave one of her good answers: her "complementary skills" response, dressing it up to say that the team's talents blended like a chorus, making one sound out of many voices. But her answer ended up on the cutting room floor.

Dr. Homer Fairbain was under orders to smile a lot and say nothing except, "The taxpayers are very proud." He asked Dr. Rohmer if he could say, "We are very proud of these youngsters." No. Just "The taxpayers are very proud." How about, "Everyone is very proud of this team?" No. Just "The taxpayers are very proud." And smile. Smile for Holly, the camera, and the sake of ed-you-kay-shun.

So the session was almost over when Holly Blackwell tilted her coif and turned her baby-blues on the deputy superintendent and asked him how the trip to Albany would be financed. Homer Fairbain smiled and replied, "The taxpayers are very proud." Dr. Rohmer grew as pale as the paper of his unsigned contract.

Having followed orders, Mr. Fairbain provided the only real news that came out of the news conference. Mrs. Laurencin immediately called the school bus dispatcher and reserved six big yellow ones to take the Epiphany Boosters to Albany.

Dr. Rohmer said that the taxpayers were proud but not that proud. He said that unlike football matches where he could charge admission to the games, there was no precedent for charging admission to the Academic Bowl. Taxpayer money would pay Mrs. Olinski's expenses and The Souls', would even pay Mrs. Laurencin's and, of course, his own, but he would not, could not, pay for chartered buses to take the entire town of Epiphany to Albany. He would allow the buses to be used, but he would not pay for the gas or the driver.

And that was when Century Village came through.

Noah's mother had taped the press conference and sent it to Noah's Grandma Sadie and Grandpa Nate who, in turn, shared it with everyone in the clubhouse at Century Village. They commissioned Bella Dubinsky to design a T-shirt. At the suggestion of Mrs. Froelich, she drew a noose. Nothing else. Sadie Gershom suggested that she put the name of the school under that.

Bella refused. "Less is more," she said.

"Not if it's wins over losses," Sadie answered.

But she liked the design, after all, and they arranged to have it silk screened on five hundred red T-shirts, which they shipped north. They sold for ten dollars apiece, and the profit paid for the gas for the buses. The drivers donated their services.

Mrs. Olinski drove to Albany, taking Julian and Mr. Singh with her.

10

• • •

The judges adjusted the score for the acronym question, which put Epiphany ahead. Then Maxwell answered: Who was the first president to live in the White House? and the score was even. Then Epiphany answered: What is the waste product of photosynthesis? Maxwell named the three major food groups, and Epiphany answered, "Who was the first Spanish explorer to reach Florida?" The lead ping-ponged back and forth as the teams took turns answering.

• • •

Mr. Singh said, "You are a very good driver, Mrs. Olinski." The rhythm of his speech was something between a chant and a birdcall. "I have not myself a high degree of skill for driving automobiles. For many years we lived on a cruise ship, and so I was a fully mature man before I passed my first driving test. Did you require many lessons to learn to drive a handicapped vehicle?"

"I had a few," Mrs. Olinski replied. They rode in silence, listening only to the muffled thump and whirr of the tires riding over the interstate before Mrs. Olinski added, "After my accident it took more courage to get back into the passenger's side of an automobile than it took for me to learn to drive again."

"I can understand that," Mr. Singh replied. "It often takes more courage to be a passenger than a driver. Of course, Mrs. Olinski, I am in no way making reference to this trip."

Julian sat alone in the back seat and read the trees and houses and road signs. He said almost nothing, but Mrs. Olinski was never not aware of him. Finally, she said, "Julian makes each mile a journey of quarter inches."

Mr. Singh replied, "It is a skill he learned when we lived on the cruise ship, Mrs. Olinski. He learned to be a passenger. He learned to read the ocean by the cupful. He also learned to regard each port of call as part of the journey and not as destination. Every voyage begins when you do."

"When you fill your pen," Mrs. Olinski said.

Mr. Singh smiled. "Yes, Noah told us."

• • •

Suspense grew, and the commissioner did his best to sustain it. He took his time between questions. He looked over at the judges, nodded, reached into the bowl, and slowly, slowly unfolded the paper. "This question is Maxwell's." Everyone knew that. Maxwell would have to answer correctly to tie it up again. The commissioner tugged ever so gently at his French cuff. He adjusted his glasses. He cleared his throat. He read, "In what work of fiction would we meet the original Humpty Dumpty, and who wrote it?"

The answer came. "*Alice's Adventures in Wonderland* by . . ."

"No!" said the commissioner of education before they could supply an answer to the second part and throw the judges into a panic about the possibility of having to award Maxwell half credit and create confusion about the score.

There was an audible gasp from the audience. Didn't they all believe—those who had actually read *Alice* and not just said they had—that Humpty Dumpty came from Wonderland? Behind her Mrs. Olinski heard Grandpa Nate Gershom whisper to Grandma Sadie, "I think it's Mother Goose. Logic tells me that an egg would come from a mother and a goose."

The commissioner of education tapped on his microphone and demanded quiet. While the audience waited, he took his Mark Cross pen from his inside jacket pocket and wrote on the back of the question in question: To be discussed: The use of compound questions for match point. He replaced his pen in his inside jacket pocket, turned to his right and asked, "Epiphany, can you answer?"

Nadia, Noah, and Ethan looked at Julian, inviting him to give the correct answer. "*Through the Looking Glass* by Lewis Carroll."

It was match point. Epiphany must answer a follow-up to be declared the winner. The commissioner looked again at the paper in his hand. Several spaces beneath and printed in italics was the follow-up: *What was the true name and occupation of the author?* Julian knew: Reverend Charles Lutwidge Dodgson; math teacher, Oxford University.

It was over.

• • •

Between reality and realization, there was a pause. It was over. There was a beat—time for hearts to skip. There was a gap—time for hearts and minds to connect. There was a moment for joy to find its home. It was over. And Epiphany had won.

The Maxwell side of the room was the first to clap. Epiphany, the first to cheer.

The team from Maxwell walked over to The Souls, shook their hands as they had been taught to do, and smiled the parched way that losers do.

The Souls smiled triumphantly. At the audience and for the cameras. There must have been a hundred cameras flashing and whirring. With spots dancing in their eyes, they walked to the edge of the small stage and stood in front of Mrs. Olinski and applauded her specifically until everyone else got the message and stood and faced her and applauded her, too. Mrs. Olinski smiled and said thank you and smiled and nodded and said thank you, thank you, over and over again, wheeling her chair in small circles until her smile and her words floated like a frieze around the room.

The Souls came down from the stage then and, two by two, stood on either side of her wheelchair, so the commissioner had to come down off the stage to give them their trophy. They didn't want it unless Mrs. Olinski was there with them.

And The Souls and Mrs. Olinski shared the trophy that is called a loving cup. And it was.

And then it was all over.

11

They had no sooner made it to the interstate than Julian fell asleep.

Mrs. Olinski and Mr. Singh were quiet, too. Mrs. Olinski felt a strange sense of loss. She did not feel like a loser, but she did feel a sense of loss. She drove for miles worrying about it. Finally, almost involuntarily, she said out loud, "Win some. Lose some." She glanced at Mr. Singh and laughed. "Why did I say that?"

Mr. Singh replied, "Because it is how you feel at this moment, Mrs. Olinski."

"I am happy that we won, Mr. Singh. But I don't understand why I feel a sense of loss. This is not like my accident when my loss was overwhelming. Why, after this wonderful victory, do I feel that something is missing?"

"Because something is." Miles hummed past before his voice floated back to her. "For many months now, you have been in a state of perpetual preparation and excitement. Each victory was a preparation for the next. You are missing future victories. Have you enjoyed the journey out, Mrs. Olinski?"

"Very much. Every cupful. Like Julian on the ocean."

"Now, you must put down anchor, look around, enjoy this port of call. Your stay will be brief. You must do it, Mrs. Olinski."

Julian did not wake up even when they stopped for gas in Oneonta. He had stretched out in the back, and the bright lights of the service station shone through the rear window. His lips were slightly parted. His eyelashes cast semicircles of shadow on his cheeks.

"What do you see, Mrs. Olinski?" Mr. Singh asked.

"I see that angels have landed on his eyelids."

"Yes," he answered, pleased. "Angels have."

A car pulled in behind Mrs. Olinski. Its lights hit her rearview mirror, which she adjusted and then said abruptly, "Mr. Singh, do you know how I chose The Souls?"

Mr. Singh laughed. "I believe you have several good answers. Which would you like?"

"I am not asking for my answers, Mr. Singh. I am asking for yours."

Mr. Singh replied, "The Souls have all returned from a journey, Mrs. Olinski."

"A journey, Mr. Singh? All of them?"

"Yes. Each of them. Noah was first."

"Well, yes, he was the first chosen."

"And the first to return from his journey. From Century Village."

"Nadia?"

"From the Sargasso Sea."

"Ethan?"

"Ethan took a little longer than the other two, yet his journey was the shortest. It was a ride on the school bus."

"And Julian was last."

"Yes. Julian was last. His journey has been the longest."

Mr. Singh said nothing more. Mrs. Olinski drove past several exits on the interstate, waiting. As they approached the ramp that would take them to the state highway that would lead to Epiphany, he had still said nothing. She could stand it no longer. "Mr. Singh," she demanded, "you must finish. You must tell me what you know about their journeys."

"They found something, Mrs. Olinski. Noah at Century Village; Nadia on the Sargasso Sea; Ethan on the bus." He hesitated. "Think about the question that Maxwell missed. They did not know that Humpty Dumpty was not in Wonderland because they never journeyed through the looking glass to find him. How can you know what is missing if you've never met it? You must know of something's existence before you can notice its absence. So it was with The Souls. They found on their journeys what you found at Sillington House."

"A cup of kindness, Mr. Singh? Is that what I found?"

"Kindness, yes, Mrs. Olinski. Noah, Nadia, and Ethan found kindness in others and learned how to look for it in themselves. Can you know excellence if you've never seen it? Can you know good if you have seen only bad? Julian knows—perhaps even more than the others—about kindness. We have, my son and I, been most fortunate. We have found much kindness when we journeyed on the ship. When sixth grade started, my son found malice. Spite and malice. Mean things were done to him. Julian has told me many stories. Many stories." The music of his voice faded and stopped. He looked at, not through, the windshield as if it were a small screen showing one of the many stories, and then back in focus, he said to Mrs. Olinski, "Each of The Souls has had a journey, and so have you, Mrs. Olinski."

Eva Marie Olinski thought back to the day she had chosen Julian. That was the day she did not choose Hamilton Knapp. She had seen something as she scanned the rows in the auditorium. Something that made her not choose him. She had seen how mean he was, and that was the day she went to tea at Sillington House.

They were riding down Gramercy Road now, and Mr. Singh started to turn toward the back of the van to awaken Julian. He stopped and quietly asked, "Do you know, Mrs. Olinski, how Julian first invited The Souls to tea?"

"How?"

"He sent them invitations hidden in a book."

"What book might that be, Mr. Singh?"

"The book was *Alice's Adventures in Wonderland*. He would never make the mistake of looking for Humpty Dumpty there."

They said nothing more except good night.

As tired as she was, Mrs. Olinski took her copy of *Alice's Adventures in Wonderland* down from the shelf. She found the Cheshire Cat but no Humpty Dumpty. As Mr. Singh had said, if you've not seen something, it's hard to know what is missing. She took down *Through the Looking Glass* and found Humpty Dumpty sitting on a wall.

Humpty Dumpty had a great fall.
All the King's horses and all the King's men
Couldn't put Humpty Dumpty in his place again.

All the king's horses and all the king's men could not have done for Mrs. Eva Marie Olinski what the kindness of four sixth-grade souls had.

She closed her book, put it back on the shelf together again with *Alice's Adventures in Wonderland*. She went to bed with a grin, which like the Cheshire Cat's, remained for some time after. For a considerable time after.

12

Eva Marie Olinski let herself down out of her van and wheeled herself to the bottom of the front porch ramp of Sillington House. The Souls were waiting. They opened the front door for her.

And that is when she knew that they knew that she knew.

They made their way to the big familiar table in the back of the dining room.

Mr. Singh had opened the windows along the side wall, and a breeze from the lake breathed sweet spring air into the room. At last the weather had caught up with the calendar. Then Mr. Singh took a seat opposite her at the far end of the table. She waited until they were all in their usual places, and then she asked, "Did I choose you, or did you choose me?"

And The Souls answered, "Yes!"

FIFTEEN QUESTIONS WITH THIRTY-SIX ANSWERS

What is the meaning of the word *calligraphy* and from what language does it derive?

Calligraphy derives from Greek.
It means beautiful writing.

What is the name given to that portion of the North Atlantic Ocean that is noted for its abundance of seaweed, and what is its importance to the ecology of our planet?

The Sargasso Sea.
Its relatively still waters and its abundance of seaweed allow many species of marine animals to feed and grow.

What famous American women are associated with the following places in New York State and why are they important?

Seneca Falls

Elizabeth Cady Stanton.
Called the first women's rights convention here in 1848.

Homer

Amelia Jenks Bloomer.
Was born here. Was editor of Lily, *a paper devoted to women's rights and temperance. She wore a short skirt and full trousers whenever she lectured, and they became known as the Bloomer costume or bloomers.*

Rochester

Susan B. Anthony.
Led a group of women to the polls here in 1872 to test the right of women to vote. She was arrested, tried, and sentenced to a fine.

Auburn

Harriet Tubman.
One of the most successful conductors of the underground railroad, she lived here for many years.

How many quarters in twenty dollars?

Eighty

If one man can paint an eight feet by twelve feet wall in a half hour, how long would it take three men to paint a wall that is eight feet by twenty-four feet?

Twenty minutes

A masterpiece by the artist Rembrandt was recently stolen from a museum in his native country. What is that country?

The Netherlands

What is its capital?

Amsterdam

Name the parts of the human eye in the order that light reaches them.

Cornea, aqueous humor, pupil of iris, vitreous humor, retina

Name the famous fathers of:

Queen Elizabeth I of England.

King Henry VIII

Esau and Jacob

Isaac

Alexander the Great

Philip of Macedon

Our country

George Washington

Name the tribe associated with each of the following Native American leaders and name a major accomplishment of one.

Sequoyah

Cherokee.

Created a system for writing the Cherokee language; the giant tree, sequoia, is named for him.

Tecumseh

Shawnee.

Great organizer and leader, was made a brigadier general by the British in the War of 1812.

Osceola

Seminole.

Resisted the removal of Native Americans to the West.

Geronimo

Apache.

Led a group of followers into Mexico resisting resettlement of his group to an arid reservation.

What is the origin of the phrase, "to meet one's Waterloo" and what does it mean?

Napoleon's last battle was at Waterloo in Belgium. He was defeated by the Duke of Wellington in 1815.

To meet one's Waterloo means to suffer a resounding defeat.

What is SONAR an acronym for?

SOund NAvigation Ranging: using sound waves for locating submerged objects and for communication with submarines.

Who was the first president to live in the White House?

John Adams

What is the waste product of photosynthesis?

Oxygen

Name the three major food groups.

Proteins, carbohydrates, fats

Who was the first Spanish explorer to reach Florida?

Ponce de León

Turn the page for a look at
The Mysterious Edge of the Heroic World,
another triumphant novel by
E. L. Konigsburg.

1

In the late afternoon on the second Friday in September, Amedeo Kaplan stepped down from the school bus into a cloud of winged insects. He waved his hand in front of his face only to find that the flies silently landed on the back of his hand and stayed there. They didn't budge, and they didn't bite. They were as lazy as the afternoon. Amedeo looked closely. They were not lazy. They were preoccupied. They were coupling, mating on the wing, and when they landed, they stayed connected, end to end. They were shameless. He waved his hands and shook his arms, but nothing could interrupt them.

He stopped, unhooked his backpack, and laid it on the sidewalk. Fascinated by their silence and persistence, he knelt down to watch them. Close examination revealed an elongated body covered with black wings; end to end, they were no longer than half an inch. The heads were red, the size of a pin. There was a longer one and a shorter one, and from what he remembered of nature studies, their size determined their sex—or vice versa.

The flies covered his arms like body hair. He started scraping them off and was startled to hear a voice behind him say, "Lovebugs."

He turned around and recognized William Wilcox.

William (!) Wilcox (!).

For the first time in his life Amedeo was dealing with being the new kid in school, the new kid in town, and finding out that neither made him special. Quite the opposite. Being new was generic at Lancaster Middle School. The school itself didn't start until sixth grade, so every single one of his fellow sixth graders was a new kid in school, and being new was also common because St. Malo was home to a lot of navy families, so for some of the kids at Lancaster Middle School, this was the third time they were the new kid in town. The navy seemed to move families to any town that had water nearby—a river, a lake, a pond, or even high humidity—so coming from a famous port city like New York added nothing to his interest quotient.

Amedeo was beginning to think that he had been conscripted into AA. Aloners Anonymous. No one at Lancaster Middle School knew or cared that he was new, that he was from New York, that he was Amedeo Kaplan.

But now William (!) Wilcox (!) had noticed him.

William Wilcox was anything but anonymous. He was not so much alone as aloof. In a school as variegated as an argyle sock, William Wilcox was not part of the pattern. Blond though he was, he was a dark thread on the edge. He was all edges. He had a self-assurance that inspired awe or fear or both.

Everyone seemed to know who William Wilcox was and that he had a story.

Sometime after William Wilcox's father died, his mother got into the business of managing estate sales. She took charge of selling off the contents of houses of people who had died or who were moving or downsizing or had some other need to dispossess themselves of the things they owned. She was paid a commission on every item that was sold. It was a good business for someone like Mrs. Wilcox, who had no money to invest in inventory but who had the time and the talent to learn a trade. Mrs. Wilcox was fortunate that two antique dealers, Bertram Grover and Ray Porterfield, took her under their wings and started her on a career path.

From the start, William worked side by side with his mother.

In their first major estate sale, the Birchfields', Mrs. Wilcox found a four-panel silk screen wrapped in an old blanket in the back of a bedroom closet. It was slightly faded but had no tears or stains, and she could tell immediately that it had been had painted a very long time ago. She priced the screen reasonably at one hundred twenty-five dollars but could not interest anyone in buying it. Her instincts told her it was something fine, so when she was finishing the sale and still couldn't find a buyer, she deducted the full price from her sales commission and took the screen home, put it up in front of the sofa in their living room, and studied it. Each of the four panels told part of the story of how women washed and wove silk. The more she studied and researched, the more she became convinced that the screen was not only very fine but rare.

On the weekend following the Birchfield sale, she and William packed the screen into the family station wagon and tried selling it to antique shops all over St. Malo. When she could not interest anyone in buying it, she and William took to the road, and on several consecutive weekends, they stopped at antique shops in towns along the interstate, both to the north and south of St. Malo.

They could not find a buyer.

Without his mother's knowing, William took photos of the screen and secretly carried them with him when his sixth-grade class took a spring trip to Washington, D.C. As his classmates were touring the National Air and Space Museum, William stole away to the Freer Gallery of Art, part of the Smithsonian that specializes in Asian art and antiquities.

Once there, William approached the receptionist's desk and asked to see the curator in charge of ancient Chinese art. The woman behind the desk asked, "Now, what business would you be having with the curator of Chinese art?" When William realized that the woman was not taking him seriously, he took out the photographs he had of the screen and lined them up at the edge of the desk so that they faced her. William could tell that the woman had no idea what she was seeing, let alone the value of it. She tried stalling him by saying that the curatorial staff was quite busy. William knew that he did not have much time before his sixth-grade class would miss him. He coolly assessed the situation: He was a sixth grader with no credentials, little time, and an enormous need. He squared his shoulders and thickened his Southern accent to heavy sweet cream and said, "Back to home, we have a expression, ma'am."

"What's that?" she asked.

"Why, back to home we always say that there's some folk who don't know that they're through the swinging doors of opportunity until they've got swat on their backside."

William waited.

It may have been because he returned each of her cold stares with cool dignity, or it may simply have been the quiet assurance in his voice coupled with his courtly manners that made it happen, but the receptionist picked up the phone and called the curator, a Mrs. Fortinbras.

William showed Mrs. Fortinbras the photographs, and Mrs. Fortinbras was not at all dismissive. She said that the photographs—crude as they were—made it difficult to tell enough about the screen. But they did show that it might be *interesting*. She suggested that William bring the screen itself to Washington so that she could arrange to have it examined by her staff.

When school was out for the summer, William convinced his mother to pack up the screen again and drive to Washington, D.C., and have Mrs. Fortinbras and her staff at the Freer give it a good look.

And they did take it there.

And Mrs. Fortinbras and her staff did examine it.

And Mrs. Fortinbras and her staff did recommend that the museum buy it.

And the museum did buy it.

For twenty thousand dollars.

When they got back to St. Malo, William called the

newspaper. The *Vindicator* printed William's story along with the pictures he had taken. The article appeared below the fold on the first page of the second section.

William was now standing above Amedeo as he crouched over his backpack. Taking a minute to catch his breath, Amedeo examined the lovebugs on the back of his hand and asked, "Do they bite?" He had already witnessed that they did not.

"They're harmless," William said. "They don't sting or bite."

"Are they a Florida thing?"

"Southern."

"I haven't ever seen them before."

"They swarm twice a year. Spring and fall."

Amedeo pointed to one pair that had just landed on his arm. "Is that all they do?"

"From about ten in the morning until dusk." William raised his shoulder slowly and tilted his head slightly—like a conversational semicolon—before continuing. "The females live only two or three days. They die after their mating flight."

Amedeo laughed. "Way to go!"

William smiled.

Amedeo picked up his backpack and started walking with William.

"Do you live here?" Amedeo asked.

"No."

"Then why did you get off at my stop?"

William's smile faded. "I didn't know it was your stop. I thought it was a bus stop."

"I meant that I live here. So it's my stop."

"I'm not gonna take it away from you," William replied, and his smile disappeared.

They had reached the edge of Mrs. Zender's property. Without a whistle or a wave, William headed down the driveway.

Amedeo stopped to watch.

William lifted the back hatch of a station wagon that was parked at the bottom of Mrs. Zender's driveway. No one who lived on Mandarin Road owned a station wagon. Mrs. Zender drove a pink Thunderbird convertible: stick shift, whitewall tires, and a car horn that pealed out the first four notes of Beethoven's Fifth Symphony.

Amedeo watched as William removed a large brown paper bag from the back. It was not a Bloomingdale's Big Brown Bag, but a no-handles, flat-bottom brown bag from a grocery store. He could tell from the way William lifted it that the bag was definitely not empty. He carried the bag up to Mrs. Zender's front door and walked right in without ringing or knocking. He knew that he was being watched, but he did not once look back.

Amedeo waited until William closed the door behind him before he walked down the driveway himself.

Amedeo had been inside Mrs. Zender's house once. Two days after moving to St. Malo, they still didn't have a phone, and his mother had sent him next door to ask the lady of the house permission to use her phone to "light a fire" under them. *Them* being the phone enemy.

Amedeo's mother was an executive with Infinitel, an independent long-distance telephone company that was a competitor to Teletron, St. Malo's communications provider. To his mother, the telephone was as vital a connection as the muscle that connected her hand to her arm. If St. Malo already had had access to cell phones, she wouldn't be in this predicament, but then if St. Malo already had access to cell phones, they wouldn't be in St. Malo at all. The only thing neutralizing her indignation about not having a working phone was the embarrassment the local company was suffering at not being able to properly service one of their own. But on this morning there was also the pool man (whom she secretly believed to be the one who had cut the line) to deal with. She chose to wait for the pool man herself and to send Amedeo next door to deal with the phone. Amedeo had been happy to go.

A wide threshold of broken flagstones led to the front door of Mrs. Zender's house. There were no torn papers and dried leaves blowing up against a ripped screen door as in the opening credits of a horror movie. Her grounds were not littered with papers but with pinecones and needles, fallen Spanish moss, and big leathery sycamore leaves. Her lawn was cut but not manicured; her shrubs were not pruned, and except for the holes through the branches that the electric company made to protect the wires, her trees were wild. The paint on her front door was peeling. Her place looked shabby. Shabby in a genteel way, as if the people who lived there didn't have to keep up with the Joneses because they themselves *were* the Joneses.

Amedeo wiped a moustache of sweat from his upper lip with the sleeve of his T-shirt. Like a performer ready to go on stage, he stood on the threshold and took a long sip of the hot, moist gaseous matter that St. Malo called air. He lifted his hand to ring the bell.

The door swung wide, and the entire opening filled, top to bottom, with a sleeve. The sleeve of a silk kimono. "Yes?" the woman said, smiling. Her smile engaged her whole face. Her mouth opened high and wide; her nostrils flared, and her eyebrows lifted to meet a narrow margin of blond hair. Just beyond the hairline, her head was covered by a long, gauzy silk scarf—purple—that was tied in an elaborate knot below her left ear but was still long enough to hang to her waist. She wore three shades of eye shadow—one of which was purple—and heavy black mascara. Her lips were painted a bright crimson, which feathered above and below the line of her lips and left red runes on three of her front teeth.

It was nine o'clock in the morning.

Amedeo had never seen anyone dressed like that except when he was in an audience.

"Hello," he said. "My name is Amedeo Kaplan, and I would like permission to use your phone."

Mrs. Zender introduced herself and commented, "Amedeo. Lovely name."

"Thank you. People usually call me Deo."

"I won't," she said. "*Amedeo* is Italian for *Amadeus*, which means 'love of God.' It was Mozart's middle name."

"It was my grandfather's first name. I'm named for him."

"Lovely," she said, "lovely name, but how did you get here, Amedeo?"

"I walked."

"You walked? From where?"

"From next door."

"Oh," Mrs. Zender replied. "I didn't know there was a child."

"There definitely was. *Is.*"

"I didn't know."

"I was at camp."

"Music camp?" Mrs. Zender asked.

She smiled expectantly, waiting for an explanation. Fascinated, Amedeo watched her upper lip squeegee away one of the red runes. When he didn't answer, she told Amedeo to follow her, and with a sweep of sleeve, she pointed the way. The underarm seam of her kimono was split. Mrs. Zender was not a natural blonde.

As they traveled the distance of a long center hall, they passed two or three rooms so dark it was hard to tell where one ended and another began. Every window was covered with heavy drapes, which dropped from padded valances. The word *portière* from *Gone With the Wind* came to mind.

In several windows, the drapes had been shortened to accommodate a bulky window air conditioner that was noisily waging war with the heat and humidity. And losing. They passed a dining room large enough to be a ballroom. In the semilight, Amedeo could make out a *Phantom of the Opera* chandelier hanging over a table that looked long enough to seat the guest list at Buckingham Palace. Opposite the dining room was a room with a baby grand piano; its open lid reflected the few slits of light that pierced the parting of the drapes. The darkness and the drawn drapes added a dimension to the heat. It was August. It was St. Malo. It was hot. Hot, hot, hot.

But the thickness of the air carried the sound of music—opera—out of the rooms and transformed the hallway into a concert hall. Amedeo slowed down and cocked his head to listen.

Mrs. Zender said, "So you like my sound system."

"Definitely."

"One of a kind," she said, "Karl Eisenhuth himself installed it."

"Karl Eisenhuth? I'm sorry, I don't know him."

"Then I shall tell you. Karl Eisenhuth was the world's greatest acoustician. He had never before installed a sound system in a private home. He had done opera houses in Brno and Vienna and a symphony hall in Amsterdam. Mr. Zender, my late husband, contacted him and requested that he install a sound system here. Karl Eisenhuth asked Mr. Zender why he should bother with a private home in St. Malo, Florida, and Mr. Zender replied with three words: *Aida Lily Tull.* That was my professional name. Those three words, *Aida Lily Tull*, were reason enough."

Amedeo said, "I'm impressed." He was.

Mrs. Zender said, "I'm pleased that you are."

And for reasons he did not yet understand, Amedeo was pleased to have pleased.

Mrs. Zender swept her arm in the direction of the back of the house. The hallway was wide enough to allow them to walk side by side, but Mrs. Zender walked ahead. She was tall, and she was zaftig. Definitely zaftig. She was also majestic. She moved forward like a queen vessel plowing still waters. Her kimono corrugated as she moved. There was a thin stripe of purple that winked as it appeared and then disappeared in a fold of fabric at her waist.

Amedeo was wearing a short-sleeved T-shirt and shorts, but the air inside the house was as thick as motor oil, and perspiration soon coated his arms and legs and made his clothes stick like cuticle. Mrs. Zender seemed not to be sweating. Maybe she followed the dress code of the desert and insulated herself with layers of clothing. Arabs and motor oil had been in the news a lot lately.

The combination of heat, music, and the mesmerizing rock-and-roll of Mrs. Zender's hips made Amedeo worry about falling unconscious before reaching the door at the end of the hall. What were the names of clothes that desert people wore? *Burnoose . . . chador . . . chador.* His mother did not approve of chadors.

The rock-and-roll stopped when Mrs. Zender arrived at the door at the end of the hall. She waited for Amedeo to catch up, and then with a flutter of sleeve and a swirl of pattern, she lifted her right arm and pushed the door open. For a minute, she stood against the door, her arm stretched out like a semaphore, beckoning Amedeo to pass in front of her.

He walked into the kitchen, and Mrs. Zender quickly closed the door behind her.

The music stopped.

An air conditioner was propped into the kitchen window and was loudly battling the throbbing pulse of heat that bore into the room. Like his house, Mrs. Zender's faced east. By August, the afternoon sun was too high to make a direct hit on the kitchen windows, but was still strong enough to bounce off the river and push yellow bands of heat through each of the slats of the Venetian blinds.

The kitchen itself was a time capsule. The counters were edged in ribbed chrome and topped with pink patterned Formica that was peeling at the seams. Near the sink sat a set of metal cylinders labeled FLOUR, SUGAR, COFFEE. There was a toaster oven, but no microwave. The stove was the width of two regular stoves, eight burners, two regular ovens, and a warming oven. It was gleaming bright, clean, and obviously had not been used in a very long time. It would take courage to turn it on. Cold cereal and vichyssoise would be better menu choices.

On the countertop in the corner of the kitchen near the dining alcove, there was a small telephone. Turquoise. Rotary dial. Not touch-tone. Amedeo had seen people in the movies use a rotary phone, and he knew the phrase "dial a number," but he had never done it.

Mrs. Zender said, "That's a princess phone."

"Does it work?"

"Of course it works. Except for my cleaning service, which is not here today, everything in this house works."

Amedeo lifted the receiver. The part of the phone he held to his ear had yellowed from turquoise to a shade of institutional green.

Mrs. Zender sat at the kitchen table. Amedeo felt he was being watched. He turned to face the wall of cabinets.

The cabinets reached to the ceiling. It would take a ladder to reach the top shelves. The cabinet doors were glass, and Amedeo could see stacks and stacks of dishes and matching cups hanging from hooks. Behind other glass doors there were platoons of canned soups—mostly tomato—and a regiment of cereal boxes—mostly bran. Everything was orderly, but the dishes on the topmost shelves were dusty, and the stemware was cloudy, settled in rows like stalagmites.

Finally, he heard, "Your call may be monitored for quality assurance," and was told to listen carefully "to the following options." He realized that he could not exercise any of the "following options." He could hardly press one or two when there were no buttons to press. He held his hand over the mouthpiece and whispered, "I'm supposed to push one for English."

Mrs. Zender smiled wide. The last of the red runes had been washed away. "Do nothing," she said. "Just hang on. When you have a dial phone, they have to do the work for you." She threw her head back and laughed.

Amedeo didn't turn his back on her again.

As soon as the call was finished, they returned to the long, dark hall, where the heat and the music swallowed them. Mrs. Zender paused to say, "I suppose you put central air-conditioning into your place."

Amedeo hesitated. Until that moment, he had never thought of central air-conditioning as something a person put in. He thought it came with the walls and roof. "I suppose so," he said.

"Sissies," Mrs. Zender said. Then she laughed again. She had a musical laugh. "I chose a sound system over air-conditioning."

"But," Amedeo replied, "I think you're allowed to have both."

"No," she said crisply. "Karl Eisenhuth is as dead as my husband."

"Oh, I'm sorry."

"Yes, a pity. There never will be another sound system like this one."

Reluctantly, Amedeo left Mrs. Zender, her veils, her house.

Now, Amedeo watched William walk through that peeling, painted front door without stopping or knocking and enter Mrs. Zender's world of sound and shadow.

e. l. konigsburg

is the only author to have won the Newbery Medal and been runner-up in the same year. In 1968, *From the Mixed-up Files of Mrs. Basil E. Frankweiler* won the Newbery Medal, and *Jennifer, Hecate, Macbeth, William McKinley, and Me, Elizabeth* was awarded a Newbery Honor. In 1997 she won a second Newbery Medal for *The View from Saturday*. In 2004 she published *The Outcasts of 19 Schuyler Place,* which was an ALA Best Book for Young Adults, a *Kirkus Reviews* Editor's Choice, and a *School Library Journal* Best Book of the Year.

After completing her degree at Carnegie Mellon University, Ms. Konigsburg did graduate work in organic chemistry at the University of Pittsburgh. For several years she taught science at a private girls' school. When the last of her three children started kindergarten, she began to write. While writing *From the Mixed-up Files of Mrs. Basil E. Frankweiler* and *Jennifer, Hecate, Macbeth, William McKinley, and Me, Elizabeth,* Ms. Konigsburg took art lessons in New York City. She would first drop her children off at the Metropolitan Museum of Art, take her lessons, and then meet her children back in the MMA. She currently lives on the beach in North Florida.